Him

J.M. Elliott

This book is a work of fiction. All the characters, organizations, and events portrayed in this novel are used fictitiously. Other names, characters, places, and events are products of the author's imagination, and any resemblance to actual persons, living or dead, occurrences, or locations is entirely coincidental.

Copyright © 2020 by J. M. Elliott

All rights reserved. No part of this book may be reproduced, or portions thereof in any form whatsoever without the copyright owner's written permission to use quotations in a book review.

First paperback edition: 2020

Cover design by Coven Design

Cover image by Michael Coven

Interior Design by Classic Interior Design

ISBN 987-0-578-79219-4 (paperback)

Published by Short Mag Books

Short Mag Books

For my late Grandmother

She was my biggest supporter and my number one fan. My grams would be incredibly proud of me for fulfilling a dream of mine. I love and miss you so much. I will always be your little Boo Bear!

Him

chapter one

A deer runs out in front of my car, bringing me back to reality. I forgot how much wildlife the scenic route has. The forest has grown a lot, and I find it hard to recognize the scenery around me. I have been in the city for so long that I have forgotten how beautiful the countryside is.

I've been away for six years, college, then settling into my first job. I haven't made time to come home much. I've been so consumed in my own life to care about anyone else's. I wish the circumstances that finally pushed me to go home were different. If I had perhaps come home more often, my father might still be alive. I may have been there at the time he took his last breath.

I wipe away a few tears that have tumbled down my cheek. I had so much fun with my father as a child. He taught me so much. Even though he was a single parent and it was us against the world, he was the best father anyone could ever ask for.

I am still driving the same 1967 Shelby Mustang GT500 we rebuilt together back when I was in High School, Junior High, and part of Elementary. I remember rushing home from school to work on it with my dad every day. I did not think we were ever going to finish it. The mustang was gifted to me, freshly painted and in all its glory, as my graduation present.

I TRAVEL DOWN MY FATHER'S DRIVEWAY; CARS LINED UP on each side of the road. I pull up closer to his house; it hits me. My father is gone. He will not be greeting me when I get out of my vehicle, nor will he have that ridiculous smirk on his face that he used to have when I would pull up in the mustang. He loved this car, and he loved that I still drove it.

I flip down the visor and check my makeup before opening my door. I dab under my eyes to fix my runny eyeliner, throw on some lip gloss, then toss my hair back in a low ponytail. I take a deep breath before I get out of my car. I pull down my black dress to try and release some of the wrinkles from sitting—what seemed like forever. I notice that there are a lot of people here. My father was very well-liked, so I can only smile, knowing they are all here to pay their respects. My heart sinks as I walk closer to his house.

I notice a row of classic cars parked on the lawn. My father loved classic cars. He would search the countryside for one and restore it. It was his passion. He even opened a tiny shop just outside of town to devote his time to those rust buckets. He always said, *why should they sit and rust?* He looked at life so differently than most. He took the bad and saw the good, he took the old and saw the new, he took the lost and made them found.

As I walk up the driveway, I can hear my father's friends and my family's chatter while conversing with one another about their lives and memories with my father. I see a group of men wearing the same shirts; gray collared shirts with short sleeves. There is red, white, and black writing on the back. *Rob's Classic Restoration* it reads. My dad's shop. Are they all his workers? I do not remember that there were this many when I left for college. All I remember is him, Ernie, my uncle Dave, and a couple of others that would come by and help from time to time. Now, there is at least twenty or so. I've missed a lot since I have been away.

"Allison!" I hear my aunt squeal, as she rushes over to hug me.

I smile and say, "Hey."

"How was the drive?" she asks sympathetically.

"It was good. Long but good," I reply. "Thank you so much for putting all of this together."

"No problem, sweetie. That is what I am here for," she says with delight.

My aunt is quite the social butterfly. She is always the first to put on a social gathering or a funeral in this case. I sit down, and I can feel everyone staring at me like I am a celebrity. As the pastor starts to talk about my father's wonderful characteristics, I cannot help but drift off into memories of my favorite times with him. We did everything together. We were the best of friends. We fished, hunted, and went camping. He taught me how to ride a bike, drive a car, change the oil on vehicles, and even beat up boys. My father was all I needed, and he never made me miss not having a mom. He played both roles quite well.

Since I am not paying any attention to the eulogy, while off in la-la land reminiscing over years of memories with my father, I smile.

"Allison!"

My aunt snaps me back to reality.

"We need to go over your father's will sometime this week. That is whenever you're ready."

This week? I was not planning to stay here for too long. I need to get back to the city.

I give her a polite nod as I walk behind my father's house to my old swing set. I grab hold of one of the rusty swings and think about how it is something he never restored, considering he made restoring classic cars his life's work, but never restored a swing for me. I giggle and sit down on one of the old, worn out swings.

The thought that you do not know what you've got until it's gone is all too real. I am unprepared to live in a world without my father. I am not ready to deal with what comes next. I miss my father and never thought this day would come. Now that it's here, I am clueless about how to embark on the next chapter of my life—a world without a dad.

IN MY FATHER'S HOUSE, THERE IS A FESTIVE ATMOSPHERE. People are consuming little sandwiches and other finger foods. A basket of cards is spilling out over a table near the fireplace and flowers litter the living room. There are so many people here that I do not know or remember. They give condolences and it is tough to strike up a conversation, so I say thank you and smile.

I sit on the bay window watching people leave. I can hear my aunt being the *hostess with the mostest* as always. The same questions haunt me. What am I going to do now? I no longer have a father. Who will I discuss my problems with? Who will give me the worst advice ever on men and dating? Who will I call to discuss issues with my car?

"Alicat!" I hear a gruff rumble.

I turn to see one of the best people ever to be associated with my father. My dad's best friend, Ernie. I jump excitedly and wrap my arms around this husky fellow. He hasn't changed a wink.

"Hey, ya, old fart. How the hell are ya?" I ask.

"Oh, you know I'm doing as well as can be expected considering," he says softly.

It's a time to celebrate my father's life, but I cannot help but feel excited about seeing Ernie after so long. He is wonderful man and the next best thing to a father.

"Yeah, it's a sorrowful day. Thank you so much for being here. It means a lot to me. My father would be grateful," I say.

He hugs me again then asks about my job and life in the big city. He tells me he still cannot believe I am grown. I am no longer that little tomboy hanging around, learning about cars. I smile as he brings back cherished childhood memories.

A lot has changed since then. I am a woman now, and I haven't gotten my hands dirty under the hood of a car in a long time.

"Maybe, I will come by the shop tomorrow and see what you guys have got going on. Get my hands dirty," I say to ease the mood.

"We would love that. It's great to see you, Ali," he says before kissing me on the top of my head.

I begin to gather the plates and cups as guests continue to leave. The mess is smaller than one would except. My aunt and uncle walk up to me as the last guest and family member leaves.

"Are you okay here tonight?" my uncle asks.

"You know you are welcome to come to stay with us," my aunt chimes in.

"I am fine staying here. Thank you for the invite," I reply with a smile.

It couldn't be further from the truth. Am I fine? Am I okay staying in my childhood home where my father won't be walking through the front door after a day full of restoring old yeller?

I hug my aunt and uncle then watch as they get into their vehicle. I walk back into the living room, perusing my dad's knickknacks and collectibles. I never paid much attention to them before, but now they hold meaning. They are tiny pieces of my dad.

Maybe, I should take a shower, get this makeup off, get out of this dress. I head to the bathroom and pass a large photo in the hallway. It's new, and I don't remember seeing it before. The large frame holds small pictures, the center picture bigger than the rest. Each photo is of my father and me through the restoration process of my mustang. The images span from the day we found it out in bum fuck Egypt to the day he gave it to me, fully restored, for my High School graduation. The smiles on our faces are still contagious. Tears threaten and the moment is broken.

As I step into the shower and the hot water hits my body, I lose it. Crumpling under the sobs, I rock back and forth. My dad is gone. He's gone forever, and I am all alone.

chapter two

I open my eyes and look around, forgetting that I am back in my old room. The house feels still and quiet. I wish this were a dream, and my father would be downstairs at the kitchen table, with his coffee in his hand, looking through the classifieds for cars.

I roll out of my bed and wander over to my closest. I know that there should still be some clothes here. I skim over my shirts, grabbing my worn and faded black *Guns n' Roses* t-shirt. They used to be my favorite band. I walk over to my dresser and grab a pair of faded jeans with some rips on the knees. I laugh, reminiscing how I used to dress this way on purpose.

I gaze at myself in the mirror, feeling quite comfortable. What am I going to do with this mop on top of my head? Since I'm just going to the shop, it doesn't need to be perfect. I grab a trucker hat off my dresser, throw my long black hair up through the hat's back into a messy bun. I then grab a flannel and tie it around my waist before heading downstairs.

I'm overly excited to head over to my father's shop. I cannot wait to see what my dad and the guys have been up to. I get my boots from the closet in the entryway that I lived in throughout High School, then I head out the door.

I make my way down the driveway in my car. What better way to pass the time then to jam out to a little *Sweet Child of Mine* and *Welcome to the Jungle*. The drive is lovely and peaceful, despite bringing back a flood of memories from when I would drive to my dad's shop every day.

I PULL UP TO THE SHOP, AND I NOTICE THAT NOTHING MUCH has changed since the last time I saw it back in High School. I've been home a few times since I left but I never came out here. I lost my interest in the whole car scene.

I walk around the back to one of the large garage doors. It's open, and I can see a gorgeous Chevelle parked right in front of it with the hood up. It looks incredible, with the candy apple red paint glistening in the morning sun. The chrome is sparkling from a new wax.

As I walk closer, a shirtless man steps back from the hood. I don't remember any shirtless guys working for my dad the last time I was here. All the guys my dad had working with him were middle-aged like him and never worked shirtless, that much I recall.

His skin is nicely tanned. His muscular arms are beaming with beads of sweat with a couple of tattoos covering his body but not overwhelming. If I knew my dad had guys that looked like this working for him, I might have come home more often.

The shirtless guy catches me off guard when he notices me and asks, "Can I help you?"

He's rather tall; his dark hair is under a backward black cap. He has a nicely chiseled body that I cannot stop staring at.

"Ugh... no, I'm good, thanks," I reply rudely.

However, I am more embarrassed as I walk past, knowing he caught me staring.

"Ahh, hey. You can't just walk in there. It's employees only," he yells.

I keep walking, ignoring his pleas. I can hear his footsteps as he comes up behind me.

"Alicat!" Ernie screams in excitement as he sees me from across the shop.

The shirtless guy comes to a halt. I turn around and look at him.

"What?" I say harshly.

He looks at me with a glare then turns to Ernie.

"Sorry, man, she just walked in here," the shirtless guy says.

I roll my eyes at him. He probably has no clue who I am.

"It's perfectly fine, Luke. She's family," Ernie boasts.

So, finally, shirtless wonder has a name.

"Ali, this is our head mechanic Luke. Luke, this is Rob's daughter Ali."

His demeanor seems to shift a little while grabbing the back of his neck and wiping it with a rag. He extends his hand. I extend my hand to meet his and give him a firm shake.

"Nice to meet you," he says.

I nod and give half a smile. I take my hand away quickly, wiping it on my pants. He smiles at Ernie then turns to walk away while glaring at me. I ignore his side-eye, not wanting to make it look like I am interested in watching his sexy ass walk away. I focus on Ernie to engage in a conversation.

"Did you bring the Mustang with you?" Ernie questions.

Surprised by his question, I say, "Yeah, it's out in front."

His eyes light up, and he smiles.

"Luke, you have to see this thing."

Luke stops at the doorway of the garage as Ernie walks over to him. They both walk out of the shop.

Well, that was awkward. When did my dad hire a hot guy? How long has he been here? When did he become head mechanic? He must have been here a while to attain that title. Why did my dad never mention him to me? And where is his damn shirt?

I make my way over to my car. Both Ernie and the shirtless guy are walking around it. They look like two giddy High School girls. Luke runs his hand down my vehicle from the front to the back, which makes me cringe. I want to open my mouth to yell some rude comment about not touching my car.

Before I can get a word out, Ernie says, "Ali, pop the hood, will ya? I want to show Luke the engine work."

I toss him my keys from my pocket. He pops the hood. Both of their faces light up again as they dive underneath. I've taken great care of my car, and she's clean as a whistle. Ernie was there during the restoration of *Eleanor*. My father and Ernie gave it that name from the movie *Gone in Sixty Seconds*, even though my car is not silver like the one in the film. They were so proud of the work and time spent on this car; I'm still surprised that it was given to me.

I break from my thoughts just as I am lifted into the air and swung around in a circle. I scream before being set back down to earth.

It's Jason, Ernie's son. He is two years older than I am. That makes him twenty-six years old now. We grew up together and were best friends throughout our childhood. I was three grades behind him. When Junior High and High School hit, we drifted apart. He became more interested in girls and partying in High School.

Since I've been away, we've talked here and there, but I haven't seen him in a while, not even when I'd come home during the holidays. Jason looks a tad different than I remember. He no longer has his *Troy Bolton* hair from the theatrical production *High School Musical*. Now, Jason is clean-cut, sporting the latest men's hairstyle, and is no longer a string bean. He's still cute, quite handsome now.

"Alicat, it is so good to see you! I see you haven't changed since I saw you last," Jason says while looking me over before giving me a huge bear hug.

I forgot that I pulled out some old clothes from my closet. I'm not wearing what I usually wear nowadays.

"Oh my Gosh, Jay, it's so good to see you!"

I ignore the comment about my current attire.

"I heard you graduated on top of your class and were offered a professional job right out of college?"

"Yea, I did. The city has so much to offer. I love it!" I beam.

The city does have a lot to offer, and I do love my job. However, I miss the countryside, cars, seeing these guys, and my dad. Even though my dad isn't here, these guys—Ernie and his family—are like my own family.

"Where are you working these days?" I make small talk as I kick the gravel underneath my boots.

I am trying not to look over at the hot shirtless guy bent over under the hood of my car.

"Here. I am still working for your da—" he looks at me with pain in his eyes.

"I'm so sorry about your dad, Ali," he says softly. "We all miss him a lot around here. He was such an amazing man and like a second father to me."

"Thanks. I miss him too," I reply, trying to hold back my tears.

I do miss my dad, something fierce. Being here is tough, but, at the same time, almost therapeutic. It's weird being at my father's shop without him here. I can still feel his presence. I'm glad to see that it's still running smoothly without a hitch. I know my father wouldn't want it any other way.

"What are you up to tonight? We need to catch up. It's been a long time," Jason smiles.

"I don't know. I'll probably be hanging out at my dad's and watching TV."

"I'm having a small get together with some friends if you want to drop by. I'm sure the gang would like to see you. Please try to make it. It will mean a lot to me," Jason begs.

The gang? Am I the only one who left this place? Maybe they came back to attend my dad's funeral, but I don't remember seeing them there. I was sort of off in my own world yesterday; I must not have noticed them.

"Yeah, that sounds like fun. At your parents, then?" I ask.

He laughs and says, "No, I live with a few buddies out past highway fifteen. I will text you the address. Come by around eight."

"Okay, sounds good," I reply.

It will be good for me to hang out with Jason and the others who I haven't seen in so long. It will be way better than being alone at my dad's place, thinking about the fact that he is gone. It will be a nice change of scenery and a worthwhile distraction. I've missed Jason.

chapter three

I see a bunch of guys walking out the garage. A few of them are carrying lunchboxes and thermals. They look so young. There are a few older gentlemen, but most look around my age.

How could I not have known about all these young workers? Did my father not tell me, or was I that consumed in my new life to pay attention to his?

"It's lunchtime!" one of them blurts out.

A few of the guys head over with Ernie and Luke to where my car is parked One of them comes over by Jason and me and jumps up to throw him into a headlock.

"Dude, don't mess with my hair," Jason demands, with a broad smile while fixing it in the way any girl would.

"We going to Mary's today?"

"Where else would we go, man," exclaims Jason.

They still go to Mary's Cafe every day for lunch. I love this. My dad and Mary's daughter had a little crush on each other and spent a lot of time canoodling while I was in High School.

"This is Rob's daughter Ali. You may remember her from High School," Jason tells the guy who joined us.

"Yea, I remember her. You were a few years behind us, right?" he claims.

I do not remember him at all. I should, shouldn't I? High School ended only six years ago, but I've been too focused on college and my job. I have blocked out a lot.

"Hey, you should come to Mary's with us. It will be like old times," Jason smiles.

"I'm there, and I'm hungry," I shout.

Mary's Cafe is a small restaurant that has been around for as long as I can remember. I would frequently dine there with my dad. The best home-cooked meals come out of that little place.

Walking across the street with Jason and a few of the other guys, I cannot help but look around for Luke. He and Ernie are no longer near my car. Ernie goes home every day for lunch and spends that time with his wife. I assume he is still doing so, as he is nowhere around.

I overhear Jason and some of the other guys' talking. They're discussing the party at his house tonight plus what alcohol they're planning to bring and what females might be there.

We reach Mary's Cafe across the street and down a block from my dad's shop. I notice that she has a new sign hung outside her restaurant, while fake red shutters still hug the two large windows.

As I walk inside Mary's Café, the aroma hits me like a ton of bricks. Oh, how I've missed this smell of pure taste bud fantasy. It feels great to be back. I feel instantly at home. The inside still looks the same. There are old wooden benches with tables on one side and wooden tables in the back. The wooden counter, with malt shop stools from the fifties, rests alongside it near the kitchen.

Jason and the others head toward the tables at the back. About five of them and I crowd around before sitting down. I notice that Luke is sitting by himself at one of the booths near the window. He is wearing a shirt. However, it's not a regular shirt, the sleeves are missing, and you can see down the sides of his rock-hard body. I take a seat within his view but still blocked by one of my dad's workers. Therefore, he cannot see me. I think, anyway.

A loud screech overpowers my ears at that very moment. The lady behind the screech is Mary, who comes hurling around the corner.

"Allison Garrett!"

I stand up and walk towards her. She is wearing a long yellow dress and a white food-stained apron. Her gray hair is pulled back in a bun, and she is wearing her black cat eyeglasses. She looks exactly how I remember her. She throws her arms around me. It is the warmest hug anyone has given me since I've been home.

"Mary!" I mumble.

When our hug parts, her hands are still locked in my arms. She looks me up and down.

“Allison, you're so beautiful and all grown up!" Mary projects joyfully. "It's so good to see you, my dear. We've missed seeing your friendly face around these parts."

"I've missed being home and your amazing cooking, of course," I say with a huge smile.

She hugs me again while squealing. I sit back down in my seat while she hands us each a menu. The menu looks a little different from before, but it still has her usuals. I skim over the front and flip to the back. I run my hand down to where it says sandwiches and locate Robby's Delight. My eyes begin to fill with water, and my heart sinks into my chest.

My dad came here so much and had Mary make him a specialty sandwich every time. She added it to the menu and named it after him. The Robby's Delight is a lot like your everyday club sandwich; the only difference is the addition of dijon mustard and pickle.

"What can I get you ruffians and Allison to drink?" Mary chuckles.

As everyone gives their drink order, I cannot help but look over at Luke. He is scrolling through his phone while sipping on what I can only imagine is perhaps coffee or tea. A plate with a half-eaten slice of pie sits in front of him. His profile is flawless. He is no longer wearing his backward cap, which means he is respectful. That is more than I can say for my group. The boys are still wearing their hats, bandanas, or welding caps.

Luke looks so mysterious, sitting all alone. His hair is a tad messy, but it looks great how it lays flat all over the place.

"Allison? Allison? ALLISON?" Mary shouts.

"Yea?" I say, put on the spot.

"What would you like to drink, dear?"

"A raspberry tea, please."

The guys all burst out laughing and rip on me a little bit for being off in a daze, a daze over a guy I just met an hour or so ago. I have so many questions in my mind about him. Why is he so intriguing to me? I haven't let a guy intrigue me in a long time. I've been too busy reaching my goals to give my time to one.

Why is he sitting by himself?

Mary brings out our drinks and begins to take our orders. I start.

"I will get the Robby's Delight, please," I say to Mary.

Mary, Jason, and the guys all stop talking. It becomes silent as all eyes are on me. I look around in the awkward silence.

"Sweet potato fries with no tomato."

"A side of barbecue sauce for your fries, dear?" Mary asks with sympathetic eyes.

"You remember!" I gleam with a smile.

I look over at Luke again and realize that his seat is now vacant. A few bucks lie on the table. He must have gone back to the shop.

chapter four

I pull down the long driveway, and my dad's house comes into view; I cannot help but see it in a different light. I have pulled up to this house a million times. It looks much different today. As the sunbeams overhead, the place looks so serene. Goosebumps travel up my body as I stare at this beautiful little farmhouse.

I get out of my car and make my way over to the old barn my dad used as his shop. I unlatch the hinge and slide open the doors. I look around and see that everything is neatly organized. All my dad's tools hung so nicely. His silly signs are hanging all around, and his crazy stereo that plays everything from CDs, tapes, and even albums.

I run my hand down his workbench that reaches along one whole side of the barn. It is covered with brown heavy-duty construction paper for easy cleanup, and you can still see all my doodles from when I would be out here doing my homework.

I continue walking around the barn. I see an engine hoist with what resembles a big block that has been taken apart halfway. The back end of a Ford Pinto is sitting a few feet from it and my dad's favorite piece of equipment, a car lift. A 1967 Oldsmobile Cutlass on top and a 1978 Ford F150 underneath. They were vehicles from my father's youth. The Cutlass was his first car. It's in immaculate shape, and everything is original except for a new paint job. A few other classic trucks and cars litter the barn along with his rusty but trusty plow truck.

My pocket begins to vibrate, and a ding sound follows. I pull my phone out and open a text from Jason.

2242 old hwy. 15. Be there or be square, Alicat!

I almost forgot about the party at Jason's tonight. I text him back before heading into the house to get ready.

I will be there!

I walk into the house. It's so quiet in here. My dad's awful old-time country music isn't blaring throughout the house. I take off my boots and head to the shower. I should take a bath instead since I need to shave my legs. It's hot out, so I think I will wear shorts tonight.

I start to blow dry my hair after I successfully shaving my legs. I have no clue how to wear my hair tonight. I decide to straighten it and put a few curls at the end. I apply some foundation, brown eyeshadow to accent my green eyes, black eyeliner, and the mascara everyone is going gaga over, that makes your lashes look longer and fuller. I step back from the mirror to apply a light brown matte lip gloss then head to my room.

I grab my suitcase and plop it on my bed. I go through what I brought from home, realizing that I mainly packed business casual clothes. I dress in business attire for work, and when I go out with colleagues, I dress in a business casual fashion. My wardrobe is for the working girl, not the country gal.

I turn to my closet for ideas. I will be out in the woods at a house party, no need for business casual. I pull out a light green crew neck sweater. I pull it over my head and flip my hair out from under it. I forgot the neckline is extended, causing one side to slip slightly off my shoulder. I remember I used to love wearing this sweatshirt.

I head over to my dresser and grab a pair of whitewashed jean shorts and grey socks. I slide on my shorts. Woah, I don't remember these being so short. My ass cheeks are just shy of spilling out underneath them. However, it doesn't matter much to me. I glance at myself in the mirror, and the sweater/shorts combination looks cute.

I check my phone, and the time is seven-fifteen. My stomach starts to fill with butterflies. I can't understand why I am so nervous. I used to attend parties when I lived here, granted not as many as Jason. I was busy studying and helping my dad with my car. I guess I am just nervous to see everyone.

LOWERING MY MUSIC AS IF IT WILL HELP ME SEE THE FIRE numbers on the side of the road better, I come upon 2242. I take a left and head down a long driveway. This one is even longer than my dad's. I can hear music and people hooting and hollering as I pull closer to Jason's house. A large bonfire blazes in an equally large yard; behind it is your basic rambler home. There is a basement with the main floor. A two-stall garage is situated not far from the house.

I pull up behind a line of cars. I thought Jason said it was going to be a small gathering. It looks like a full-blown frat party. I should know never to trust Jason when he says it's going to be a small party. They're always sublime with a lot of people and booze.

I flip down my visor to check over my hair and makeup. I look down at my purse in the passenger seat and start to grab it. I put it back down, realizing I don't need to carry my purse around with me. It's better to keep it in the car just in case I lose it at the party. I step out of my vehicle, locking the doors, slide my keys into my front pocket, and my phone into my back pocket.

I make my way up the rest of the driveway. When I pass the fire, I don't see many people there. I head over to the house; only one light is on. I wonder where everyone is. I see a few people coming out from behind the garage.

"Ali?" I hear someone call my name.

I see a tall, skinny, blonde girl walking towards me.

"Hi," I say back. She makes the most annoying screech and runs up to hug me.

It's a girl from High School named Bridget, who was always at every party. She always needed every guy's attention and had the hots for Jason.

"OMG, girl! You look amazing! How are you?" she screams in excitement.

"I am well. Thank you. How have you been?" I reply, and no sooner than that, her posse of equally annoying girls join her.

"Hey, Ali." Hi, Ali," they say, smirking.

Here are the same groups of girls together like in High School, who were nice to me, yet mean at the same time. Every girl wanted to be them, and guys wanted to, well, you know. Bridget, Nikki, and Mindy still look the same as they did back in High School, and they still seem to have that stuck up bitchy attitude.

"Jason is around here somewhere. Come with us. Some of the guys are bullshitting in the garage. Everyone is above it. There is a pool table, beer pong, and beer!" Bridget says, sounding like she is forecasting the weather.

I smile and follow them to the garage. I notice the driveway goes a short distance past the garage then turns. I cannot see much past that; the sun is starting to set, and the sky is becoming darker. I walk through the group of people with Bridget, Nikki, and Mindy as they say hi to everyone. I am not surprised to see the guys hugging them or grabbing their ass. I do not see Jason amongst these people nor recognize them. He must be down in the garage area.

Nikki hands me a drink.

"What is this?" I ask.

"Jeremiah Weed and Pink Lemonade," she replies.

I've never heard of Jeremiah Weed, so I ask the girls about it.

"What's Jeremiah Weed?"

The girls giggle as they look at each other.

"It's a sweet tea whiskey," chimes Mindy.

"So delicious," Bridget says as she smiles, taking a sip from her cup.

I look down at the light brown colored liquid in my cup. I've been drinking Moscato and Chardonnay for the past four years. I'm positive hard liquor is going to kick my ass tonight. I take a sip and find it surprisingly impressive; I cannot taste the whiskey as its light and tastes precisely like sweet tea. These will go down rather easily.

The girls walk off and mingle amongst the piles of men that have staggered around. I skim the room again looking for Jason. Since I can't see him, I make my way back to the stairs to head down to the garage. Someone grabs my arm, and I turn around. I realize that it's the guy who works for my dad who put Jason in a headlock earlier today.

"Hey. Remember me? I never got a chance to introduce myself. I'm Austin," he says as he sways back and forth.

"Hey, Austin! Nice to meet you. Again," I reply with a smile.

"Are you looking for Jason? I'm pretty sure he went back into the house with a girl not too long ago," he laughs.

I giggle.

"Yeah, I am, and I see Jason hasn't changed at all."

Austin walks with me out into the garage. I recognize more familiar faces; the guys I had lunch with today and a few faces from High School. Everyone is amicable and half in the bag already. I guess I am a little late to the game.

I watch as a few guys participate in keg stands and chant as they take shots of *Fireball* and *Wild Turkey*. They manage to get me to take a few shots too. *Fireball* burns all the way down and leaves a warm but fuzzy feeling. I'm not too fond of this stuff.

Jason appears in the garage after my fourth drink of this fantastic sweet tea and a couple of fireballs. He lifts me over his shoulders, and I get a sudden urge to pee.

"About time you showed your face," I slur with a smile.

"I was getting lucky," he boasts as guys chant around us, and a few of them give him fist bumps.

"I have to pee!" I shout.

Jason whispers in my ear while he throws his arm around my shoulders, "Everyone has to piss outside, but you can go in the house. It's the second door on the right."

I feel glad I do not belong to the "everyone" category, considering how close we are. I am also not comfortable popping a squat outside while intoxicated. Jason takes his arm from around me and smacks my ass as I start to walk away. I turn around, giving him the middle finger and stick my tongue out at him. I have to pee so bad.

I make my way to the house and notice the driveway that goes past the garage. I can see the light shining through the trees. My curiosity takes the better of me, and I head down the road, forgetting that I need to use the restroom. At times like these—peeing takes a backseat to curious adventures.

chapter five

I follow the dirt road, for what seems like forever. However, I have not ventured too far from Jason's house. When I look back, I can still see the garage light through the trees. The loud headbanging music fades as I travel further down the dirt road. I stop when I see a ginormous pole barn.

The light shines brightly from the top of the pole barn. As I walk closer, I can hear the faint sound of music coming from the building. There are three large doors across the end, with a small main entrance on the side. I reach for the handle and can make out the song *Are the Good Times really over?* by *Merle Haggard.* The kind of music that my dad listened to.

I open the door.

"Hello?" I say softly as I step inside.

I looked around this vast building and notice that there is nobody in sight. I am surprised to see a pole barn with a concrete floor instead of a dirt one. I see a black Dodge Charger in front of me. As I walk further in, there is another car that I am not quite sure of, because it's so rusted and smashed up. In front of it is a lifted Denali truck. I spot a few dirt bikes, two four-wheelers, a side by side, a boat, and a motorcycle filling the rest of the space.

This place is phenomenal—all the tools, toys, and cars. Even the workbench is astounding. Is this Jason's too? I notice out of the corner of my eye that there is a car under a sheet. I am surprised that

I didn't see it earlier. I'm feeling nosey, so I make my way over to it. I lift a part of the sheet to see collector plates. The plate reads *ALIS HERO*. Now, my curiosity is stoked further. This plate is very familiar. My mind is buzzing with questions. Why is it on this car? I had it made for my dad one year for Christmas when I was in High School. Why does Jason have it?

"What are you doing?" I hear a voice coming from behind me.

Startled, I drop the sheet and turn around, quite buzzed from all the drinks and shots. I look up to see Luke standing with a wrench and an angry look on his face, which quickly fades into shock.

"I— I, why are my dad's plates on this car?" I fire back at him.

Uninterested in his answer, I turn back to the car, and as I remove the sheet, Luke says in a concerned voice, "I wouldn't do that, Ali."

I rip the cover from the car; it's my dad's Ranchero. It was his favorite vehicle out of all the ones he owned. Tears fill my eyes as I run my hand across the hood while walking over to the side. I drop to my knees when I see the crumpled-up door panel. My mind starts to turn, and flashes of my father come across it. There is a reason why the door panel is crumpled.

My father was on his way home from work when a young woman t-boned him. He pulled out from the intersection, and she side-swept him. She was going so fast that it spun their vehicles around, causing hers to go into the ditch. Her car flipped a few times before ending up on its roof. My father rushed over to see if the young woman was okay.

There was water in the ditch, and she was trapped inside her vehicle. Unbeknownst to them, one of the telephone poles nearby had a loose cable laying in the water. As my father was pulling her out of the driver's side window, both he and the young woman got electrocuted, and my father was killed instantly. My father taking the brunt of the shock, the woman they say, received the shock through him. The young woman ended up dying from head trauma a few days later.

I feel a hand on my shoulder. I turn to look at Luke. I push his arm off me as I stand up and take off running. I can hear the muffled crackles as he yells my name, but I keep running. I run out of the building, past Jason's house, and all the people partying until I reach my car. I am crying so hard that I drop my keys while fumbling to get into my vehicle.

"Ali, wait!" Luke pleads as he grabs my arm.

I turn to yell at him to leave me alone, but I bury myself into his chest. He wraps his arms around me and holds me tight while I cry the hardest I have since the news of my father's death. I've felt so alone since I have been back, and I've reached my threshold. I break down, and it feels therapeutic in a sense. I push my hands against Luke's chest, pushing myself away from him and out of his grasp.

"Sorry," I whimper while wiping my face and under my eyes with my shirt sleeve

. "It's okay. I needed a shower anyway," he says with a smirk, while trying to lighten the mood.

I giggle. I guess Luke isn't the asshole I have assumed he was from the day we met. He's quite sweet.

"Have you been drinking?" he asks.

"Yes, I have had a few," I reply.

"Would you like me to drive you home?" I nod politely and hand him my keys before walking around my car to get into the passenger side.

I figure I need a ride home since I am not in the best condition to drive. I've had a few drinks, and my recent outburst in front of Luke are two good reasons for that.

We are silent during the whole drive to my dad's house. I lean my head against the window, staring out into the darkness as tears spill down upon my cheeks.

We pull up at my dad's house, and I run inside without even saying 'thank you' to Luke. I run-up to my room, slam the door shut, and lie down on my bed. I pull a pillow to my chest and cry myself to sleep.

I WAKE WITH A SUDDEN URGE TO PEE. I REMEMBER THAT I didn't go to the bathroom while I was at the party. Flashbacks from what I saw in the building at Jason's fill my head. I walk downstairs to see if my car is here. I look out the window; my car is in the driveway.

I grab myself a glass of water from the kitchen and walk into the living room. I'm startled to see Luke on the couch, and almost drop my drink. There is light shining on his face from the moonlight poking through the window. He looks hot even while he sleeps.

I walk over to the couch, grab the blanket off the back, and cover him up. I look at him for a moment, then head back to my room.

chapter six

My ringing phone awakens me. An *unknown number* flashes across my screen. I hit the silent button, lie my head back on my pillow, and fall asleep.

I sit on the couch, watching TV. My dad is in the kitchen, frying fish he caught on a great weekend at the cabin. He comes into view as the sun is shining through the dining room window before supper time. "Dad, do you need any help with dinner?" I call out to him. He doesn't reply to me. I call out to him once again, and there is still no response. He doesn't even turn to look at me. He's just standing there staring out the window. Beams of light shine on him as the sun is setting. I leave the couch and walk toward him.
As I approach him and place my hand on his shoulder, I softly say, "Dad?"
He vanishes, and dust particles float around through the air in the beam of sunlight where he was standing.

I spring awake in a panic, dripping with sweat, and start to cry. It is the first time I have dreamt about my dad since he passed away. I am confused as to why he did not look at me in my dream nor answer me. The dream felt so real. It was like he was there staring out of the window.

I walk to the bathroom while collecting myself from the bizarre dream. The light at the top of my phone is blinking. I swipe the screen to unlock it; I have a missed call from Jason and an unknown number. There are text messages from Jason, my coworkers, and Troy.

Are you still here?
Where did you go?
Are you okay?

All three are from Jason. I left his party last night without finding him to say goodbye. I reply.

Yea, I'm fine, Jay. I came home from the party. Call you later.

There is a message from my coworker/roommate Larissa. She likes to go by Ris.

How are you doing, girl? Thinking of you and miss you. Mwah.

Ris is great. We've become very close friends. When I started my job at Facade, we were both fresh out of college. She came from a high-class upbringing and studied at a prestigious college; however, she is nonetheless warm and very kind. We get along very well. It's the best friendship I have ever had with any female.

I've always had more male friends than female friends. The female friends I did have in High School only seemed to like hanging out with me because I was always surrounded by boys.

Ris and I live in a cute little two-bedroom apartment near downtown Milwaukee. It's about twenty or so blocks from work. I wish I could see her right now. She is so caring and compassionate when I need a shoulder to cry on.

She'd fit right in here with all the guys. She pulls off sheik to geek at the snap of a finger. Therefore, she could pull off hot business chick to countryside hick, no problem. She is quite wild when she is in party mode, that's for sure. She's a tad bit on the promiscuous side. Ris and Jason would easily hit it off.

Hey, sorry I've been so quiet. It's been a bit crazy the past few days. Miss you too. Call you later.

I reply to her message.

The next text is from Troy, a guy I'm kind of seeing back in the city.

Goodnight, beautiful, sleep well!

Troy has messaged me numerous times since I came home to attend my father's funeral. I've been short with him since I got here with one or two-word replies to his sweet little greetings, such as "Good Morning," "Have a great day!" and "Good Night."

We met about six months ago at a Gala Night for a fundraiser that my boss puts on every January. Troy is a fantastic guy. He's so sweet and a thorough gentleman. I've mainly only seen him in slacks, a button-up shirt, and a suit jacket. I've seen him a time or two in jeans and a t-shirt, but still with a suit jacket. He seems to be quite proper and high class.

We started seeing each other about a month ago. We're not officially dating. Everything is fresh and new now that I have finally given in. Troy chased me from the moment we met, but I played hard to get, very hard to get. We've only kissed once since we started seeing each other. He doesn't seem to mind that, at least as far as I am aware.

I hear a car door slam outside, and I rush from the bathroom to the window across the hall. I completely forgot about last night. I got wasted at Jason's and had Luke drive me home in my car. He must have called someone to pick him up. It doesn't seem to be Jason, though; it looks like a girl. I hope I did not cause any drama regarding staying here last night if he has a girlfriend. I must thank him for his kind gesture. Judging by his appearance alone; you wouldn't think he has one respectful bone in his body. Most good-looking tattooed men are arrogant assholes, and that's just putting it lightly.

I was quite drunk last night and was caught off guard by seeing him in that pole barn with my dad's vehicle from the accident. I cannot seem to stop thinking about him since I met him yesterday. I need to know a few things about him. Does he live with Jason? I didn't notice another fire number when walking to that building. However, I was also intoxicated and not paying much attention to what was going on.

My phone rings. It's Jason.

"Sup Alicat?" he says

A little too chipper for eight o'clock in the morning, which is a little bit surprising since he was probably drunker than me at the party last night.

"Hey, Jay! What's up?"

"Did you get super shitty last night and drive home?" he questions.

"I got pretty drunk, but I didn't drive home," I tell him.

"Phew, that's good. My dad would've killed me if he found out that I let you drink and drive. Next time, you should just stay the night. I have a guestroom with your name on it, or you can always cuddle up to me." he laughs.

"I'll remember that!" I reply sarcastically.

"How long till you're ready?"

"What? Ready for?" I say, feeling quite puzzled.

"I will be over in ten minutes to pick you up to head to my parents for breakfast! It's the best hangover cure ever, remember," he proclaims.

"Oh, okay! I have to go change quick," I say.

"See ya in a few," he says before hanging up.

I scramble around to brush my teeth, throw my hair up, and fix my makeup from crying last night. I throw on some jeans and a t-shirt. I hear a honk coming from outside. Shit. He's here already. I look terrible. I resemble a dog that just threw up.

I hop inside Jason's truck, and he gives me a stare.

"What?" I say to him in annoyance.

"You look fucking hot!" he grins.

I roll my eyes at him and pull my purse onto my lap.

"A purse? Since when you lug around a purse?" Jason laughs.

"Shut up! I am a girl, you know, and we do use purses for our shit," I reply.

"I know that, but, honestly, it's weird to see you with one," he chuckles.

I look at him and flick him off before gazing out the window. It's so pretty out here, so many trees. It's so different from the city, and even the smell is distinct. I see birds flying around, bugs buzzing by, and wildlife roaming all over. The country is so peaceful.

"How did you get home last night anyway?" Jason asks.

I was dreading this question, but perhaps it will help me find out more information about Luke. I fidget with my fingers in my lap.

"Um... Luke drove me home in my car."

I can see the anger building on Jason's face. Why is it a big deal to Jason that he gave me a ride home? It was very nice of him to do so.

"Did you sleep with him?" Jason barks.

"What? No!" I reply in a pissy voice. "He slept on my couch and was picked up this morning by some chick."

I can see the blood boiling in Jason. He grips tightly to his steering wheel and clenches his jaw together. He looks cute when he's angry. But damn, he's pissed. I wonder what grudge he has against Luke.

"Stay the hell away from him, Ali, I mean it," Jason says, straight-faced as he looks at me dead in the eye.

"Why? He was nice enough to bring me home when I was drunk and upset last night."

"He's not a good guy, Ali. He's a piece of shit, and to tell you the truth, he should've never come here." Jason says fuming.

I clearly do not know the history between these two, but I could tell something is amiss. I give Jason a concerned, yet confused as hell, look.

"He pulled up to the shop one day on his stupid ass motorcycle and never left. If it weren't for your dad, Bridget and I would still be together," he says, looking at me like a lost but angry puppy.

"What do you mean if it wasn't for my dad?" I demand.

"Your dad took Luke under his wing. They did everything together, and your dad taught him a lot about cars. Granted, Luke knew a lot already, more than most of us," Jason says.

"We hit it off pretty good at first, and I even had him move into my house. The one you were at last night. I was having one of my parties, and Bridget and I got in a fight because she was flirting with Luke and was all over him."

I can see Jason getting more and more worked up as he continues to tell me the story. I wasn't aware that he and Bridget were in a relationship. All he did was sleep with her many times back in High School, along with a bunch of other girls. They never had anything serious since she slept with other people too. All of this comes to me as a surprise. So much has changed in the past six years.

"A few buddies of mine told me about Bridget disappearing from a party. I went to look for her. I ended up finding her butt ass naked in Luke's bed. I threw a punch, and we began to fight. It was a huge fight, and a lot of stuff got broken at my house. My dad and your dad came to intervene and break us apart."

After hearing the story, I feel sorry for Jason. I would like to know Luke's side of the story, but I need to be sympathetic toward my friend.

"Oh, my goodness, Jay. I'm so sorry," I say while I grab his hand.

That explains why Luke was sitting all alone yesterday at Mary's.

"Luke moved all of his stuff out and into the pole barn. Your dad helped him fix it up and add a living quarter to the back. I wish he would've just left town. I hate that motherfucker," Jason retorts.

I feel awful for Jason. How could a friend do such a horrible thing to you after you welcome them into your home? Why was my dad so close to Luke? I have so many questions. I cannot for the life of me understand the relationship between my dad and Luke. At the same time, I keep wondering why my dad never told me about him at all. I need to find out more about that mysterious hunk of deliciousness.

Why would my dad help him? I know my dad had a kind soul. However, I know that he'd never help someone over Jason. Bridget must have been the girl who picked up Luke from my house this morning.

"Please, just stay away from him, Ali." Jason pleads.

I am quite shocked and clueless. I agree with Jason so that he will calm down.

"Okay," I reply, looking at him.

Jason turns up the music, and we ride the rest of the way to his parent's house in silence. I cannot get out of my head that Luke must not be that bad if my dad was willing to help him. He even made him the head mechanic at his shop. Did that piss Jason off too? There could be more to this than what Jason is saying. I know my dad would never be this kind to anyone without good reason.

We pull into Jason's parents, and my phone rings.

"I will come in right after I take this," I say to Jason as he hops out of his truck and heads into the house.

"Hello."

"Good Morning, sweetie," my aunt says joyfully.

"Good Morning," I mutter.

"Tomorrow, we are meeting with your daddy's team of lawyers to go over his will. We can postpone until next week if you aren't ready," she exclaims.

I run my hand across my forehead because I know I'm not ready. I don't think I will ever be prepared to hear who gets whatever is left of my dad's shit. I need to get back to work, and next week will be too long to be away from my job.

"Tomorrow is fine," I reply with a sigh.

"See you tomorrow then, sweetie. Make sure to dress in your Sunday best! Hugs and kisses," she says, making smooching sounds before hanging up.

I look up from my phone to see Ernie and Jason on the deck.

They are standing with their shirts tucked under their chins and pinching their nipples while they're sticking out their tongues. Those two dorks have been doing shit like this since I was little, which most definitely lightened the mood. I laugh as I hop out of Jason's truck, shaking my head.

chapter seven

I feel very much at home inside Ernie and Gladys' house. I used to come here every Sunday for breakfast and a few of Jason's parties when they'd be out of town. Gladys is Ernie's wife, and she is quite the woman. She doesn't take any shit from anyone, and she's hilarious as hell.

This family is my second family. My dad, Ernie, and Gladys spent almost every day together since I was born. Gladys greets me at the door and gives me a huge hug. She tells me to fix myself a plate before I waste away. On the counter in the kitchen is a buffet-style breakfast, just like how I remember. Eggs, ham, bacon, sausage, hash browns, potatoes, and fruit are displayed in foil pans. There is also a pitcher of orange juice at the end of the counter, surrounded by glasses. I scoop up a little bit of everything and pile it on my plate. I head for the table and take a seat.

"Here, Ali," Gladys says as she hands me a large glass of milk. "You still like milk, right?" she asks with a smile.

"Yes, thank you!"

Aww, she remembered that I don't care for orange juice and was once obsessed with milk. My dad would have to buy me a separate gallon because I drank so much of the stuff. I still do drink it a lot but not in such an obsessive way anymore.

I feel I need to discuss the lawyer meeting that my aunt called me about with everyone at the table. I am not sure if this will be bad timing because we have just sat down for breakfast. I do not want to ruin the meal, but I must mention it since it is fresh on my mind.

"My aunt called and said we are meeting with the lawyers tomorrow at one. We need to go over my dad's Will," I spurt out.

Everyone goes quiet and stares straight in my direction. You could hear a pin drop if it weren't for the faint sound of music coming from the kitchen. Gladys looks at me with the most loving eyes. I always loved it whenever she did that. Ernie breaks away from his stare to focus back on his plate before bringing a spoon full of eggs to his mouth.

"We will be there with you tomorrow, Ali," Gladys says as she squeezes my hand.

I give her a light smile, then bring my attention back to my plate.

"Guess who brought Ali home last night?" Jason belts out like a colossal dick.

I kick him from under the table. Now, this is what I call bad timing. Jason is being a prick. Whatever his issues with Luke are, this is not the time for it.

"Luke brought her home. He even drove the mustang."

Ernie looks up at me from his breakfast with the most God awful look on his face. I melt in his expression; I feel like my dad is scolding me. Is he disappointed in me for drinking last night? Having Luke bring me home or that I let him drive my car?

Jason goes off on a tangent about how much he despises Luke. Ernie, without saying a word, stands up from the table. He walks into the kitchen, slamming his plate on the counter, then walks out the door. I give Jason a slight glare to indicate, "*why the hell did you say that*" then look over to Gladys. Gladys is staring at Jason. He gets up, slamming his chair against the table before stomping out the door. Like father, like son. I can hear Jason as he peels out of the driveway.

What in the sam hell just happened?

"I will give you a ride back to your dad's, Ali. Please finish your breakfast before it gets cold," she says as she starts to clear the table.

I promptly finish my breakfast and help Gladys clean up in the kitchen. I know my way around this kitchen just as well as I do around my dad's. I walk around the house looking at all the pictures. I see a few of Jason and me when we were younger. There are also pictures of my dad and Ernie. I need to consider that I am not the only one who lost my dad that day.

ON THE WAY BACK TO MY DAD'S, GLADYS TELLS ME HOW LUKE came along. She said he was passing through one day and had engine trouble with his bike. My dad and Ernie helped him work on it, and in return, Luke helped at the shop to repay them for the parts they bought for his bike. She went on to say that Luke is very reserved, and he does not say much, but he took a liking to my dad almost instantly. He came from California to get away from a life he wasn't proud of.

What kind of life was that? Jason did say he wasn't a good guy.

Gladys continues to say that she would've never known any of this if Luke hadn't confided in my dad. She went on to say that my dad let him stay at his house until his bike was fixed, but he ended up staying longer. That was almost two years ago now.

My dad never told me about Luke, not even once, since we spoke pretty much every day on the phone. He never even mentioned it when I'd come home occasionally, either. Is Luke that bad that my dad had to hide him from me? All of this isn't very clear, and I hope I will learn the truth soon.

Gladys mentions details of the story that I already knew about between Jason and Luke. She talks about how they got in a huge fight causing my dad and Ernie to break it up. The battle was mainly over that floozy Bridget, Gladys says, but partly because my dad made him his head mechanic. She went on to say that Ernie was not upset about it as they collectively decided to give Luke the position. He did show up to work more than Jason and would work whenever they needed him to, even if it was seven days a week.

Gladys said that they didn't kick him out of Jason's house because technically they own the property. My dad helped ease the tension by building Luke, a living area behind the pole barn. Jason never used it anyway, and it's also where my dad stored some of his stuff he wasn't currently working on at home or the shop.

chapter eight

I give Gladys a tight squeeze before getting out of her car. I was glad she did not react like Ernie and Jason. I felt relaxed with her in the car as well as on the drive home.

"Would you like us to pick you up before we head over to the lawyer's tomorrow?" she asks.

"Yes, that would be great! Thank you!" I reply.

We say our goodbyes, and I head into my father's house. I set my purse on the chair in the entryway and head for the living room. I sit down on the couch and flick on the TV. While flipping through the channels for something good to watch, I fall asleep.

I'm walking into the barn to bring my dad a plate of fresh-baked cookies and a glass of milk. He is bent over under the hood of his 1967 Ford Ranchero. He is talking to someone, and as I get closer, I can see who it is. It's Luke. They are working together on my father's engine.

"Dad, I brought you some milk and cookies!" I say excitedly. He doesn't reply and continues working and talking to Luke.

"What are you doing here?" Luke asks.

I open my eyes and sit up frantically. I look around to see that it's dark out now and that I was merely dreaming, again. Why am I dreaming about my dad and Luke? Why won't my dad look at me in them? I need to find out why Luke has my dad's Ranchero. These are all burning questions that I want answers to. I know I shouldn't be taking these dreams to heart because they're just that, dreams. Regardless, this one did shake me just like my previous dream; my father would not talk to me in that one either. He ignored me. I wonder if this is some sort of sign.

I check the time on my phone, and it's 8 p.m. Wow, I must have slept the day away. I have a few text messages to go over and reply to. I respond to Ris and Troy right away before setting my alarm for tomorrow. I'm not ready to meet with my dad's lawyers, but I don't have much choice, since I have already agreed to meet them. I read over Jason's text again before replying.

I'm sorry for what happened at breakfast. I don't like that guy. I didn't mean to upset you and my dad. Can you stay longer and come to the cabin with us next weekend? Please.

I don't know if I plan to stay through the weekend. I may leave back to the city after meeting with the lawyers tomorrow. I need to get back to work.

It's okay. I will think about it. Nite.

MY ALARM GOES OFF, AND I INSTANTLY REMEMBER THAT today is the day my father's death gets real. Today, we will be sitting down in front of his lawyers while they read off a piece of paper; what parts of my dad's life will go to who. I do not know how people can be excited about this sort of thing. I would rather have my dad back instead of his property.

I know when there is money or expensive collections involved, people become greedy, and that becomes their primary focus. It is no longer the death of their loved one. My feelings have not changed. I would give up all my dad's assets to have him back, even if it were only for a day. I want him here with me. To talk with me like he used to, unlike the dreams I am having where he won't even look in my direction.

I sit up from the couch and stretch my arms in the air. The reading of my father's Will today is making me sick to my stomach. Can I skip this part? I'm hungry, but I don't think I can manage to eat; I feel like throwing up. Why does this have to be done so soon after his death? Can't we wait a while, like forever? Everything is happening so fast that my heart's skipping a beat. I do not know how to handle this situation.

I head to the bathroom to take a shower. The hot water feels terrific against my neck and back, but I'm frozen in place while staring off into space. I'm numb from the feeling of what I have to go through today. I want to cry, but I can't. I want to crawl into my bed and not do today at all.

When am I going to grieve over the death of my father? Am I grieving? I've cried a few times, but I feel like I haven't grieved as I should. I know everyone grieves differently, but I thought I would take this way worse than I am. My father was my world. I should be more miserable then I am. I'm overthinking everything. I need to relax and take it easy.

I step out of the shower, soaking wet. I stare at myself in the mirror. Who are you? How are you not crying over your father? You're selfish. Am I?

I start to shiver but stay standing here, staring at myself. I give myself a blank stare as if I've turned into a zombie. I finally snap out of it and wrap myself in a towel then head to my room. I sit down on the edge of my bed and sob hard into the palms of my hands. I need to cry; I need to let my emotions out. It's necessary. I miss my dad so much. Why was he taken from me?

I cannot do today; I'm not ready for any of this.

I collect myself a bit and lift my suitcase off my floor before hurling it on my bed. I grab a pair of my seamless panties and a nude bra. I slip them on and sit on the edge of my bed again, staring at the floor, dragging my toes back and forth over the carpet. You can do this; you need to do this for him. You can do this; it's now or never. I prefer never.

I dig through the clothes I brought. I pull out a white button-up blouse, navy blue pencil skirt, and nude heels. My dad loved blue, especially dark blue, though he hated it when I dressed up as a businesswoman. He preferred when I was full of grease and anti-seize.

I head back to the bathroom before getting dressed, to do my hair, and some light makes up. I need to cover up these dark circles under my eyes from crying and lack of sleep. However, I have slept surprisingly well and quite a lot, despite a few odd dreams, since I've been home. If my dad was here, it would be early to rise, not waste the day or the sunlight, he'd say. He wanted to make use of his entire day to maximize his productivity. He was a consummate professional or overly motivated.

I straighten my hair and push it back in a low ponytail, apply some concealer under my puffy eyes, and brush on some mascara. I head back to my room and get dressed. I do not check myself in the mirror before heading downstairs. I drift off back into a numb state as I cannot recall much of myself walking down the stairs and into the kitchen. I do not feel like myself at all, but I need to get hold of myself.

I come back to when I realize I'm standing in front of the fridge, and the cold air hits my face. I grab an apple and milk and pour myself a glass. I sit down at the dining room table and stare out the window. The dream comes flooding back, the one I had a few days ago about how my father was standing here and staring out of the same window. This dream keeps playing over and over in my head.

A knock at the door releases me from my thoughts. I head over to open the door. Jason stands before me in khakis and a black button-up shirt, with his hair combed perfectly. He looks so handsome. Jason knows how to carry himself. He is a ladies' man, and despite the fact I do not have any feelings for him other than brotherly, he always impresses me with his dress sense. He usually dresses like a country boy, but he loves to dress to impress when the time comes.

I smile at him and wrap my arms around his chest. He holds me tightly in silence while resting his cheek on top of my head. We embrace for what seems like five long minutes before we part.

"Are you ready?" Jason asks.

"As ready I can be, I guess," I reply, trying not to cry.

I have cried enough already, and now it is time for me to take care of business. Business that I quite frankly do not wish to be part of, but I must be. I grab my purse, and we head out the door. Jason rests his hand on the small of my back as we walk towards his parent's car.

"You look beautiful today!" he says.

I turn to him and thank him with a slight smile.

"I still prefer you in those shorts, the ones your ass hangs out of, but this, this outfit is sexy." Jason laughs.

I give him a good smack and laugh, calling him a perv.

chapter nine

The drive is quiet yet peaceful as we make our way to the lawyer's office in another town. I lose myself in the beautiful summer scenery as I drift off daydreaming about—Luke! Why do I think about him so much? My mind becomes consumed by him, and I flashback to seeing his shirtless body the first time we met, his flawless profile as he sat alone at Mary's, and the look of his face after he held me while I cried on his chest. I wonder if he has soft, firm lips. Is he a good kisser? Woah, what is going on with me? I feel myself becoming more attracted to him the more I think about him.

My mind snaps back to reality as the car comes to a stop.

"We're here," Gladys says as she releases a massive sigh.

Jason grabs hold of my hand and looks at me with a smile before he exits the car. I stay back for a moment to work on my breathing. I see that my aunt and uncle are already here. We walk inside, and my aunt walks over to me. She hugs me, then turns to hug Gladys and Ernie. My uncle gives me an awkward side hug before he shakes Ernie and Jason's hands then gives Gladys a peck on the cheek. We all take a seat in the waiting room. I can tell everyone is quite uncomfortable, and no one wants to be here, but we all need to be. I'm glad I am not alone today.

The door opens as Luke walks through. He looks disheveled. His black button-up shirt is unbuttoned, revealing a white t-shirt, and is untucked from his gray slacks; his hair is scattered all over his head.

Ernie stands up and heads over to shake his hand. Luke stops buttoning up his shirt to shake Ernie's hand then my uncle's.

He asks the receptionist where the restroom is before excusing himself. I want to know why he is here, but for some reason seeing him just now and knowing that he is here sets me somewhat at ease.

"Why is he here?" Jason asks bitterly.

"Not now, Jason," Gladys mumbles.

I can cut the tension building in the air with a knife since Luke walked through the door. I grab hold of Jason's hand, and he puts his arm around me. I lean into him and close my eyes as we wait for my father's lawyers to call us into their office.

Luke walks back out from the bathroom, his shirt buttoned except for the top one, and neatly tucked into his pants. His hair is laying perfect across his head.

He sits by himself over by the window and takes his phone out of his pocket. I cannot help but stare at him. He looks insanely handsome the way he's dressed. Not that he doesn't look just as good in jeans and a t-shirt or just work pants, but right now, he looks perfect. I find myself looking him over from head to toe.

Even his shoes are perfect; they are black cap toe dress boots. Until now, all I've seen him wear are his dirty old work boots. His outfit is so debonair and sophisticated. I bring my eyes further up his body, studying every inch of him. He has long fingers; they are masculine, not too skinny but not sausage-like either. His broad shoulders are so sexy, and his jawline is defined.

I bring my eyes up to meet his.

Holy Shit!

Oh, God! Shit! Shit! Shit! He's looking right at me. What an idiot I am, caught like a deer in headlights practically undressing this man with my eyes. He gives me a slight smile, and I look away quickly without returning the gesture. I smile and look back over at him, but his face is down, looking back at his phone. His skin is beautiful too. He's so mysterious to me. There must be so much more to him then the eye can see.

I break free from my inappropriate sexual gaze and impure thoughts as I hear a voice.

"They are ready for you now," the receptionist says. "Right this way, please."

We all get up from our seats and head into a decently sized conference room with an oval mahogany table surrounded by fancy chairs. The room is decorated warmly with many works of art hanging from the walls. A bookcase is full of legal books and cascades along the back wall. Flowers lie centered on the table in a large vase. I take a seat furthest from my father's lawyers; on one side of me is my aunt, and on the other is Gladys.

Luke sits beside my uncle with an empty chair on both sides of him, almost directly sitting across from Jason, who, I'm sure, is secretly plotting his death. Jason is uncomfortable, but he has no choice but to deal with the situation. Both lawyers sit at the opposite end from me, a folder and manila envelope displayed out in front of them. The receptionist brings in a pitcher of water, some glasses, and a few boxes of tissues.

"Shall we begin?" one lawyer asks as he stands to introduce himself and his partner to us.

"You have all gathered here today to hear the final Will and Testament of Robert Allen Garrett," the other lawyer says.

He hands the receptionist a folder, and she starts to pass out a sealed envelope to each of us.

"Robert prepared a letter for each of you to be read at your leisure, whenever you are ready," the lawyer exclaims.

I can feel the tears well up in the corners of my eyes, and I reach for a tissue. Gladys and my aunt both reach to rub my back as I dab the corners of my eyes. I take the letter from the receptionist and place it on the table in front of me. Written in my father's handwriting, it says:

To my Little Lady

I'm unable to stop myself as tears flow down my face. My dad always called me his "Little Lady," and I always called him "My Hero." I grab the letter from the table and slide it into my purse. I wipe my eyes, wishing I hadn't worn mascara or at least wore the waterproof kind. I am blessed with the moral support here with me today.

"We will start by reading Robert's personal portion of his Will then end with his business portion," proclaims one of his lawyers.

Here we go. My father's lawyers will start naming off his personal belongings, the things he worked so hard for, and that he treasured. I take a deep breath and close my eyes. I open them and look over at Luke, who is staring at the table. He looks up at me with the most caring and sympathetic eyes. I look away as the lawyers begin to read my father's Will.

"I, Robert Allen Garrett, resident of the City of Baronette, in the State of Wisconsin, being of sound mind, body, and soul, not acting under duress or undue influence, fully understanding the nature and extent of all my property and this disposition thereof, do hereby make, publish, and declare this document to be my last Will and Testament."

I fade off into memories of my childhood. Memories of my father teaching me the proper way to hold a baseball bat, wiping away gooey marshmallow from my cheek after eating a s' more he had just made, and hanging my straight-A report cards next to my drawings on the fridge. I remember him picking the gravel from my wounds before bandaging my hand and knee after taking a digger from falling off my bike and learning to braid my hair as mommies do for their daughters.

I can see my dad jumping up and down as I ran out of the DMV the day I received my driver's license, his mouth wide open as I walked down the stairs in my Prom dress, taking me for ice-cream after my first broken heart, and helping me pack my car while tearing up as he hugged me before I left for college.

chapter ten

"I devise and bequeath my property, both real and personal and wherever suited as follows:

To my daughter, Allison Paige Garrett, I leave my home at 3891 Oakwood Trail in the City of Baronette, in the State of Wisconsin, and all equity found on and within my property.

My half of the family hunting property in the City of Effie, in the State of Minnesota, with my brother, David Patrick Garrett, to my daughter, Allison Paige Garrett.

My half of the cabin property on Kawaguesaga Lake in the City of Minocqua, in the State of Wisconsin with Ernie Michael and Gladys Elaine Anderson, to my daughter, Allison Paige Garrett.

My tools, equipment, scrap metal, and junked cars found in the large pole barn at 2242 Old Highway 15 in the City of Baronette, in the State of Wisconsin, as well as my 1967 Ford Rancho, to Lucas Mitchell Jameson."

A loud gasp is let out, and Jason gets up from his seat, storming out of the room with his hands clenched in fists. I watch, baffled, as he leaves. Gladys grabs my hand as she closes her eyes, shaking her head in an embarrassing disappointment towards her son. I look over at Luke, who has a tear trickling down his cheek. His hands are clasped together and pressed against his face while he is leaning his elbows on top of the table, looking downward with his brows knitted in a frown. My father must have meant something to him.

"We will now go over Robert's business portion of his last Will and Testament," one of the lawyers' states.

Grabbing another tissue, I look over at Ernie, rocking lightly in his chair while staring at the table. This is not only hard on me, but on everyone who is sitting here. I love them all, and that includes Luke. Astounding as it may be. I feel a sudden connection with him, considering how my dad has included him in his Will. Their relationship, it seems, must have been very close. Almost family like.

"My body shop, known as Rob's Classic Restoration at 1300 Highway 63 and 30th Avenue, in the City of Baronette, in the State of Wisconsin, is free of debt. All expenses and upkeep will be bestowed upon those listed below and will be distributed as follows:

Co-Owners, splitting the profits and losses, will be given to my daughter, Allison Paige Garrett, and my lifelong friend, Ernie Michael Anderson.

His son, Jason Robert Anderson, will receive his father's share in the time of his passing.

My friend, Lucas Mitchell Jameson, will receive ten percent of the business as long as he continues to work for Rob's Classic Restoration.

Ernie Michael Anderson and Lucas Mitchell Jameson will take over my business in its entirety with the assistance of my daughter, Allison Paige Garrett."

The lawyers continue with information on how my father wanted to leave his business. I knew he would leave it to Ernie and myself, but Luke too? I can see that my dad considered Luke a friend and trusted him enough to uphold this responsibility. So, shall I. Although, there is something I am surely missing. Jason and Gladys' stories about him don't seem to add up. In two years, my dad made him a part of the family, and I knew nothing about it.

I need to find out more about Luke, and more importantly, about my father's relationship with him. We couldn't be related, could we? Could he be my brother? It wasn't stated before his name in my father's Will that we were of any relation. Oh God, I hope that's not the case as I have been fantasizing about what he looks like naked lately.

I look over at Ernie. He has lost it and is sobbing profusely as Gladys comforts him. Jason has not returned since he stormed out some time ago. My aunt and uncle are sitting calmly listening to the lawyers speak as if they were listening to the church's hymnal. My eyes make their way to Luke again, and he looks like he's ready to lose it.

I get up from my seat, walk over to Luke, and sit down. He looks at me so empathetically. I put my hand on his arm as I continue listening to the lawyers as they finish my dad's Will. Luke places his hand over mine and removes it from his arm. He then grabs it with his other hand bringing both our hands under the table and onto my lap. He interlocks his hand in mine.

I look at him while he's looking at me. We give one another a slight smile then turn towards the lawyers. I feel comfortable with my hand inside his. Please, God, do not let us be related. I would dread for that to be true.

"Last but not least. Robert's final wishes," the lawyer says as he looks around the room at us.

"It is my last Will and Testament, and so I direct, that my remains shall be cremated, and some of my ashes are sprinkled at my hunting property, my cabin, and my shop. For my final resting place, I be placed inside an urn. My remaining ashes enclosed in the urn will be given to my daughter, Allison Paige Garrett.

This concludes the last Will and Testament of I, Robert Allen Garrett."

"A copy of Robert's Will is available to you at the front desk on your way out," one of the lawyers says.

The other lawyer notes, "We need everyone involved in Robert's Will to stay and sign documents before heading out."

I let go of Luke's hand and head over to the lawyers to sign the paperwork. When I finish, I head out the door and into the waiting area where Jason is standing. I grab a copy of my father's Will from the receptionist before walking over to hug him.

I excuse myself to find the restroom. As I return to the waiting area, everyone is standing around talking, except for Luke. I wonder where he went. My aunt hugs me, and we all head outside to the parking lot. Luke is standing at his truck. Ernie walks up to him, they shake hands, then embrace in a light hug.

Luke opens his door, about to climb in his truck, but stops and walks towards me. I look around for Jason, but I notice he is in his parents' car talking with Gladys. I look back at Luke.

"Can I give you a ride home?" he asks.

I look at Ernie, and he gives me a "go ahead" nod and smiles before turning to shake my uncle's hand.

"Sure," I reply.

A spark of excitement ignites through my body. Finally, I may be able to find out more about him. I say goodbye to my aunt and uncle, hugging them both tight. I wave to Ernie and Gladys, then walk with Luke to his truck. He opens my door for me and helps me up inside. He walks around the front of the vehicle and climbs up into the driver's seat. He closes his door and lets out a slow breath.

"I bet you have a lot of questions you would like to ask me," Luke says as he looks over at me.

He must have read my mind; I have a plethora of questions to ask him. I'm glad that he took the initiative. I look at him and nod. He turns the ignition, starting his truck, then shifts it into gear, and we begin to leave the parking lot.

chapter eleven

As we sit in silence, I notice how nice Luke's truck is. The inside is spotless with a light grey leather interior.

"What year is this?" I speak up, trying to break the quiet.

Luke looks over at me, with a raised eyebrow and a puzzled stare behind his eyes wondering why I might be asking something that is so far from the topic we need to discuss.

"It's a twenty-seventeen," he replies.

I can tell he is searching for the words to begin his story- how he came about here and his relationship with my father. I notice his apprehensiveness as he grips his bright orange steering wheel with both of his palms as he rolls them forward and back. Patiently, I wait for him to start talking.

"I'm not a bad person, contrary to what you've heard," Luke says as he grips tighter on his steering wheel. "Honestly, if your dad were here, he'd back me up on that."

I listen, without saying a word, while he tells me his entire story. He begins by saying that he is originally from San Diego, California. He was born and raised there. He got into some trouble and was sentenced to seven years in prison.

He was in a toxic on-and-off-again relationship with a girl who repeatedly accused him of cheating. Luke assured me that he had never cheated on her. They broke up, and three months later, she came back, claiming that she was pregnant. She demanded he take her back and help her raise their baby. His mother told him that he could still be a man by being there to help raise their child, but he did not need to put himself through that toxic relationship again. Since the girl was upset with his decision, she had her brother and a group of guys go after Luke. They jumped him one night after he got off work.

A few days later, he came home from work to find his mother's house, engulfed in flames. His mother was trapped inside. She received severe burns to her arms, chest, and face.

In a burst of rage, he went to the girl's house to find her brother. Luke beat him within an inch of his life, and he would've killed him if it weren't for the police ripping them apart. He was sentenced to seven years in prison for first-degree assault with an attempt to kill. However, he was released after only three years for good behavior. His mom came to visit a few times once she healed from her burns, but she decided to move to Arizona to live with a friend. Luke hasn't seen his mother since but speaks to her quite often; he goes on to say.

The baby was born while he was incarcerated, and he took a paternity test to find out that the baby was not his. The girl had been the one cheating, not Luke. When released from prison, there was nothing left for him in San Diego, and he wanted to leave his past behind him.

So, he took whatever little money he had and hitchhiked across the country. He stopped here and there along the way. When he arrived in Colorado, he stayed for a few weeks with a guy who picked him up in Las Vegas. He took on doing odd jobs to make a few bucks. He also traded work for a motorcycle before leaving Colorado and making his way to Wisconsin. He said that he was passing through when his bike broke down, and my father picked him up.

My father gave him a meal, a warm place to sleep, and even offered to help him fix his bike. Luke continued to tell me that he told my father he had no money to pay for the parts, but my dad said it was fine. He could work the debt off. Luke worked night and day for my dad, and anytime my dad needed help. He would also work when someone did not show up for their scheduled shift at the shop.

Eventually, he and my dad grew a quick and healthy bond. My dad was like the father Luke never had.

I am blown away by Luke's story and stay silent as I sit and listen to him. Tears roll down my cheeks when I hear about what happened to his mom and what he went through. Hearing him speak about the kindness of my father warms my heart. My father was a saint, and he'd give the shirt off his back.

Luke proceeds to tell me that my father talked about me a lot, and he wanted us to meet, but he wasn't quite sure how to break the news to me. He said it was probably due to his troubled past and not knowing how long he planned to stick around. Luke tells me he spent his holidays at Ernie and Gladys's, due to his growing friendship with Jason.

He liked my dad, Ernie, and Jason so much that he decided to stay once his bike was good as new. He and Jason eventually moved into a house that Ernie and Gladys bought to give to Jason with some help from my father.

Then Luke starts to talk about what happened the night of the fight between him and Jason.

"Bridget came into my room after I left the party to go to bed. She woke me up and started doing a striptease even though I asked her to stop and leave. She vomited all over my bedroom floor, and when I was in my bathroom, getting some towels to clean up the mess, Jason walked in to see Bridget passed out naked on my bed. That's when chaos ensued," he mutters.

Luke continues to tell me that he never touched Bridget that night. Since then, they've kissed a few times but are only friends and who hang out from time to time. He wanted to pack up his stuff and leave after the fight. He was worried about possibly going back to prison, but my dad talked him out of it, telling him that he's family and Jason would eventually get over it. My dad then helped him build a living quarter attached to the back of the pole barn and made him head mechanic a few months later at his shop, in the hope that he'd stay.

"We would work on vehicles together at the shop, your dad's old barn, and my pole barn. Your dad told me often that it was something he used to do every day with you, so it was nice to have a partner again." Luke says with sadness in his voice.

"Your dad helped pick out this truck that we are in, set the chrome accents on it, and put the lift kit in," he boasts.

"He planned to finally introduce us on the fourth of July when you came home for the holiday and his birthday," he sighs.

My eyes are blurring and filled with tears. Luke spilled almost his entire life story to me, well at least the past five or so years. I feel as if I've now known him my whole life. His mysterious persona has dissipated some, and he is more attractive to me than ever before. It's safe to say that Luke and I aren't related.

My dad always saw the good in everyone. He never judged people and always gave them the benefit of the doubt. My father knew that Luke was a good man, or he would never have helped him beyond fixing his motorcycle. I wish he would have told me about Luke, though. Nearly two years is a long time for my father to keep something from me. I am sure he thought I would fall for Luke and did not want me to get hurt if he left or want me to drop what I've worked so hard to achieve to move back home.

chapter twelve

I wipe the tears from my cheeks and flip down the visor in Luke's truck to check my makeup.

"I'm sorry for dropping all that on you, like that," he says while looking at me.

I needed to hear all of it, and it made me emotional. My father treated him like a son. He never had one, so he formed a relationship with Luke, which was heartwarming to hear.

"Thank you. It's exactly what I needed to hear!" I reply.

I give him an awkward smile, not knowing what else to say or how to show sympathy for what he went through without looking more like a complete weirdo.

"Are you hungry?" Luke asks.

I look over at his gorgeous face.

"I could eat!" I reply with confidence that screamed cockiness.

I want to slam my forehead into my palm or throw up in my purse in embarrassment. I am sure my cheeks are flush. Thankfully, he smiles and laughs under his breath before pulling into Mary's Cafe. Luke opens my door and helps me out of his truck.

"It's a beautiful truck," I say and add, "Why the color white?"

"I live down a long dirt road, so white looks clean the longest," he says as he smirks.

A sexy smirk at that. We sit down by the window, and Mary greets us as she passes out some menus.

"Two days this week! How did I get so lucky? Glad to see you are still here, Ali," Mary declares.

She gives me a devilish smile and raises her eyebrows twice as she looks over at Luke then back at me.

"Tell me a little bit about yourself. Your dad said you're brilliant, and you received an amazing job right out of college." Luke conveys, looking very interested in knowing a little about me.

"I attended Stout, majoring in Architecture with a minor in Graphic/Interior Design. I was blessed to receive an internship my sophomore year based solely on my grades and one of my professors' recommendation, whose good friend happens to be the CEO of the company where I work. After I graduated, I was asked to stay on as a full-time Designer. Currently, I design the lighting concepts mainly for commercial businesses but sometimes for personal clients." I take a breath, smile, then study his face.

Luke looks amazed after hearing about my achievements, and I continue to talk about what exactly my job entails as we dine. We also talk about what we enjoy; favorite past times, foods we like and dislike, cars, fishing, and laugh until our faces hurt. It's the most fun and magical time I've had eating lunch. Plus, he's easy on the eyes.

———

ON OUR WAY TO MY DAD'S HOUSE, WE LISTEN TO MUSIC AND jam out to almost every song on the radio. His singing voice is nicer than I expected. I'm not surprised by what I am learning about him anymore because he keeps surpassing the usual persona that accompanies most guys like him. I am starting to dig him, and more than just his insanely good looks.

He turns down the music blaring throughout his cab as we arrive at my dad's. I'm kind of sad our ride is over, and we now part ways.

"Thank you for everything today!" I say with a big smile.

"My pleasure!" Luke replies as he gets out of his truck.

I watch as he walks around the front of his truck to open my door like a thorough gentleman. He helps me down, and we walk to the front door of my dad's house. I turn around and look up at him, into his dreamy light blueish-green eyes. I open my mouth to say something, but I am caught deep in his trance. He puts his hand on the door above my head, then leans in toward me.

A strange excitement fills my body. I break my eyes free from his and look at his perfect lips. They look so kissable. I bite down on the corner of my bottom lip as I lean in closer to him and bring my eyes back to his. We are so close that I can feel his warm breath on my cheek. I close my eyes and take a deep breath.

My phone rings, and we get jolted apart from almost kissing.

"Sorry," I say, embarrassed and disappointed that our intimate moment was disrupted.

I quickly reach into my purse and take out my phone.

"It's Jason!"

Luke sighs as he grabs the back of his neck with his hand then takes a few steps away from me.

"I should get going now anyway," he states, looking at the ground.

My heart melts a little, and I hit the silent button on my phone and look up at Luke. He has since started walking back to his truck. He stops, then looks back at me.

"Would you like to see a movie tomorrow, after I get off work?" he asks with hope in his eyes.

I am screaming with joy inside.

"Yes, I would love to see a movie!" I reply with a smile.

Which I am sure is creepily huge. Luke smiles, then turns back around and walks towards his truck. I turn to open the door of my father's house.

"I will be here by about seven-thirty to pick you up," he yells from his truck.

I turn towards him, "Sounds like a plan. See you tomorrow!"

"Goodnight, Ali."

"Nite!" I respond.

He waves at me before leaving my father's driveway. I wave back and head into the house. I close the door and rest my back up against it. I let out a massive squeal as I smile from ear to ear as excitement travels up my body from my toes. I want to scream and jump around like a giddy little kid who just received some candy.

I must call Ris. I need to tell her everything that has been going on. I need to tell her about my dad's Will reading and my afternoon with Luke. How we almost kissed. Eeek!! She'll be ecstatic once she hears this! Okay, maybe not as stoked as I am, but close.

My phone rings again, it's Troy! Sigh!

chapter thirteen

I have not spoken to Troy on the phone or had an actual conversation with him since I've been back in my hometown. He texts me every day and has called a few times, but I have let his calls go to voicemail. I should probably answer it, but I'm still shaking over the twitter-patter of my heart, from the way Luke had made me feel just now.

I know Troy likes me, and I like him too, but Luke makes me feel a lot different; he makes me feel alive. He makes me feel closer to my dad and closer to myself, my old self, the one I left here when I went off to college.

I answer Troy's call right before it goes to voicemail.

"Hi, Troy! How are you?" I answer, hoping to keep this short and sweet.

"Ali, it's so great to hear your voice finally! I'm staying busy, but I miss you very much! How are you doing?" he says, surprised I answered my phone.

His response amuses me, but I won't blame him because I have been ignoring his calls. I've been busy taking on everything with my dad and quite frankly preoccupied with fantasizing and thinking about Luke.

"I'm doing alright. I just got back from my dad's lawyer's office. They read his Will today," I say while making small talk.

I cannot help but think of Luke the whole time while talking to

Troy. He's become a guilty pleasure for me. I feel bad as I refrain from telling him that I spent the last few hours having a fantastic time with another guy.

"I bet that was tough. I wish I could've been there with you during all that. If you need anything, you know, I am here for you," Troy proclaims.

"Yea, I know," I say.

A few moments of silence pass before Troy speaks again.

"What are your plans for the rest of your day, beautiful?" he asks.

"I think I may go see some friends or stop by my aunt and uncles to see what else needs to be done before I return to the city."

Without skipping a beat, Troy blurts out, "When do you think that will be? I know I should be empathetic, but I do miss you. I am sorry for what you're going through. I know you'll need your time, but I hope it's not too long."

"When what will be?" I reply.

I completely forget what he just said as I fantasize about Luke's perfect lips pressed up against mine.

"Coming back to the city?" he says as his voice is filled with excitement.

"I'm not sure, but soon, I hope. I am planning to return within the next few days, if not early next week. I need to get back to work," I ramble.

The tone in Troy's voice shifts, "You know you have recently gone through a huge loss in your life and taking time for yourself is not a bad idea, Ali."

He's right, and he is repeating what he said earlier that I did not pay any attention to. However, it is none of his business, to be honest. Who is he or anyone for that matter; to tell me about what has happened and how I should be taking time for myself? I am the one who decides when that happens, not him, my aunt, Ris, no one. I need to get back to work; it will keep my mind off having to deal with everything. My life can go back to normal, and I can move forward. My life here is such a mess right now. At least I think it is, although I am not so sure. On one end, there's Luke, and on the other a feeling of emptiness that I have felt for the past few days.

A little irritated by Troy's comment, I reply in a snarky tone, "Yeah, I get that, but they need me back at Facade."

Not leaving any time for Troy to talk down to me about what is currently going on in my life and how I should take time to heal, I say, "Uh, my aunt is beeping in, I should take this. It's probably something relating to my dad."

It happens to be a bald-faced lie, but I'm done talking about my father's death or anything that accompanies it.

"Oh, okay. It was nice to talk to you, Ali. Keep me posted on your return, please." Troy says in the sweetest, most caring voice. "I miss you and cannot wait to see you!"

I reply, "Me too," before hanging up.

I put my phone on the armrest of the couch and sit down. I run my hands through my hair as I bring my chest to my thighs. I can't believe I just lied to Troy to get out of talking to him. I used to get so excited when he'd call or even text me, how things have changed since I've been back. I am so focused on Luke now, and I can't help myself. He just came out of nowhere and has taken my breath away.

My mind strays away from what just took place on my phone call with Troy back to Luke. He has the most beautiful light blueish-green eyes; it's like looking at the ocean. He also has perfect lips. I think they may even be more perfect than *Michael Keaton's.* He romanced with Hollywood beauties *Kim Basinger* and *Michelle Pfeiffer* in his *Batman* movies with those superb lips! I have always tried to find a guy whose lips could even come close to Michael's. It's hard to explain, but I mean, come on, he has the best-framed lips in history.

My phone buzzes. It's a text from Ris!

Girl!! I am off soon. Call me in twenty, okay! 😘

Ris and her silly emojis!!

I wonder if Luke is going to the cabin this weekend with Jason and his parents. Probably not, because Jason hates him. Maybe Ris could come to visit this weekend and distract Jason for me to spend some more time getting to know Luke. Jason will be pissed once he finds out I am keen on Luke, but he will have to deal with it, as it's none of his concern.

Excited about what I just conjured up in my mind, I call Ris. She answers on the first ring.

"Girl, give me all the deets!! What's going on with you?"

I start off telling her what happened at the reading of my father's Will and how my father gave Luke some of his stuff, including ten percent of his business. I already told her about how Luke and I met while he was shirtless and how incredibly good-looking, he is, along with the issues with Jason. I also mention that he brought me home the night of Jason's party plus the details of that night. I then tell her every detail of my ride home with him today after the reading and our amazing lunch.

She screams into the phone, yelling annoyingly, "Ali has a boyfriend," before asking if I humped his brains out.

I let her down gently when I tell her we almost kissed but were interrupted when my phone rang.

"Bitch, you should have hurled yourself on to his lap and fucked him silly or at least sucked his dick while he was driving," she blurts out bluntly.

She is one of the biggest horn-balls, I know. I mention that I talked to Troy right before calling her, and she asked if I told him about Luke. I tell her I hadn't. She says good, fuck them both, before going off on one about how she wants to meet my hot shirtless beau. That reminds me of the idea I had come up with.

"Hey, is there any way you could come here this weekend and accompany me to my cabin?" I say in anticipated excitement.

"Jason, his parents, and I'm sure a few of his friends are going. I'm not sure if Luke is, but if you come, Jason will be too preoccupied with your pussy power to pay any attention to his hatred for Luke," I laugh, realizing I just told my best friend I practically want to pimp her out.

"Jason is your hot childhood friend, right?" she asks.

"Yes, I've told you about him numerous times, remember?" I boast.

Laughing, Ris replies, "Okay, I will take Friday off and come wrangle some men with my magical poon!"

We burst out in laughter as we continue to refer to her vagina as the *Great Bambino.* Its charm has sucked in many men. We chat a little more about what she should bring with her. What skanky outfits and suits she should pack to make sure she reels Jason in on the first day. I tell her she could do that wearing a burlap potato sack.

She talks a little about work and how everyone misses me and what projects are taking place right now and what gossip has struck the office. I miss not being there and having the assignments to occupy my time. She assures me that everything is under control, and I will be back before I know it, complaining about our co-worker's annoying habits.

"I'm going to pack my slutty ass thong bikini," she belts out.

We both burst out laughing, call each other derogatory names like "skank" and "whore" then say, "I love you" as we end our call. I cannot wait to see her this weekend; it's going to be a blast, whether Luke is there or not.

chapter fourteen

I am awoken abruptly by a knock at the door. Who'd be waking me up so early? I rush downstairs to see who is knocking this early in the morning. I open the front door.

"Good Morning, Ali," Gladys says with a smile.

"Good Morning! Come in," I say while half asleep.

"Is something wrong?" I ask, not remembering if we made plans to do something today or not.

"No, nothing is wrong. Well, not entirely. It slipped my mind yesterday when we were together to mention this to you and when I remembered, it was too late to call," Gladys says with a little worry in her voice.

A little concerned now, I reply, "What's going on?"

"Your dad's secretary, Maureen, is retiring in a few weeks, and I need your help in hiring a new secretary," she continues.

Maureen is the backbone of my father's shop; she keeps it running day-to-day. She does everything from answering phones, scheduling appointments, invoicing, payroll, paying bills, etc. Maureen has been my dad's secretary since he opened the shop almost thirty years ago. She was kind of his right-hand woman as she took care of all clerical matters.

Gladys reminds me that she did some work with Maureen a few years back when she had shoulder surgery, and I would cover for her when she'd occasionally go on vacation. Maureen has a lot to teach

Gladys and me before she leaves, given that we are unable to find a replacement right away. Gladys used to work at the hospital a few towns over but retired last year.

"I am on my way to the shop now; would you like me to wait for you, or do you want to drive yourself?" Gladys asks as she walks back towards the door.

"I need to get changed and stuff. I will meet you at the shop," I mutter.

She turns to open the door, "I will see you when you get there then. See you soon!"

Gladys smiles and gives a wave before leaving to head to my father's shop. I need to shower and look halfway decent since I will see Luke there. I rush back up the stairs to take a quick shower and get myself somewhat presentable.

Freaking out, as I cannot find anything that I want to wear, I fling myself into the back of my closet. Sliding shirt upon shirt across the clothing rack, I come upon a shirt much like the ones I saw the guys wear at my father's funeral. Although it did not have the new logo for the shop on the back, it was still one of his shop shirts. My name is sewn neatly in white on the front. I slip it on over my black tank top then grab a pair of my ripped jeans.

I head into the bathroom to blow dry my hair and put it in a ponytail. I throw on some quick makeup; shadow, liner, and mascara before heading down to the kitchen. I open the cereal cabinet, knowing I don't have time to sit and eat a bowl of cereal right now. I grab a cereal bar, put my boots on, and walk out the door.

I jump into my car, forgetting my purse, so I take off back into the house. I knew I had forgotten something in the excitement of seeing Luke again.

ON MY WAY TO THE SHOP, I DON'T PAY MUCH ATTENTION TO THE beautiful morning scenery because I am in a hurry. I make a quick stop at the gas station and grab myself milk and bottled water.

I pull into my dad's shop and drive around back to where the employees' park. I can feel my nerves start to go when I see Luke's truck. I am excited to see him but freaking out at the same time. I throw the milk and cereal bar into my purse before I get out of my vehicle.

I walk up to the back of the shop. It's a gorgeous summer morning; all the doors are open. I walk into the shop and make my way back to the offices. I skim the shop looking for Luke, Jason, Ernie-anyone, but no one is around. I get back to the offices and notice that all the guys have crowded around in the breakroom.

Before the guys start to walk out, I dip into the office where Gladys and Maureen are.

"Ali!" Maureen shouts.

She gets up from her desk and rushes over to hug me.

"Hi, Maureen! Congratulations on your soon-to-be retirement," I murmur.

"Thank you. I know it's not the best time to be leaving but your father."

She sighs.

"But your father and I had my retirement planned for months before he had his accident," she says sympathetically.

Feeling awful for her, as she appears to cry, I assure her that we understand and will not hold anything against her for keeping her retirement date. It's not her fault, and she's given so much to the shop and my dad already. She deserves to retire and will be terribly missed.

TIME GETS THE BEST OF ME WHEN ERNIE COMES INTO THE office to get Gladys to go home for lunch. We've been working diligently learning Maureen's ropes, that I didn't even take time to eat my cereal bar or drink my milk. I am sure it's become warm now. I walk out of the offices through the shop to head to my car.

I look up to notice Luke, resting himself up against my mustang. He has his shirt on today, but it's unbuttoned and untucked from his work slacks. His black ball cap is on forward, and he's wiping his hands on a blue shop towel. As I get closer to him, I notice he is looking at me with a gorgeous smile. Those lips! Ugh, those lips! I cannot believe he is right in front of me.

"Hi," I gush.

"Hi," he replies.

We look at each other and surge into endless smiles. I may have never smiled this much before in my life.

"What?" Luke says with a smirk.

I shake my head, "nothing," then look at the ground.

"Lunch?" he asks.

"Yes, but I'm driving," I babble as I walk past him and get into my vehicle.

Luke opens the door and gets into the passenger side. He closes his door and smiles at me. So far, the day has gotten off to a good start. Luke looks hot as usual. I am trying not to squeal!

I look at him and say, "Where do you want to go?"

"I don't care, anywhere, but Mary's." he says turning on my radio.

We drive a little way before he tells me to turn back to the shop as he forgot something. So, I turn around and head back. He gets out of my vehicle and walks over to his truck. He comes back with a large cooler between his hands. I roll down my window.

"Pop your trunk, please," he shouts.

I pop my trunk, and Luke sets his cooler down then closes it gently before getting back into my vehicle. I look over at him with a confused look on my face. I wonder what he is planning to do with it, but it must be good knowing him.

He looks at me, smiles, and says, "Just drive!"

"Where are we going?" I ask.

"I will tell you when you need to turn," he laughs.

Hmm. I am puzzled, but I drive along. We head a little further out of town then turn off on a dirt road. We go down the dirt road a bit before Luke tells me to stop. He gets out of my car, and I do as well. He tells me to pop my trunk open to grab his cooler and asks if he can take the blanket from my trunk.

I nod, and he hands me the blanket while he takes the cooler. He sets off, walking into the woods. We are walking down a narrow little trail then come upon a lake. My eyes look around in amazement at how beautiful the view is. I wonder what this place is. Luke is full of surprises, the good kind!

"Can you hand me your blanket, please," Luke asks.

I hand him my blanket after he sets his cooler down near a little spot where someone had previously set a fire. I watch as he unfolds my blanket and places it on the ground. He picks up his cooler and puts it back down on one of the edges of my blanket. He looks at me, giggling.

"You can sit, Ali," he smirks.

"Oh," I giggle.

Mesmerized by him, I sit down on the blanket and continue to watch him as he gathers sticks and branches. I look over at the lake for a minute then look back at him. He starts a fire then sits down next to me. He stares off in the direction of the lake. While the scenery is beautiful, my eyes are fixated on Luke; a perfect view all on its own.

I look over at him and study every inch of his face before looking back at the lake. I can feel his eyes on me, and I cannot help but smile.

"What?" I say as I turn to look at him.

In the softest, most heart-pumping voice, he says, "You're beautiful!"

I blush a little. Luke smiles while looking into my eyes and I smile back then look down at my blanket. He gets up and opens his cooler.

"A burger and chips okay for lunch?" he conveys.

I nod politely and look back at the lake. I'm on cloud nine right now, considering that I am on a technical picnic date with the best-looking guy in the world. I look back toward him and watch as he smiles at me and makes burgers for us. His arms are so muscular, and his face is more visible since he has turned his hat backward. Man, he's handsome, and he enamors me.

He hands me a plate, then he sits beside me as we eat our lunch. He finishes his burger in no time, then lays down on my blanket on his side with his arm propped up under him.

He stares at me while I finish the rest of my food. Nothing like being put on the spot and having the guy you have the hots for watching you eat. I put my plate aside and thank him for cooking lunch. He tells me it was his pleasure.

"You have a little mustard on your cheek," he chuckles.

Embarrassed, I quickly slap my hands to my face to remove the mustard. Luke moves closer to me as he reaches his hand towards my face.

"I got it," he says with the most beautiful smile I've seen him give yet.

Our eyes lock, and we stare at each other for what feels like an eternity. Luke breaks our stare as he looks to my mustard-stained cheek. His hand is a little coarse but soft, as he gently removes the mustard from my cheek with his thumb. We lock eyes again before he breaks our stare as he looks down at my lips, I look to his. He leans in closer to me, puts his hand behind my neck, and presses his lips against mine. I close my eyes.

I feel my body go weak. Luke's lips are so soft and firm. He removes his lips from mine, looks me in the eyes, smiles, then kisses me again. Not using his tongue but a pure innocent kiss. It's just as passionate and perfect as I imagined it would be. I am warm and tingly, with screams of joy radiating on the inside. I am feeling completely breathless.

He ends the second kiss and says, "We should get back to the shop."

Unable to speak, I nod and smile at him. He smiles back as he gets up from my blanket to pack up the food. He walks over to the lake and fills up a water bottle. I grab my blanket and shake the grass from it before folding it up. I watch as Luke puts out the fire and grabs his cooler. He smiles at me then turns; I follow him as he takes off back through the woods to my car.

chapter fifteen

The whole drive back to the shop, I am floating outside my body. Luke makes me feels so beautiful, and I am starting to become comfortable with him. I catch him looking at me a lot on the way back while we sing to the radio just like we did yesterday. His voice is incredibly sexy when he tries to sing instead of being silly about it. Today has been the best day I have had in a long time. Luke is fantastic, and he is everything I could want in a guy.

Luke grabs the volume button and turns the music down a little, "What movie do you want to see tonight?" he says, looking at me while he fidgets with one of the air vents.

"I was thinking since it's a nice day and should be a nice night, most likely, we'd go to the drive-in instead of the theater." I smile.

"Where is there a drive-in?" he asks.

"Not too far from the shop. Every summer, well, at least when I still lived here, they would open the old drive-in for the summer," I say, feeling unsure if they even still open it anymore.

Hopefully, I am right.

"That would be cool! I could pick you up in the Charger. If it happens to not be open anymore, we can do Plan B and head to the theater," Luke states.

I pull into the shop and park back where I was this morning.

"Sounds like a plan," I say in excitement.

Luke gets out of my car, but he bends down before he closes the door and says, "See you tonight at seven-thirty! Oh, and pop your trunk, would ya."

He winks and closes his door. I sink back into my seat and soak up every moment of what took place at lunch before collecting myself and heading into the shop to finish working with Gladys and Maureen.

I walk into the shop, and the first person I see is Jason. I hope he did not see Luke and me together just now as I do not need him starting a fight at work.

"Alicat! What are you doing here?" Jason says with a confused look on his face.

"I've been here all day working in the office with your mom and Maureen," I reply.

He chuckles, "For reals!?"

"Yeah, we are going over everything she does for the shop before she retires in a few weeks," I explain.

I am so glad I did not have to defend my whereabouts with Luke. Jason is in a good mood, and I prefer it that way.

"What? Maureen's retiring?" he says.

I am a bit surprised that he does not know. I swear sometimes talking to Jason is like talking to a wall. He's cute, but most of the time, the hamster is asleep at the wheel. Luke peers around the corner and walks to a stall where a truck is lifted into the air. He must be changing a rear differential or something.

He's so hot when he is full of grease and sweat. I wish he had his shirt off, so I could gawk at him. Not that his face isn't more than enough. I turn my attention back to Jason as I completely missed most of what he said to me about Maureen. I am so obsessed, ugh, is that the proper word for what I am feeling right now. I have been ignoring most of what others say to me when I think about him. Okay, yes, I'm obsessed.

"Are you coming to the cabin with us this weekend?" he says, well more so, pleads.

"Who all is going?" I reply, already knowing the answer, but I want to see if he will say if Luke is or not.

I'm not even sure if he is. I forgot to ask him during lunch.

"Well, Friday will just be me, Austin, my parents, and... fuck face over there," he says as he looks in Luke's directions.

Yes! Luke's going! It does not matter that Jason loathes him since I already have a contingency plan for that. I hope they don't get into any fights while we are at the cabin. Breaking stuff there would be awful because a lot of the decorations are priceless antiques. Hopefully, Ris will keep Jason occupied enough for that not to happen.

"Then a few other guys, Nikki, and Mindy will be coming up Saturday," he finishes.

I blurt out, "Bridget too?"

"No, she has to work, and I don't want to hear her whiny ass all weekend," he bellows loudly.

I am so mean for being tickled pink, jumping up and down inside, knowing that Bridget will not be coming to the cabin this weekend, and I will not have to compete for Luke's attention.

"I'm coming but won't be there till later Friday night. I have to wait for my roommate Ris to get here."

"You're bringing a friend? She hot?" Jason says as his face lights up.

"Well, she ain't ugly," I laugh as I start to walk away.

"She better not be," he says in all seriousness.

Jason knows of Ris, so he will be looking forward to meeting her. I feel more relaxed and excited about the weekend now.

I make my way back to the offices and get back to working with Gladys and Maureen. I never realized just how much she does for this shop behind closed doors. I am so glad she stuck around with my father for so long.

CONSUMED BY MOUNTAINS OF KNOWLEDGE, paperwork, and filing from Maureen as she goes over every detail of her daily routine, I check the time; it's four-thirty now. Shit. I should head home to get ready for my date with Luke tonight, but I don't want to just up and leave. I wonder what time Maureen usually heads home for the day, as I know the shop closes at 5 p.m.

"We can pick up here tomorrow, ladies. It's time for me to get home and soak my feet," Maureen says as she slips off her work shoes and puts her everyday shoes on.

They do not look much different from each other. I grab my purse and take out the milk I bought this morning then toss it into the trash. What a waste that was! Tomorrow if I get milk, I must remember to put it in the fridge as soon as I get here.

I tell Gladys and Maureen to have a great rest of their day then head out to my car. As I walk through the shop, I notice Luke finished the truck he was working on when I was last out here and is now under the hood of a different classic car. I can tell he loves doing his job, just like my father did.

Here at my dad's shop, they work on nothing but classic vehicles, so anything newer than 1996 must go to a standard auto body shop. My dad dedicated a good portion of his life, keeping the classics on the road. He didn't want them to be forgotten. Luke told me that they added a paint booth to the shop's side because my dad was getting sick of sending cars out for paint jobs that he'd have to wait forever to come back. My dad and Ernie hired some incredible auto painters, which has brought in a lot more business.

chapter sixteen

I rush from my vehicle into the house. I need to get ready. I fly up the stairs to get into the shower, while ripping my clothes off from today. As I wash my hair, I cannot help but daydream about what might happen on my date tonight with Luke. Will we kiss again? Will it be a full-on make-out session? I'm sort of nervous.

Will it go further? Am I ready for it to go further? I know I have been secretly fantasizing about what he looks like naked. However, when it comes down to it, I'm scared as hell thinking about it. I don't want sex to change anything or ruin what we have built up so far. We've come a long way in such a short time and having sex now may complicate things.

That is if he even wants to have sex with me. What if he doesn't want to? Oh, who am I kidding, every guy wants to get laid. Right?

I step out of the shower and put on some of my nourishing *Pure Romance* body lotion. I love the smell of this stuff, and it makes my skin so smooth and silky. I skip down to my room like an overly excited child. I grab some sexy lace boy shorts and my nude strapless bra before heading back to the bathroom to do my hair and makeup. I check the time, five forty-five.

Ugh, he's going to be here in less than two hours, and I do not know what I'm going to wear. I open my music app on my phone and select a pop station from *Pandora.*

I blow dry my hair, straighten it, then add some curls to give it a little volume. I apply a subtle smoky eye, not too over the top and trashy, though. I put on a light pink lip gloss and cover it with my twenty-four-karat gold flake lip gloss. I blot my lips, do a hair flip while running my hand through it before flipping back up and heading to my room.

I dance down the hallway as I jam out to the music blaring from my phone in the bathroom. I enter my room and have no clue what I plan to wear tonight. I do not want to wear business casual, and I do not want to dress like a tomboy, which I have been doing lately. I graze over the clothes in my closet and come across the dress my father bought me for my High School graduation. I have not worn it since that day. It's practically brand new.

It's a cute little yellow floral sundress with spaghetti straps. It's mid-thigh length, has a high low ruffle hemline, and the back-tie strings lace-up to the waist with a cinched look. I slip it over my head and look at myself in the mirror. It still fits; my body fills it out a lot better now than when I graduated. I grab a necklace, my jean jacket, and light tan sandal heels. I head back into the bathroom to check over my hair and makeup. I apply some fragrance mist to my hair, dress, and lady bits before shutting off the light and making my way downstairs to wait for Luke. I check the clock, proud of myself that I am ready with twenty minutes to spare.

I sit down on the couch and turn on the television while I wait for Luke to arrive.

My phone buzzes.

Good luck on your date tonight! Do everything I would do!! 🤪

I laugh while reading Ris's text. She's such a dirty whore, but I love her to bits. I take a selfie and sent it to her. I anticipate an even dirtier reply.

Girl, you're so getting fucked tonight. You look smoking hot!! 🥒
🥒🥒🥒🥒

I hear a door slam and rush over to the window; it's Luke. My chest starts racing, my heart starts thumping, and I pace back and forth as he walks up to the door. His hair is laid nicely on top of his head, and he is wearing a tight white t-shirt with dark blue jeans. I step away from the door and head back to the couch to turn off the TV. I am going crazy inside.

He knocks at the door, and I walk over to open it. I open the door with a smile on my face and quietly say, "hi". As he takes in the sight of me before him, Luke's face is alarming yet flattering at the same time.

"Damn. You, you look stunning," he says as he looks me over.

"Thank you!" I reply, still smiling.

We walk to his car; he drove the Dodge Charger. He is walking a few steps behind me. I turn around and look at him. He's practically drooling like a dog who just received a bone.

"What?" I say a tad embarrassed while loving the fact that I engulf him.

"Sorry, it's just that dress- it's-ugh- you're beautiful in it," he replies as if it seems I may have caught him off guard on what to say.

I am immensely proud of my choice in attire tonight. Who knew my old graduation dress would one day serve a greater purpose?

He opens my door for me, and I sit down. I watch as he walks around to the other side and gets in. He sits and stares at me, smiling. I blush while smiling at him then look away

"We should probably get going before we miss the movie," I say.

"Ugh, yea." he sighs.

"You look amazing," he says again, and we head down the driveway.

I smile then turn up the music. I am so happy that we are together right now, Luke makes me forget all that is going on in my life, and I catch a break from my current depressing reality.

WE ARRIVE AT THE DRIVE-IN, AND I'M HAPPY TO SEE IT IS

open and still showing summer movies. I think a drive-in film is way more romantic than watching one at a theater. You are alone in a vehicle instead of sitting next to strangers. It allows the chance for more intimate moments.

"Sweet, it's open!" Luke says in excitement.

I reach into my purse to grab some money. I hand him twenty bucks.

Grabbing my hand Luke says, "No, put that away, I got it. It's on me."

"You made me lunch, I will pay for the movie," I say sternly.

"I asked you out to the movies, so I'm paying," he replies as he looks at me and puts my money back into my purse.

He pays the guy at the toll booth, and we head over to find a spot to park.

"I forgot to ask what is playing. But the guy did give me this paper for the radio channel we need to be on," Luke says as he hands me the paper.

"It's not 80's movie night; those are on Thursdays and Saturdays it says," I blurt out.

"I love 80's movies!" Luke shouts.

What are the odds that he and I would love the same genre of movies? I'm usually the only one in the crowd.

"Me too! What's your favorite?" I ask.

"I have too many. But if I had to pick one. It would have to be *Caddy Shack*." He chuckles. "That movie is hilarious. Which one is your favorite?"

"*Solarbabies* or *Spaceballs*." I ramble.

"I'm a Mog! Half Man, half Dog," he laughs as he references *John Candy's* character in the movie, *Spaceballs*. "I completely forgot about *Solarbabies,* though. That's a good one too!"

We continue talking about our favorite 80's movies and how we should have a movie night Thursdays or Saturdays to come to the drive-in and watch them this summer. It's so odd how much he and I have in common. I never thought I would end up with someone so reserved and rugged. I always saw myself more with a nerd or jock type, but he's different.

He reminds me not to judge a book by its cover, just like my dad always did. My dad would tell me if you judge something by its appearance, you will miss out on its authentic and inner beauty. He was not wrong there. Luke is nothing like his 'bad boy' outer shell. He's sweet, caring, and honestly, he is perfect.

chapter seventeen

I fumble through the radio channels to the one written on the paper that Luke gave me for the movie. I can feel his stare taking over my body like a laser attack, and it makes me fumble even more and almost lose my concentration. I finally reach the right station and look over at Luke. He is leaning against the window with his arm propped up on the car door's armrest, and his hand tucked somewhat under his chin.

"What! Do I have mustard on my face again?" I giggle.

I know I don't, but I love the way he looks at me. He says nothing then moves toward me. Leaning over the center console and reaching towards my face, he touches my cheek, sending a tingle through my body and tucks a piece of my hair behind my ear. I look into his beautiful blue-green eyes as he slides his hand to the back of my head. I lean backward with my head as I tilt it up towards his.

He smiles at me then presses his lips against mine. This time he opens his mouth almost immediately, and his tongue enters mine. He massages my tongue with his, and I return the maneuver. His kiss is soft and gentle; he's a good kisser.

Our heads change positions from side to side as our kiss deepens with every passing of our tongues over one another's. Luke places his other hand on my upper thigh, slightly under my dress. I feel goose-bumps rise throughout my body and let out a tiny sigh in his mouth. He moves farther over the center council, and his hand inches up my thigh, resting gently upon my hip as he runs his finger under my lace panties. I grab hold of his shirt and squeeze it roughly in my fists as I begin to twist my hands.

I want him to climb into my seat and take me right here, right now. He has me so hot and bothered; I can feel my heartbeat faster and faster.

A voice comes over the radio, "Our show starts in eight minutes!".

Ugh, such horrible timing. We were having such an incredible moment. Luke pulls his face away from mine and lets out a sigh through his nose. Then we both burst out in laughter. He sits back in his seat, and I fix my dress.

"Please, visit our Snack Center for all your snacking needs. We have fresh popcorn, cold soda, an array of candies, ice-cream, and more," the voice continues.

"Are you hungry or thirsty?" Luke asks.

I am hungry but not hungry for food, hungry for him! I need to simmer down and collect myself.

"Not really," I reply.

"I'm gonna grab a soda. Do you want one or a water?"

"Water would be fine. Thanks," I say with a smile.

Luke gets out of his car, and I watch him as he strides to the Snack Center. I flip down the visor to check my hair and makeup. My face is red from the erotic adrenaline rush I just had. My heart is beating back to normal now. I turn to look at Luke at the Snack Center. I wonder if he had to adjust himself before heading over there. I giggle thinking about it. I couldn't have been the only one strongly affected by that steamy make-out session.

Luke comes back with water, soda, and a small popcorn. I give him a raised brow look.

"It smelled good," he says while he fishes out a popped kernel with his tongue.

I grab the water and soda from him so that he can sit back down in the car. Dinner and movie dates cannot get any better than this, rather snacking and movie dates!

"They announce what is playing while I was gone?" Luke asks.

"Not yet, but you did miss the dancing snack foods and condiments," I reply while laughing and performing a little dance number in my seat.

That was always a highlight of the movies whenever I saw them here with my dad.

Luke laughs, "Bummer, the dancing hotdog is my favorite!"

We laugh some more over the silly commercials they use. The evening keeps getting better and better. I love Luke's gorgeous smile, and his laugh is contagious.

The radio's voice comes on again after the little commercial ends, "Enjoy tonight's screening of *Smokey and the Bandit!* It will begin momentarily."

I can sense the excitement growing in Luke through the pure joy on his face when he hears what is playing tonight. It is priceless and super cute.

"No way! This is only the best movie ever!" he shouts in pure glee.

"It was my dad's favorite movie! *Easy Rider* coming in a close second, following *Gone in 60 Seconds,*" I say, smiling as I look away from Luke and to the screen.

I am glad we have the same taste in movies, as he also does with my dad. I can tell his excitement fades a tad, knowing I am a little upset about the movie and my father. He places his hand on my lap; I look at him and smile, then place mine over his. It's a sign from my dad that he approves of me with Luke. Love you, Dad!

The movie begins, we are laughing almost from the moment it starts. We laugh at how crazy *Carrie* is at the beginning while running out on her wedding then getting picked up on the side of the road by *Bo*. Luke talks about how amazing the Trans Am is that Bo drives and his suburb driving skills. He laughs when the Bandit gives Carrie the nickname *Frog*.

"I need to give you a silly nickname like that," Luke laughs.

"I'm no runaway bride, hitchhiking for a way out!" I giggle.

Laughing more, Luke snickers, "I'm gonna call you, Turtle!"

"Turtle?!" I snort from laughing, which causes Luke to laugh even harder.

Trying to catch his breath while tears are present in the corners of his eyes, he says, smirking, "Turtle, it is—it's funny and cute! Just like you."

I laugh and smack him. He grabs the side of my face and cups my cheek in his hand. He leans in toward me and kisses me. This time he goes straight for it, full tongue action and all. Our kissing is more heated as we massage each other's tongues more aggressively, and both our breathing is heavy. I lift myself and crawl on top of him in his seat. I slide myself lightly down onto his lap, and he flips up his steering wheel. I dive back into our kissing as I bite his bottom lip gently and give it a light tug. He groans softly, then grabs my head with both his hands, and we kiss vigorously. The movie continues, but our attention is toward one another. Luke's hands travel down my body, grazing across my chest, and stopping as he gets to my ass. He lifts my dress as he grabs a firm hold of each cheek. I rock my hips into his lap.

"Oh, my God!" Luke says in a low, shaky voice.

"You're so fucking sexy," he mumbles in my mouth as we continue making out.

I wrap my arms around his shoulders and persist rocking back and forth in his lap. Luke moves his hands from my butt and up to my hips then pushes me back towards his steering wheel to stop me. He breaks our kiss, and I look at him with concern. I don't understand why we would stop this, as things are about to get hot and heavy. What did I do?

"What's wrong," I ask.

Luke brings his hand to the back of his neck and looks down, "We need to stop. I don't think we should go any farther Ali."

I want it to go further, why doesn't he? Does he not like me? I'm embarrassed and feel incredibly uncomfortable now. I need to get off his lap.

"Why not? You don't—" Luke stops me before I can finish my sentence.

"I want to trust me, I do. Boy, I do. I don't want our first time to be in my car with people around." he says in the sincerest voice.

Phew! I am glad that he wants what I want, but I am a little weirded out that he stopped us. Maybe, he is thinking we are going too fast. Are we? I don't know what to think right now; my mind is all over the place. I give him a polite smile, lift myself off his lap, and sit back in my seat. I fix my dress and my hair. Then attempt to collect myself and focus back on the movie.

"Are you mad?" he says as he grabs my hand.

"Turtle?"

I burst out laughing.

I turn to him and say, "I agree! Now, be quiet and watch the movie."

He laughs and gives me that stunning perfect smile of his while putting his hand on my thigh. He is amazing.

chapter eighteen

We continue watching the movie. Luke's hand is still on my thigh, my hand on his, and our fingers are interlocked. We glance at each other often and smile. His smile and those perfect pearly whites of his; I could sit here watching him all night.

The last half of the movie is the funniest, and Luke only stops laughing a few times between looking at me and taking sips of his soda. The movie ends, and everyone starts honking their horns. I reach over Luke's lap and give his horn a few honks while I give a quick "whoop, whoop" shout.

I don't want our date to be over, and I do not want to go home yet. Although it is late and we both have to be up early in the morning for work.

"Do I have to bring you home right now?" Luke says.

I am glad to hear he does not want our date to be over yet either.

I turn to him with a smile, "No, you don't." I smiled!

"Good, I have something I want to show you," he replies.

My mind starts to wonder what that might be. Luke has a strange way of taking me to perfect places while keeping me in suspense. We leave the drive-in and head back through town, then out of town again in the opposite direction. I want to ask where we are going, but Luke looks so peaceful, humming to the song on the radio and playing drums with his thumbs on the steering wheel.

We come upon a hill, and he turns down a dirt road at the top. I have no clue where he is taking me. He smiles at me while singing then turns back to watch the road. Luke looks so hot right now; I want to rip his clothes off and have my way with him. I've become infatuated with him; I can't help myself.

Is he bringing me somewhere private so we can have sex? Did he mean he didn't want to have sex at the drive-in because of the people around us, or did he mean in his car period? We come to a stop, and he parks his car.

"You may want to put your jacket on," he says before giving me a peck on the lips and getting out of his car.

Where is he taking me? I grab my jacket from the back seat and slip it on. I flip down the visor to check over my hair and makeup. Not that it matters because it is pitch black outside. The car shakes slightly, and I turn around to see that Luke has popped open his trunk. Luke is holding two blankets under his arm. He grabs hold of my hand. My heart starts beating in wonderment.

"Come on," he demands.

I follow him up a little path. It's hard to see in the dark what seems to be a wide-open field at the top of the hill we turned on. Luke is using his phone flashlight to guide us down the path. He stops, and let's go of my hand. He hands me one of the blankets then takes the other. He unfolds it and places it on the ground. Luke walks over to me and grabs my hand again, bringing us over to the blanket. He pulls me down, and we sit on the blanket. I'm a little confused about the hell we are doing until he points up into the sky.

I look up.

The Northern Lights shine across the sky above us. The gorgeous glow of reds, blues, pinks, and purples dancing overhead wash a wave of peace over me. I'm taken aback by the view. I forgot how beautiful the Aurora Borealis is and that I cannot see them from the city, or the stars. This moment is tranquil. It's just him and me under the stars, stargazing, and it's very romantic. I can sense my father looking at us from up in the heavens, giving me a thumbs-up or an A-Okay gesture with his hand while giving me that creepy wink of his.

I watch the sky as the colors change and shift above me. I almost forget where I am and who I am with for a second. I turn to Luke; he is lying flat on his back with his arms behind his head. I lay down beside him and gaze back into the sky. This moment, right here, right now, is perfect and intimate, without needing to be touching, kissing, or engaging in any physical contact. Lying next to Luke is so magical. It's unbelievable. Luke reaches down and grabs my hand. We lock our fingers inside each other and continue to stare into the sky in silence.

I can hear the bellows of frogs and toads and the sweet melodies of crickets off in the distance. Being here with Luke is the most surreal experience I have ever had with any man. We lay in silence for what feels like hours before we decide to head back to town.

Walking back down the path to Luke's car, I cannot help but feel warmth and happiness throughout my body. I am content right now.

"I had an amazing time tonight," I say to Luke as we head back. "Thank you!"

"I had a great time too. I always do when I am with you," he replies as he looks at me and smiles.

I melt every time this man smiles at me. I love his smile, and he makes me turn to mush every time he speaks.

HE OPENS MY DOOR FOR ME, AND I STEP OUT OF HIS VEHICLE. He walks me to my door, just like he did the first time he brought me home. He puts his hands on my waist, then presses his lips against mine. I put my hands on his chest and lean into his kiss.

"Goodnight, Turtle! See you tomorrow!"

I giggle.

"Goodnight, Luke!"

He walks back to his car and waves before he drives away. I wave back and smile as I head into my father's house.

chapter nineteen

I lay in my bed and stare at the ceiling; I'm not tired at all. Today was amazing, from the mini barbecue/picnic to the drive-in then the northern lights. Most guys would not have stopped going all the way with a girl in the manner we were going at the drive-in. Luke is different. I could tell that he respected me a lot. I know he likes me but also respects me more out of his association with my dad, I'm sure. I am glad he stopped us from going any further as it's too soon to have sex. We've only been hanging out less than a week, but it does feel a lot longer. I've gone farther with him than I have with Troy, and he courted me for six months. While Troy is sweet, Luke is something else.

I feel bad about ignoring Troy today, but I was somewhat preoccupied. I need to tell him about Luke and let him know it's not going to work between us. I don't want to hurt him, but do I have a choice here! We would be better off just friends. Wait, are Luke and I going to become something? Are we going to date? It seems to be headed in that direction as of now. Do I want it to lead that way?

What will happen to my job? Would he move to Milwaukee with me? If he does, his ten percent of my dad's business would be null in void. Would I move back here, work at the shop, and quit the job that I worked so hard to achieve? I love my job. I wonder if I could work from home and go to the city once a month or so. I don't know if I could handle a long-distance relationship right now. Being five hours away from Luke would be difficult. Ali, you need to stop; you've only been around the guy a few days, it may end up as nothing. It could be just a small fling, although I hope that's not the case.

Now, I have added more to my plate than before. More tough questions I need to think through and decipher. I've gotten a bit carried away with some guy. A bit is an understatement, but I must keep my head on straight now. A conundrum such as this must have been why my father never mentioned Luke to me. He's clouding my brain, and I'm thinking about our future together over my own. I refrained from being consumed by a guy, mainly after my first broken heart because it was too painful. I focused most of my time at school. Leaving this small town and making something of myself was my main goal. I've accomplished that, so I am not sure if I can give it up.

Not that my father didn't make something of himself but working at an auto shop and being female is not perceived well by society. Not that being a female architect is any different, but I feel more accepted and respected. I've paid my dues, but I miss being around those classic cars and watching as they go from basically a rusty nothing to a beautifully restored something.

It's after midnight, and Ris is probably asleep. I wish she'd text me back so we can talk about my date and how my mind is all over the place over a guy for once and not work. She'd laugh and say, welcome to the club. I'll have to go with the flow and see how things progress.

I AWAKE TO MY ALARM SEEMING LOUDER THAN USUAL, OR maybe it's because I didn't fall asleep until an hour or so before it was to go off. I was thinking about Luke and my work for so long I do not know when I slept. I should go back to bed as technically they don't need me at the shop today. Then again, it's now half mine. Ugh, I better get my ass in gear.

I roll out of bed and stumble my way into the bathroom. Oh God, I look at my hair and see that it's a mess. I giggle while checking myself over in the mirror. I must have dozed off hard during that hour of sleep to have my hair stick straight out like this.

My shower feels incredibly fantastic this morning, and I almost fall back asleep, leaning against the wall. I check my armpits; they're suitable for another day or so. I shaved my legs and lady bits yesterday, so they should still be fine. I must be mad to think that Luke and I will have another intimate moment so soon, but its best to be safe just in case.

I step out of the shower and dry myself off. I am so not in the mood to do my hair or even put makeup on. I need to do so, though, as I will be seeing Luke. Ugh, why does he have to work at the shop; I want to show up ugly today. He has never seen me without makeup.

I throw on some liner and mascara. I should get my eyeliner tattooed on; then, I would not have to worry about repeating the lines that I mess up one hundred times before they're even. I start with a subtle line then get to the other eye, and it looks like a Kindergartner did it. Then the lines end up thick once I finally get them even.

I don't bother to blow dry my hair. I throw that bitch up on the top of my head. I lay on my bed for a few minutes.

My phone buzzes and I jump up with a few ninja moves as I must have nodded off. I've not had enough sleep, but either way, I check my phone, hoping it's Ris replying to what I sent her last night or even Luke.

Good morning, beautiful! Have a good day! Miss you.

It's Troy and his stupid "Good Morning" shit he does every damn day. I need to talk to him about what's going on with us and soon. I used to love his little morning gestures, but now I wish they were coming from Luke instead. Luke hasn't texted or called me once since we exchanged numbers at Mary's when we had lunch after my dad's Will reading.

I wonder if he texts Bridget. He did say they hang out but are just friends. Does that mean "just friends" like him and I are? Does he bring her, or has he brought her to the places he brings me? I need to stop overthinking things. I've been doing a lot of that since my date with Luke last night already.

This is what getting involved with men does to me. It makes me an insecure little girl, and I lose focus. I'm not too fond of it, but at the same time, I can't help myself because Luke is so unbelievably infectious.

I skip grabbing something to eat from the kitchen and head straight to the shop instead. I sit in silence the whole way there, staring off in a blank state, not thinking about anything. I pull into the shop ten minutes after eight. I do not see Luke's truck or his Charger; I wonder where he is. I park my car and walk toward the shop.

I look around, but I do not see Luke anywhere. The guys are busy working on their tasks for the day. I continue through the shop back to the offices. Maureen's office is right when you come in, past the waiting room area. Ernie's office is shared with Maureen, and my dad's office is a little bit behind it, tucked back in its only area.

I haven't been to my dad's office yet, but I should go there sometime today. I'm scared to; I don't want to cry in front of all these people. I want to stay strong and be professional. My dad wouldn’t want it any other way.

chapter twenty

Maureen, Gladys, and I are working together again today. We dive right into more of Maureen's daily routine. We go over daily, weekly, and even monthly tasks. Then, we sit down with Maureen as she goes over how to use Google Calendar to schedule appointments, time off, vacations, etc. We also cover QuickBooks, where all business expenses, invoicing, and other financial information are kept.

Maureen tells me if I want to take any of this home, it is all programmed to my dad's laptop. I turn and look at the door to my dad's office. I get up and walk towards the door. Now is a better time than any to go inside it. I have a strange feeling that I will sense my dad's presence in it. I stop at the door to my dad's office then turn to Maureen and Gladys.

"I'm going to work from here today," I say.

They both look at me, smile, then turn back to what they were doing. I turn the handle and enter my dad's office. It smells like him. He always smelled like swisher sweets and pine needles. He'd smoke those little cigars to keep bugs away from him but mainly because he wanted to have something in his mouth. I close the door and look around. His office is a pigsty. There's paperwork everywhere, clothes, jackets, and boots piled up in every corner. You cannot even make out his couch under all the mess. His dusty trophies are displayed on shelves towards the ceiling from all the contests he's won with his classic car collection. Pictures on the wall from when his shop was built. The first cars he and Ernie worked on, and the first dollar the shop made in a frame from June 7th, 1989.

The shop looked so different back then. It's incredible how far it's come from these pictures. I make my way to my father's desk and see that it's cluttered as well but has pictures spread across it of me. One from when I was, I'm not sure how old I am here, but I am quite little sitting on the hood of his Cutlass. I look as if I just started sitting up in the picture. There are a few other pictures of me when I was younger too.

There is one graduation photo of me with his car and another picture of me the day he gave me the Mustang we restored together. I smile looking back at these pictures; my father was so proud of me. I tidy up his desk a bit before I turn his computer on. His backdrop is a photo of him and me on the day of my graduation with the Mustang. It's the same photo in the middle of the frame he has hanging in the hallway at his house.

I lose it and cry hard, so hard that I cannot see or hear. My father was my rock and my world. I feel so empty and alone without him. I feel numb like the same way I did the first few days I came back home. I grab the picture from his desk of him and me, hugging it tightly as I lay my head down on the desk. I can't control myself; I'm a blubbering mess. I miss my dad so much. How will I continue my life without him?

I know that the shop management and its staff will always be my family, but no one can replace my dad or what he means to me. It's tough not having him here and being with all his stuff and our old pictures make me miss him even more.

I am startled by a sudden knock at the door, and I quickly wipe my eyes.

"Yes," I shout with a hoarse tone to my voice.

Ernie opens the door, and Gladys is right behind him.

"It's lunchtime!" Gladys says as she looks at me with sad eyes.

They could see I am missing my dad a lot, and this entire affair has been exceedingly difficult for me. Ernie walks into my dad's office and straight over to me. He wraps his arms around me, and I sigh loudly into his shirt before I lose it again. Gladys comes around behind me and hugs me from the other side. These two people are the most amazing people I know, they are my family, and I love them. I am so glad they're still around. They make me feel a lot less lonely, and I always pray for their long lives.

We embrace silently for a while before letting go of our special moment in memoriam of my father. Ernie looks around my dad's office before tears trail down his cheeks, and he excuses himself.

Gladys grabs my hand gently and says, "Would you like to come with us for lunch?

I politely decline her offer and look at the ground. I need some time to myself, and I'm not feeling hungry. Gladys lets go of my hand and rubs my back before leaving my dad's office and closing the door behind her. I sit back down in my dad's chair and look around. My eyes fill with water again. I continue to go through the paperwork on my dad's desk and organize it to be correctly entered into the system and filed.

I hear a light knock at the door. I'm not even sure if I heard a knock, but I walk to the door and open it. It's Luke. I turn away from him and wipe the tears from my face, I'm sure I look real attractive right now. I am glad he is here. He can lighten my mood and make my day a little brighter. Luke hugs me from behind tightly, and I turn around in his arms, wrapping mine around his hips.

"Shhh," Luke whispers as he rocks us side to side and kisses me on my head.

Why is he so perfect? He knows exactly what to do every time we are together. He knows how to make me laugh and when to hold me when I'm sad, and when to show lust at the appropriate times. I'm a mess when it comes to my emotions. Right now, I am an even bigger mess, but he makes me feel so relaxed and comfortable.

"Are you hungry, Turtle?" Luke says in the most adorable way possible.

I giggle, almost choking from the built-up spit and snot in my mouth from crying. I look up at him and smile.

"Yes!" I reply.

He hands me a tissue, and we walk out of my dad's office, through the shop, and out the door.

"Mary's okay today?" he asks as he grabs hold of my hand.

I nod, and we make our way across the street towards Mary's.

We reach the entrance to Mary's, Luke, lets go of my hand, puts his arm around me giving me a side hug before opening the door. We head in and walk over to a booth by the window. Luke grabs my waist before I sit down and pulls me towards him. He presses his warm, soft lips against mine. Instant warmth and tingles grow throughout my body as I kiss him back. I immediately start to feel better than I have since I stepped into my father's office. I've been in a haze for most of the morning. But Luke always makes me feel warm and fuzzy. I fall for him more every time we are together.

We are abruptly broken apart. I watch as Luke is slammed into the booth by Jason, who appears out of nowhere.

"What the fuck are you doing, you fucking piece of shit. Don't ever fucking touch her again!" Jason screams at Luke as he points his finger at him.

Luke is half sitting, half lying in the booth from Jason pushing him away from me. His face is red with anger, but he calmly keeps his composure. I'm unable to open my mouth to tell Jason to stop. Luke stands up and gets in Jason's face. Luke is a tad taller than Jason, but they are practically nose to nose right now. I'm frozen.

"It's none of your fucking business, Jason," Luke spits as he growls back at him.

The groups of guys Jason came with, rush over to our side and separate them from each other. I am shaking by what I just witnessed. What the hell is Jason's damn problem? I'm pissed.

"Come on, guys, let's not do this right now," Austin says as he pulls Jason away from Luke, then looks over at me.

"What the fuck are you thinking, Ali? I told you to stay away from this trash," Jason yells at me as he looks Luke up and down.

Things are about to get very ugly: I can sense it. I look at Jason, ready to speak just as Luke grabs my hand, and we head for the door.

Jason reaches toward me, but the guys pull him back. He screams out at me, but I ignore him and keep walking.

"You're a fucking dead man. You hear me. A dead man!" Jason spews.

I never would have thought going to Mary's may have been a bad idea. I was in my own little world filled by Luke that I did not take into consideration Jason may be here, and that an issue would most definitely arise. I know Jason thinks that Luke is bad news because of what happened between him and Bridget. I forgot I also promised him I would stay away from Luke. Shit!

We get outside of Mary's, and I stop Luke. I look up at him, and he's looking forward.

"I'm so sorry that just happened," I say as water fills my eyes.

"It's fine, Ali. Let's go!" he replies.

His face is still red, his breathing is heavy, and his hands are in fists. We walk back to the shop. I can see the anger on Luke's face more prominent now and the pain behind his eyes. I'm sure he's hurt because he doesn't want to fight with Jason, especially not over me. Luke stops and looks at me, and I give him a pleading gaze. His blue-green eyes are so vivid and sharp. He's so fucking hot when he's mad, it's unbelievable.

"I'm taking the rest of the day off. Will you come with me?" he asks.

I smile at him then head into the shop to grab my purse as he walks to his truck. I let Maureen know what's going on and make my way to Luke's truck. We leave the shop and head out of town. Luke stays silent. I feel awful as I look at him. He's tense, his jaw clenched, and is white-knuckling his steering wheel. What do I say right now? What can I say not to make matters worse? I want to calm him down. I grab my phone and skim through my apps. I sync my phone to Luke's truck then turn up the volume. I search for the perfect song to ease the current mood. I press play and look over at Luke.

Eastbound and Down from *Smokey and the Bandit* begins to play.

Luke smiles while looking forward, watching the road. The tension in his jaw and hands lessens. He looks over at me, smiles again, then places his hand on my thigh. I set my hand on his. He is calming down, and everything is becoming less tense. I let out a sigh of relief.

chapter twenty-one

We head down the same road that Luke brought me down yesterday when we had lunch at the lake. He parks his truck, smiles at me, then gets out. He takes off down the trail without grabbing anything from his truck. I get out and jog to catch up with him. It's hot out, and the bugs are being exceptionally annoying right now as they buzz by and crash right into my face. I swat at a few before I fall over into the grass. I roll around for a little bit before sitting up.

"What are you doing?" Luke laughs while extending his hand out to me.

"I got hungry and stopped for a bite to eat," I reply sarcastically while grabbing Luke's hand as he helps me to my feet.

Luke laughs more as he pulls grass, dirt, and leaves from the mess up top on my head; I like to call my hair. I brush the dirt and grass stains off my pants. I guess that is a way to break the awkward silence and tension lingering since we left Mary's.

"Were you late for work this morning?" I question.

"Yea, about an hour. I had a dentist's appointment at eight," he replies.

Now, I know why his smile is so gorgeous, and his teeth are so perfect. He takes good care of them. But I wonder why he didn't tell me last night or at least a quick text this morning. I am technically his boss. Oh shit, having any relationship with him now would technically be unprofessional. Wouldn't it? But do I care? Not one bit!

Luke starts walking down the trail again but holding my hand this time. I'm sure he's worried I might get hungry again. I like walking behind him as it gives me a straight shot to check out his ass. Although his work pants are a little on the baggy side, they still sit nicely off his hips and make his rump look amazing. I don't think there is anything he could wear that doesn't look sexy on him. I want to kiss him so badly right now. I could give him the perfect distraction to take his mind of the heated dispute with Jason earlier.

We get to the grassy opening where we had lunch yesterday, but we keep walking and head over to another trail just past the picnic area. Where the hell is he taking me this time? We keep walking, and I keep getting dive-bombed by bugs. Those fuckers are going to be the death of me today. Man, they're so annoying.

It's so hot out, and I can feel the sweat drip down between my boobs. I can feel the part of my shirt where my underboob area has started to become soaked, real sexy. Luke stops and reaches his hand up over his head, grabbing hold of his shirt. He slips it over his head and tucks it in his back pocket, then grabs my hand again, and we continue walking. Oh. My. God. Luke's upper body is glistening in the sun. Major eye candy.

I can see his tattoos more closely now than when I saw them the first time we met. His tattoos run down from his rib cage, over his pec and shoulder, then down his arm giving him a sleeve. The tattoo is almost like a mural. It's beautiful and without any color. The grayscale ink is amazingly done. His body is molded perfectly in all the right places. He stops as we arrive at another opening. He turns to me, and I see the front of his tattoo. Underneath his pec not connected to the sizeable themed tattoo, it says *Ma Mere, Mon Amie* in cursive writing right over his heart. I run my fingers over it then look up at him.

"What does this say?" I ask.

I patiently wait for him to tell me. He looks deeply into my eyes then bends down a little and gives me a gentle kiss on my lips. I close my eyes, taking in his kiss and ignoring the ferocious bugs trying eagerly to ruin this moment.

"Ma Mere, Mon Amie. It says My Mother, My Friend in French. I got this and the rest of the tattoos while I was in prison," he replies, looking at me then walking away.

Luke and his mother are incredibly close, just like my father and me. He pulls me into his body and grabs my waist then leans down to kiss me again. My mouth opens almost instinctively as I know this is an intimate moment we are sharing. He gently slides his tongue into my mouth and massages my tongue with his. I gently massage his tongue back with mine. We break from a short but meaningful kiss. I really like kissing him.

"Damn, you're short!" Luke laughs as he pats me on the head.

"You're an ass," I grumble.

I go to smack him, but he takes off running. I chase after him but am unable to catch him. While he runs away from me, he starts to unbuckle his belt, then unbutton and unzips his pants. I stop dead and watch him strip before me. Luke lets his pants drop around his ankles then steps out of them. He stands before me wearing only his sexy as fuck, light blue and white striped boxer briefs, which don't hide his large bulge but hug it nicely.

"Too tired to come and get me, shorty pants!" Luke laughs while he crouches down to my height.

I take off like a bat out of hell after him, and he takes off running. I almost reach him before he jumps. I freeze in place as I watch him drop down a cliff and right into the water. A few seconds later, he pops back up. I almost shit myself.

"Jump! The water is perfect," he shouts.

I inch closer to the edge and look down. I've cliff jumped before when I was a kid, but it seems high. I don't know if I can get myself to do it. I'm scared to jump.

"Come on, Turtle, jump!" he yells in a girly voice as he laughs.

"Come jump with me," I yell down to him.

I think I can do it with him by my side. Maybe. Luke dips under the water and swims to the side. He begins the climb up the cliff. I take a few steps back and take a deep breath. I take my shirt off, my tank top, and my pants. When Luke reaches the top, I am standing there in my bra and panties. He stands up and stares at me. Shy. I cover myself with my arms and look at the ground while digging one of my toes into the ground.

"Ali, you have a beautiful body," Luke says.

He walks over to me and removes my arms from covering my chest. He grabs hold of my hand.

"Are you ready?" he asks.

I am scared out of my mind but as ready as I will ever be, I think. I nod, yes, and we take off running. We jump, and I close my eyes. I feel lifeless for a while before hitting the water. He doesn't let go of my hand until we are under the water. Luke was right. It feels amazing against my hot, sweaty skin. I pop my head up from under the water and wipe under my eyes. Luke splashes me immediately, and I splash him back. We swim around a while before we climb back up and jump a couple more times. Each time we jump is more fun than the last—a perfect way to spend the rest of the afternoon under the blaze of the hot sun.

chapter twenty-two

We drive up my dad's driveway, and I can see the sun still shining but getting ready to set behind his little farmhouse.

"Do you want to stay for dinner, then maybe watch a movie?" I ask.

"What you gonna cook for me?" Luke replies.

"Spaghetti and meatballs!"

"I can't say no to that," he smiles and puts his truck into the park.

We make our way into the house. He excuses himself to the bathroom, and I head into the kitchen. I wash my hands then grab a pound of ground beef from the freezer. I plop it in the microwave to defrost. I grab a pot and pan from the cabinet and place them on the stove. I reach into the spice cabinet for a few seasonings, then walk to the pantry and look for some spaghetti noodles.

While in the pantry, I can overhear Luke talking to someone while he's in the restroom. I tiptoe closer to the bathroom and bring my ear to the door. I wonder who he is talking to. I know it's impolite to eavesdrop, and I would like it if it were done to me, but my curiosity has gotten the better of me. I can hear Luke's muffled voice while he converses with whomever he's speaking to. I don't remember hearing his phone ring. He probably made the call.

"It's none of your business what I do or who I do it with. I can be with whoever I want."

I can hear him say in a deep angry voice. Is he talking to Jason? Maybe, its Ernie. Who is he talking to?

"Yes, I do happen to like her. But like I said, it ain't any of your goddamn business. I'm not talking about this with you anymore. Bye!" he whispers rudely.

I rush back to the kitchen, so he doesn't know that I was eaves-dropping. Was he talking about me? He likes me. Well, I knew that already but who does he need to clarify it to? I take the beef out of the microwave and unwrap it as Luke walks into the kitchen.

"Can I help you with anything?" he asks.

He grabs my waist and kisses me on the cheek. He's quite chipper for just arguing with someone on the phone. I want to know who he was talking to. I'm sure if he wants me to know, he will tell me. Right? Well, I can't say no to his help, and I need a distraction.

"Um... you can fill that pot with some water, please," I reply.

Luke stands over me as we stir the meat into the sauce together, and he helps me make the salad and set the table. Cooking dinner with Luke in my father's kitchen is uncanny but unbelievably fun. We dish our plates and sit down to eat. I'm starving, and I am sure he is too since we did not eat lunch due to Jason's unruly antics. The sun is just setting, and it looks beautiful out the window of my father's dining room. I wish he were here to enjoy spaghetti with Luke and me. I would love to listen to them talk about classic cars and watch as my dad's face lights up when he'd talk about them. He loved cars and could talk about them for hours.

"It looks delicious! We are an amazing team," Luke says as he takes a bite of his salad.

"I have to agree with you there," I reply.

We engage in everyday conversation as I assume an average couple that lives together would do. I've never lived with a guy beside my dad. I'm not saying that I want to live with Luke right now, but I imagine it would feel like this.

“Are you going to the cabin this weekend?" Luke asks.

"I'm planning on it, and my roommate, Ris, is coming from the city on Friday to come with," I reply.

"Are you?"

I know he is going, but after the fight with Jason today, he may not be. I hope he still plans to go, or my weekend will be so dull. Once Ris and Jason hit it off, they will be too busy fornicating all weekend to keep me company.

"Yes, I need to help Gladys with her flowers, and I'm sure Ernie will need me for something. I can take you and your roommate, after work, if you want," he says softly, then shovels spaghetti into his mouth.

"Great! I hate driving back from there after a weekend in the sun," I reply.

"Thanks, just going to use me as your own personal chauffeur. I see how I rate!" he laughs.

I laugh, not having anything witty to say back. So, I focus on finishing my meal. Luke finishes his, then we clean the table. Surprisingly, he helps me with the dishes. I may have to slap myself to make sure I see clearly. Could he be any more perfect? We sit down on the couch. I grab the remote and flip on the TV.

"What would you like to watch?" I ask Luke.

"Anything but reality TV," he replies.

I flip through the channels. Luke slides closer to me, putting his arm around me, then grabs the blanket off the couch and places it over our laps. I stop at one of the *Batman* movies. We watch in silence for a while before Luke lifts me up and scoots me forward. He lays behind me, then pulls me down to lay in front of him, wraps his arm around my waist, and continues to watch the movie as he rests his chin on top of my head. I try to stay focused on the movie but cannot help how comfortable I feel lying here inside his body, wrapped in his arms. He is like a comfy blanket, and before I know it, I fall asleep.

chapter twenty-three

I wake, having to pee. I realize I am on the couch and still wrapped in Luke's arms. I gently slide my way out of his grip and tiptoe to the bathroom. I do my business and make my way back to Luke, who is still sound asleep. He looks so peaceful, I do not want to wake him, but the couch is so uncomfortable. We would be better off sleeping on a bed.

I nudge his shoulder a few times before I can wake him.

"Luke, LUKE!" I say, starting in a whisper, then rising to my normal voice.

He startles awake and sits up on the couch, stretching his arms over his head as he looks around.

"What time is it?" he groans.

"It's two thirty-eight in the morning," I whisper.

"Do you want to go up to my room. My bed is more comfortable than the couch."

He nods, yes, and I grab his hand. I lead his sleepy ass up to my room. He plops face first down on my bed and is out like a light. I remove my pants and slide under the covers. I turn off my lamp and drift back to sleep.

MY ALARM BUZZES LIKE A FREIGHT TRAIN AT FIVE-THIRTY,

causing both of us to jump up in my bed. Luke removes his arm from around me as I reach over to silence my alarm. I want to lay back in bed with Luke all day, but I need to get ready for work. Not only me, we both need to get ready for work. His body is so warm, and I enjoy snuggling with him. I start to get out of my bed, but Luke pulls me into his chest.

"Where do you think you are going?" he asks, then yawns.

"To take a shower," I reply.

"Lay here with me for a little longer," he demands as he wraps his body tightly around mine.

I lay there, and it feels heavenly, my body tucked into his. He is holding me like he never wants to let me go. I back into him a little bit and can feel his morning wood against the small of my back. He begins to kiss the back of my neck lightly as he gently rubs himself on me. I cannot get enough of him. It's starting to get me a little excited, and don't want to be a killjoy, but I don't want to have an intimate moment with him right now. I feel gross, and I'm sure I have the worst morning breath ever from eating spaghetti and meatballs last night, then not brushing my teeth. I roll back a little toward him and look at him over my shoulder.

"I have to shower now," I say, then pop out of bed and jog to the bathroom.

I can hear him yelling for me to come back and cuddle him, but I ignore it. I close the bathroom door and turn on the shower. I slip my shirt, tank top, bra, and panties off, then grab my toothbrush and toothpaste before climbing into the shower. I brush my teeth then start to wash my hair and face. I close my eyes to wash the shampoo out of my hair then turn to the water to make sure all the soap is off my face. I open my eyes as I turn myself back around. I jump and scream as Luke peers in the shower while the rest of his body is behind the curtain. I quickly cover myself in embarrassment the best I can with only two hands

How long has he been there? I put one hand over my lady bits and my arm across my breasts. I must have forgotten to lock the door before I came in here. He just saw me naked.

A huge smile stretches across Luke's face as he says, "I'd join you, but I don't have clean clothes to change in."

I stand here frozen, unable to collect any thoughts to reply to his comment. I was not ready for him to see me naked yet. I'm so self-conscious about my body. I don't like it. I am sure my face is eight shades of red right now. He could have given me a warning of some sort, something, anything other than just popping his head in here like that.

"I am going to head out, and I will see you at work. Turtle!" he winks with a gorgeous smile then closes the shower curtain.

I drop my hands from my body and sigh as I look toward the ceiling. Completely Embarrassed. Then the other end of the shower curtain flings open, and I scurry to cover myself again.

"You look very sexy naked and wet, by the way," he says with the biggest shit grin on his face.

I give him a blank stare as I am about ready to cry in humility. He grabs my arm, pulling me towards him and kisses me on the side of my head then shuts the curtain. I listen to him walk out of the bathroom and close the door behind him. I stick my head out to make sure he's not still in the bathroom. I quickly step out, run to the door, lock it, then run back into the shower. Holy shit balls, he saw me fucking naked, and we haven't even had sex yet. He should've just come in here and had his way with me instead of teasing me and making me feel super insecure about my body. I'm so embarrassed. But he thinks I am sexy naked.

I shut the water off and step out of the shower. I dry myself and clean the water from all over the floor. I unlock the door and head to my room. Still wrapped in a towel, I search through my suitcase for some panties and a bra. Time to get over myself and get dressed! I head back to the bathroom to blow dry my hair. I straighten it and throw it back in a braid. I put on some light makeup.

I check the time on my phone, and it's a little after seven. I notice I have a few messages to look over, but I will do that later. I walk into the kitchen to grab myself something to eat. I can hear voices coming from the TV. I thought I shut that off this morning. I walk into the living room and have the shit scared out of me once again when I see Luke sitting there.

"What are you doing here?" I ask as my heart is beating out of my chest.

"I thought you were going home to shower and change for work."

"I did, then I came back," he replies, smiling while focused on what he is watching.

"Your car is at the shop; I came to give you a ride," he states as he looks over at me.

I completely forgot I had left my car at the shop when we left after his altercation with Jason at lunch yesterday.

"Oh, yea," I say.

I turn to head back into the kitchen, still embarrassed over the fact he saw me naked not too long ago.

"Do you want anything to eat?" I yell as I am bent over in front of the fridge, fishing out a pear from the crisper.

"I'm good," Luke says.

He grabs my hips while standing behind me. I turn around, and he closes the door to the fridge then pushes me up against it. His hands still on my hips. I look up into his dreamy eyes. He bends his head down towards my face.

"I can't stop thinking about your naked body," he whispers in my ear.

He gently kisses my neck, and I instantly feel goosebumps travel up my body. He runs his lips up my neck, kissing my jaw, then the corner of my mouth. I drop the pear from my hand and bring my hands up to his hips. His hands cup me behind my head, and he looks into my eyes then down to my lips. I bite the side of my lower lip, and he presses his lips against mine. Our mouths open, and we engage in a deep passionate kiss. Luke bends down and grabs me under my ass, lifting me on to his waist. He spins us around and walks back to the counter then sets me down on it. We begin to kiss more aggressively as I wrap my legs tighter around him. Luke's hand travels under my shirt and up my ribcage, then underneath my bra. I let out a small moan in his mouth as I drop my head back while he lightly squeezes my breast. He begins to kiss my neck under my chin. I let out another tiny moan.

Luke's phone rings and our moment is interrupted.

He fidgets for the silence button while still kissing my neck, and his hand firmly attached to my breast. I release my grip from around him while pushing him away from me, then removing his hand from my breast.

"We should get going before we're late for work," I say, smiling as I adjust my girls and fix my shirt.

Out of breath and adjusting himself, Luke pulls his phone out of his pocket.

"It's Ernie, and it's seven-fifty," he says as he swipes his screen to take the call on his phone.

He walks out of the kitchen to the entryway to get his boots on. I can hear him telling Erie he's on his way and that he had to stop to pick me up first. I grab my pear off the floor, wash it quickly, then head to the door to put on my boots. Luke opens the door for me, I grab my purse, and we head for his truck.

chapter twenty-four

The first half of work goes by quickly as I plan to get most of my father's office cleaned today to start designing a new one. His office is big enough to provide enough room for two or three people in it. I have not designed something in over a week, being away from work, which will be fun for me. I'm excited to do a little remodeling of my own.

I've been so busy cleaning, organizing, and filing that I haven't thought about what happened between Luke and me this morning at my house, how embarrassed I was, or the fact he had stayed the night. It's almost lunchtime, and I will be reminded as soon as I see him, I'm sure.

I leave my father's office to go find a small ladder or step stool to take the trophies down from the shelves to clean them and pack them away until I need them again later. I notice Maureen and Gladys are not in her office. I make my way to the supply closet, grab a small ladder, then head back to my dad's office. I get back, and Jason is standing there with his arms crossed.

"Hey," I say as I walk through the door.

I have a strong feeling this will turn out to be an awkward conversation. What happened yesterday between him and Luke over me was a little over the top.

"We need to talk," Jason says with anger displayed across his face.

"I'm not in the mood to discuss Luke with you today," I reply.

I walk past him and unfold the ladder underneath the trophy shelves. I do not want to deal with another crazy day like I did yesterday at Mary's Cafe. I don't care to hear what he has to say about the situation, either.

"Are you two sleeping together? Are you guys dating or something?" Jason demands.

Where he thinks he has any right to ask me these questions is beyond me. I understand he cares about me. But seriously, what in the fuck!

"Jay, it's none of your business what I do with Luke, or anyone for that matter," I snap back at him.

"He's—"

I interrupt him before he can go off on his rant over Luke.

"He's a bad guy blah blah blah. All because you caught your slut of a girlfriend trying to fuck him. But you didn't catch them in the act or even catch Luke in the goddam room while she was passed out in his bed," I scream.

I just had to let it out. Enough is enough. This issue between them is so childish and not my fucking problem; it's theirs. Fury vibrating my very being, I glance at Jason. He looks at me as if I just took away his beer. I stand there with my hand on my hip, irritated and pissed.

"He's not good enough for you, Ali," he yells.

Did he seriously just go there? Anger ripping through me like a vortex of rage. I'm ready to snap. He is about to get a piece of my mind.

"Who's good enough for me then, Jay? You?" I scowl.

"No one has ever been good enough for me when it comes to you. You can't control who I like, date, or fuck. Stop ruining shit for me, please," I sneer.

Jason's face turns white as he looks at the floor, defeated and hurt by my harsh verbal rant. But it's true. All through school, he prevented me from going on lots of dates and guys liking me. We are adults now, and he can't control what I do or who I do it with. It's not fair to me or anyone who wants to be with me, including Luke.

Speaking of Luke, he walks through the door.

"What's going on?" he asks as he looks at Jason then over at me.

"He's going to hurt you, Ali," Jason says, then walks past Luke stopping for a moment to glare at him.

They both stand tall and puff their chests up as they stare at each other. I roll my eyes over the annoying, childish banter. Jason looks back at me and leaves my father's office. Luke watches him go, then walks over to me and wraps his arms around me.

"You okay?" he asks.

"I'm fine. Sick of his shit. He won't come after you anymore," I say while I lean my head into his chest.

"You want to talk about it?"

I shake my head as I nuzzle more into his chest

"Hungry?" he says.

"I am always hungry," I reply with a giggle.

He whips out some sandwiches that I assume he made for us when he went home this morning—equipped with string cheese, some crackers, cookies, and juice pouches. Damn, he got all them snack time favorites. He sits down at my dad's desk, and I sit on his lap. We watch silly YouTube videos as we eat our fabulous lunches.

THE SECOND HALF OF WORK GOES BY JUST AS FAST AS THE morning half did. I have my dad's office almost completely under order. A few areas need some love yet, but at least I took care of all the paperwork that was scattered everywhere, and now you can see his brown leather couch again. That thing is hideous, and I know why he had it covered. My dad was no dummy! He made an ugly couch look less hideous!

Gladys comes in to tell me that she is heading home and won't be in tomorrow because she will be packing up for the cabin. She says that Ernie and Jason will only be working in the morning and would then be leaving for the cabin. I told her I'd be there about dinner time with Luke and my friend Ris. She seems happy to hear that I am bringing a friend. She mentions that they are taking their motorhome so us kids could have the cabin to ourselves at night.

Oh boy. I cannot believe she and Ernie trust us to have the cabin to ourselves. I will take my dad's room, and I'm sure Jason will take his parent's. Austin and the rest can share our loft that has a few sets of bunk beds. I wonder where Luke will sleep, I want him to sleep with me, but if Ris does, I don't know where he will go.

I hope she and Jason hit it off so I can be alone with Luke. After last night and this morning, I think I'm ready to have sex with him now. The time feels right to take whatever our relationship is to the next level. I grab my purse and head out of my dad's office to talk to Maureen.

"I'm heading out for the day," I say to Maureen.

"Bye, Ali, have a lovely evening," she replies.

I'm just about to head out when she asks if I can cover for her tomorrow so she can take the day off to bring her dogs to the groomers. I politely tell her that I will do it without a problem and to enjoy her weekend. I walk into the shop when I notice Luke is out front in the lobby area, talking to a blonde woman. I walk over by the window to peek a little closer and see he is talking to Bridget, making me feel a bit apprehensive.

chapter twenty-five

That skanky ass bitch has her hand on his arm and is all goo-goo eyed at him while wearing an outfit from sluts-r-us. I know I shouldn't be so mean, but she was such a harlot in High School, one can only assume that she still is, knowing what happened between herself, Jason, and Luke.

What is he smiling about? What on earth could she say that he would find the least bit amusing? Get a grip, Ali. You and Luke aren't together? You're just friends, and they are just friends. Stop being a jealous little girl and walk away before someone catches you staring out the window like a creeper.

I was thinking about taking our relationship, friendship, or whatever it is to the next level. After seeing him with her, I am not sure anymore. I do not want to think that he may do intimate things with her as he does with me. Although he told me he hasn't, it's there in the back of my mind, haunting me. Things between him and I have moved quite fast, and I have not been able to exercise any self-control. He consumes me every time he is near me, and I forget about everything. I cannot help that he has that effect on me.

"I'm headed out, Ali. See you Monday. Thank you for covering for me tomorrow!" Maureen says with a smile.

"No problem. See you Monday," I reply.

I turn back toward the lobby and notice that both Luke and Bridget are gone. I settle down some and head through the shop. I look around for Luke but do not see him. Where did he go, and is he still with Bridget? I was hoping we'd possibly hang out today after work, but he has just vanished. I keep walking to the parking lot toward my car. Luke is standing at his truck with Bridget leaning up against it. Ugh, she is such a fucking- whore! Luke looks over at me and waves; Bridget turns around and looks at me. I do an awkward wave back and smile like a dork.

"Hi, Ali," Bridget yells in her annoying bitch voice while waving.

I smile, say hi back, then get into my car. Feeling uneasy and not sure what to do, I drive off. I try not to look back at them through my rearview mirror. Oh boy, I hope Luke does not think I'm a psycho jealous girl right now or something. Ugh, I should've just walked over there and made small talk or stayed in Maureen's office until I saw him back in the shop. Something.

My phone rings, and Luke's name flashes across the screen. Should I answer it or let it go to voicemail? If I let it go to voicemail, he will know that I'm mad and jealous. Shit.

I answer, awkwardly giddy, "Hello!"

"Hey, you didn't come talk to me before you left," Luke says.

"Sorry, I didn't want to interrupt you and Bridget," I reply.

Smooth! Nice one Ali, he doesn't need to know you're a little disturbed by what you saw, and you needed to get the hell out of there before making a scene.

"We were just talking about our weekend plans. She dropped off some stuff for Maureen," he states.

"That's cool," I mutter.

"I'm off soon if you want to get dinner with me," Luke inquires.

"I would love to, but I need to pack for the cabin this weekend, talk to Ris, and get to bed early. I'm covering for Maureen tomorrow since she has the day off," I sigh.

It sucks to say no to him, but what do I do! I still feel weird about seeing him with Bridget and them being so buddy-buddy.

"Yea, I need to pack too. You still want me to pick you and your roommate up after work tomorrow?" Luke questions.

"Yes, she should be here about three or four."

"Okay, I should get back to work. I will miss not waking up to you in the morning, Turtle!"

I giggle.

"See you tomorrow, Luke."

"Bye!" he laughs before hanging up.

I would not mind Luke distracting me again tonight. He has such a kind soul. I wonder if he was this amiable in his past life, the life he had lived in California. Did prison help him change from a bad boy into a good one, or the fact he wanted to start a new life afterward, or has he always been this way? I hope that the more time we spend together, the more I learn about who he is and was. I'm curious to know about his life growing up and what he was like before. I'd love to see pictures of him when he was younger, although I am sure those got burnt in his mother's house during the fire. I want to ask him about his past, but I'm afraid to open old wounds. He seems to have worked hard on himself to get to where he is today.

I think I am starting to fall hard for him. Seeing him today with Bridget, knowing their history, and what she is capable of, really bothered me. I wonder if they have done more than kissing, which is why he keeps stopping us from having sex. Then again, I don't think he was going to prevent it from happening this morning. I may just be overthinking.

I wonder if he called me while Bridget was standing next to him today. What would happen if she found out about him and me? Was she who he was talking to last night at my house when he was in the bathroom? I did overhear him say that he likes me. It could very well have been her on the other end.

I need to call Ris; she can talk me down from my overthinking and irrational thoughts. I grab my phone. I wish I had voice activation in my car like Luke does in his truck, so I can ask it to call Ris for me. It would be so much easier than having to pull over to call her. I'm just feeling lazy today. I scroll through my contacts and click on Ris's number.

"Eeek girl, T-minus twenty-four hours, and I get to see my favorite bitch!!" she screams into the other end of the phone without even saying hello.

I can sense her excitement; I cannot wait to see her either. I need my bestie.

"I know I'm so excited to see you. A week has been way too long to be apart," I shriek back.

"I packed and repacked my shit so many times; it's unreal. I think I'm just going to bring our whole apartment," she laughs.

She has a corny sense of humor, and it always makes me smile. I giggle. I'm sure she will pack our entire apartment. We've gone on a trip for the weekend, and she had four bags to my one. She's the type that needs to change outfits a million times a day.

"Speaking of packing, can you please pack my orange bikini for me? I don't know if I still have suits at my dad's. I'm sure if I do, they are just lame one-pieces," I say.

"Girl, I bought you a new suit, but I will grab the orange one right now and throw it in one of my bags. I know how much you like that one, plus it makes your boobs look, killer!" she cackles.

"Thanks. You're too good to me," I reply.

"I'm pumped to meet your childhood friend. What's his name again?" she asks.

"His name is Jason, and he's excited to meet you too. He asked me if you're hot," I giggle.

"You best have told him, that I'm fucking Filet Mignon and will rock his world this weekend," she laughs.

She would do it too, and that's a fact—my overly promiscuous friend.

Laughing, I reply, "I told him you aren't ugly!"

"Way to make me sound mediocre, bitch," she giggles.

"You need the wow factor when he sees you. If I hyped you up too much, he wouldn't be in suspense," I joke.

Jason needed an excellent sales pitch. You cannot just go straight for the sale; you need to work up to it, plus I am sure Ris will exceed his expectations. She's a knockout in the looks department, and her figure is mind-boggling.

"What time are you planning to leave tomorrow?" I ask.

"I'll leave as soon as I wake up," she replies.

"So, that would be noon?" I burst out laughing.

She tends to sleep the day away and be late for everything.

Laughing, she says, "No! I plan to leave no later than ten."

"Great, you should be here about three or four then!" I say.

Knowing Ris, she will have to stop many times to pee and buy snacks, so it will take her a little longer. Plus, she's not the greatest with direction even when she has a GPS right in front of her.

"I can't wait to meet your sexy tattooed guy. Have you fucked him yet?" she chuckles.

"Shut up. We're, well, he's taking his time," I reply.

I don't have a better answer. He is taking his time, and it's driving me insane. Although I do have to say the boy has some serious self-control. I, on the other hand, do not.

"What fucking guy takes his time? He must like you if he has not fucked you by now," she states.

"We were pretty hot and heavy this morning in my kitchen," I say before she interrupts me.

"Wait. What? In your kitchen? Girl, did he sleepover at your place?" she asks.

I go into detail and tell her about yesterday, last night, and this morning. She yells at me for stopping what could have been great sex in her words on the kitchen counter. I continue to tell her about Bridget and how she came to the shop. She reassures me that Luke likes me and that she will know for sure after meeting him because she thinks she can read people. She knows how to calm me and make me understand. She is my voice of reason. If she can greenlight Luke, that's all the assurance I need.

Ris changes the subject to talking about herself, which is the norm for her. She tells me about what she is planning to wear tomorrow and some of the outfits and swimsuits she packed before we end our call.

"See your bitch ass tomorrow. Love you! Mwah." Ris mumbles.

"Love you too. Text me before you leave," I reply.

chapter twenty-six

I dig through my closet to find a bag; I do not want to dump my clothes out of my suitcase and lug that thing around. I finally find one and a pair of my old flip flops. I wonder if I still have clothes at the cabin, not even sure if they'd still fit me. I grab a few t-shirts, tank tops, shorts, sweatshirts, and a pair of jeans.

I dig through my dresser for some cute pajamas. I am sure I will end up wearing shorts and a tank top to bed, but you never know. I head to the closet by the bathroom and grab a couple of beach towels. Then, back to my room to grab my dirty laundry.

I should probably wash some of my bras and panties since I'm almost out of clean ones. I hope Ris brings my orange suit as it's my favorite, and it does make my chest look good. I grab my laundry basket and make my way to the basement. I start a load of clothes in the washer and check the dryer.

A load of my dad's clothes is in here. I stare at them for a moment, then pull them out, put them into my empty basket, and head upstairs. I put the basket down in the living room and flick on the TV. I graze through the fridge for something to eat, but nothing looks appetizing. Maybe, dinner with Luke would have been better. I should have taken him up on his offer.

I check in the freezer and see a box of pizza rolls; I haven't had pizza rolls in forever. I look in the fridge to make sure there is

Western dressing to dip them in. I place them on a baking sheet and slide them into the oven after the preheat timer chimes.

I start to fold my dad's clothes from the dryer. What am I going to do with all his clothes? He won't be wearing any of them ever again. I can feel the tears well up in the corner of my eyes. He's gone, but everything belonging to him is still here and will continue to remind me of him. I miss him so much.

A knock at the door breaks my sadness. I wipe my eyes with my shirt and make my way to the door. I look out the window and see Luke's truck. What is he doing here? I am surprised but glad to see him; he will distract me from missing my dad.

I open the door.

"Hi!" I say, smiling.

"Hey, I thought maybe you'd want some ice-cream?" he says with a perked brow

I give him a "what the hell do you think" look while he stands in my doorway holding a quart of chocolate ice cream. Come on, what woman says no to ice cream

"Ice-cream is good. I never say no to ice cream," I giggle.

Luke laughs and comes into the house. We walk into the kitchen, and I grab some bowls from the cabinet.

"We can share," he says while putting one of the bowls back.

"Fewer dishes to do later," he smirks.

The oven dings, and I grab a hot pad to pull the pizza rolls out then place them on top of the oven to cool.

"Pizza rolls, hey," Luke giggles.

"What's wrong with pizza rolls?" I ask, looking at him funny.

"Nothing. I love pizza rolls. Those guys and chocolate ice cream are the perfect combo!" he laughs.

"Shut up!" I say, then nudge him.

He lunges toward me, and I take off running. He chases me into the living room then back into the kitchen. I run back out in the living room; he catches me and tackles me to the floor. I try to wiggle free, but I can't, then he starts to tickle me, and I squirm even more.

He stops and stares at me, then pushes my hair out of my face before leaning down toward my face. I am flat on my back, and he spreads my legs apart and slides himself in between my thighs then holds himself up by his forearms. He gently brushes his thumb across my cheek as he looks deep into my eyes. I need to hold myself together before I scream, "take me now" at the top of my lungs.

"I like you a lot, Ali," he whispers while still staring into my eyes.

"I know!" I reply, overly confident.

He lets out air from his nose while releasing a humph sound and smiles.

I know? He just told me he likes me a lot, and I reply with, I know. I'm spread eagle with him between my legs, gazing deeply into my eyes, and that is what I have to say. Man, I am so stupid. Say something to him; save yourself.

"I'm glad you do," he says with a smile.

He leans down and presses his lips against mine. His kiss gentle, delicate like a flower's petals yet strong. He takes his lips away from mine.

"I love kissing you, Turtle!" he laughs.

I love kissing him too! I could kiss him forever.

"Shut up!" I giggle.

I grab his shirt with my fist and pull his lips back to mine. I want him and do not feel like letting go, so I am going full steam ahead. Our mouths part as I slide my tongue into his mouth and across his tongue. I am rough but sensual as I smash my lips and tongue against his, soft and moist and hot and breathy. Our tongues dance in unison, battling back and forth like wrestlers.

I bring my hand down his chiseled stomach that I can feel through his shirt then down across his belt. I place my other hand on his rib cage.

There is zero distance between us at this very moment. His hands are still cupped behind my ears as he holds himself up by his forearms and knees. I guide my hand over the bulge in his jeans and grab firmly. Through his pants, his penis feels quite girthy. I play around down there, rubbing my hand up and down over his pants. I can feel his warm breath against my skin as we kiss and can hear his breathing become more solemn.

He groans in my mouth, and I smile as we continue to kiss. He removes a hand from my face and slides it down my body, across my chest, traveling further down. He grabs my hand and stops me. He breaks free from our kiss and looks at me while brushing my cheek with his thumb from his other hand.

"The ice cream is going to melt!" he says, smiling.

He gives me a peck on the lips, stands up, then reaches out his hand to help me up. Ugh, why does he keep stopping us? Why can we never make it past kissing and a light grope here and there? I'm going to explode if he doesn't fuck me, and soon.

I follow Luke into the kitchen. He grabs the bowl of slightly melted chocolate ice-cream, and I dish myself up some pizza rolls then head for the living room. I am frazzled while sitting on the couch and have lost my appetite. I attempt to eat my pizza rolls in between Luke spoon-feeding me chocolate ice-cream. We watch a movie, and as the credits start, Luke says he should probably head home. I want to tell him to stay the night, but I walk him to the door instead. We share a brief kiss, and he departs.

chapter twenty-seven

I wake up a half-hour before my alarm is set to go off. I'm too excited about today, and this weekend, so I am unable to fall back asleep. I need to shave my legs if I'm going to be in a swimsuit and shorts all weekend. I have enough time to chill in the tub and relax with some bubbles before I need to get ready for the day.

There is something about a bath that makes you feel at peace. I close my eyes and play all the intimate moments I've had with Luke thus far over in my head. We've had quite a few, but they don't seem to go past heavy kissing. Am I reading too much into it, or is there something drastically wrong?

Yesterday was the first time we went a smidge past making out, where he felt me up, and I touched him over his pants- like we are in Junior High. Our date at the movies, he said he didn't want our first time to be in his car. We've been numerous places that would have been ideal for our first time together but to no avail. What is he waiting for? Does he think it's too soon? Is it too soon? It is too soon, right? Why is this shit so undeniably abstruse?

LUKE AND I PULL IN AT ABOUT THE SAME TIME. HE WALKS over to meet me and gives me a side hug with a kiss on the lips.

"Good Morning, Ali. Luke." Ernie says as we enter the shop.

"Good Morning," I reply.

"Morning," Luke says. "What we are working on today?"

I part from Luke then head to Maureen's office to put my stuff down. I turn on her computer and go through her morning checklist. She's so organized. I mosey on into the lobby to brew some coffee for clients and tidy the public restroom. I unlock the door, flip on the open sign, then head back to Maureen's office. I continue my way down her checklist. I work on invoices that need to be sent out on Monday, so Maureen doesn't fall behind from having today off.

My phone buzzes. Ris's name and text message flash across the top of my screen.

I just woke up. I'm packing up my shit and will be on my way to see you soon!! 😘

It's before ten; I'm so proud of you! Drive safe, see you soon.

I reply.

I am proud; she never gets up this early when she doesn't have to work. I hope the day doesn't go by slow now that I'm waiting for her arrival. I scroll through my messages and see that I have a few unopened ones from Troy. I'm sure they're just his usual, "Good Morning and Good Night" texts.

Good Morning, beautiful!
Are you mad at me? I know you're dealing with a lot, but you've barely talked to me all week.
Ali?
Talk to me, please.
Goodnight. I miss you.

All sent by him yesterday. I don't know what to say to him. I need to talk to him about what is going on but not over a text, and every time I'm sort of free to speak, I'm with Luke. I need to tell Luke about Troy, now that he told me he likes me, he deserves to know.

I give Troy a quick reply before diving back into my list of invoices. I should at least ease his mind until I can figure out a good time to talk to him.

Morning! I'm not mad at you. I have a lot going on that you wouldn't quite understand. I will tell you everything when I see you next. Have a good weekend!

He replies almost instantly, but I stay focused on the invoices. I think I am doing them correctly. It's nice that I don't have to print off too many to send through snail mail because most are delivered electronically through email. I finish the invoices that Maureen left and grab the mail from the pile on the basket in her desk corner. I open them, scan, and file them. I separate the client invoices and the bills for the shop. She can show me what to do with these on Monday.

Luke pops his head in the door. I love it when he does that.

"Hi, handsome!" I say with a smile.

"Hey, beautiful. Ernie, Jason, and Austin just left for the cabin. Where do you want to do lunch today?" he asks.

I look at the clock; it's noon, already.

"Um... I was thinking about working through lunch since Ris should be here in a few hours. I need to leave early to finish packing." I reply.

"Do you mind if I go to Mary's with the guys then?" he asks.

Can he get any hotter? He's asking for my permission to eat lunch without me. That's so cute! Well, I guess we've had lunch together every day this week, so why not. He looks so sexy today. I love it when he wears his hat backward.

"Not at all, go with the guys!" I smile.

He walks over and kisses me on the cheek.

"Want me to bring you anything back?" he says before leaving Maureen's office.

"I think I'm good. Thank you, though." I reply.

Luke leaves, and I continue with what I was doing.

BEFORE I KNOW IT, I HEAR A GIGGLE THAT SOUNDS LIKE RIS'S coming from the lobby. I look up, and she is walking across the waiting area with Luke. I check the clock, and it's a little after three. She made great time.I head out to the lobby. Ris and I scream, then hug each other while jumping up and down. I look at Luke, and he's shaking his head laughing.

"What?" I say to Luke.

He shrugs his shoulder, lifting his palms to the ceiling, grinning.

"I see you two have met!" I say to Ris and Luke.

"Yes, we did!" Ris yells. "He was outside and was nice enough not to make fun of my non-classic car."

"She drives a goddamn brand-new Mercedes! Those don't fit in around here," Luke laughs.

He winks at me and tells Ris it was nice to meet her then makes his way back into the shop.

"Girl, you said he was hot but not that fucking hot. He's gorgeous." Ris says as she hugs me again.

I love that she's already stamped her seal of approval on him. I was not lying when I told her he was unbelievably attractive. Okay, hot as all fucking hell!

"I know. I melt into a puddle every time I'm around him," I convey between my teeth.

I am also not lying here; it's so true. Luke makes me weak in the knees.

"Fuck, me too. My panties are soaked just by looking at him," she spouts.

We bust out laughing. Boy, I missed her and her lack of a filter. I bring her into Maureen's office and shut everything down. I let Luke know I'm leaving, and I will see him when he gets off. He tells me not to worry about locking up; he will do it before he leaves.

chapter twenty-eight

At my dad's, I give Ris the tour of the barn before we put our cars in the garage by the house. I help her haul all her bags from her vehicle, four to be exact. She grabs a bag to change her clothes while I can finish packing. She continues to talk about how hot she thinks Luke is and how jealous she is of my find. Ris is gorgeous and draws any guy's attention with her long legs, dishwater blonde hair, big boobs, and bubbly attitude. She's loud, doesn't give two shits what she says, and always has guys eating out of the palm of her hand. I hope Luke doesn't fall under her spell. Ris knows how I feel about him, so she will turn it down some when it comes to him. I'm sure of that.

"How does this look?" Ris says.

She presses her lips together and checks out her ass in my mirror. She does have a nice one! Ris is wearing a super cute romper that accentuates her perfect long legs.

"That's fucking hot, your legs in that! Mmm, mmm, mmm," I reply as I snap my fingers in front of my face.

I change out of my jeans and work shirt into a pair of jean shorts and a yellow tube top.

"How do I look? Besides my pasty skin," I say, laughing.

Grabbing my boobs, she announces, "The girls are perked right up. Take the bra off to give them more attention!"

She laughs while raising an eyebrow. Stellar idea, but no! I'm not one to go braless and flaunt my boobs for the world to see.

"No, I will not go without wearing a bra. I will wear a strapless if anything," I press.

"You want to get Luke in the mood to fuck you sideways this weekend. Right? Lose the bra!" she shouts.

"Fine, you win," I grumble as I remove my bra and pack it in my suitcase.

I hope she's right and it works!

I leave Ris in my room to admire herself in the mirror, to grab my clothes from the dryer. I can hear mumbles upstairs from the basement. I see Luke talking to Ris when I reach the top of the stairs. She is doing her usual hair whirl on her finger thing to make her seem innocent while begging for attention. Luke doesn't seem to pay much attention to it as he grabs her bags. He looks over at me, and his face lights up.

"Woah, you look hot!" he says.

The bra trick worked! Winning!

"Doesn't she. I told her to ditch the damn bra," Ris boasts

Way to embarrass me, as usual. She winks at me then gives me the two fingers up to your lips with the tongue wiggling between them gesture when Luke isn't looking. I mouth, "stop" to her, and she laughs.

"Thanks," I reply, a little embarrassed.

"I have to run upstairs and grab my bag."

Luke heads out the door with Ris's three bags. She and I head upstairs to grab my bag and her other one. We get to my room, and Ris grabs my arm.

"Girl, he did not check me out once. I even flirted and not a darn thing. He is really into you!" Ris beams.

I smile then finish putting my hair and makeup stuff in my bag. I'm so relieved that Luke didn't pay any attention to Ris or her charm. I know he likes me for sure now and wasn't just saying it in the heat of the moment.

Ris has a straw floppy hat on and her huge ass, *JLo,* sunglasses. We hand Luke our bags and follow him out the door; Ris climbs into the back seat of Luke's truck. I run back into the house to grabs my sunglasses and keys. Luke comes behind me. He pushes me up against the wall, planting a soft kiss on my lips, then grabs my breasts from under my tube top. I push him away, point to the door, and tell him to go. He laughs.

"What? Your tits look amazing right now."

"Shut up and go!" I bark at him, giggling.

We head out of my dad's house, and I lock the door. We walk to Luke's truck; he opens my door and helps me in. As he walks around the front to his side, Ris whispers.

"He opens fucking doors too. Girl, you better slob on that nob, tonight."

"Shhhhh!" I laugh as Luke opens his door.

"Whore!" Ris growls.

"Skank!" I hiss.

"Woah, there, ladies. Now simmer down!" Luke chimes in.

Ris has definitely set the mood for our drive. We head down the driveway, and I look over at Luke. He's looking back at me with his gorgeous smile. He looks equally hot with his black hat backward, tight white t-shirt, colorful board shorts, and globe shoes. They are different than his usual work boot; I normally see him in. He even has shorty socks on that barely peek out under his ankles from his shoes. His sleeve pops nicely with his shirt and the blue, orange, white, and black of his shorts. His tattoos are so captivating. The artist who did them is talented.

I realize Ris is off doing her usual babble about nothing when Luke interrupts her.

"We have to stop at the liquor store to get some ice and beer for Ernie. And whatever you two want," he says.

"We getting' lit, bitches!" Ris shouts as she dances around in her seat.

We pull into the liquor store a town over. Ris and I jump out and head inside. We walk around with our basket as we giggle over ridiculous jokes we crack about the different alcohols we pass. Ris puts a bottle of Kinky, Blue UV Vodka, Malibu, and Cherry McGillicuddy's into our basket. Ris likes to party.

I look down an aisle to see Luke grabbing a few cases of beer and a bottle of Jack Daniels. I walk down by the freezers to grab some Tang, Sprite, and pink lemonade. Luke comes up behind me and wraps his arms around me before grabbing two of the bottles. We walk to the counter, where Ris is standing with her basket, the beer Luke grabbed, and ice.

"I got it," Luke says as he takes his wallet out to pay for everything.

We haul it all to his truck, fill his cooler, then head on our way to the cabin.

chapter twenty-nine

We finally make it to the cabin as the sun is about to set. Luke offers to bring everything in, but we help him haul all our stuff. Everyone must be out in front around the fire, getting ready to eat since I do not see anyone inside.

The A-frame little cabin looks exactly as I remember. It's so cozy and peaceful here. I give Ris a quick tour of the cabin after dropping off our bags in my dad's room. The cabin is small, but it is enough for five people. The open kitchen layout is Ris's favorite because you can sit at the island and look out at the lake. The view is phenomenal. Directly across from the kitchen is a little living room that has a small couch and two recliners. A loft overlooks the kitchen where Jason and I had our sleeping quarters, two bunk beds, and a dresser. A small bathroom separates my dad's and Ernie and Gladys's room on the main floor.

I tell Ris the real attraction is outside. Luke puts his stuff up in the loft for now because Ris will be bunking with me until Jason decides to steal her away. We all wander outside. The screen tent is set up, as is the volleyball net and other yard games. The firepit is on the opposite side of the yard, surrounded by a few lawn chairs and a picnic table. Jason and Austin are nowhere to be seen, so they must be down by the lake or something. Gladys is in the screen tent, setting up the table for dinner. I am getting hungry just thinking about food.

"About time you all arrived!" Ernie says, smiling as he walks around the corner carrying a bag of charcoal.

Luke grabs the bag and follows him over to the grill but winks at me first before he walks away.

"I love this place! I could live here. You could go naked all day!" Ris shouts.

She runs and does a cartwheel in the grass. I laugh, then head over to Gladys; Ris follows me.

"Do you need any help?" I ask.

"Everything is just about ready. You could grab the napkins off the table by the firepit.

The flies are terrible today, so we are going to have to eat in here," Gladys replies.

"This is my roommate, Ris. We work together at Facade," I say as I introduce Ris and Gladys to each other.

They shake hands then converse about Ris and the city. I head out of the tent over to Luke and Ernie to grab the napkins.

"What's on the menu?" I ask Ernie.

He lifts the grill.

"Shish-kebabs!" he boasts.

"They look amazing!" I say.

They do. Red pepper, green pepper, yellow pepper, onion, potato, and steak displayed perfectly across the skewers. Ernie is such an excellent cook. My dad loved everything he made, especially when we were here. I am missing my dad a little now since it's the first time I am here without him. Luke is here; he will help me to not think of my dad too much.

Luke smiles at me, then he and Ernie continue with their conversation as I head back to Gladys and Ris. I love being here; it was the only place I ever saw my dad relax and be somewhat lazy. I wish he were here right now.

"Ris want to go down to the lake quick?" I say as I interrupt her and Gladys.

"Yes, let's finish my tour," she says in excitement.

We head across the lawn to the stairs to make our way down to the docks. Ris talks about how sweet Gladys is and how much she likes it here already. We get down to the docks, and I show her the boathouse first. Inside is my dad and Ernie's huge pontoon boat, many life jackets, fishing supplies, water toys, and other miscellaneous things.

I notice that Jason's boat is still in here, but the jet skis are gone. He and Austin must be out on them. We head out of the boathouse, and Ris runs down to our sandy beach on one side of the boathouse. She runs in the water up to her knees.

"It's cool but feels great," she shouts.

I smile and sit down on the sand. I cannot help but think about the last time I was here. It was my dad's birthday six years ago. Since I've been away, I selfishly made him visit me for his birthdays, breaking the tradition of spending them here. I am sure it broke his heart, but he would never say so. Why did I become so self-absorbed and make everything about me? I barely came home for him or anyone, and I made my life seem more important than my dad's as well as those two people up there cooking. Now, I am here without my father. I should have made more time for him, for here, to come back home.

I am released from my little pity party as I hear the jet skis draw closer. I can see Ris bent over, picking shit up from under the water. I wave at Jason as he and Austin park themselves up on the beach. I laugh as both their eyes bug out of their heads when they see Ris. I walk over to her as they make their way towards her.

"Jason!" I yell while waving.

He runs over to scoop me up and give me a huge hug. After the recent tension between us, I am glad we are starting off cordial.

"She's smoking hot!" he whispers in my ear.

I had expected this reaction from him.

"I told ya she wasn't ugly," I whisper back, giggling.

He puts me down and walks over to Ris and introduces himself. Austin introduces himself as well.

"Let's go play some volleyball until the food's ready," Jason shouts.

We all make our way to the docks. Ris gives me a big smile then walks off with Jason and Austin as they look overly interested in what she has to say. They need to pick their jaws up off the ground from drooling over her.

I stop before heading up the stairs and walk to the end of the dock. I sit down on the bench and watch as the sun continues to set over the lake. The view is spectacular right now. It's stunning. My mind goes back to my dad, my selfishness, and how much I miss him. Tears trickle down my cheeks as I look at the water. It is times like these that I miss my dad most. I wish he were here sitting next to me.

"Ali. You okay?" Luke says from behind me.

I wipe my face and stand up.

"Yea. I'm good," I say with a smile.

Luke knows I'm not and grabs me pulling me into his chest, hugging me tight as he rests his chin on top of my head. We embrace in silence for a few moments.

"Dinners ready," Luke says.

We break free from one another and walk back up to everyone. Luke is leading the way and holding my hand. We reach the top of the hill, and everyone, except for Ernie, is gathered under the tent. Luke grabs my waist, kisses my forehead, then heads over to assist Ernie. I walk into the tent and take a seat right next to Ris, who is already all up in Jason's shit. She is practically sitting on his lap, while Austin looks like he wishes it were his. She's working her Ris magic! Hopefully, it will ease the tension between Jason and Luke, and Jason will be too preoccupied with Ris to care about what I am doing. Ris grabs my hand, smiles at me, then looks back at Jason as if she's way into what he' has to say. Luke and Ernie come in with trays full of shish kebabs. They set them on the table, and Luke takes a seat next to me.

"It looks delicious," Ris says.

"Thank you, and thank you for joining us," Ernie replies to her.

We all dig in. I sit and listen as everyone engages in conversation. Ernie and Gladys talk to Luke about what they have planned for tomorrow. Jason is telling Ris one of his many "I'm the most remarkable humans on the planet" stories. I smile, and for the first time in over a week, I feel like I am finally home.

chapter thirty

After dinner, I help Gladys clean up. Luke helps Ernie, and Ris goes off with Jason and Austin. We all gather back together around the firepit. Ernie starts to talk about old times up here when Jason and I were little kids. I look over at Luke, standing next to Ernie, laughing at the embarrassing yet silly stories. Those were such simple times when things weren't so complicated.

He walks over to me, and I get up from my chair. He sits down, and I sit on his lap. Ernie is still talking about the good ole days. Gladys is back at their motorhome; I assume getting ready for tomorrow or settling in for the night. Ris is sitting between Jason and Austin, all laughing on mine and Jason's account.

"You smell good," Luke whispers in my ear. "I want to kiss you so badly, right now."

I look at him, believe me, the feeling is mutual. I smile, then lay my head on his shoulder, and he wraps his arms around me. Jason looks over at us then stands up from his chair. All I can think is, here we go. I thought Ris's charm would keep him occupied, but sadly, that's not the case tonight. He walks over to Ernie.

"Dad, are you okay with this?" he yells as he points over to Luke and me.

"You're okay with this piece of shit moving in on Ali?" he shouts.

Things are about to get bad, real bad. I can feel it. Ernie stands up, and Luke takes me off his lap, standing up as well. Ris comes over to me and grabs my hand. Austin stands up next to Jason. A confrontation is about to ensue. However, Ernie seems to be the voice of reason among these hotblooded boneheads.

"Jason, it's not our business. If they want to be together, it's their business, and there is nothing you can do or say about it. So, let it go, son." Ernie says in a loud stern voice.

I'm surprised by Ernie and his comment, but he's right. What Luke and I do or what we are is no one's business but ours. I am so glad Ernie spoke his mind.

"That's fucking bullshit. He comes here and takes everything from us," Jason screams.

Luke does not like what's going on and moves closer to Jason. His face quickly changes, displaying a confused yet angry expression.

"Woah! Take everything? What the fuck are you talking about?" Luke barks.

"That's enough!" Ernie yells.

Ernie does not want trouble any more than I do, especially when everyone is together to have a good time. He's had enough apparently, and so have I; I'm over this shit.

"No! He comes here looking for a handout. Then, he takes our women and is now taking over the shop," Jason screams.

Great, I can see this is not looking like it will end well, despite Ernie's clear and stern warnings to Jason. Luke looks heated as well. Ris grabs hold of my hand tighter as she watches the guys scream at each other.

I stand up. That's it, this shit is ending, and it's ending right fucking now.

"You all need to stop, and I mean it. This is so fucking stupid. If my dad were here, he would be livid at all of you for ruining such a beautiful night here at the cabin." I say, outraged, then take off towards the cabin.

"Ali! Ali! Ali, wait!" Ris shouts from behind me.

I do not even stop to wait for her. I keep walking to the cabin. I'm so unbelievably pissed right now. I get inside, walk to my dad's room, then slam the door shut out of frustration. I sit on the bed and start to cry. I tend to do that when I'm angry. Ris comes in and sits down next to me and gives me a big hug.

"Are you okay, Ali?" Ris asks as she hugs me tighter.

"I-I'm just tired of Jason and his bullshit. I'm tired of everything," I say.

I have not had it easy since I came back, and Luke has been the light at the end of a very dark tunnel. He's become someone I turn to, to lose myself in, sort of like my knight in shining steel toe boots. I'm falling for him, and Jason is ruining everything for me, just like he did when we were in High School. I know he's trying to look out for me, and he thinks what he is doing is best, but I make that decision, not him. I hate that this weekend is turning sour so quickly and that Ris is witnessing it. On top of that, I miss my dad like crazy, and being here puts the topping on the cake. What else could go wrong this weekend?

"I miss my dad; being here brings back so many memories. I should've made more time for him," I say, almost hysterical.

Ris lays me down on the bed and rubs my back while I cry my heart out. I wish I had been there for him more instead of focusing on my selfish pursuits to make it big in my career. I know he was proud of me, but it was also vital that I was there for him. He made me his number one priority; I should have made him mine.

"Ali, your dad understood. He was so proud of you, he loved you more than anything in the world, and he is here. He's always with you. He's watching over you every day," she says in the most comforting way she's ever been with me.

I thank her and cry myself to sleep.

chapter thirty-one

I wake to the smell of bacon and coffee. I look over, and Ris is still sleeping, arm over her head, mouth wide open, and releasing tiny snores. I quietly get out of bed, change out of my clothes from yesterday into something comfy. I look back at Ris; she is still fast asleep.

In the kitchen Gladys and Luke are making breakfast. Everyone else must still be asleep, most likely. Luke turns and smiles at me; I smile at him back.

"Good Morning!" he says as he walks over to give me a hug and a kiss.

"Morning," I say, still half asleep.

Last night seemed like a terrible nightmare. Today doesn't seem so bad, not yet at least. I hope it stays that way.

"Morning, Ali," Gladys chirps. "Coffee?"

"Yes, please," I reply with a smile.

I love Gladys. She's like a mother to me. I love her warmth and care when she speaks. Gladys pours a cup of coffee and hands it to me. She turns to Luke, talking about the flowers she is planning to plant today and where. I sit down at the island and stare out of the window at the lake. It looks like glass right now. I bet its prime fishing time out there. I am sure my dad would be down at the end of the dock, rod in hand.

I glance back at Luke, who is flipping scrambled eggs. His hair is messy. He has a white tank that shows his rib cage and gray sweat-pants-style shorts. He's still looking hot, more so since he's cooking. I trace my eyes down his tattooed arm losing myself in all the detail.

"Ali. Ali! Turtle!" Luke says with a giggle.

"Huh?" I reply as I am lifted from staring at him.

"You want some breakfast?" he asks.

"Yes, please," I smile.

Luke dishes Gladys, me, and himself a plate. Gladys takes her plate into the living room, and Luke sits down next to me. He looks at me and smiles as he rips a piece from his bacon.

"You look beautiful," he says with a mouth full of bacon.

I smile.

"So do you, *Martha Stewart,*" I giggle.

We continue eating our breakfast as we stare at each other and laugh lightly, between him stealing bites of my bacon and me stealing bites of his right back. Gladys walks into the kitchen and rolls her eyes then begins to clean up. She places the leftover food on a plate, slides it into the oven, and wipes down the counter.

"I got the dishes," I say.

"Thanks, Ali," Gladys says and smiles, walking toward the door.

Luke kisses my forehead then heads out after her. I grab our plates and bring them to the sink to start the dishes. I fill the sink with hot, soapy water; I hum quietly to myself while I wash each dish and silverware. Jason walks into the kitchen and sits down. I turn and look at him, then turn back to the sink.

"Want some breakfast?" I say.

"Yea," he replies.

I wipe my hands, grab a plate, and dish him up. I slide it across the counter then turn back to the dishes. It's silent for a while, and I can hear Jason chew. I don't have anything to say to him right now; last night is still very fresh on my mind.

"I'm sorry," Jason says.

I don't reply or turn around. I pretend like I didn't hear him. He gets up, grabs something from the fridge, then takes his plate into the living room. I finish the dishes and head back to my dad's room. I open my bag and dig out some clothes to wear today. I wake Ris up and ask her where my orange suit is. She sits up, says it's in one of her bags, then heads to take a shower. I find my suit in the last bag I search through of hers.

I throw on my orange bikini. The bottom has a slight ruching on the sides, and the top is a halter style with a twist in the fabric across the bust, which makes my chest look perfect. Perfect enough for Luke to keep his eyes on me at all times! I put on some jean shorts and a tank top. I brush my hair and throw it back in a ponytail, then apply some light makeup. Ris comes back with wet hair and wrapped in a towel.

"Will you french braid my hair, bitch?" she says, laughing.

"Yes, slut," I snort.

That's how we've always talked to each other, calling one another vulgar names. She's like a sister. Ris sits in front of the mirror behind the door and applies gallons of makeup as I brush her hair out and french braid it. We laugh as she commentates while putting on her face. Ris finishes and digs out her white thong bikini from her bag. She rocks it! Jason will be eating out of the palm of her hand by lunch.

"I told you I was going to bring this," she winks at me and laughs.

She puts her suit on. It fits her like a glove and makes her look super-hot. She grabs a sheer wrap and ties it around her waist, then pulls her floppy hat down onto her head and grabs her sunglasses before walking out of the room. I grab my sunglasses and our towels then head out after her.

We walk out front, and I can see that more people have arrived. Nikki and Mindy are here with another guy I recognize, but I don't know his name. I search for Luke and see he is down at the flower garden with Gladys. He has his shirt off and his hat on backward, my favorite. I am sure he has figured it out by now that I like seeing him this way, well any female does for that matter!

"Hey, ladies, are you coming on the boat with us?" Austin yells.

Everyone looks over at us, and I can see them all gawking at Ris. Which I knew they would. I can tell Nikki and Mindy are intimidated by her beauty; they are hatin' pretty fierce right now.

"Hell yes!" Ris shouts and runs over to the boys.

Luke doesn't follow her with his eyes but stays focused on me as he smiles and puts down a potted flower. He walks over to me and looks me over.

"An orange swimsuit! Hot!" he says, then bends down to kiss me. "Orange is my favorite color, by the way."

He winks. I am so glad I chose to wear this today. That explains why the steering wheel in his truck is bright orange. I smile at him while checking out his sweaty rock-hard body. So that's great. We have an affinity for the same colors, even though my favorite color is green, orange comes in a close second or third.

"Are you going out with us on the boat?" I ask.

I figure he won't go because of the tension between him and Jason, but I ask anyway, so he knows I want to spend time with him today.

"No, I have lots to do around here with Gladys and Ernie. You go with your friend. Save her from being mauled by those morons," he laughs.

I kiss him then rush over to everyone. I look back at Luke as he smiles and gives me a wave. I smile and wave back then head down the stairs to the dock. We all pile into Jason's boat. It's a fancy one, mainly for pulling a tub or wakeboard; it's not an ideal fishing vessel.

"Who wants to board first?" Jason yells.

"Why don't you, I'll drive," I say.

Jason agrees and jumps out of the boat to gear up. I figured he'd be all for being the first to show off his skills for Ris and his friends. He was pretty good the last time I was here. I am sure he's still got it. Jason is ready, and I start to take off toward open water.

chapter thirty-two

We come into shore after a crazy day on the lake. We did wakeboarding, skiing, and tubing. No one got hurt, and only Austin lost his trunks a few times. It was so much fun. Jason and Ris got a little cuddlier throughout the day, which gives me hope for tonight.

Nikki and Mindy were not too bad either, I don't know if it was because of Ris putting them in their place a lot or that Bridget is not here, but I still had fun hanging out with them regardless. Everyone is hungry and hyped up, ready to get their drink on. Ris is glued to Jason, and they are flirting something fierce. Mindy and I walk to the boathouse to hang the soaked life jackets as everyone heads up the hill.

"Are you and Luke a thing now?" Mindy asks.

I turn toward her, a tad surprised at her question.

"What?" I reply.

I wonder why she's so inquisitive. She's been pretty cool today, why ruin it now.

"He and Bridget were like together, then you came home, and he didn't want to be with her anymore," she says in her snarky bitch voice.

There she is, she must have held this in all day. Her true self is coming out now that she has me alone and without Ris. I don't even know what to say to her. What Luke and I are is none of her concern at all.

"They were hanging out and sleeping together until just a few days ago. Bridget called him because he didn't show up at her house, but he was with you. He told her he didn't want to be with her anymore," she says slyly.

I don't react to her comment. Luke told me they've only kissed and have never slept together. When I was eavesdropping on his conversation, I don't remember hearing him mention not wanting to be with someone. Maybe, that is why he took the call in the bathroom so I wouldn't hear him end it with her. He didn't want to raise any doubts, and that's respectful. I guess.

"We should head up to where everyone else is," I say without replying to her last comment.

I believe ignorance should be ignored, and that's why I don't care. Well, not entirely. We get to the top of the hill, and Mindy takes off over to Nikki and the rest of the clan. I skim the yard for Luke but don't see him anywhere. I walk over to Ris and grab her arm.

"I need to talk to you," I say.

I need her to help ease my mind. It's best not to leave any doubts, and my best friend can at least guide me and tell me I am overthinking. I hope! We head back into the cabin, and I tell her about what Mindy said. She told me to ignore the bitch as she is trying to get a rise out of me and do Bridget's dirty work. She reassures me that Luke wants me bad and to forget about it, precisely what I needed to hear. I love Ris!

"Let's get our drink on!" she shouts.

We head back outside, and Luke is at the grill with Ernie. He looks at me and waves. I smile and wave back. Ris runs over to Jason, and they start a game of volleyball. I sit in a chair next to Gladys. I ask her how her flower planting went, and she tells me about all the flowers she and Luke planted. She loves to plant flowers around the cabin, she does it every year. Gladys continues to say she found some neat red, white, and blue flowers to plant around the flagpole. She said she couldn't have finished it without Luke's help.

I look over at him. He and Ernie are flipping burgers while chatting. Jason has never been much help to his parents as he is always worrying about his friends and partying. I'm sure they enjoy Luke's help and company just as much as my dad did in my absence. Luke truly is a great guy.

The food is done, and we all sit down to eat. After dinner, Luke and I help Ernie and Gladys clean up while the others play another yard game and continue drinking. I'm glad Ris is fitting right in and having a great time. I knew she would. It was a great decision to bring her here. I am also glad that Jason and I are cool now too. Hopefully, he won't be such a pain in the ass tonight.

The sun starts to set, Luke starts a big fire and we all crowd around it. I've started drinking, and Luke has had a few beers. Mindy is watching us like hawks, and I'm sure she will report every second back to Bridget. I try to ignore her stares and have a good time. The guys start chanting "shots." Everyone starts to take shots from the mini shot glasses stretched out across the picnic table. Ris and Jason talk me into taking two of them. Jason runs into the cabin and brings out his boom box. The girls start to scream as the music begins to blast across the lawn. It's time to party, and everyone has joined in the fun. Us girls are having a great time despite Mindy's snarkiness.

Ris, Nikki, and Mindy get up to dance as the guys watch in amusement. Luke grabs my face and kisses me while I'm sitting on his lap. Quite buzzed, I drop my cup on the ground and wrap my arms around his neck. I get into our kiss. I don't care who is watching us.

We break from our kiss to screams from Ris, Nikki, and Mindy as a song starts to play. The guys get up and start grinding on them. It looks like one big orgy on the lawn as Ernie and Gladys excuse themselves from us crazy kids. Ris comes over and grabs me from Luke's lap, and we dance like dorks to a few songs. Luke doesn't seem mind and is quite amused.

I walk back over to Luke. I notice Ris has started making out with Jason, and they are all over each other. It's safe to say he will leave Luke and me alone tonight!

"Get a room!" Austin shouts as everyone laughs and continues to dance.

I look at Luke. His eyes are so gorgeous, I can see the flames from the fire dances in them. Man, he's hot as hell. I press myself against him. He is still shirtless, and I'm only in my swimsuit. I push my chest to his chest as I slide my tongue gently into his mouth. He grabs the back of my head with his hands and kisses me hard. I start to feel tingly all over, hopefully from his touch and not because I am drunk now. I don't care. Either way, this is steamy, and I'm way into him. I desperately want him to pick me up and bring me to a bed.

"I love you bitch!" I hear Ris scream.

I break myself free from Luke's lips and look to see Ris heading into the cabin with Jason. I bring my eyes back to Luke's.

"Do you want to go inside?" he asks.

"Yes," I practically moan.

I am glad he finally got the hint. Luke grabs my ass then gets up out of his chair, carrying me to the cabin as we attempt to keep making out. He puts me down, and we walk inside. I have a hold of his hand, leading the way to my dad's room. We enter my dad's room, and I close the door. I push him on to the bed, then climb onto his lap. I bring my arms around his neck as I slide my tongue back into his mouth. He slides his hands from my hips up my back. I bite his lip and give a playful tug. He moans.

We kiss hot and passionately as our breathing draws heavy. Luke brings his hands farther up my back, undoing the clasp of my bikini top. I grab the front and slide it over my head and throw it to the floor. He kisses my neck then brushes his lips across my collarbone. I arch backward as he trails his lips across one of my breasts then over to the other. He circles his tongue gently around my nipple then bits down softly, pulling away with a light suck. He continues onto my other nipple as he lays down onto the bed. My body follows his, and I start to kiss his neck, making my way down his chiseled abs. His body is well built. It's incredible.

He moans as he puts his hand on the back of my head. I reach his shorts and stick my hand down them, under his briefs. I grab hold of his already hard penis. It is quite large as I can barely touch my fingers tips as I start to move my hand up and down in a figure-eight motion. I pull his shorts down more as he wiggles to help me and groans from my touch. I lick my lips and slide my mouth over the enormous head of his huge cock. He stops me as he sits up and grabs me under my arms, flipping us over. I am now on my back, and he presses his mouth to mine, aggressively massaging my tongue with his.

He runs his hand down my body and slides his fingers in the side of my bikini bottoms, pulling them down. I lift my hips to help him remove my bottoms. He takes his hand, spreading my legs, and lowers himself to me. I can feel his penis as it rests against my hip and up past my belly button.

He stops kissing me for two seconds to suck on his finger before returning to kiss me and brings his hand down between my legs. He gently rubs his thumb over my clit, and I instantly break out with goosebumps across my entire body. My heart starts to race, and my breathing deepens. He slides his finger into me, and the feeling is exotic. I let out a slight gasp in his mouth before he lets out a deep breath.

"Holy fuck, you're tight," he whispers in my mouth.

He continues to kiss me aggressively and starts moving his finger in and out of me slowly, then picking up the pace as I become wetter. I let out a loud moan in his mouth, and he kisses me more passionately but aggressive at the same time. I can feel his penis throb against my thigh. I've never felt like this before.

"You're so fucking wet. My God!" he whispers in my ear.

He removes his fingers just as I'm close to climaxing. I grab onto his wrist. He smiles then grabs hold of himself and runs his penis up and down the opening of my vagina.

chapter thirty-three

He stops at the opening and starts to ease himself into me gently. He lets out a loud moan then stops. He moves his lips from mine, lets out a growl, then puts his head down on the pillow next to the side of my face. He takes the tiny bit of the tip of his penis out of me. I fling open my eyes and grab his wrist. I look straight into his eyes.

"What- what's wrong? Why'd you stop?" I asked, concerned.

What now, what could possibly be the reason why he is stopping this. He lifts himself onto his forearms, putting his hands on my cheeks, and stares into my eyes before pecking me on the lips.

"You're wasted. I've only had a couple of beers. I promised myself that I would never have sex with you when your drunk. I want you to remember this, more so because it would be our first time together," Luke replies, gazing into my eyes.

I am not sure what to say, because he's right, I'm drunk as shit. Fuck, I want him badly, but I want to remember every moment of our first time together. Ugh, why must he be so respectful?

"Okay," I say, smiling and kiss him.

"Please, don't be upset with me. I promise I will make it up to you when you're sober," he says with sincerity in his eyes.

I smile back at him, giving a nod of approval.

The door bursts open, and we are startled from our beautiful moment to Ris crying and holding her face. I hop out of bed and throw a shirt on. Luke grabs his boxer briefs, slides them on, then walks over to flick on the light. Ris is standing there, holding her nose, butt naked, with blood all over her face, chest, and arms. What in the hell?

Luke grabs a towel from the floor and wraps it around her and leaves the room. I hold her nose and walk her to the bathroom. Jason shows up in just his boxers, and he's covered in some of Ris's blood.

"What the fuck happened?" I scream at him while holding Ris's bloody face as she cries.

Jason looks concerned for Ris. I feel bad for them both. At least she had somewhat decent timing when she rushed in here.

"She was on top, and I flipped her over to nail her from behind, then she fell off the bed. She smacked her face off the bedside table," Jason shrugs his shoulders, trying not to laugh.

"You've got to be kidding me," I burst out laughing.

Only Ris! Of course, something this retarded would happen to her. Drunken sex can lead to crazy disasters sometimes. I do not know whether to laugh more or feel sorry for her as I hold her nose while she is wrapped in a towel, crying. Luke comes in with a few wet washcloths and an ice pack and hands it to Jason. I tell Jason to hold one on her nose as I take the other to clean the blood from her chest and arms.

"Can you grab Ris a shirt from the room, please?" I yell at Luke.

Luke and Jason look each other over before Luke turns to leave the bathroom. I tell Jason that he can go and that I've got it covered from here. I ask him to clean himself up and any blood he sees in his room. Luke returns with a shirt, laughs, then kisses me before leaving again. I wipe the blood from Ris's face and place the ice pack on her nose.

"You've got to take it easy on the hard-core fucking," I laugh.

She giggles as she throws her arms up in the air. I am so glad Ris took it all in good spirits; I am sure she is used to this sort of thing happening.

"Did I interrupt you and Luke?" she questions.

"No, we were pretty much done," I sigh.

I wish he wouldn't have stopped us, but we may have been interrupted by Ris and Jason anyway. She kicks me and lets out a squeal, squinting and groaning when it hurts her nose. I look at her and shoosh her.

"I will tell you about it tomorrow when we're sober," I say.

There's a lot for me to tell her after tonight. I help her get the shirt on that Luke brought. I leave her in the bathroom to get us some water. I walk into the kitchen and notice Luke is out cold on the tiny couch in the living room with his feet hanging over the end. I walk over and put the blanket from the back of the couch over him. He is such a cute sleeper.

I head back to the bathroom with the waters. Ris takes a drink of her water, downing the whole glass in seconds. We walk into my dad's room and crawl into bed together. I cannot help but chuckle at what just happened. Ris punches me and tells me to shut up. Who gets a bloody nose from bouncing their face off the nightstand during sex? Ris does, that's who! Ris and I lay in bed, talking for quite a while about anything and everything before we fall asleep after a great but bizarre night.

chapter thirty-four

The morning sun beams through the window, shining directly on my face. I open my eyes to look around. Behind me is Ris sprawled out in a shirt, pantyless, and snoring away. Her face looks quite bruised. I giggle a little because I'm reminded of the events that led up to her misfortune. I grab my phone and see that it is only a quarter to seven. It's so early, why am I awake. I am surprised I don't have much of a hangover. Maybe, I didn't drink as much as I thought last night.

I get dressed and grab a sweatshirt, check myself in the mirror quickly, then pull my hair through the loop of my hat and head out into the kitchen. I can hear Luke's adorable snores from the living room. He is on his back with one leg off the couch, his foot on the floor and the other leg hanging off the end, still wrapped in the blanket I covered him in.

I set up the coffee maker to brew some joe for the hungover clan. They will be looking for it when they wake. I quietly open the fridge, grab myself an apple juice, and the styrofoam cup full of worms. I snatch a granola bar from the counter and make my way down to the lake—time for some me-time.

The grass is still wet from the morning dew as I walk across the lawn. It's so quiet and peaceful right now. It is the best time to be out here. I saunter into the boathouse and grab my dad's fishing rod, tackle box, and a net just in case I happen to catch something of decent size. I sit down on the bench and look out over the lake before setting my rod up for fishing. Every time we came here for a weekend, my dad would fish from this bench every Sunday morning. He would say it's his church. He'd sit down here for an hour or two even if he didn't catch anything.

Now, I see why he did. The view is stunningly beautiful, and it smells divine. The birds are chirping, the lake is still, and the bugs aren't too bad yet. I can feel my dad's presence. It's surreal. I bait my hook and stand up to give it a cast. My dad liked to fish with a bobber, so I put one on. I can hear a slight crinkling coming from the front pocket of my sweatshirt. I pull out an envelope, the writing on it is in my dad's handwriting, and it reads,

To my Little Lady.

I forgot about the letters given to us during the reading of my father's Will. I must have shoved it in the pocket of this sweatshirt from my purse. I wasn't ready to read it then. Now is as good a time as ever. I flip over the envelope, slide my finger under the flap, pull out the tri-folded paper, and open it.

Dear Allison Paige,

I write this letter because I have been told a personal message is more meaningful than being read off guidelines on what to do with someone's personal belongings. I have to agree. I hope I am in my old age at my passing, and you are all grown with a beautiful family of your own that I was able to be a part of. I want you to know how proud of you I am. I am so proud of your hard work and dedication you've shown while in school and life. You worked fearlessly to achieve your dreams. Allison, you can do anything you set your mind to. You have a huge heart, and you're so beautiful. I hope I was able to watch you graduate from college, settle into your career, see you move into your first home, walk you down the aisle, and watch you become an amazing mother. Time is not measured by the rise and set of the sun, but by the moments we share with those we love. Please, know I love you with every piece of me, and I will continue to love you when I am no longer on this earth. Take care of yourself, sweetheart.

With all my love,

Dad

Tears heavily cascading down my face, I fold the paper back up, put it in the envelope, and slide it back into my pocket. Reading my dad's words hurt my heart so much. He died so young and will not witness a lot of what he mentioned in his letter. He won't be there when I purchase my first home, and he won't be walking me down the aisle, or wrestle around giving horsie back rides with my children. He was taken too soon. He deserved a longer life. I should be angry with God, but for some reason, I'm not. He needed to take my dad home, and I'm somewhat at peace with that.

"Fishing this early, Alicat?" Ernie asks from behind me.

"Nah, I'm in church," I reply with a slight smile and wipe the tears from my face.

Ernie smiles and takes a seat next to me. He grabs hold of my hand then looks out over the lake. I can sense that he feels dad is here too.

"We all miss him, kiddo," he sighs.

I know Ernie misses him a lot because they've been friends for years. We sit in silence as we have Sunday church together with my dad. Ernie gives me a huge hug before excusing himself and strolling back up the hill. I start to cry again, and my rod falls onto the dock. I grab it and notice my bobber is gone. I set the hook and begin to reel. The fish seems slightly bigger than what I am used to catching from the dock, usually sunnies, bluegill, perch, or an occasional northern pike. But this one is putting up a fairly good fight, as I reel it in closer to the dock.

"I got something big!" I shout to Ernie.

He makes his way back to me and notices the bend in my dad's rod as well as my tired struggle from reeling. The fish comes closer to the surface as I continue to reel it in. It jumps frantically out of the water then back to struggling to swim away.

"Woah!" Ernie shouts in excitement and grabs the net.

He scoops under the water with the net and pulls up the fish. We hoot and holler as I just reeled in one of the largest walleyes I've ever caught in my life. I dance around in victory while Ernie laughs. I wish my dad were here with us, but Ernie being here makes me feel like he is.

"Hold this while I get a tape measure," Ernie says and digs through my dad's tackle box.

I pull the walleye out of the net and hold it up. Ernie takes a quick picture then measures my fish. The beast measures just over thirty-three inches long. What a pig! A definite wall mounter, but I decide to remove the hook and release it back into the water to swim another day. I am blessed to have caught it and have a picture taken with it. Ernie pats me on the back, tells me "great catch," then heads up to the cabin. I grab my dad's rod, tackle box, and the net to put back in the boathouse. I grab the container of worms and set off for the cabin. Before I reach the top of the hill, I turn back to the lake. I look out over it and smile.

"Thanks, dad! Love you!" I whisper.

chapter thirty-five

When I enter the cabin, Ernie is sitting at the island talking with Luke while Gladys is cooking breakfast. No one else is awake yet. I am a little nervous to see Luke after our awkward moment last night, which ended in him stopping us from having sex again. However, he doesn't seem to think it's as uncomfortable as I do since he is smiling those gorgeous pearly whites at me. He looks striking, as usual.

"Nice fish you caught this morning," Luke says.

"Thanks, it was the biggest walleye I have ever caught. It was a lot of fun to reel in," I reply.

"Hard to believe I caught it off the dock."

I walk past everyone and head to my dad's room to check on Ris and grab my phone. Ris is sitting on the bed and looks in rough shape. The corner of her eye by her nose is quite puffy and blackish purple, her nose is pomegranate red, and her upper lip on the same side as her slightly black eye looks as though she has received lip fillers. I want to laugh but know I shouldn't, although the situation leading up to her MMA debut is one to put in the record books.

"How are you feeling, Ris?" I ask as I sit down next to her.

"As good as I look," she laughs.

I smile back at her.

"I seriously look like *Kim Kardashian* just got her ass kicked by *Ronda Rousey*!"

I wasn't going to argue with her there. She clearly does, but at least we can laugh about it now.

"What time do you want to get going today?" I ask.

I know she's very hungover and has a five-hour drive ahead, after our two-hour drive back to my dad's place to get to the city.

"I'm way too hungover to give a shit about going home today. Plus, no makeup in this world can fix this," she replies as she points to her face.

"You're going to leave tomorrow morning, then?"

"Yea, if that's okay with you. I will call into work tomorrow. This way, I can spend some more time with my bitch!" Ris grunts and throws herself back onto the bed.

"So, what happened between you and Luke last night before I interrupted you two love birds with my naked circus antics?" Ris asks sarcastically while sucking air in-between her teeth in pain as she touches her bruised face.

Last night was all kinds of craziness. Luke stopping us when he practically had it in then Ris naked and all bloodied up.

"I don't know how to explain what took place between him and me last night. He stopped us from having sex again, though," I say with a sigh.

Ris flings up from the bed.

"What? What the fuck is wrong with him?" she shouts.

I wish I knew the answer to give to her, but I don't even know it myself.

"It's just so strange that he keeps stopping us from having sex. Last night was the farthest we've made it. Like he was in but not in, in," I say while picking the polish from my nails.

"What the fuck is not in, in?" Ris questions with the most awkward, confused look I've ever seen her make.

"Well, we were naked. I attempted to suck his dick, and when I put my mouth on him, he flipped us around then fingered me before he went to insert himself. He was barely in, and there was no penetration or anything before he stopped it all completely," I explain, quite embarrassed.

Ris looks at me as if her mind is blown, and she is literally clueless as to why Luke is acting the way he is when it comes to us being intimate with each other.

"Um... Woah! Did he say why he stopped from fucking you silly? Is it big?" she asks.

"He said something about how I was wasted, and he didn't want to have sex with me while I was drunk. It was also that he wanted me to remember our first time together," I reply feeling just as stupid saying it out loud as I felt when Luke said it to me.

"Oh, and he's huge!"

Not even listening to the first part of what I said, Ris holds her hands up to give me a measurement gesture of Luke's dick size. I adjust her hands, moving them farther apart, and her mouth drops. Of course, she would be more interested in his penis instead of why it hasn't been inside me. I give her a detailed description of it before she could ask me for one.

The way her eyes light up and the facial expressions she displays as I describe every inch of Luke's dick to her make the unfortunate situation I was in last night a tad more bearable. After I finish describing the massive appendage Luke has between his legs, Ris begins to tell me her theory as to why he may keep preventing us from going all the way. She mentions that he may really like me and not want to ruin anything by going too fast. Either that or he's nervous about our first time together. Then she mentions something about the shop, my dad, Ernie, and Jason. It could be a whole lot of things, but I've got the gist of where she is going with her speech.

I never thought about Luke and I being in a relationship, whether it was purely sexual or becoming something serious, affecting the shop or something my father may disapprove of if he were still here. I have a lot of work to do on myself and to realize that not everything revolves around me. I need to consider the way things may affect others, as well.

I ask Ris if she wants to get some breakfast and see what Luke wants to do since we are no longer in a hurry to get back to my dad's place. Ris puts on a pair of my comfy shorts and sets her hair up on top of her head.

When we enter the kitchen, everyone is up and crowding around the island. Gladys, Ernie, and Luke must be outside.

"Holy shit, what happened to your face?" Austin asks, looking at Ris.

"Well, you see, Jason and I were working on our Las Vegas show act in the bedroom last night; I'll let you ponder on the details," she replies without skipping a beat, dishing up a plate for herself.

Ris always has the best comebacks to everything, and her reply to Austin was fucking classic. Jason's face is in pure shock, and I can see him turning red from the words that just spewed out of Ris's month. Everyone starts laughing and making fun of Jason. He looks so embarrassed, and it's priceless.

chapter thirty-six

I leave everyone to their chewing and go outside to find Luke. Ernie and Gladys are down in her flower garden, but Luke is nowhere around the yard. I proceed down to the lake to see if he is down there. He isn't on the dock or over by the beach; I decide to check the boathouse and see if he may have taken one of the boats out. I open the door and walk inside; Jason's boat and the pontoon are still here. Where the hell could he be? Maybe, he went for a walk. I turn to leave the boathouse when Luke comes around the corner of the changing area. I gasp.

He is naked and looks drop-dead sexy without his clothes on. His body is so hard not to sit and stare at. Every part of his body seems finely sculpted. His muscular physique, a little tanner than when we arrived on Friday, is cascading with beads of water. His abs perfectly display his six-pack plus another six-pack, the Ken Doll lines lay to perfection, and his limp baby arm looks so thick and tough dangling there.

I'm speechless as I stand and gawk at the sight before me. Luke bends down and grabs a towel from the bench, wrapping it around his hips, then walks toward me. He grabs me around the waist, pulling me towards him, and kisses my forehead.

"You just missed the shower," Luke says with a raised brow.

Still picturing his impeccable body and that ginormous penis of his, even when it's not erect, I stay silent but give a ridiculously big smile.

"When do you and Ris want to get going?" he asks.

Thank God he changed the subject to something else before I was about to explode and either attack him or faint. I need to let him know there is a change in plans.

"She is staying until tomorrow due to being hungover and her face," I reply.

Finally, able to open my mouth and remove my mind from the gutter.

I notice the mannerisms change in Luke's face as he ponders over what happened last night to Ris. He's so hot when he's deep in thought. I must admit he looks hot whatever he's doing. He starts laughing.

"Oh man, I forgot about what happened to her face," he chuckles.

He puts on his clothes for the day, solid red boxer briefs and blue shorts.

"Jason gets a little too carried away in the bedroom!" I cachinnate.

"How does her face look today?" he inquires.

"Well, she looks like she got beat up, to be honest," I giggle. "She has a black eye, a fat lip, and a swollen nose."

Laughing and shaking his head, Luke counters, " Ouch, that's rough!"

He hangs his towel, walks back over to me and gives me a peck on the lips, then grabs my hand, and leads me back up to the cabin. Before we reach the hill, he stops and turns to me.

"Are you upset with me about last night? Luke asks.

"No, I understand where you are coming from. You were being respectful, even though I was not as drunk as you thought I was. It will happen when it's supposed to happen, right." I reply.

I wrap my arms around his waist, burying my face into his shirtless chest and embracing him with a firm yet gentle hug. Of course, I'm shook over the events from last night and that we've come so close to having sex a few times without any luck. However, I thought for sure we would have accomplished it at the stage we were at this last time. He has way more patience then I do and a lot more self-control. If it were me, I would have never been able to stop myself last night or any of the times we've been together, even though I am the culprit to one of the stoppings.

IN THE CABIN, EVERYONE IS LYING AROUND THE LIVING room. Mindy, Nikki, and the guy who came up with them whose name I can never remember are getting ready to leave. Mindy and Nikki look like hell, and so does Ris, but she has an excuse at least. Did we party that hard, last night? Maybe they did, but I tried to take it easy since Luke wasn't drinking much.

It's nice to see Jason is finally over his embarrassment and is cuddled up to Ris on the couch. They truly make a cute couple, but I know Ris, and she won't settle down with anyone. In her words, she likes to play the field and keep her options open. She may bang Jason a few more times after this or never speak to him again. It depends on how she feels. She is a bit unpredictable that way. I don't know how she can just shut off an attraction to someone.

I do not have anywhere near the experience or numbers that she has, but I cannot shut it off after being intimate with someone. I always end up feeling something for that person. I've only been with one guy that turned me off so bad after we had sex that I could not bring myself to do it again. However, I still spoke to him, and we've become quite good friends. Ris can brush it off as if it never happened. She may call Jason just another one of her weekend flings. He does the same shit.

"Hey Jay, I think I'm gonna catch a ride with them unless you need some help down here," Austin says.

"You're good, man, see ya at home," Jason replies.

Austin puts his arm around Mindy right before heading out the door with the others. Mindy and Austin? I do remember them being quite this cozy last night. Good for them, hopefully, she was too preoccupied with him then to report Luke's every move yesterday to Bridget.

"Bye, Ali!" Nikki says before leaving.

"Bye, Nikki. Bye Mindy, Austin, and the other guy!" I yell as they walk out the door.

"His name is Chris," Luke whispers.

I snap my finger.

"That's right! I can never remember his name," I giggle.

I notice that Jason and Ris suddenly get up from the couch and head to his room. Other than maybe helping him make the bed and pack, I can only assume they will try and finish what they started last night minus all the face bashing and blood. Luke and I head up to the loft to make the beds and pick up any garbage left from last night. I am quite impressed to see the beds made, and only a single condom wrapper is littering the floor.

Luke and I make our way into my dad's room, and he makes the bed while I pack mine and Ris's stuff up. I stand up, and Luke wraps his arms around me from behind. I put my hands on his arms and smile back at him in the mirror. He rests his chin on top of my head and grins back.

"I had a fun weekend with you, and you look beautiful right now," Luke says as he continues to look at me in the mirror and smile.

"Thank you, and I did too," I reply, smiling.

I turn around in his arms and lift myself on my tiptoes to plant my lips firmly against his. We go past a simple peck into a sensual kiss, with a little tongue action but not quite enough to cause erotic electricity like last night. Luke grabs my bag and a few of Ris's and strolls out to the living room. I grab Ris's last bag and look around my dad's room to ensure that nothing is left behind before catching up with Luke.

You can easily hear Ris and Jason going at it from the living room, so Luke and I decide to give them some privacy by taking our stuff up to his truck.

chapter thirty-seven

On our way back to Baronette, Ris is passed out cold in the back seat while Luke and I quietly jam out to some tunes on the radio. His hand is resting on my thigh, and I catch him glancing over at me here and there. I drift off in thought, thinking about the weekend and how much fun I had with everyone, especially Luke. I replay everything that had happened between us last night in my head.

I can still picture every detail, how he made me feel, as well as everything about his huge penis. He made me feel comfortable and beautiful, despite all my insecurities. I am sure the alcohol had a hand in that since I am not too keen on giving a guy head unless I've been dating him for a while. His penis is like, holy shit, it's enormous. I could barely touch my fingertips when I had my hands around it, and I struggled to fit it in my mouth.

I want to know what it feels like and if it will hurt when I have it inside me. Will I enjoy it, or will it be too much to handle? Everything about his dick is big, the length is long, and the girth is thick. Everything about this man is turning out to be questionably perfect. He's too good to be true. They do not make a lot of guys like him.

WE FINALLY ARRIVE BACK AT MY DAD'S; LUKE HELPS US

haul our bags inside. Ris heads into the house while Luke and I say our goodbyes and have another sensual kissing moment but nothing too hardcore. I can tell he is hesitant to leave, and I do not want him to, but I need some alone time with Ris.

Once Luke leaves, Ris and I veg out on the couch watching movies for the rest of the afternoon as she works through her hangover.

I must have nodded off when the smell of something burning wakes me. I sit up and notice that Ris is no longer next to me on the couch. I can hear her trying to be quiet in the kitchen as she fumbles with things. I get up from the couch to see what it is she is up to.

"Are you trying to burn down the house?" I ask, sarcastically.

"Bitch, I'm cooking us some Alfredo, but I dropped some sauce on the burner thing. I've never cooked without the glass top before," she snarls.

I giggle and thank her for her kind gesture. I'm surprised that she even attempted to cook at all. I usually do all the cooking back home, or she orders out for us. It looks quite tasty.

"You and Luke seem like you are becoming pretty serious. Are you going to start dating him now?" Ris asks, seeming quite concerned.

"I don't know what is going on between us or what's going to happen. I still have to talk to Troy about everything as have not completely ended shit with him yet. There are loose ends to tie up and kinks to iron out," I reply.

“What? You're still with Troy? Ooo, scandalous,” she boasts.

She loves any opportunity to pick on me and poke fun at my relationship choices or lack thereof.

“No, there's no scandal. Troy and I are not together technically, but I don’t think telling him over a text is the right thing to do. I haven't had the time to call and talk to him about it yet.”

“Yeah, 'cause you’ve been preoccupied with *Mandingo*!” Ris bursts out in laughter while poking her tongue out the side of her cheek repeatedly and humping the air.

She is so obnoxious. I roll my eyes in disgust at her use of gross bodily actions and laugh.

"Shut up!" I shout.

I do need to talk to Troy. He's messaged me numerous times this weekend, and I have not replied to one of them. Maybe Ris can help me talk to him while she is here, so I won't feel so inapt to weaken and retract what I want to say to him. She can be my moral support. There must be a reason why it took me so long to consider seeing Tory when I am here for merely a week and can't keep my legs closed around Luke.

Troy is very handsome and has a nice body, one I've never seen, not fully clothed. So, who's better looking doesn't have any play here. There is just something about Luke that makes me want to be with him every second of every day. He's simply enthralling. On the other hand, I could go days, even weeks without seeing Troy.

I believe in the month since we started seeing one another, we've only seen each other twice. I've seen Luke every day since we met, granted he works at my dad's shop. That does help a lot, but that's also how we became close. We both were close to my dad in our own ways. Something, I would like to find out more about.

Ris talks me into calling Troy while we sit down to eat the dinner. He answers after the first ring. I start the conversation out very nonchalantly and ease my way into letting him know that I am not in the right state of mind to be seeing anyone right now. It is partially true, but I want to be with Luke at the same time. I'm not even making any sense to myself. I need help.

Troy assures me he understands and that he will wait until I am ready because he likes me a lot and thinks we are great for each other. He makes me feel awful and want to spill the beans about Luke to him, but Ris helps me fight the urge to do so before ending the call. Feeling like an absolute asshole, I sit on the couch, ignoring Ris's philosophical speech and flip through the channels on the TV.

My phone buzzes, assuming it's Troy having more to say about our conversation, but it's Luke.

I can't stop thinking about you. I miss you right next to me. Goodnight Turtle!

I'm over the moon. Luke has never texted me, and his first text is so cute. Who knew the rugged bad boy would fall for the little semi goody two shoes? Who knew I would fall for the bad boy? Well, he's not a bad boy; he just looks that way. I never thought when I first met him that I would fall for him. It was quick and quite scary. I've never had this much natural chemistry with any guy before.

One thing is for certain; he is still a mystery to me. I want to know everything I can about him. I want to uncover who or what made him the man he is today. I want to build trust and grow with him.

chapter thirty-eight

I open my eyes, feeling refreshed and rested, but also a tad warm. The sun is shining in my room, making it warmer than it usually is in the morning. Ris is next to me, still sleeping hard on her stomach with the bed covers pulled over her head. I grab my phone to check the time, but it's dead. I must have forgotten to charge it last night. I plug my phone in to charge.

The sun is shining through the window in the hallway, which seems a bit odd for the morning. I make my way downstairs and into the kitchen. It's already after noon. Shit, I slept in. I should've been to the shop at quarter to eight this morning. I rush back upstairs to see what percent my phone is. Three percent is good enough to turn it back on and see if I received any calls or texts. I turn my phone on and hear a knock at the door.

I run to the window in the hallway and see Luke's truck parked outside. He must have been trying to reach me all morning. I bet that's why he came here or maybe he came for lunch. Either way, I am excited to see him. I wake up Ris and head down to answer the door. I try to make myself look halfway presentable before opening the front door. I open it to see Luke standing there in his work uniform.

He has on black slacks, a black t-shirt underneath a Rob's Restoration button up with his name on a patch on the side, and his hat is on forward-facing. I haven't seen him wear one of my dad's shop shirts yet. It looks good on him and hugs his muscular arms very nicely. I notice that he has some grease on his arms and face; he must have been working hard this morning.

"Hi, your phone is off, and you weren't at the shop this morning. I couldn't remember if you said you were planning to come in or not today. So, I thought I would come to check on you," he stammers.

I try to pull myself together in the best way I can after just waking up. I can only imagine how disheveled I look right now. My shadow on the ground proves my thought. I look like *Beetlejuice*!

Slightly embarrassed by my appearance, I reply, "I just woke up, I forgot to charge my phone last night, and it died."

Luke steps into the house and wrangles me by my waist.

"Is Ris still here?" he asks while looking around the house.

"Yea, she's upstairs either sleeping or packing up her stuff," I reply while looking into his gorgeous bluish-green eyes.

Luke kicks his boots off and walks us back to the couch; he smells of Aqua Di Gio, old spice swagger, and a dap of grease. He presses his lips against mine. I don't want to make out with him since I have just woken up and haven't brushed my teeth, but I don't want to deny his affection right now either.

"Ali, Ali, it's Barrett!" Ris yells as she comes barreling into the living room with my phone in her hand.

Luke looks at me, confused, then over at Ris. She is slightly clothed but wearing more than what she had on at the cabin when she barged into our room.

"My boss, Barrett Azguard," I whisper to Luke.

I grab my phone from Ris and go into the kitchen to talk to my boss.

"Good Morning, Barrett," I say.

"Good Morning, Allison! How are you doing?" he replies.

We engage in conversation about how everything is going with me here since I left for my father's celebration of life over a week ago. I receive ten working days of paid leave for such an occasion. I am technically supposed to return to work this Thursday. I tell him about what is going on at my father's business and how it has now been handed down to me. He asks what I plan to do now, and I told him that I honestly did not know because everything is still so fresh. He says that I will always have a job at Facade since I am one of the best new designers there, and a lot of clients specifically ask for me. Barrett mentions that I should take a short leave of absence until I can get everything figured out with my dad's shop. He tells me to come back to the city on Thursday, and we will get the paperwork started with HR for my leave, and he will have IT work on getting something set up so I can work from home. What a great idea! I won't be out of the loop, and it will be like I am still at work, only remotely. I agree with Barrett's proposal and tell him I will see him sometime Thursday afternoon.

I head back into the living room where Ris is laying on the couch watching TV, and Luke is sitting on the bay window, staring outside.

"So, what did the boss man want?" Ris asks as she sits up on the couch.

Luke turns to me, just as interested in what I am about to say.

"I am going back to work Thursday," I reply.

Luke's face saddens, and he looks toward the floor then back out the window. I expected Luke to react this way but was not sure he would be affected at all.

"Barrett is going to have one of the IT guys set me up with a way to bring everything back here so I can take a leave of absence for a while until I figure out what's going on here and with my dad's shop," I say smiling and feeling quite excited.

Luke looks a little upset that I am going back to the city period, but he should be happy that I am here at least another three months. Ris is excited as she has missed me at our little apartment and work. She rushes upstairs to shower and get ready to head back to the city. I walk over to Luke and grab his arm. He puts his hand on my hip.

"Glad to hear that we have some more time to spend together," he says, smiling.

"Yes, I believe we do," I reply.

I give him a peck on the lips and wrap my arms around him, laying my head on his shoulder. I need more time with him before I go back to the city for good.

"You better go get dressed so you can come back to the shop with me," Luke demands.

I give him a raised brow, kiss his cheek, then run upstairs. He smacks my ass before I leave the living room. I change quickly. I will probably get dirty today, so I will shower tonight. Plus, Ris is in the bathroom doing her hair and putting on her face. Luke is in the kitchen, making some grilled cheese sandwiches when I return. I love it when he cooks; it makes him ten times sexier. What girl doesn't love a man that can cook?

chapter thirty-nine

I hug Ris tightly before she gets into her car to drive back to the city. I wave as she travels down my dad's driveway. I'm going to miss her, but I will be seeing her on Thursday, when I go back to work. I'm sure she will want me to stay and party for the weekend, but I want to get back to spend more time with Luke. I already know as soon as I get there, I will want to be back here.

I hop into Luke's truck, and we leave for the shop. Luke turns on the radio and starts playing the drums on his steering wheel with his thumbs. It's bizarre to think that I couldn't wait to get back to the city and my job when I got here, but now that I'm here, I want to be quick in the city when I go so that I can hurry back home

"How long will you be in Milwaukee?" Luke asks me, turning down the music.

"Only a few days. I will leave Thursday morning and will be back Saturday afternoon at the latest," I reply.

I am intrigued that he is so interested in how long I will be gone. I wonder if he will miss me; I know I will miss him.

"Two days without you. What will I do with myself?" he chuckles, then places his hand on my thigh.

We pull into the shop, and Luke kisses me before we leave his truck and head inside. It feels like we are in a relationship, with all the kissing we do before we part ways from each other. I walk through the shop and see all the guys diligently working on their jobs for the day. I make my way back to the offices.

Gladys isn't here, and Maureen is out in the lobby talking with some customers. I dart into my dad's office and get started on where I left off. I am excited about having Façade's IT personnel set me up with an at-home program, so now I can design the perfect office for Ernie and Luke. Maybe, I will add a spot for myself or redo Maureen's area to make a nice place for me.

Wait. I'm acting as if I am going to stay here and help run the shop. Would I still feel this way about being here if it wasn't for Luke and my sudden attachment to him? I have a lot of deliberating to do about what my plans will be after this leave. I love being an architect and my job. I also love the thrill of my life in the city, but I love being here at my dad's shop, with Luke, Ernie, and the others. I miss the country and going to the cabin.

I do not know what to do. If it doesn't work between Luke and me, it will make being here and at home awkward. I don't want that. I don't want to make my decision based on my feelings for a guy that may only be lukewarm and temporary. I detract myself by focusing on the remodel. I start hauling things out of my dad's office. I want it to be bare so that I can start from scratch. That's the best way to go about it.

"What are your plans for your dad's office?" Maureen asks as she watches me carry box after box out of the room.

"I want to surprise Ernie and Luke with a brand-new office! When I'm done, I can maybe surprise you with a new one too before you leave," I reply with a cheesy smile.

"That would be lovely! Ernie and Luke will love their own space. Thank you for all your work on Friday and for covering for me," she says.

"You're welcome. You need to show me what to do with paid invoices and that other stuff in the bottom basket that I went through on Friday," I say as I walk back toward my dad's office.

"I can show you now if you want to take a little break from your project," she smiles.

Maureen's such a kind soul. I will miss her when she leaves. I take her up on her offer and have her show me everything that I had questions about last Friday. I am becoming quite confident that Gladys and I can handle Maureen's job after she retires until we find a replacement for her. I think we will be able to train them without her help, maybe. We'll see when we cross that bridge.

The time passes quickly, and I head back to my dad's office when Maureen leaves for the day. I still have a half-hour to work until the shop closes. I decide to pass the time by paying some shop bills through the program that Maureen showed me today. I see a folder on my dad's computer that is titled "LJ." It strikes my curiosity and the noisy person I am; I double click on it. Up pops information about Luke.

Perhaps, this will tell me more about him and his relationship with my dad. The folder has Luke's personal information and filed copies of all the receipts from the parts for his motorcycle, from his truck, and a few miscellaneous documents I don't understand but assume have to do with his home attached to the pole barn. Has my dad been paying for everything for Luke? He must be making decent money here, as the head mechanic. Maybe, my dad kept part of Luke’s pay to reimburse himself, completely understandable if he did.

A small knock at the door startles me as Luke walks in. I quickly click out of the folder.

"I'm off now. You ready to go home?" he asks.

I hope I did not look suspicious while clicking out of the folder on my dad's computer.

"Um... yeah, I think I'm good to go," I reply.

"I'm going to go wash my hands if you want to go lock everything up," Luke says with a smile.

I meander out into the lobby, lock the door, and switch off the open sign. I cannot stop thinking about the receipts and documents I saw in the folder. I didn't pay attention whether they said that they've been paid back or what those other papers were. I'm not going to worry about them because they were something between my dad and Luke, and frankly speaking, it's none of my business. But then again, part of me is dying to know.

I walk into the shop and notice Luke has taken his shirt off and is walking toward me. If I were a cartoon character right now, I'd be that wolf who whistles as his eyes bug out of his head when he sees a sexy female wolf or woman. Looking at him without his shirt on while he's all dirty and sweaty never gets old.

"Do you want to go swimming?" he asks as we leave the shop.

"You do look and smell like you need a bath," I laugh.

Luke chases me to his truck before grabbing me and pushing me up against it. He removes a strand of hair from my face as he grabs the back of my head and bends down to kiss me. I gently massage his tongue with playful circles as he smiles and giggles lightly through his nose. He brings his other hand behind my head and kisses me passionately while massaging my tongue seductively. I push him off me as the guys start trickling out of the shop to go home for the day. Luke nudges me, then opens my door and helps me up into his truck.

He opens his door and yells, "yea, see ya tomorrow," to one of the guys on the other side of the parking lot. He looks at me with a crazed look in his eye.

"What?" I say, weirded out by his stare.

He leans toward me, pecks me quickly, puts his truck into drive while looking at me, smiles ridiculously, then faces the front and takes off. He's so weird sometimes.

chapter forty

Luke is singing loudly as we travel down the gravel road toward the lake. We stop, Luke gets out and opens the back door of his truck. I noticed that his bag from the cabin is still back there. He then pulls out a towel and grabs the blanket from the back seat.

I get out, and we trek toward the lake. Luke is leading the way while holding my hand. We walk past the clearing, where we had lunch the first time we kissed. We then walk over to the other trail that leads to where we cliff jumped the other day. We reach the top and come out into the opening. He lets go of my hand and unfolds the blanket, laying it on the ground, then throws his towel on top of it. He takes his boots and pants off and is standing in his briefs. He looks at me and smiles, then he walks over to me and pecks me on the lips.

"You best be damn near naked when I get back up here," he demands then takes off running.

He does a front flip off the cliff. I hear a splash as he hits the water, then a "woo-hoo" shout after he pops back up. I take off my boots, then my shirt and pants just as he reaches the top of the cliff. Standing in my bra and panties, he first looks me over, smirks, then shakes his hair off on me while extending his hand out. I grab hold of it, and we take off.

We jump, and I look over at him. Pure joy parades over his face, as he looks at me with a gorgeous smile just before we hit the water.

It's surprisingly warmer than the last time we were here. We splash around a bit before we climb back up the cliff. Luke pushes my ass as he helps me up. We reach the top and jump a few more times. We do a couple together and some by ourselves. Every time we go up the cliff, Luke is behind me, I'm sure to stare at my ass, but probably more for safety reasons in case I lose my footing or something. I am glad I can at least do it on my own now, even if it's under his watchful eye.

We sit down on the blanket, and I dab my face off with his towel. I look at Luke, and he's giving me a stare that causes me to lose myself in his eyes. He scoots closer to me and reaches behind my head with both his hands, then kisses me. I put my hands to his chest and kiss him back. He becomes aggressive with his tongue as we change positions with our heads, and he slowly lowers me to the blanket.

He uses his legs to spread mine apart as he brings his body between my legs and closer to me. We continue to kiss heavily as he runs his hand up and down my body. It's the most sensual feeling ever. I bring my knees up toward my face and slide my big toes into the waist of his briefs, then gently maneuver them down his hips, exposing his semi-flaccid penis, which falls across my stomach. I press my tongue farther into his mouth as I massage his faster with mine. I start to get worked up and want him unbelievably bad right now. He runs his hand under my bra and grabs hold of my breast, massaging and squeezing it lightly. His other hand removes his briefs then reaches back up to my panties as he grabs hold of the side and gently tugs them. I lift my hips as he slides them further down my body. My heart is beating faster at the thought of finally going all the way.

He puts my panties aside and lowers himself back between my legs. He inserts his finger inside me as he lets out a sigh through his nose and a slight moan into my mouth. He slowly moves his finger in and out as I squirm a little from the slight discomfort until I become wetter. He starts to move his finger faster in and out of me. My body starts to tingle, and my goosebumps heighten. I arch my back and moan into his mouth. My heart is beating fast, and my breathing has now become panting. He removes his finger and kisses me the deepest he ever has. He grabs himself and rubs his head up and down my clit before inserting his penis into me. I gasp as he presses himself into me slowly, letting out another sigh from his nose.

"FUCK!" he groans into my mouth.

Oh, my God, he's not stopping. He pushes farther into me; it hurts but feels amazing at the same time. He presses a little farther in before drawing himself back slowly then back in farther again. His pelvic thrusts are so satisfying despite being painful as well. I can feel myself stretch out as he moves in and out while I become wetter. The pain subsides a little but is still apparent as he begins to move in and out more quickly.

I let out a strange moan.

"Are you okay?" he whispers.

"Yea, it just hurts a little," I say while I breathe out another more sensual moan.

"Do you want me to stop?"

"No."

I close my eyes, taking in the out of this world sex we are having and how he feels inside me. I begin to kiss him again, and we return to aggressively massaging each other's tongues. He starts to thrust his tumescent penis inside me harder and faster. It almost unbearable, but I'm too aroused to do anything about it. I dig my nails into his back.

"I'm going to cum!" he moans as his voice shudders.

He grabs his briefs and pulls out, grabbing hold of the head of his cock. He lays his head on my chest as he shakes and groans while ejaculating into his boxer briefs. I can feel the burning sensation from my vagina as it pulsates from being penetrated by a larger than average dick. He certainly has a huge one, and it's not like I've seen or been with a lot either. I lay there, catching my breath as Luke returns from his mini seizure.

chapter forty-one

After collecting himself, Luke lifts his head off my chest and kisses me softly.

"I'm sorry I didn't last very long. I am kind of embarrassed about it. It's been a while since I've had sex, quite a long while, and you felt awesome," he says, shyly.

I want to ask him how long it's been and how many people he's slept with, but part of me doesn't want to know the answer. I want to know if he's been with anyone since he's been here. I'm sure he has; going two years without sex is a long time. He may not have lasted long, which is fine, but we finally had our first time together.

"It's okay. It's been a while for me—too," I reply, still in shock, as we finally just had sex without being interrupted or stopping.

It was exactly how I imagined it would be, only better. Granted, it was mid-day, and we were out in the open where anyone could have easily stumbled upon us, yet it was magical—even though it was in the grass on a blanket.

Luke rolls himself off me, and I sit up next to him. I'm still a little tingly, even though I didn't climax, but I'm super sore. He hands me my panties, then asks if I'd pass him his pants. I slip on my panties and stand up to put my pants on. Luke has already put his pants on and rolls his cum-stained boxer briefs up in his towel. I slide my shirt over my head as Luke hugs me from behind. I stop what I'm doing and grab hold of his arms while he hugs me tight.

I help Luke fold up the blanket, and we head back down the path to his truck. The walk back is quiet. Neither of us speaks a word to each other. It's not an awkward silence but taking in what just happened between us, silence. I am not sure if he is as high on life as I am right now. I am jumping with joy, and I have goosebumps all over me. I feel closer to him, pleased, and content with everything. I hope he is feeling more than embarrassed or disappointed that he didn't last long.

I can't tell as he hasn't spoken to me since he asked for his pants and apologized for being quick on the trigger.

We reach his truck, and he opens my door for me. He smiles but doesn't say a word or kiss me. I watch him walk around his truck, opening the back door to put the blanket and his towel on the seat. Now, it's become a little awkward. I don't know what to say to ease this strange tension that's growing.

"Are you hungry?" he asks, while reaching his arm back over his headrest reverse his truck down the gravel road.

"Yes," I reply.

He's looking out the rear window as he continues down the road. He stops and turns us around to face forward. He stops the truck then looks at me.

"Will you stay the night with me?" he begs, with the most adorable puppy dog eyes.

I look at him like a lovesick little girl, give him a nod, then a big grin like an idiot.

"We can stop at your dad's so you can grab your stuff and shower, or you can shower at my house. I'll cook dinner on the grill," he discloses.

"Okay," I reply.

He smiles and turns up the music, then places his hand on my thigh. I look at him; I think I'm falling in love. I correct myself, because you do not fall in love with someone simply because you just had sex with them.

chapter forty-two

We turn onto *2242 Old Hwy 15,* making our way down the long driveway and past Jason's house. My phone buzzes, it's a text from Ris. I smile as I read her message. I was just thinking of her.

Just made it home. I had a great weekend, thanks for inviting me! Love you bitch. See you soon. 😘

"Ris made it home safely," I announce.

"That's good—long drive," Luke counters.

He parks in front of one of the large garage doors of the pole barn. We get out of his truck, and I follow him inside. We walk through his vehicles, toys, and past my dad's Ranchero to the back of the building. We walk through a door into his house, and he flicks on the light. The first room we enter is like a mudroom/entryway, where his footwear and jackets are displayed and a laundry area.

One side has a bench with a shelf above it lined with jackets and sweatshirts. Shoes and boots line the wall from the floor. A door to the outside is at the end of the room. The other side has a counter with a single long cabinet above it, and a stackable washer and dryer across from it. He keeps himself quite organized, and he's relatively tidy for a guy.

I follow Luke down a short hallway that ends with a small bathroom on the right and a fridge to the left. An open layout of the kitchen and living room comes into view. The design is somewhat like that of the cabin, but a bit bigger. Two doors lead off the end of the kitchen and living room.

Luke walks to the door off the living room and opens it. Once he turns on the light, I can see that it's his bedroom. It's quite a decent-sized bedroom. Plain but looks cozy. The walls are a very light tan, almost cream color. A queen-size bed and dresser seem to be the only furniture besides a bow rack, and a picture of a forest scene hung on the wall. A cute little closet with louvered doors is across from the bed.

"You can put your bag in here and go take a shower while I cook us dinner if you'd like," Luke says.

I put my bag down on the bed. His bedding is all camo, and the headboard looks to be made of pine or something with a cutout bear silhouette. I turn and look up at him. I give him a snarky smile.

"Want to take one with me?" I ask, batting my eyes.

Luke arches his eyebrow up and instantly starts to remove his pants. I giggle as he kicks them to the side. He is now naked, grabs me, and throws me over his shoulder. We walk out of his room, through the living room, and into his bathroom. It's not as small as I thought, it's narrow but long. The size is perfect for a single guy living by himself.

He sets me down and turns on the shower, then he grabs me and pulls me close to him, tilting his head down to kiss me. He starts to unbutton my pants as he slides his eager tongue into my mouth. My pants drop to the floor, and I step out of them. His hands grab the bottom of my shirt, and he pulls it up over my head. We continue kissing as he puts his hands on my shoulders, sliding his fingers under my bra straps, and pulls them down, unclasping my bra as he kisses down my neck. My bra hits the floor as Luke makes his way down my chest to my breasts.

He grabs a firm hold of them and latches on to my left breast with his mouth, sucking hard between his tongue circles around my nipples. I can feel goosebumps on my arms as I start to breathe heavier. I let out a closed mouth moan. He makes his way over to my other breast as his hand travels down to my panties and pulls them down. I am starting to get wet.

My panties fall to the floor, and I step out of them. I push Luke away from me and step into the shower as I look back at him very seductively. He follows me in, and we continue making out. Luke kisses my neck while the shower falls upon his face. He stops at my breasts again and plays with them a little bit. Biting and sucking on my nipples gently but in an aggressive manner. He kisses my belly button, and I bring my hand to his head, running my fingers through his hair.

He has me going insane on the inside, my breathing has increased, and my heart has started to pound. It's like a blast of electricity going through every inch of my body. He travels farther down lowering on to his knee. Luke begins to kiss my vagina, tenderly running his tongue up and down my clit. Instant stimulation ignites my body, and I throw my head back; picking up the pace as he switches between circular movements with his tongue and light sucking. It sends me into tiny jolts throughout my body.

He inserts a finger slowly while continuing to eat me out. I steady myself against the wall of the shower with one hand as I pull his hair with my other. I let out a deep moan as my voice shudders in a slight euphoria. He inserts another finger, moving them quickly and in sync with his tongue. I can't handle it anymore and start to moan uncontrollably while my thighs begin to shake. I reach climax and thrash my body as I cum in his mouth. Oh my God, this is intense!

Luke removes his fingers and grabs my ass. Pecks, my vagina, then stands up. Still high and numb from my orgasm, I try to catch my breath and regulate my breathing. He looks into my eyes and smiles a mischievous smile then reaches behind me and shuts off the shower. We haven't washed up yet, so I am not sure what is going on in his head. We're completely soaked. He kisses me and grabs underneath my ass, pulling me up onto his hips, then turns to step out of the shower. Soaking wet, he places me down on the sink counter and grabs me behind my head with both of his hands. He stabs his tongue into my mouth, assertively massaging my tongue. It's quite erotic.

I feel his huge cock growing between my legs. I reach my hand down, grabbing hold of it, and start making a figure-eight motion as I move up and down his thick shaft. He groans into my mouth then removes a hand from behind my head. He moves my hand from him, grabs hold of himself, and inserts his erect penis into me. I'm still a little sensitive from my orgasm in the shower that I feel like I could cum again at any moment. He feels bigger than when we were at the lake. It's a tad painful again, but I don't care; I'm way too aroused to care. He starts picking up speed sooner this time.

I let out a scream type moan within a moan, due to the position we are in, and I can feel more of him hitting my cervix than I did our first time. I start to shake, moaning profusely, then begin to convulse in the pain as his momentum grows deeper and faster. His arms begin to shake as I'm holding on to them, with my nails digging into his skin. He lets out a deep groan. I lose it and orgasm for the second time.

He does a few more thrusts, kisses me hard, then pulls out and ejaculates all over my stomach and part of his. This time I was taken to another world of intense sensual pleasure; I had never imagined I would ever in my life feel such severity. Luke takes the entire experience to a whole new level.

chapter forty-three

I finish soaping up my body and rinsing the conditioner out of my hair before stepping out of the shower at Luke's house. We just had the most amazingly intimate moment in his bathroom, and he more than redeemed himself from earlier today at the lake. I step out into the steam-filled room and wipe the hazy condensation from the mirror. I look at myself; I am glowing and feel like I'm floating.

I feel so comfortable with him, even during our first time. This time was more enjoyable and lasted longer; I felt like I lost all my senses. I felt things that I've never felt with anyone before, very unexplainable things. I don't even know how to comprehend it or explain it, it's mind-blowing to me.

I've waited longer before sleeping with someone I liked, even loved, but never felt the way I do right now. Nor has anyone made me feel the way Luke has on an intimate or even a normal level. There is something about him that makes me feel safe, at ease, and I can be myself, all of myself.

I collect my thoughts and head out into Luke's living room. I don't see him in the kitchen. I figure he's outside grilling. The smell from whatever is on the stove is heavenly and fills the entire room.

I notice he set the table for two already, and a candle is lit in the center. I get dressed then head back to the bathroom to hang the towels I used. Luke is standing in the kitchen with his back toward me now. He is wearing light gray sweatpant-looking shorts. He is humming as he continues to cook. It makes me want to jump him, but right now, with how tender I am down there, I don't think I could handle it.

He turns and notices me walking across his living room. He smiles and walks up to me, grabbing hold of my waist, then bringing me into his arms. He bends down and kisses me, then holds me tight. I wrap my arms around his waist, resting my head against his bare chest. I love it when he has me like this.

"I've got to go check the steaks," he says.

I hang the towels I use in the bathroom and glance at myself in the mirror. It is the first time Luke has seen me without my eye makeup. Some of it is still visible and was not completely removed in the shower, but enough to almost be my natural look. I walk into the kitchen to see what else he has going on for dinner.

I see a pot with onions and mushrooms, another with potatoes and carrots, and notice that the oven is going as well. I open it a tad to see a pan with green beans and Brussel sprouts. Damn, this boy can cook. I walk over into the living room and look at the single picture he has that does not hang on the wall, and is not of a forest scene, car, or animal. It's a framed picture of him and a very pretty, dark-haired woman. Her smile is a lot like his. Luke looks younger in this photo but still very much a man, not a boy. He is smiling, but his eyes look sad, and in pain, I don't see that in his eyes now.

I wonder if the woman is his mother.

"That's my mom," Luke says from behind me, as I am startled and almost drop the frame.

"She's beautiful. How old are you here?" I ask, quietly.

"Yes, she was. I'm twenty or twenty-one, I think," he says, walking back to the stove.

What does he mean by was? She was pretty? Did he mean she is older now, and her face has aged or that the burns she received from the fire caused a lot of damage to how she looks now? I want to ask, but I want him to mention it.

"Dinner is ready. I'm not sure how you like your steak, so I cooked it medium-well," he states.

"That's perfect. Thank you!" I reply.

I take a seat at the table, unfolding my napkin and placing it in my lap. I look up at Luke and smile.

"What would you like to drink? Wine, soda, water?"

"Milk, please, if you have any," I say politely.

Luke opens the fridge and pulls out a half-gallon of milk then pours me a glass. He brings the glass and my plate full of food, setting them down in front of me. It looks so delicious. I'm so hungry and excited to devour all this fantastic food.

"I hope you like mushrooms and onions on your steak? How about steak sauce," he says.

He brings his plate to the table and sits down.

"I love them on my steak, and I will let you know if I need any sauce," I reply as I cut up my steak into bite-size pieces.

Luke smiles, places his napkin in his lap, then picks up his fork and knife. I hadn't realized before that he is left-handed. I love finding out little things about him in these surprising ways. I take a bite of the steak. No sauce needed, it's juicy and perfectly seasoned, and melts in my mouth. Damn, he's a phenomenal cook. The potatoes and carrots are equally scrumptious, as are the green beans and brussels. He even has a little custard cup filled with different fruits; melons, grapes, strawberries, and pears. I am not sure if I will be able to finish it all.

I wonder how he learned to cook so well. Perchance, he has been by himself all this while, so he had to teach himself. *Pinterest* has done wonders for my cooking skills! Maybe, Ernie taught him? Or even my dad! I keep looking at him while we eat. He's so unbelievably handsome, how am I here right now and how did I get lucky enough for him to want to be with me—scrambles my brain. Consumed by his aura, I drift off, not touching a single morsel on my plate.

"Ali? You okay?" Luke asks, looking at me funny.

I snap back to reality, looking down at my plate then back up at him. His plate is almost completely empty.

"Yes, sorry," I reply, a little embarrassed.

I continue eating my meal.

"What were you thinking about?" he questions.

Do I fib and tell him something other than I was off in a daze over the gorgeousness of his face and his outstanding culinary skills?

"You," I say shyly.

He smiles and blushes a smidge.

"What about me?" he asks, looking somewhat interested in what my answer will entail.

"Um... how good looking you are, your cooking skills, and what we did in your bathroom earlier," I murmur.

I cannot believe I just said all of that out loud. I bring my eyes up from the table to look at him. He brings his head down toward his plate, then looks up at me, with his eyes only. The way he is looking at me right now is causing goosebumps to rise all over my entire body. He smirks, then full out smiles, a gorgeous smile but says nothing.

I break free from his stare and finish my dinner while he keeps staring at me, having put his hand under his chin now. It feels a little awkward eating while he stares at me like that, but I'm too hungry to care, and this food is so tasty.

chapter forty-four

A buzzing sound is muffled in my head but grows louder and more annoying with each buzz. I open my eyes, reaching for my phone to shut off my alarm. I look around the darkened room. I almost forgot that I stayed the night with Luke at his place. I roll over to find out that he is not lying in bed next to me. I rub the sleep from my eyes and sit up. I want to go back to sleep; Luke's bed is extremely comfortable with the pillow top mattress he has. I sink right in it, and it wraps right around me. I don't know how he can get out of it every day.

I stand up and walk to the door when an alarm goes off again. I walk back over to the bed, but my phone is not going off, Luke's is. I walk over to the other side of his bed and disarm the alarm on his phone. I forgot that I asked him to set it sooner than he usually does for me in case my phone were to die since I didn't bring a charger. I see a little envelope at the top of his screen before it goes black. I wonder who that message is from. He's not big into texting, at least not with me anyway.

I hit a button on his phone, and it lights up, asking for a password. I need to walk away and stop being nosey. He's not my boyfriend, and he can talk to whoever he wants. I turn and walk to the door; his phone makes a 'bing' sound, and I rush back over by it. Flashing on the top of his screen, it shows that it's a message from Bridget.

Why didn't you come over last night? Are you—

Luke's phone goes black. Why was he supposed to go to her house last night? What does it say after "are you"? Does it say are you coming over tonight? I thought they were just friends. I thought Mindy said that he told her he wasn't interested in her anymore. Is he with both of us at the same time? The more time I spent with Luke, the more I think I am getting to know him, but then his mysterious side keeps popping up.

The door opens, and I quickly fall back on the bed. Luke turns on the light. I look up at him. He is still wearing the light gray sweatpant shorts from last night, and his hair is a tad on the messy side.

"Good, you're awake. I made coffee and some breakfast for us," he says.

He grins, then walks over to me. He bends down, putting his hands on the bed on each side of me and kisses me on the lips, then grabs for his phone. Do I bite my tongue or blurt out what I saw on his phone from the text he received from Bridget, literally ten seconds ago? I don't want to start the morning off unpleasant.

"Your alarm went off on your phone, but I dismissed it," I say in a calm, yet firm way.

He looks at me, then at his phone, slides it in his pocket, and walks out the door. I follow him into the kitchen; it smells delightful again. He made waffles, eggs, bacon, and sausage.

"Wow, you and your cooking skills. I might have to keep you after all," I chuckle.

He smiles as I walk up closer to him. I touch his arm, and he turns toward me; I wrap my arms around him. I want him to know I want him to be mine and mine only. That's only natural considering how far we've come in such a short time. He wraps his arms around me, holds me for a while, resting his chin on top of my head. I can hear his heart beating; it's soothing and makes me forget about wanting to ask him about Bridget. The bacon smells amazing right now, making me so hungry, but I don't want him to let me go.

The door to Luke's house flings open, and Bridget comes barreling inside. Luke and I break free of our embrace. He turns toward her as I am standing somewhat behind him. What the fuck is she doing here?

"What are you doing here?" he questions, angrily.

"So, this is why you didn't come over last night because she's here. Are you fucking her too?" Bridget yells.

My eyes widen, and I take a few steps back from Luke. My mind is blown; this is unexpected. She parades in here like she owns the damn place. I want to know what her deal is. I want to know what the fuck she is talking about and what the hell is going on.

"What the fuck are you talking about? I'm not fucking you, and I never told you that I was coming over last night," he shouts back at her, then turns to look at me.

His facial expression looks worried. I don't know what to do or how to feel right now. I want to leave.

"Fuck you, Luke. You told me you were coming over, and you just fucked me the other day, and you're fucking her now," she yells.

She throws her arms up in the air, causing her already tiny shirt to show even more of her midriff. Luke puts his hand on the back of his neck and breathes out his nose heavily.

"You need to leave. Please get the fuck out of my house! Now!" he screams at her.

"FUCK YOU! You'll be back for more, and you know it. Enjoy my sloppy seconds, Ali," she spews.

Bridget gives me a gruesome smile then slams the door, not once but twice. Luke goes after her; I'm sure to watch to make sure she doesn't mess with any of his stuff in the pole barn. I stand speechless in the middle of his kitchen. I want to cry, but my emotions are frozen. I don't know what to think or what to do. Everything seems like a cluster fuck right now. Bridget is more than likely acting like a jealous and possessive ex who can't stand to see her once-significant other with another girl. But they never dated or were even intimate with one another beyond kissing, at least that's what Luke told me. But now I'm not too sure.

She could be making a scene to cause friction between Luke and me because she wants him, and he doesn't want her back. I hope I am right about this part because if there is more to this story, I want to know. If he was sleeping with her before, that's fine; I wasn't a part of his life, and he wasn't a part of mine. But if he's sleeping with us both, that's a different ball of wax. I prefer honesty, and knowing Luke, he does too. He will explain what the hell is going on.

I am numb over this dumb situation. I decide to get ready for work. I walk back into Luke's room and grab my bag. I go into his bathroom to change for work and grab the rest of my stuff. I want to cry, and it takes everything inside me not to as I look at myself in the mirror. I brush my hair and put on some light makeup. A knock on the door startles me.

"Ali?" Luke says in a soft voice.

I brush my teeth and put the rest of my stuff in my bag. I open the door. Luke is standing there with a sad and concerned look on his face. I look up at him. I don't want to talk about this now. It's all too much for me to handle.

"We need to get going. I don't want to be late," I say.

I grab my bag and walk past him toward the small hallway.

"Ali? Can we talk about this?" he questions as he grabs my arm.

I turn to him and look up into his eyes. The bluish-green eyes of the man from the photo with his mother are apparent right now. I don't know what to say to him.

"What is there to talk about?" I scuff.

"Talk about what just happened," he counters.

"I don't want to know what's going on between you and her, I just want to go to work," I say, then turn away, heading down the hallway.

Luke follows me. I stop, turn to him, there's anger in my face and voice.

"Please, go get dressed, or I will walk down to Jason's for a ride."

He looks at me like he's about ready to either punch the wall or cry. I'm not sure which one it is, as I'm not sure if I know who he is at all. I thought I did not too long ago, well that I was getting to know him at least. I know I should hear him out, but with my mindset the way it is right now, I won't hear what he has to say anyway. I'm not even sure if an explanation can fix things right now. I need time to process everything.

"Can we please talk about this, please?" Luke begs.

"I don't want to," I shout and walk away.

I look back at him as he turns and walks back down the hallway. I put on my boots and head out into the pole barn. I walk over to my dad's Ranchero and remove the sheet that covers it. I open the passenger side door, slide myself into the driver's seat, and sit down. I rest my arms on the steering wheel, lay my head in between them, and stare at the floor

chapter forty-five

The ride to the shop is unusually silent; not even one song plays on the radio. I stare out the window the entire way to work. We pull into the parking lot, and I get out as soon as I can. I hear Luke say my name, but I ignore him. I walk straight back to the offices, not acknowledging anyone on the way there, even if they say hi or good morning to me. I want to be left alone. I'm relieved when I see Maureen is not at her desk. I proceed to my dad's office, close the door, and lock it behind me. I walk over to his couch and sit down. I need a few moments to myself. I run my hands through my hair as I bend the top half of my body toward my thighs, looking at the floor.

Luke and I are not together as there has never been any dating talk or talk about having a relationship. It was merely just sex, and he is sleeping with other people. I am only one of those people on his list. I was overthinking and got overexcited, thinking he wanted to be with me exclusively. I need to stop thinking there was more to the situation than that. I need to let go of what I feel for him and focus on finishing the remodeling of my dad's office, hiring a new secretary, and getting back to my life in the city. Luke has clouded my head long enough, and I need to get back on track.

I call Ris, but of course; she doesn't answer. I need to talk to her right now; she would set me straight. I'm sure she is getting ready for work or on her way there and has the music blaring in her car. I will text her a short-summarized bit.

Hey Ris, call me when you get a chance. I really need to talk. I had sex with Luke twice yesterday and stayed the night with him at his place. Bridget came by this morning and flipped out on him because he did not go to her house her last night. Also, I want to talk about how he's fucking us both. I'm freaking out. Love you.

I get off the couch and dawdle to my dad's desk, power on his computer, and grab my coffee cup. I didn't get coffee or eat any of the deliciously appetizing breakfast that Luke made me this morning. I walk into Maureen's office, and she is on the phone; I smile and wave at her as I pass by. There is coffee in the breakroom, but I don't feel like running into Luke right now. I want to avoid him for the rest of the day. My stomach growls, I'm hungry but not in the mood to eat. I put a french vanilla cappuccino into the customer Keurig machine. As the water heats for brewing, I look out the window watching traffic as it passes by.

The steam sounds and gurgles as it's ready to brew my cup. I press start then hear the door from Maureen's office open and close. I turn around to see Luke walking toward me. He is wiping his hands on a rag, his work shirt is unbuttoned, and his hat is backward. He looks delicious but distressed.

"I don't want to discuss this morning with you at work," I tell him sternly.

He says nothing and keeps walking toward me. I stand there staring at him, and he continues walking. He stops with a finger worth of space between us. I look at his chest, which is at my eye level, then look up at him. His eyes are glossy and reveal so much pain behind them. They look so sincere that I can't help but feel sorry for him. I look back and forth between them as they do not change their appearance.

"I'm falling in love with you," Luke chokes out.

He looks as though he will start crying any minute. My mood shifts from anger into concern over the sadness in his eyes. Luke brings his hands up toward my face and places them on my cheeks.

"I mean it, Ali," he whispers earnestly.

His eyes lock in on mine, and he kisses me. His kiss is passionate. I can feel the raw emotion behind it as well as the words he spoke. I look into his eyes.

"I'm falling in love with you too," I reply as a single tear leaves my eye and rolls down my cheek.

I am, undeniably so. He kisses me again, wiping away my tear with his thumb, and we hug each other tightly. We break free from each other, and I grab my coffee. Luke and I walk to my dad's office. I close the door and sit down on the couch.

"I'm not sleeping with Bridget. I've slept with her, yes, but not sexually," he begins to say.

I don't interrupt him; I let him talk. He sits down next to me and continues talking about his relationship with Bridget.

"We've stayed the night with each other a few times but have never had sex. We've had some gnarly make-out sessions, and she's given me head twice. The last girl I had sex with was a friend from Colorado that I would meet up with every few months. The last I saw of her was over seven months or so ago. Bridget and I stayed together the night before your father's Will reading. She was drinking with Jason that night then ended up at my house. She slept in my bed, and I slept on the couch," he continues.

"I told her the next morning I wasn't interested in her the way she is in me. She found out about us and called me while I was at your house the other day, and I told her I like you. She's been inviting herself over and asking me to come over almost every day since. I don't reply to her calls or texts or show up. I was supposed to go there last night to change the oil in her car but wanted to be with you instead," Luke finishes.

He takes out his phone and shows proof of the messages from last night, explaining the one I saw this morning. The rest of the texts asked if he was coming to change her oil. I believe him now as I know how she can be when it comes to a guy, more so with one that doesn't want her the way she wants him. I've watched how crazy obsessed she can get and the shit she did to Jason when we were in High School.

I'm glad Luke came clean and was honest, so we can move forward from the entire Bridget drama.

chapter forty-six

It's always more complacent showering in your own home, not that my shower at Luke's wasn't enjoyable. My mind fades into dreariness, and everything becomes a foggy illusion. The hot water calms me, and I can do my best thinking; it's very therapeutic.

Work sped by today after my early morning talk with Luke, clearing the air over Bridget and her whorish antics. He told me everything about his past sex life, even the last time he had sex before me. He also confessed that he's falling in love with me.

A little over a week is relatively soon to be falling in love with someone, but I feel the same way. I do, because he makes me feel different about myself and life in general. I don't put myself first as much since I've been infatuated with him. Things seem to have more meaning now, and there's more to life than being focused on sheltering myself from the world and those I care about most.

Ris called me back on her morning break, and I told her everything, including my amazing sexcapades with Luke yesterday and what happened with Bridget this morning. She wants to claw her face off, to put it nicely. Ris said that she can usually call a guy's bluff because men lie to get what they want, well, so do women, but she wholeheartedly believes Luke. She called Bridget every term for "slut" you can think of, and that she will be a problem since she can't take a hint.

I leave soon for Milwaukee, and I'm excited, yet apprehensive, about the trip. I don't want to leave Luke where Bridget is hot on his trail, and I don't want to be forced to face Troy once he finds out that I'm back for a few days. I need to get in and out when I get to Facade. If only Luke could come with me, then I could relax a little, and my mind would be somewhat at ease.

I'm pretty sure I've been in here almost an hour, just rambling over my thoughts. I'm surprised the water is still hot; usually, if I take longer than my regular twenty-minute shower, the water starts to turn lukewarm then slowly runs cold. I should get out anyway; Luke will be back from his house anytime to stay the night. I don't have to worry about cooking dinner; we ate at Mary's. I'd be wasting my time trying to one-up the exquisite dinner he made me last night. The spaghetti I made him was no match for his cooking talents. Popcorn and a movie sound perfect right now anyway.

I step out of the shower; my fingertips are starting to prune. My skin is red and splotchy. I can see the steam lift from my arms and head in the lightly fogged mirror. I dry my hair and body, then let the towels slump to the floor. I look over my naked body in the mirror before applying lotion. I don't harshly rip apart my body as I have done every time before. I stare into the mirror, imagining Luke's hands running up and down my naked body, and I can feel goose-bumps rise as I continue staring at myself. I can feel the touch of his soft yet calloused worked hands, the warmth behind them, and the heightened stimulation they bring.

Luke opens the door, and I snap my head toward him. He stares at me as I stand before him, completely naked with damp hair. His bottom lip falls open as he takes in the sight of me. I walk toward him, stopping within inches of our bodies touching. I cannot even describe what he's wearing right now because I'm so ready to tackle him, my blinders are on. I put my hands under his shirt then grab hold of the bottom, lifting it up. He grabs the back of his shirt from behind his neck and pulls it over his head. I run my hands up his rock-hard abs as I start to push him back into the hall. He brings his hand up and puts a finger under my chin, lifting my head toward his. He bends down and kisses me, and I dive right in his mouth with my tongue. I bring my hands down to his pants as we stop against the wall in the hall. I slide the zipper down, still passionately kissing him while standing on my tiptoes.

I reach my hand down his pants, grabbing hold of his semi-erect penis. I want to feel it grow in my mouth, so I part from our kiss and travel my way down his chiseled body, licking and kissing almost every inch of it. I get to his stomach and blow a raspberry just over his bellybutton. I look up at him and smile; he giggles slightly then watches as I take a knee and slide his pants and briefs down. His penis flings in excitement from his briefs, almost smacking me in the face. It seemed that it was primed ready to surprise me. I grab hold of it, he's a little more than semi-hard now. I lick my lips as I look up at Luke, staring at me with eager eyes. I spread my lips apart and maneuver his dick into my mouth, tracing the head of his penis with my tongue a few times.

I can hear him let out a deep moan. I begin to take his growing penis farther into my mouth, making lights sucks, as I tease him by backing off it entirely then bringing it back into my mouth. He grabs my hair, and I know he's wanting more than my playful teasing. He is fully erect now, and it's challenging to keep my mouth around his huge cock, but I try my best. I bring my hand to his shaft as I make figure-eight movements and follow suit with my head as I move back and forth, just shy of halfway down his throbbing penis. He grips tighter on my hair, and his moans become more frequent. I move faster with my hand as I continue bobbing up and down. I can feel his legs tense, and tiny jolts flicker from his abdomen.

"Stop, STOP!" Luke whisper shouts in a crackling voice.

He pulls my hair to remove my mouth from around him, then bends down and grabs my arm, bringing me to my feet. He reaches under my ass and pulls me onto his hips. He looks into my eyes then takes off toward my bedroom. He lays me down on my bed, removing his pants and boxer briefs, then crawls on top of me and begins to kiss me. He inserts his finger in me. Instant tingles arise throughout my body as I am already aroused. He does a few slow in and out movements then speeds up until I'm wet.

He takes his finger out of me and slides his huge cock inside me. Every time he enters me for the first time, the feeling that travels throughout my body is out of this world. I immediately feel an indescribable sensation, where I want to scream. It's orgasmic!

"You're so fucking tight and soaking wet," he groans.

He pulls out and flips me over, quickly sliding himself back in. I lean my upper body down toward the bed and raise my back end toward his chest. Luke grabs hold of my hips, slowly sliding into me from behind. Oh my God, the way he feels from this position sends me into instant shakes, and my jaw begins to chatter heavily. I can tell he's not in very far yet, as he can barely go over halfway when he's on top before I'm in a lot of pain. He slides in deeper, and the pain starts to build slowly. I try to bear through it as he feels unbelievable in this position. Luke begins to pick up the speed, and my body goes numb. I orgasm, and he must be able to tell because he fucks me harder.

"Owe, owe! Stop!" I scream as I tighten my thighs and push at him.

"Too far in?" he questions me.

"Yea!" I say, trying to catch my breath.

"I won't go that far in, okay?" he says.

I nod, and he keeps going. He thrusts faster and faster; our skin slaps against each other. I get an intense tingly numb feeling again, then start to convulse. I arch my back toward Luke and throw my head up. I let out a series of moans as I orgasm again. He grips my hips tight and starts to shake as he pumps faster. I can feel the entire bed move. He pulls out, coming all over the small of my back as he groans uncontrollably and brings his upper body to rest against my back. We fall to my bed, desperate to catch our breath.

chapter forty-seven

I draw a somewhat perfect line of black over my top eyelid. It's not as perfect as the one I drew on my other eye but close enough. It's so hard to make your eyes match. The black liner makes the green in my eyes pop, or so I've been told. My green eyes are my best feature. I receive a lot of compliments over their shape, color, and overall appearance from family, friends, and strangers, yet Luke has not said anything at all about them. I shouldn't be one to talk; I haven't said anything about his to him either.

His eyes are so different. The color itself is fascinating. I've never seen the color of his eyes before. The bluish-green hue is like the colors seen in the Caribbean ocean, crystal clear and crisp though soft and dreamy. When he looks into my eyes, I melt and lose myself. I turn submissive and vulnerable under his gaze.

The past few days with him have been very unforgettable. We kept it low key yesterday after work. We changed the oil in my car and checked all the fluids. It was fun working together like I used to do with my dad. He slept over, but we didn't have sex last night or this morning because I was sore from the night before.

Luke got up before me this morning; he made us breakfast and called into work for the first part of the day to hang out with me before I go. He's changing my windshield wipers right now as I get ready. Although, I would like to have sex before I leave for

Milwaukee in a few hours. I would be sore driving, and it would make for an uncomfortable five hours, but it'd be worth it.

I finish my makeup when Luke walks in the doorway of the bathroom. He leans in, watching me as I start curling my hair. I love how he looks at me.

"You going to watch me get ready?" I ask.

"Yes, you look sexy standing there in just your bra and panties," he says.

He looks me up and down with a stare that makes me weak in the knees. I roll my eyes at him and continue to curl my hair. He walks over to me and stands behind me, staring in the mirror; I stare back at him and smile. He puts his hands on my hips and kisses the nape of my neck.

"Stop it," I giggle, moving my head away from him. "You're going to make me burn myself."

Luke grabs my curling iron and puts it down on the counter of the sink, returning his hand to my hip. I put my hands on the sink, leaning into them, and stare at him in the mirror. He stares back at me with a devilish smirk. I watch him in the mirror as he brings his hands up the sides of my body, then slowly under my bra, grabbing hold of my breasts. I love it when he touches me; I instantly receive an embodied sensation.

I look at him as he stares back at me. He looks at his hands on my breasts as he gently begins to massage them and lightly pinches my nipples. They become hard as I start to feel tingly down in my lady bits. He knows how to turn me on. I want to do dirty things to him right now, but I don't want to get all sweaty before I leave. I look away from what he is doing to me to his eyes; he's staring at me now, seductively. I bite my lower lip and watch him bring one of his hands back down my body, tucking his fingers under my panties, exposing only his thumb. He leans forward toward me and inserts a finger inside me; I gasp slightly as I look up at him. He watches his hand move in my panties and looks at me. I've never watched myself get fingered before, and it's so hot.

My breathing goes heavy, and I watch his hand move faster and faster in my panties. I drop my head down and grip tightly onto the sink, breathing heavier as my heart starts to pound. I look up at him in the mirror when he removes his other hand from my breast and down to his pants. Not skipping a beat from penetrating me with his finger, he unzips his pants and pulls out his turgescent phallus. Holy shit!

He brings that hand into my panties and slides a finger in me, moving it in and out a few times in sync with his finger from his other hand, before removing it. He rubs his finger up and down his cock then grabs hold of it. He begins to jerk off while fingering me in front of the mirror. I'm more intrigued in watching him masturbate than I am in him, pleasuring me, causing me to become even more aroused.

I watch him continue to touch himself. I cannot take it anymore and grab his hand that is inside me. He looks up at me in the mirror and stops fingering me. He stops touching himself too.

"What?" he questions, bewildered.

I take his hand out of my panties and turn around facing him.

"Go sit on the toilet," I demand and push my hand against his chest.

He walks over to the toilet and sits down. I pull my panties down and step out of them as I walk toward Luke. He slides his pants and briefs down around his ankles. I straddle him as I grab hold of his thick cock and slowly lower myself onto him. I wrap my arms around his neck and look into his eyes. I let out a moan through my nose as I lower myself down farther onto him. He grabs my ass and helps me slide down more. I suck hair through my teeth as I am still a little tender from the other night when he took me from behind. I kiss him as I bring myself back up his shaft and bite his lower lip. He moans and squeezes my ass tightly. I slide back down slowly.

"Oh, my f-f-fuck!" he stutters through a moan.

I continue moving up and down teasingly slow until I become wetter, and the tenderness of my vagina dissipates. Luke's eyes are closed when I look at him and begin to pick up the pace, only taking half of him, which is all I can handle right now. I let out a gasp when he squeezes my ass and pushes me down farther on him. After a little bit, I start to tingle more and lose control. I move up and down his shaft quickly. Luke moans and groans with every pass I make. My chin begins to shake, and I can barely feel my legs. I want to stop because it hurts but can't as it feels way too good.

I throw my head back and let out a low grumble as I orgasm. Luke grabs my hips, pushing me up and down him, then lifts me off his penis as he holds himself and comes. I sit down on the cold bathroom floor as I collect myself from the tingling feeling that radiates throughout my entire body. It's even in my face this time, and I feel like I'm ready to pass out. Luke tries to catch his breath as he rests his head back, still holding himself.

"You're unbelievable on top, Ali," he says, still out of breath.

I stand, still shaky, and grab a hand towel. I give it to Luke to clean himself up. I fix my hair, check my makeup, and clean myself down below. I walk over to Luke and kiss him while he is still complying himself. I leave the bathroom to get dressed and pack up my hair and makeup stuff in my suitcase. I put on my navy-blue pleated dress pants, an off white high necked, exaggerated sleeve blouse, and black flats. I head back to the bathroom to brush my teeth.

Luke is washing his hands when I enter. He looks at me and smiles; I return his smile and grab my toothbrush. I brush my teeth as he wraps his arms around my waist, watching me in the mirror. I rinse my mouth, apply some lip gloss, then turn to face him. He looks down at me and kisses me on the nose. I close my eyes, taking in the moment.

"I'm going to miss you while you're away," he sighs.

I lay my head against his chest and listen to his heartbeat. The thumps are soothing.

"I'm going to miss you too. It's only a few days. I need some time to heal anyways," I giggle.

He lets out a laugh through his nose.

"I know!"

We hold each other a bit longer before parting. Luke carries my bag downstairs and out to my car. I check to make sure everything is shut off inside before I leave. Luke is leaning against my car; he is in his work getup and hat backward. He's looking hot as usual.

"You look sexy in that professional shit you're wearing," he states.

"Thanks! You look sexy in your work clothes, " I reply as I stop right in front of him.

He grabs my waist and pulls me to him, hugging me while holding onto my ass. I hug him back as he kisses my forehead, then rests his chin on the top of my head. He grabs my hand and walks me around my car to my driver's side door. He pushes me against my car and cups his hands behind my head and kisses me with the slight passing of his tongue.

"Drive safe," he says.

"Will do," I reply.

"Text me when you get there," he orders.

"Aye, aye captain!" I joke as I give him a salute.

He gives me an "I'm not amused" look then smirks his sexy ass smirk. He opens my door, and I get into my car.

"See you in a few days," he sighs.

"Bye, handsome," I reply.

He closes my door, and I start my car. I watch as he walks to his truck and climbs inside. He begins driving down my dad's driveway, I follow behind him.

chapter forty-eight

I arrive at Façade just a little after three, just in time for the afternoon meeting. I park in my usual spot in the parking ramp, check over my hair and makeup, then send Luke a text letting him know I made it. I enter the building and immediately feel like I'm in a foreign place. Since the day I started my internship as a Sophomore in college four years ago, I haven't felt this way. I feel almost uncomfortable like I shouldn't be here. I don't know why I feel like I don't belong here now. I've only been gone a little over a week. The smell is different or something; maybe my mind was so accustomed to how my dad's shop and his house smells, it erased the smell of Facade. Perhaps, the feeling is more so coming from my time spent with Luke. I can still picture him in front of me, the sight I saw of him in my mirror this morning.

My phone buzzes. It's Ris.

"Hey!" I answer.

"Are you here yet, bitch?" she asks.

"I just walked in," I reply.

She squeals loudly, then hangs up. I can hear the fast pace clicking of heels on the concrete floor as I walk farther into Facade. Ris appears around the corner doing a little jog, quick step thing. We hug, and she walks with me to our offices. I am so glad to see her; she will distract me from my thoughts of Luke and wanting to be back at my dad's.

Ris doesn't look much different when she is dressed professionally; her business attire is just as hoochie. She is wearing a white with black pinstripe darted waist, a-line silhouette, mid-thigh skirt that falls to an edgy, asymmetrical hemline, and a tight black crew neck cropped shirt, showing a sliver of her midriff. I assumed with this outfit that she'd be wearing her suede thigh-high boots, but instead, she shows off her long ass legs with black lace-up, open-toe heels. Ris looks sophisticated with a slide of "fuck me hard" today.

I could never pull off this look, or most of her looks, being shorter than her. Sometimes, I wish I were five foot eight like her, but for the most part, I am content at being five foot two and a half.

We walk up the stairs to the second floor; Ris hates elevators and says if she's going to sit behind a desk all day, she will at least get some exercise. Ris and I reach the second floor, passing through different areas along the way before coming into the Designers quadrant of Facade. It's a massive building with two floors and eight quadrants on each floor.

A cluster of fancy cubicles fills the middle of our quadrant, and offices line up the outer wall. Those working from the cubicles are the Interns and Designer Assistants. I sat there when I was interning during college. Most Interns become Assistants before becoming Designers, but Ris, myself, and two others skipped that part. Each Designer has one Intern and two Assistants under them except for our Senior Designer, who has four Assistants and no Interns.

Our Senior Designer is Brady Adams; he's been with Facade for almost eight years now. He and Ris like to fool around a lot, causing some weird awkwardness and tension at work, more so when they're in between deciding if they hate each other or want to have raunchy sex. He is very good looking but overly cocky and arrogant. Brady is Troy's best friend; that's how we met.

My office is at the end of the quadrant, next to the Senior Designers office, the largest office. Ris's office is across from mine and three down, away from Brady, which is good. All the Designer offices have glass walls and doors. Barrett claims they open offices to light and collaboration, allowing for a more positive work environment and connectivity. A see-through office happens to be the latest rage at the workplace right now here in Milwaukee. We are on-trend for sure, well, I think we may have started it.

"Brady is in his usual dickish mood today," Ris whispers as we come closer to her office.

"So, you two are hating each other right now?" I laugh.

She curls her lip up at me and growls, then darts into her office as she sees Brady, flicking me off from inside.

"Ali, welcome back," Brady says in a smug but semi-delightful voice.

Brady is average height, around five foot ten or so, and very brawny. He is a workout, protein shake, and eat well-balanced meals type. He has sandy blonde hair shaved on the sides, longer on top, and slicked back. It is sort of like how *Zack Morris's* hair is from the classic sitcom *Saved by the Bell*. Brady has light brown eyes and a decent smile with dimples. His personality makes him unattractive and unbearable to be around. We almost match our attires today. He is wearing navy dress pants, an off-white button-up, and black dress boots.

"Thank you, but I'm only back for a couple of days," I reply with a smile then cut across the cubicles toward my office.

He follows behind me as I make my way to my office. I can feel his piercing stare, knowing that he's checking out my ass and making a disgusting look on his face. I open the door to my office and walk-in with Brady hot on my trail. I walk around behind my desk, setting my purse down.

"Do you need something, Brady?" I ask rudely.

"Not really," he replies as he sits down on the edge of my desk.

I roll my eyes. He thinks he can do whatever he wants and that every woman should swoon over him. Most do, but I'm not too fond of his arrogance at all. He bothers the living piss out of me, but for some reason, he always has his nose shoved up my ass. I'm sure it's because I'm one of Barrett's favorites or the fact that I'm the only girl in this entire building that won't sleep with him.

"Does Troy know that you're back?" he asks, picking at his cuticles.

"Not yet," I reply quickly.

My two Assistants enter. They greet me and give me my messages from the past two weeks, paperwork, and talk about my sizeable commercial account with the Christiansen's. Ignoring Brady as he watches me from my desk, I continue my work as if I am going about a typical day at the office. He looks down at his watch, then grabs the paperwork from my hands, and tosses it on my desk.

"It's meeting time," he says snarkily.

He ushers me out of my office while glaring at my assistants. I quickly walk away from him and meet up with Ris, who is waiting for me at the end of our quadrant so we can head to the conference room for our four o'clock meeting together.

"What the hell was that all about?" Ris asks, in a semi-bitchy voice.

"Nothing. Brady is just on me like a fly on shit today," I reply, sort of brash.

Ris is annoyed but can tell that I am disgusted by him and gives me a side hug, and we continue our way to the conference room for the meeting. Brady is unbelievably tacky and grosses me out by his lack of respect for women. He literally makes my skin crawl. He is like the male version of Bridget, the very definition of man whore. He has some nerve to show so much disrespect to me and my assistants. He's infuriating.

chapter forty-nine

We enter the conference room, which is in the center of all the quadrants on the second floor. A glass exterior also surrounds it. Ris and I both take a seat next to each other at the far end of the large steel rectangular table. Most people like to be the closest to the door, but we want to sit the nearest to Barrett, who sits at the end farthest from the door. A white Facade folder, a legal pad, and a pen lay in front of each chair.

There is a refreshment station at the back of the conference room with various beverages and snack-type items. I usually grab a water and a granola bar, but I don't feel like it right now, since I have only been at work for an hour. Others trickle in, including Brady and some other higher-ranked Designers. Barret is the last to arrive at every meeting.

Quite a few people have noticed my return and ask me how I am doing. It is a nice feeling to know that my coworkers, who drive me bonkers most of the time, actually care about my well-being. Brady sits directly across from both Ris and me; I'm sure to torment her as always. Barrett enters a few minutes after we have all taken our seats.

He never wears business attire like most CEOs of a company would. He always wears jeans and a sweater over a collared button-up shirt. Today is no different. Barrett is kind, yet affirmative, when it comes to business and Facade, but outside of the office, he is a riot, and his wife is the sweetest, soft-spoken person I have ever met.

He is built a lot like Brady, and they are around the same height for the most part. Barrett is very youthful-looking and handsome; his hair is always perfectly cut and styled, as if he gets it cut right before we see him every day. He is the personification of cool and collective. He has some gray on the sides, but other than that, you would never guess that he is fifty years old. I love working for him and spending time with him and his wife outside of work.

"Good to see you, Ali, "Barrett whispers.

He passes by me and makes his way to the end of the table. He takes a seat, with all eyes on him, and puts a Facade folder down on the table and opens it.

"Good Afternoon, everyone! It's great to see Ali back after her short absence. She will be here tomorrow then will be working from home for a while. If anyone has any questions for her while she is here, please feel free to reach out to her; otherwise, contact her through work email or the company chat," he announces.

Barrett's forthcoming announcement regarding contacting me once I start my leave makes me feel better after Brady being an obnoxious prick with his disheartening banter earlier. It shows how personable my boss is, as well as how he appreciates his employees. Brady should notes; he may learn a thing or two.

"Team, let's discuss new and current projects that are taking place. Brady, what is the latest news in Commercial?" Barrett asks.

Brady begins to discuss what all of us in quadrant thirteen and fourteen are currently working on. In our quadrant, we focus mainly on commercial projects. The second floor is quadrants nine through sixteen, which are Commercial, Industrial, Landscape, and Urban Architecture. The first floor consists of Housing, Research, Interior, and Sustainable Architecture.

My phone buzzes in my pocket. Trying not to look conspicuous, I slide my phone out and peer down at my lap under the table. We are not supposed to bring our phones to meetings.

I open two texts from Luke, including one with a picture of what looks like a 1950's Cadillac and the other about my safe arrival. His messages make me happy, but I miss his sexy smile, gorgeous body, and his soft touch. I've had a pretty great week getting to know him, including the incredible sex we've recently started having. I shouldn't get myself started on thinking about our sex life right now.

I look around the room to make sure no one has noticed that I am on my phone, and quickly reply to his text showing interest in the classic he is working on and letting him know I miss him without coming straight out and saying it. My phone buzzes almost immediately after I send my reply to Luke. Wow, he's quick to reply today, but it's not from Luke. It's a message from Troy.

Heard you're back. Can I take you to dinner tonight, please?

I guess he did not get the hint that I am not interested in dating him right now, or he could just be being himself and wanting to see how I am doing since I left. I did leave to attend my father's funeral and deal with what comes after losing a parent. I will text him back after I find out if Ris has any plans for us tonight. Either way, I do not want to see him while I am back in town for these few days.

Ris kicks me under the table, I jump and look at her.

"Hello? Earth to Allison?" Brady says, in a stern and loud voice.

"I'm so sorry, what was it that you asked?" I reply.

I have not been paying attention to what he has been talking about since he opened his mouth. I tend to do that when he speaks.

"Where are we at with the Christiansen account?" he demands.

"Oh, yes. The account is currently on hold, but my assistants took care of any questions or concerns during my absence," I state calmly.

"Have you spoke with these clients at all in her absence?" Barrett asks Brady.

"No, they are not my project," Brady snaps.

Barrett turns in his chair, and the expression on his face changes into disappointment.

"You're the Senior Designer, Brady, all projects are your responsibility," he says firmly.

They go back and forth, arguing over the largest Commercial project our firm has going on right now. Little does Brady know that I have a close relationship with the Christiansen's, as I do with most of my clients. Thankfully for me, they know what I was going through and that I would be away from the office for a few weeks. Barrett is also aware of all of this. My time away has given the Christiansen's enough time to get the proper documentation into us for the massive project they have in store for myself and my team.

I am the Lead Project Designer for this building design, and it pisses Brady off because he usually is the one to receive such a position on a project. My clients requested that I be the one in charge; therefore, Barrett gave me responsibility. I have all the designers on the floor, interns, and specialties needed to develop the project; however, I see fit. Brady is my bitch during this project. We will be designing a chain of five-star hotels to be built in four major cities right here in Wisconsin.

I am super nervous about the project but also very excited at the same time. I have not overseen the design of a building from start to finish. I have only led the lighting concepts for Commercial projects; this is a huge honor and change for me. I need Brady's help, but I know he will be a douche during this project because he did not receive it himself. I hope I do well, being five hours away when I leave on Saturday.

"To close our meeting, I would like to invite all of you out tomorrow evening in celebration for landing the Christiansen account. Have a great rest of your night, everyone, and see you all in the morning!" Barrett states.

The meeting ends, and we are all dismissed back to our offices.

chapter fifty

I rummage through the paperwork scattered across my desk, gathering it neatly and placing it in the middle of my desk to go over tomorrow morning. I grab my purse and head out of my office to Ris's.

"Ali," Brady calls out from his office.

What the hell does he want now? I toddle to his office and stand in the doorway.

"Yes?" I reply, sort of crudely.

He is sitting at his desk talking on his phone, giving me a "one-sec" finger. I roll my eyes at him and turn to walk away.

"Would you like to get dinner with me tonight?" he asks, in a very charming and sweet voice.

What the hell is going on here? Troy asked me, and now Brady is asking me. Ugh, Troy is relentless. I highly doubt Ris is in the mood to be around him tonight. I would rather avoid both these men and chill with Ris.

"I believe Ris and I have other plans for this evening than accompanying you and Troy to dinner," I reply.

He looks up at me, stands up from his desk, and walks toward me.

"No, it's just going to be us," he says.

"What? Why?" I ask, a little baffled.

Why would he want to go to dinner with just me? He and Ris are a thing or were, I can never keep up with their on and off again crap, plus he usually takes out one of the cute little interns. He must have a motive; he is never overly friendly for no reason at all. What is he up to?

"I just wanted to discuss the Christiansen account before you take a leave again. So, we are on the same page," he says, suspiciously casual, yet nonchalantly.

Brady is fumbling behind his door through his filing cabinet as if he is of grave importance to everyone, and we all should bow down to him. I feel he may just be using this as an excuse to show off in front of me. I don't feel like talking about work outside of work, but I am taking a leave for up to three months. I will also be five hours away. Plus, this account is significant for the company, and he will physically be here working with my team.

"Okay, sure. Where and when would you like me to meet you?" I ask.

"I'll pick you up at six, be ready, " he replies.

He shuts the light off then escorts me out the doorway of his office.

"I can just meet you myself," I say again, more firmly.

"As I said, I will pick you up," he says callously and walks past me.

He is such an arrogant asshole. I should probably grab my project folder and the Christiansen's folder to go over what I have thus far for the account. It isn't much as we technically have not even started working on it yet. I wonder if I should call and invite them to dinner with us. They cannot stand Brady, so I am not too sure if it's that great of an idea.

I shut the light off in my office after grabbing the folders I need and make my way to Ris's office, where Brady happens to be. He is standing in the doorway, and she's giving him her "I'm a tough cookie" stance while batting her "fuck me" eyes at him. I stop just outside her door, as he steps out to leave

"See you tonight," he winks then walks away.

Ish. I walk into Ris's office. I can see the piercing look in her eyes as she's ready to freak out on me for no reason at all.

"See you tonight? What the fuck is that all about?" Ris asks in her bitchy, yet very annoyed voice.

"He asked me to dinner to discuss the Christiansen account," I reply.

"Hmm," she lets out unimpressed.

Ris grabs her purse, then walks past me, and turns out the light to her office. I hate it when she acts like this. She gets all stupid jealous when she is not getting all the attention from a guy she wants to sleep with or is currently fucking. I ignore it and walk behind her until she gets over herself.

"I need a new cocktail dress, and my nails did for tomorrow's dinner," Ris finally speaks as we are almost to the parking lot.

"We're going to the mall. I suppose you need a new one too and to get those brows cleaned up. You're starting to look a little too country."

And she's back from her little jealous bout over Brady taking me to dinner tonight. I ignore her comment about my eyebrows and continue walking. My phone rings, and I tell Ris that I will meet her at the mall. She gives me a stupid wave, then gets into her vehicle and drives off. I answer my phone.

"Hi!"

"Hey, Turtle! How are you?"

"I'm good, just got off work. How was the shop today?" I ask.

"It was pretty busy today. A lot of paint jobs and bodywork," he replies.

Luke tells me about the Cadillac and how excited he is to be rebuilding the engine for it. He rambles on like a little kid explaining a story, and it is super cute. I've only spoken to him on the phone a handful of times, but I love to listen to him talk. His voice is so deep and unbelievably sexy over the phone. I wish we could talk for the rest of the day.

"What's up tonight?" he asks.

"I am going to dinner with one of my bosses to discuss details about a huge project I recently landed. Since I will be working from home, well my dad's for a while, I need to make sure my entire team is on the same page before I leave," I answer.

"Wow, that's amazing! You're amazing," he states.

Whenever he says this kind of stuff to me, I get all full of butterflies. I want to see him right now and rest my head against his chest. I wonder if he's shirtless with his hat backward. I swear whenever he looks like that, I instantly want to drop my panties.

"I, uh, um... kind of miss you," he mutters. "I know it's stupid since you have only been gone for around eight hours or so."

I smile big, all by myself in my car on the way to the mall.

"No, it's not stupid. I feel the same way. I…"

I hear a beep and see that Ris is calling from the other line.

"Um... Ris is beeping in. She is waiting for me at the mall," I announce.

"Okay, I am home now and need to hop in the shower anyway. I will text you later. Have a good time tonight!" He says.

"Thank you, I'll try!" I reply.

"Talk to you later, Turtle!"

"Bye," I sigh.

"Bye."

Our call ends, and I switch over to Ris.

"Hey!" I answer.

"Where are you, bitch?" Ris shouts.

"I'm pulling in now. I was talking to Luke when you called," I say.

"Well, hurry the fuck up!" she demands.

I park a few spots from Ris's car. She walks over to where I am and asks what Luke and I talked about then cuts me off mid-sentence, demanding I tell her about our sex and his horse cock. I chuckle and begin to tell her about the sex we had this morning and how it all started with me standing completely naked in front of the mirror in the bathroom. I tell Ris all the juicy details as we walk across the parking lot to the mall. Of course, she loves hearing every bit of it. Dirty whore!

She trips over the curb and almost face plants into a bench near the mall entrance. We both shriek with laughter as I recall a similar incident happening at the cabin not too long ago, but sex was the culprit then. We try to talk in code language, so other passersby don't get weirded out by our inappropriate sexual monologue. Although, we usually get strange looks when we are in public regardless.

chapter fifty-one

We end up in the tenth store, looking at dresses that have prices tags the size of our rent, but Ris can afford it. I found my dress for tomorrow night's dinner party back at *Macy's,* which is way more my price range after I had my eyebrows waxed. The dress is a little out of my comfort zone, but Ris suggested that I need a dress to dine and dance in. Ris has an incredible fashion sense, and she knows how to stay on-trend. I'm sure she was hinting at going to the club after dinner tomorrow night. It feels great to be back and hanging out with my best friend.

I run my hands through racks of clothing while fantasizing about my next sexual encounter with Luke. We've had some pretty crazy sex already and surprisingly, not in the usual places, like a bed. Once in a bed out of four times so far, the rest have not been normal places to have sex.

My phone rings, and I snap from my thoughts and fantasies of Luke. It's Brady. Shit, it's after six.

"Hello."

"Where are you? I'm at your apartment," Brady huffs.

"I'm at the mall with Ris. I will meet you. What restaurant do you want to have dinner at?" I ask.

"I'll wait for you. Get here now," he replies tactlessly before hanging up.

Ugh, the nerve of him sometimes. He drives me insane. I yell to

Ris as she is trying on countless dresses, that I must go back to our apartment to meet Brady. She scowls and says, bye. I tell her to grab the hoochiest one as she will look fabulous in whichever she decides. She agrees with me in her bitchy way, then I scramble off to my car.

I OPEN THE DOOR TO BRADY'S BMW AND SIT DOWN ON THE light tan leather seats. He's talking on his phone to one of his many booty calls, I'm sure. I buckle my seat belt as he takes off into traffic. I place the folders on my lap and look around his flawlessly clean car. This car is gorgeous, and the seats are amazingly comfortable. The metallic wood trim accents make the interior pop. It has a keyless push to start ignition, which I find neat on newer vehicles yet a tad confusing at the same time. There is a panoramic moon roof with a two-piece glass panel overhead. A genuinely nice car, to be honest. I am sure Brady doesn't appreciate it and is already looking for the latest luxury vehicle to blow his money on, then show off to everyone.

He continues talking on his phone while glancing at me periodically. We have passed quite a few restaurants that I thought we would have stopped at. I wonder where he is taking me. Brady finally ends his call with a tap at his earpiece. I need to know where we're going because something seems a bit off.

"Where are we going?" I ask.

I'm a little concerned now that we are away from the heart of the city. We're far from any of the restaurants that he could have taken me to for dinner. Places I know that wouldn't cramp his style and image. Places where he would have undoubtedly flashed his big bucks while providing us with the most fabulous and expensive meal.

He ignores me and makes another call. He is such a pompous jerk. I check my phone to see if Luke has sent me a message, but he hasn't. I'm sure he's probably busy working on something in his pole barn. I imagine his dreamy smile and the way he looks at me with his ocean-colored eyes. I think about his touch and the way he makes me feel every time I am with him. I miss him.

Brady begins to slow down then turns on to a nicely tarred road with high stone walls. We travel down a bit before coming to a fancy black gate. Where are we? I've never seen this place before. Brady rolls his window down and presses a white button; then, the gate slides open. He continues with his conversation with God knows who. Large trees are lining what is now a brick driveway. The trees are evenly placed apart from each other and lean inward, giving a tunnel feel. A vast white colonial house comes into view.

Large pillars frame the outside lower level of what looks to be a three-story mansion—a few balconies cascade from the second floor. The brickwork is stunning, and the landscaping is phenomenal. Whose home is this? Brady swings his car up to the entrance of the mansion on the looped driveway. He ends his call and opens his door. I grab his arm; he stops and looks at me.

"What?" he says rudely.

"Where are we?" I demand.

"My parents," he replies and steps out of his vehicle.

His parents' house? Holy shit balls. Why would he take me to his parents' house for dinner? An older gentleman, wearing a butler type suit opens my door and extends his hand to me. I put my hand in his and step out of Brady's car. He has already gone inside. I say thank you to the man, and he nods politely. He escorts me to the door of Brady's parents' house and opens it for me. I step inside, my eyes go wide, and instantly my mouth drops open.

A house that is clearly straight out of an episode of *Cribs*. This place is drop-dead gorgeous. The shiny white marble floor foyer is divine, with two staircases leading to the second level on both sides of the room, and a glass chandelier perfectly accenting the large room. The decor alone is breathtaking. His parents must be filthy rich, which would explain why Brady is such an arrogant asshole.

I continue into the house and walk into a room with light gray walls and fancy white furniture. A white grand piano sits on one side of the room, and another chandelier hangs from the ceiling. Beautiful hardwood flooring lays across the room. It must be a living room or sitting area, I assume. I wonder where Brady is. I also wonder what the heck I am doing here.

The next room I walk into is not as large as the last; it is a gold color with a long rectangular glass table that seats eight people and set for five. I walk around the room, taking in the beautiful decor and fascinating architecture. The plates, glasses, and cutlery match the gold walls and chairs. I have no clue where Brady is, so I decide to continue to the next room in hopes I may find him there. Is he trying to brag about his riches? I am not amused by him needing to show off his home life, but this house is stunning.

I enter a room that resembles your standard living room, only way fancier. I thought the room before the dining room was one, but I guess not. This room is larger than the previous two. It has a few different sized couches and chairs throughout it, and a large flat-screen television placed on the wall above a beautiful fireplace.

I can hear a woman's voice coming from the next room, and I make my way toward it. A slender blonde-haired woman dressed in an off-white business suit with a long pencil skirt stands talking with what appears to be a maid or housekeeper. The room looks different to the last few. It is an octagonal shaped room with windows that reach from the floor to the ceiling. A single Toscano bench rests between the windows, and a small bistro style table sits in the middle of the room. A small chandelier hangs over the table, and a flat-screen television is placed on the wall above the fireplace. The view from the windows overlooks the pool and backyard. I knew Brady was a spoiled rich kid, but I didn't realize he was this rich. The maid leaves the room, and the woman turns to me.

"Hello, you must be Allison! I'm Claire," she says with a very inviting smile.

She cannot be Brady's mom as she seems way too nice, but I can see a lot of him in her. She's pretty and is more charming than her spoiled son.

"Yes! Nice to meet you," I smile.

She draws closer to me and reaches out her hand to shake mine. She drops her hand into mine, and I am not quite sure what to do with how she has presented it to me. It's an awkward "nice to meet you" handshake, that's for sure.

"You're as beautiful as Brady described. I believe he is out on the terrace talking with his father," she chirps.

Brady thinks I'm beautiful, and he told his mother I am. That's strange; he pays no attention to me other than when he's a downright douche bag. I do not understand why he would bring me to his parents. I do not feel comfortable discussing the Christiansen account or any business matters in front of them

On the terrace, you can see the entire back yard, and it's a breath-taking view. Brady is chatting with his father, who is in jeans and a blue and white polo shirt. He is a tad shorter than Brady, with white hair, and is quite tanned. He is as good looking as his son.

"This must be the infamous Allison. Aren't you a sight," he says as he looks me over.

I'm becoming quite uncomfortable. The "infamous Allison"? That remark has taken me a bit off-guard. I want to be polite and respectful to Brady's parents as they're so friendly, welcoming, and charming. Although, I am confused about one thing. What has he told his parents about me, and why am I here in the first place?

"Dad," Brady scowls lightly.

"Nice to meet you," I say and give him a firm handshake.

His eyes are darker than his sons. They are shifty, almost devious.

"You work with Brady at Facade correct and are you in Commercial design too?" his father strikes up a conversation.

"Yes, I am the lighting designer for our Commercial clients," I answer his father politely.

"She recently landed the Christiansen's account," Brady chimes.

"Congratulations, that is a huge account of land," he says with a warm smile.

"Thank you, Mr. Adams," I blush while looking over at Brady, who is staring out over the yard.

I know it was an account he tried and wanted desperately to land, but I ended up landing it. We're rivals; I guess you could say, ever since I became a designer. We are continually trying to outdo the other when we should be working together, not against each other.

"Please, call me Jerry," he says.

"Would you care for a drink?" Claire asks, handing me a glass of white wine.

Not wanting to drink but not wanting to decline either, I politely take the glass of wine from her. Jerry continues asking questions about the Christiansen project. Brady answers most of his father's inquires for me. Their butler enters and informs us; dinner is ready. I wonder if he wanted his parents' input on the Christiansen project or his father has something to do with it and wants me to know.

Jerry and Claire head off the terrace. Brady walks behind them and stops.

"Would you please not tell my parents you received Lead Designer for this project. I don't feel like getting into it tonight with my dad over the fact that a woman was chosen over me," he says in a vulnerable tone, one that I have never witnessed before.

I nod in agreement. I feel bad for Brady that his father would treat him so harshly and judge him over the fact that I received the lead position on the project over him. I read his father wrong based on my first impression of him, but his eyes have me believing he may not be a very kind man. Maybe he is why Brady is the way he is. But it still does not answer the question of why I am or why we are here.

chapter fifty-two

We walk into the room I was in earlier with the glass rectangle table and the gold-accented everything. "Everything" seems to be the best way to describe it. A young girl is already seated at the table; she is blonde and looks a bit like Jerry. She must be Brady's younger sister. Jerry sits at the head of the table. Claire sits next to the young girl, and I sit across from her next to Brady.

"Hi, I'm Abagail, Brady's little sister," she whispers joyfully across the table.

I smile and give a light wave.

"I'm Ali," I whisper back.

I look down at the plate in front of me. It's a decorative plate with a single spoon lying across it. A thick slice of mozzarella cheese and a thin slice of tomato drizzled in balsamic vinegar topped with a beautiful edible pink flower and basil leaf, lie on the spoon.

"Our first course this evening is Caprese, and is taken in a single bite," the butler announces.

I dislike tomatoes, so I hope the cheese, vinegar, and basil drown out the taste and texture. It would be impolite not to eat it, considering the company at hand. I do not care for Brady, and I think he is an obnoxious prick, but I don't want to embarrass and insult him in front of his parents. I place my napkin on my lap and choke the bite down, which is rather delicious.

The butler announces that we will be enjoying a nine-course meal this evening. Nine courses, where the hell am I going to fit nine courses? I look over at Brady, who is chewing his Caprese.

My plate is removed, and another one is set down before me. It's a cup of soup, a very fancy looking cup of soup.

"Our second course this evening is Duck Wild Rice soup," the butler announces.

Duck, I like ducks, I can certainly handle this one. I scoop up a spoonful of the soup and take a bite. Oh my God, it's divine, the best cup of soup I have ever had. The duck is so tender and compliments the wild rice perfectly. I may like this even more than chicken wild rice soup.

While we eat, Brady's parents engage in conversation about his life outside of work. They begin distastefully degrading his promiscuous lifestyle and the fact he never has a steady girlfriend. His mother practically tells him he is an embarrassment to the family and that he disgusts her. I honestly cannot believe they choose to have this conversation with him right now, at the dinner table in front of a perfect stranger. I've never before seen Brady cower like a puppy about to get beat and look so helpless. A part of me is enjoying this, but a part of me also feels that it's a bit unfair. I open my mouth and say the first thing that comes to my lips without thinking it through first.

"Brady is quite a handsome, highly successful man. He cannot help that the ladies cannot keep their hands off him. If they weren't after his checkbook, maybe he'd be settled down by now," I say in his defense.

Everyone stops eating and looks at me. I may have to eat my words later, but despite mine and Brady's tension between one another at work, we're still a team, and he's still a person. He doesn't deserve to be treated in such a manner by his family.

Brady has pure shock displayed all over his face, over the fact I just talked back to his parents in a conversation that I technically wasn't even a part of. His mother gives me a slight glare but seems more ashamed of their choice in conversation. They change the subject and do not revisit Brady's sex life the duration of our incredible dinner.

The rest of the courses are exquisite. I cannot begin to describe most of what I am eating because I am too intrigued by their display on my plate rather than paying attention to their name. I finish all nine courses since they were small portions. A dining experience I will never forget, that's for sure.

After dinner, Brady takes me on a tour of the rest of his parent's house. This house has a total of twelve rooms. We end the tour in his bedroom from when he lived with his parents before taking me on the backyard tour. His room is gorgeous, and the mahogany woodwork is impressive. His bedroom at his parents is the size of mine and Ris's two-bedroom apartment. The tapestry is beautiful, and I love all the decor. The mahogany sleigh bed ties the room theme together perfectly. We leave his room, which takes up most of the third floor, to head outside.

IN THE BACKYARD, THERE IS A LOT TO LOOK AT JUST LIKE inside. I can spot a decent-sized pool, with a neat waterfall and a hot tub. There is a cute little pool house with an outdoor bar. Flowers, trees, and shrubs make the back yard feel like a park, with a tiny two-story house that sits off the yard tucked in the back corner. Brady says it is where the butler, maids, and other staff stay. We walk over a little bridge that sits over a small pond; coy fish swim around in it. I stop on the bridge, watching the fish. I wonder what they do with them during the winter.

"The pond is heated during the winter, so it never freezes, and they swim all year happily," Brady says.

I look at him, wondering if I said something out loud to make him say that just now.

"It's the first question everyone asks. Thank you for sticking up for me at dinner. You didn't have to, but it meant a lot. I know you don't like my ways, either," he says, looking at me so sincere.

I've never seen Brady this way, he may act like a hard ass and a huge jerk at work, but deep inside, I think he is possibly a charming softie.

"You're right, I don't, but I didn't think it was the appropriate time or place to be talking about it," I say.

He looks at me, and I look back down at the fish; I can feel him staring at me.

"What, Brady?" I say, looking back over at him.

"You have beautiful eyes," he says, stepping closer to me.

I look at him, taken aback by his comment.

"Thank you!" I reply.

I turn back to watch the fish and notice out of the corner of my eye that Brady is still looking at me and takes another step closer. I look at him, and he leans toward my face then kisses me. My eyes widen, and I push him away from me.

"Woah, Brady, what was that?" I say, a little disgusted in his action.

I am weirded out and feel uncomfortable. We were supposed to have a business dinner and be talking about the Christiansen account, not having a nine-course meal with is parents and engaging in inappropriate actions.

"Sorry, I just got carried away by the moment and had a few too many glasses of wine," he says arrogantly.

"Moment? There was no moment," I say rudely.

"Whatever you say, Ali. You know you want me," he says slyly.

The nerve of this man. I cannot believe what he's implying; he's unbelievable. I should have known he had an ulterior motive. I bet this was his plan the entire time. To seduce me so I would lose my focus on the Christiansen account, and he could take it out from underneath me. Not a mother fucking chance in hell I will let that happen. I earned this account, and its mine.

"Excuse you? You asked me to dinner to discuss the Christiansen account, but you end up bringing me here to have dinner with your parents. To what, try to make a move on me like I am one of the girls at work who will eat up your every word and part their legs like the Red Sea. I'm sorry, but you have the wrong girl," I bark.

I need to get the hell out of here and away from him. I'm irate.

The audacity of this motherfucker, trying something on me, is absurd. I should've seen this coming, but I thought truly he wanted to discuss the project. I scurry back toward the house. I believed in him, but I should have trusted my gut instinct. Brady took advantage of my sincerity, and he crossed the line.

"Ali, wait. I'm sorry. Will you stop for a second, please," he shouts.

Desperately needing to leave but not knowing where I am to call someone to come pick me up, plus my purse and phone are in the house—I stop and turn around. I cross my arms and wait for Brady to catch up to me. He reaches me, somewhat out of breath.

"I want to leave," I say firmly.

I turn away from him to go into the house, but he grabs my arm, and I move it to take his grip off me.

"Please, don't touch me," I growl.

He throws his arms up in the air.

"I'm sorry. I shouldn't have kissed you," he says.

I look at him with a "no shit" stare. He steps closer to me, reaching his hand up toward my face. I uncross my arms then step away from him.

"Don't fucking touch me, Brady," I hiss.

He throws his arms up once again and steps toward me; I back up and end up against the glass of the French doors to the house. I reach for the handle of the door, but he grabs my arms and tries to kiss me again. I move my face away from his. What the fuck is wrong with him? Is he that drunk?

"Brady, stop!" I shout.

He grabs hold of both my arms in one of his hands, pushing his entire body against mine, grabbing my face with his other hand. I want to scream, but I cannot get a sound out.

"Fucking kiss me, then I will let you go," he says between his teeth as he breathes out heavily from holding me against the door.

Brady has genuinely lost it. Now, I realize why we came here; its private and secluded. He can get away with a lot more here than if we were in a public setting.

"NO!" I scream through his hand.

He squeezes my face and tightens his grip around my hands; I break them free and slap him hard across the face. He stays turned to the side, and his nose flares. He clenches his hands in fists and begins to breathe heavy.

"You're going to wish you never fucking did that," he sneers.

chapter fifty-three

I reach for the door again, but Brady grabs me by my wrist and throws me to the ground. Hard. I hit the ground, winded. I try to catch my breath, hoping his parents or someone has heard all the commotion. Brady picks me up off the grass and throws me over his shoulder. I frantically kick and scream the few steps he takes to the pool house. He carries me inside then throws me to the floor. I sigh as I hit the floor, then look up at him. He closes the door and locks it as I rise to my feet.

"Let me out," I demand.

What's going on with him? Brady has crossed all lines. I do not understand why he is doing this.

"Not until you kiss me," he snarls.

He has lost it, and his desperation and perversion have gone too far. He's become a raging monster.

"Fat fucking chance. Now let me the fuck out!" I scream loud.

He lunges at me, and I take off running in the tiny pool house, yelling for him to stop. What have I done to deserve this? He catches me and throws me to the ground again, this time on my stomach, then climbs on top of me. I scream, but he covers my mouth.

"Shut the fuck up!" he growls.

I try to scream again, but I am unable to. Brady is so strong I can barely move under his weight and tight grip. I bite his hand, and he removes it quickly from my mouth but pushes my head down to the floor.

"Brady, STOP!' I scream as loud as I can. "What the hell's gotten into you! Why are you doing this?"

Brady lowers himself onto me, bringing his face down toward mine the removing a piece my hair out of my face. I try to remain calm and control my breathing. I need to regain my strength before I try to get him off me again.

"What are you trying to do?" I ask as calmly as possible while I try to catch my breath.

"You'll see," he murmurs through his teeth.

He reaches under me for the button of my pants. I start to wiggle profusely. I cannot believe this is happening to me.

"No, no, NO... STOP! BRADY!" I scream.

He gets my pants unbuttoned and forcefully pulls them down over my hips, exposing my bare skin. I try to reach behind me and grab my pants, but it's too hard. I dig my fingernails into his arm as hard as I can, but he grabs both of my hands and holds them over my head against the floor. I begin to cry.

"Brady, you don't have to do this. Please, stop. PLEASE!" I yell out.

He doesn't stop or reply. I can hear his heavy breathing and the unfastening of his belt. He pulls his pants down with one hand as he holds me down with the other. Brady lays back on top of me, and I can feel the warmth of his body against mine. He grabs my pants and panties, pulling them down farther, ripping the fabric. I'm becoming very nervous, and I am having a hard time breathing. I would never have thought that Brady would stoop to a level this low.

"Brady, please. STOP!" I scream again.

He enters his fingers in me to guide himself into my vagina. I try to squeeze everything tightly together to prevent it. He removes his fingers, and forcefully enters me. I gasp loudly. His penetration is rough and feels like he's ripping my insides. I cry and scream in pain, it's the most unbearable pain I've ever endured. I'm thankful he didn't enter me anally. That would have been torture.

I lay here numb and lifeless as he pounds me bone dry, not giving two shits about what he is doing. He doesn't seem to think what he is doing is wrong, which it is on so many levels. He thrusts faster and deeper inside me. I can hear him grunt and moan in pleasure. I want the pain to go away, but it doesn't seem as if he's stopping any time soon. I start feeling very queasy and a little shaky. My mouth begins salivating uncontrollably, and I vomit. I turn my face to the opposite side; I close my eyes and pray for him to stop.

He puts all his weight on me as he ejaculates inside of me. Brady lays on top of me while he catches his breath. He then climbs off me and stands to his feet. I lay still on the floor, listening, while he pulls his pants up, and tucks in his shirt. I've never felt this violated or helpless before; it's utterly disgusting.

"Get dressed and come inside to say goodbye to my parents. Then I'll give you a ride home," he says, calm and relaxed as if we just had consensual sex.

Brady leaves the pool house, and I curl up into a tiny ball. I sob hard as I lay here, holding my legs to my chest. I take a deep breath, and I try my best to collect myself. I pull up my ripped panties, noticing my inner thighs have some blood on them. I stand up from the floor and pull up my pants. My button is broke, so I pull my blouse down to hide it. I find a mirror in the pool house to quickly fix my hair and wipe the makeup from under my eyes.

I cannot believe that just happened. I've worked beside Brady for four years and watched him with different women through those years, and I never suspected him to be a predator. Has he done this before? Has he done this to others at work? To Ris?

I walk across the stone-paved sidewalk to the house and let myself in. Claire greets me. She is so kind and warm, and I want to cry my heart out to her desperately. I wonder if she knows what kind of person her son is and what he just did to me. I am still numb, and I want to go home.

"It was very nice to have you for dinner, Allison. I want to apologize for our topic of conversation; it was inappropriate. I appreciate you sticking up for my son and putting us in our place," she says with a smile.

I want to tell her I regret every word that came out of my mouth during dinner but instead, I give her a slight smile, trying to hide my shock and discomfort. I look around to see Brady, but he's not in the room.

"Where is Brady?" I ask eagerly, so I can get the fuck out of this house and away from him.

"He's in the sitting room with Jerry," she states as she leads the way.

I follow her. We enter the sitting room, and Brady does not acknowledge my presence at first. His mother sits next to his father on the white sofa across from the grand piano. Brady is sitting in a chair near the lit fireplace.

"Well, Mom and Dad, thanks a lot for dinner. I need to get Ali home and get ready for work tomorrow," he says as he stands up from the chair.

I stand by the piano as he shakes his dad's hand and hugs his mother. His father says goodbye to me, and his mother stands to give me a slight embrace. Brady walks over to me, placing his hand on the small of my back. His touch makes me cringe. I am disgusted. I wish I could go home on my own, but I don't have a choice. I don't even know where I am. We walk out the door and over to his car, he opens my door, and I get in quickly. I watch him walk around the front of his car and get in. He doesn't look at me or say a word. He puts his earpiece in and makes a call.

He is acting as if nothing happened. It's like he has some Jekyll and Hyde personality. He switches to predator mode, then he shuts off whatever damage he administers to women he touches. I'm afraid of him; I'm scared of what he might do to me next. He continues with his conversation as I stare out the window the whole way back to my apartment, letting tears slip down my cheeks.

Brady doesn't stop talking on his phone when he pulls up at my apartment. I get out of his vehicle and slam the door shut. He pulls out into traffic and takes off. I want to run inside my apartment and cry myself to sleep, but I don't know what to do. Should I go to the hospital and tell them someone forced themselves on me? Do I wake up Ris, and tell her? Would she even believe me?

chapter fifty-four

My alarm sounds, and I awaken, hoping last night was merely a bad dream. It wasn't. I'm not as tired as I thought I'd be with only a few hours of sleep. I couldn't sleep much last night from not being able to get the images out of my head from what happened and how nauseous the morning-after pill made me feel. I've never had to take one before, and I couldn't ask Ris about it. She was asleep when I got home last night, and I didn't want to wake her, so I ran to the nearest open pharmacy and got the Plan B pill. I didn't even want to talk to Luke last night, so I just made small talk and acted as if everything was okay when it wasn't, and it's not.

I'm terrified to go to work today and see Brady. I badly want to tell Ris about what happened last night, but I don't know how to tell her or how she might react. I am afraid she may see the situation differently since she has been involved with Brady romantically. I don't want it to get out in the open and jeopardize my job or friendship with her. I also do not want a big deal made from it, as I loathe drama, nor need any of it right now.

I leave my room and notice that Ris's door is closed, meaning she is still asleep. I make my way to the bathroom to shower. I showered last night and scrubbed every inch of my body, but I still feel dirty and violated. I hope Brady is clean and does not have any STDs. Knowing him, I cannot take any chances. He's such a loose cannon when it comes to girls.

I've never had to worry about that because I'm very picky about my sexual partners. Which isn't very many. I've also never had someone force themselves on me or have ever been raped. Raped, I was raped last night, wasn't I? What did I do to have someone I know attack me and force himself on me?

I step into the shower and somewhat relax as the hot water cascades over my naked body. I grab my loofah and bodywash then sit on the cold tile floor of the shower. I start to clean every inch of my body. As I scrub my arm, I notice I have some black and blue marks on my wrist and a little farther down my arm as well. I look at my other arm, which has the same bruising, but it's a bit darker. I scrub and scrub, trying to make them disappear, so I am not left with a constant reminder of what my co-worker/boss did to me last night. I want to cry in anger, sadness, and shame, but I've become numb to the situation. I need to be strong and show Brady what he did, will not break me.

I scrub and rinse off every part of my body once more. I step out of the shower and pat myself dry. The bathroom door opens as Ris moseys on in, while I put on a tank top and shorts, then throw my hair up in a towel.

"Morning," I say slowly.

"Morning. How was your dinner with Brady?" she asks while half asleep but still a bit bitchy.

"Fine," I reply and walk out of the bathroom.

Ris doesn't say anything. I can hear her start the shower as I enter my room. I skim over my closet for something to wear, trying not the think about last night at all.

My phone buzzes and I grab it, then sit down on the edge of my bed. It's Luke. I want to talk to him, but it's hard not to think about what I went through last night. He makes me forget about the negative in my life, but I don't know if he can heal this wound right now or if I can even tell him about it.

Good Morning! I have a question for you.

His text reads. I swiftly reply.

Good Morning to you! What's your question?

My phone rings.

"Hi!" I answer.

Slight silence is present on the other end, then I can hear Luke take a deep breath.

"Would you be mad if I took the afternoon off and came to see you? Maybe, stay the weekend, you could show me around the city," he says.

I want to cry, hearing his voice. I want to see him so badly right now and have him hold me in his arms. I want him here to protect me from Brady.

"No, I wouldn't be mad. I would love for you to come and stay here for the weekend," I reply, trying to sound excited.

Because I am excited, considering.

"Barrett, my boss, put together a dinner for tonight in celebration of my landing the Christiansen account. It will be at a fancy restaurant, so make sure to pack an outfit like the one you wore to my dad's Will reading," I ramble.

"A party with your co-workers and having to dress up. I don't know about all of that, Ali," he says.

Luke sounds unsure, but I want him with me. Does he not want to come now? I need him here; I need to see him. I am not okay. I'm a wreck on the inside. I need to have him bring me back into that world I drift off to whenever we are together.

"What? You do not want to come here now?" I ask, almost ready to cry.

He starts laughing.

"Ali, I was being sarcastic. I will be there and dressed to a 'T'. You can count on it. All you needed to do was ask," he chuckles.

My heart drops into my lap. Maybe, I would have picked up on his sarcasm if Brady wouldn't have forced himself on me last night and ruined me. I'm glad Luke was only joking and will be accompanying me to the party tonight.

"Okay, good!! I cannot wait to see you," I say eagerly.

"I better get going to pack quick and head into work so I can leave here by noon," Luke states.

"Yes, you best!" I reply.

Finally, there is a light at the end of this very dark and horrifying tunnel. Luke is coming to save me, which he has been doing pretty much since we met.

"See you in a few hours, Turtle," he says in a low tone.

"See you soon!" I reply, melting in his sexy voice.

We end the call, and I lay back on my bed, staring at the ceiling. I have to tell Luke about Troy as soon as he gets here before he's told by someone else tonight. I am sure Troy will be coming with Brady. I can also bet that Troy won't have the slightest clue about what his best friend did to me. Brady will act all calm and collective, I know it. How could Brady do that to his best friend? He knows how Troy feels about me. Drunk or not, he had no right to pin me down and violate me, all because I wouldn't kiss him.

Maybe I should've kissed him, and if I would have, then perhaps he wouldn't have forced sex on me. Did I lead him on in some way last night to make him think I was interested in him, especially in a sexual way? I did stick up for him at dinner in front of his parents, saying he is handsome and that he can't help that every woman wants him. But I did not mean that I was also one of them.

"Can you french braid my—Ali, are you okay?" Ris asks as she walks into my room, wrapped in a towel.

I hear her muffled sounds and can see that she has entered my room, but I have disappeared into a world where I am scared, all alone, and feel as if I had a hand in what took place last night. I must have done or said something that made it happen, it's my fault. I triggered something in Brady, and he acted on it. To him, he thought it was okay. But there is no justification for his actions, he acted on his carnal and animal instincts, which should be relatively controllable when we call ourselves human beings.

"Ali?" Ris says, now sitting on my bed and shaking me.

I break free from the horrid bubble I am in, consumed by what-ifs and maybes regarding last night's events.

"Yeah?" I finally reply.

"What is going on? I've been trying to talk to you for like the last five minutes, and you were just staring off and completely frozen. Are you okay?" she says, sounding very concerned.

"Um... ya, I'm fine, just tired is. That's all," I say and sit up on the bed.

"Did something happen last night between you and Brady?" she asks sternly.

I cannot look at her without crying. I want to tell her, but I don't know where to start. I get up from my bed and walk over to my closet.

"Luke is coming today to stay here for the weekend," I say.

I try to change the subject, but my voice doesn't sound very convincing at all. I can hear Ris get up from my bed and walk toward me. She places her hand on my shoulder.

"Ali, did Brady do something to you?" she demands.

Knowing her, she's not going to let up. She wants answers; thus, she has ignored the news about Luke completely. She tuned out everything I said because she knows that something is wrong. We've known each other for so long, she can see right through me. I drop my head and let out a huge sigh; I begin to cry. Ris grabs my hand and holds me tightly. I turn into her and sob like a blubbering idiot on her chest for a solid ten minutes.

"Do you want to talk about it?" she asks sincerely.

I shake my head and continue to cry.

"You can talk to me about it when you're ready?" she says softly.

I squeeze her tightly.

"Thank you. Please, keep this between us." I reply, sniffling.

"I got you, girl. Always," Ris whispers and hugs me tighter, resting her chin on top of my head.

She could tell that something majorly wrong took place last night. Maybe, she suspects what happened, or perhaps Brady has done something like this before. However, Ris is no dummy and can tell when something is not kosher. If Brady was known for such atrocity, she would have warned me. But, since I had mentioned it was a business dinner, maybe she thought I would have been safe. Either way, it's not her fault, and I am glad she is with me right now.

chapter fifty-five

Ris and I pull into the parking lot at Facade. She did not want me to drive due to how upset I was this morning, plus we usually carpool to work anyway. I was silent the whole commute to work. Ris knows something happened between Brady and me last night, just not exactly what. She knows I am not ready to talk about it, so she refrained from saying anything in the car.

Ris holds my hand tight across the parking lot and into the building. She doesn't let go of me until we reach my office. Thankfully, Brady is not occupying his right now. She hugs me and says she is only across the room if I need her. I thank her and enter my office.

I sit down at my desk and begin going through the paperwork I set in the middle of it yesterday, but I can't seem to get focused at all. I'm trembling at the thought of seeing Brady for the first time since last night. I startle when I hear a deep voice, Brady's voice. Suddenly, a shiver runs down my spine.

"Good Morning, Ali," Brady says, sounding quite chipper.

I look up from my desk, scared for my life, but trying desperately not to show it.

"Good Morning, Brady," I reply, calmer than I thought I would sound.

He enters my office and hands me two folders then smiles his devious smile.

"You left these in my car," he smirks.

It's the Christiansen folders I had brought with me to our dinner last night that we never went over. I had completely forgotten about them until now. I take the folders from my desk and hold them up to my chest to cover myself.

"You look nice today," he says with a smug look on his face.

Brady's eyes scroll up and down my body, undressing me with his piercing stare. I feel gross and uncomfortable watching the way he is looking at me.

"Thanks," I say, not amused at all by his disgusting gesture or words over my attire.

He winks at me then leaves my office. I take a deep breath in and exhale out. That wasn't as awful as I thought it would be. I think I can handle the rest of the day until Luke gets here to protect me. My assistants and interns enter my office with their notes and messages, showing eagerness for their morning tasks. I quickly collect myself from Brady's brief encounter to focus on my job before the morning team meeting. I delegate duties out for the Christiansen account and a few smaller ones that are already underway.

Ris comes to my office to walk with me to the morning meeting. My assistants and interns exit to begin their tasks. Ris closes my door.

"How are you holding up?" she asks genuinely.

I am glad she's here; otherwise, I would be feeling more helpless.

"I'm good right now," I reply.

I adjust my shirt under my little suit jacket, and we head out of my office toward the conference room. I try not to look around for Brady and act like my usual self. I need to be cordial and professional, showing no signs of weakness at all toward him. I walk to the back of the conference room with Ris. I grab a water and granola bar, and she grabs a diet soda and a muffin, then we take our usual seats. I stare at the white legal pad on the table in front of me while Ris engages in conversation about what's happening tonight.

Brady walks in with one of the Project Managers who will be conducting our morning meeting. Barrett only does the afternoon one. Brady takes a seat next to me after grabbing his usual stupid protein fruit drink thing. Why is he sitting next to me? He always sits across from Ris. There is an empty seat over there, yet he chooses to sit next to me. I elbow Ris, who is still deep in conversation about the club she wants everyone to go to after the team dinner tonight. She sits up and notices Brady is sitting next to me.

"You okay?" she whispers in my ear.

I nod, even though I want to move to another seat but can't since they've all become occupied now. The meeting begins, starting with production stats and where the company is; as a whole. I try to control my breathing and ignore Brady's presence next to me. I try to pretend that he is not there at all, even though it is tough to do so. Brady is busy taking notes on the legal pad in front of him when the production stats and other information about Commercial is read.

The Project Manager starts to talk about each quadrant, of which Landscaping is first. Brady leans back in his seat, setting his pen down, and removes his hands from the conference table. He takes his hand closest to me under the table and places it on my thigh. Trying not to make it obvious, I grab hold of his hand then remove it from my thigh. He puts his hand back on my thigh, in the crook of my pants where I am crossing my legs, and my leg meets my groin area. I take a deep breath, exhaling in short spurts of air. I'm not able to remove his hand this time since everyone is looking at the person next to him talking about the latest landscape project. Brady slides his hand farther down in between my crossed thighs, resting his pinky finger against the crotch part of my pants.

I am becoming very uncomfortable and uneasy right now, trying my hardest to keep my composure. He starts to gently rub in circular motions over the part of my pants where my vagina is with his pinky. I clench my jaw and hold back my tears, then dig my fingernail as hard as I can into his hand. I hope my face is not turning red. I cannot believe that he is doing this to me right now and at work in front of over twenty people. I want to scream, but I do not want to cause a scene. I can see him out the corner of my eye, biting his lower lip, shifting himself in his seat as he watches me become distressed. I'm sure he thinks I'm enjoying this torture he has bestowed upon me. He has zero shame.

He gradually picks up the pace with his finger, and I fling myself to my feet. My chair flies back hard into the wall. I couldn't take it anymore. I look around the room, embarrassed, then calmly excuse myself and walk as fast as I can out of the conference room. I rush to the bathroom as tears follow heavily down my cheeks. Brady is making it unbearably tough to be here. He has robbed me of my pride, my self-confidence, and my self-esteem. He has stripped me bare. Every time I think of him, I get reminded of what happened. Now, this.

chapter fifty-six

I slide down the wall of the bathroom stall, crouching in a sitting position on the back of my calves in my nude heels. I am sobbing so hard into my hands that I've cupped them to my face. I hear the clacking of heels enter, and I try to soften my crying.

"Ali?" I hear Ris call out in a concerned tone.

She stops in front of my stall and knocks lightly.

"Ali, are you okay?" she asks sympathetically.

I remain silent.

"Please, open the door. I saw, you know, under the—" she begins to say before I cut her off.

"Ris, please, shhh!" I interrupt.

I open the door, slowly bringing my eyes to hers. She grabs hold of me tightly.

"What the fuck did he do to you?" She whispers with worry.

She seems quite distraught, seeing me so vulnerable. I shake my head as I am still not ready to tell her or talk to her about it. She holds me tighter in the bathroom stall, rubbing my back, and hushing me as I sob uncontrollably. She reaches down for some toilet paper without breaking our hug and hands it to me.

"Do you want me to take you home?" she asks.

"No."

I do not want to leave; I don't want Brady to win at any cost. I need to focus on my job and the Christiansen account. I have the rest of the day, and tonight, then I don't have to see him for a while. I collect myself some, and we leave the stall. We walk over to the mirror, Ris fixes my makeup, and I straighten up my clothes, then we depart from the bathroom. The meeting has ended, and the conference room is empty when we pass by it.

Ris grabs my hand and pulls me into the "mother's" room. It's a private room for breastfeeding mothers to pump, and it happens to be soundproof. She probably feels we can talk here without anyone hearing us, and we can get much-needed privacy, especially from Brady.

"Ali, please tell me what happened," Ris says, holding onto my upper arms.

I take a deep breath in and exhale before I tell her about what happened last night.

"Brady brought me to dinner at his parent's house," I begin.

Ris drops her arms to her sides and steps back, sitting on the arm of the chair.

"Brady was talking to someone on the phone and kept ignoring me when I tried to ask him where we were going. When we passed all the fine dining and casual dining places, I was quite confused about where he was taking me. We were supposed to talk about the Christiansen account over dinner, and that was it. I had no idea he was going to take me to his parents' place," I continue.

"It was a very nice dinner, a fancy nine-course meal. His parents started belittling him about his love life and how he likes to play around with women. I interrupted them by sticking up for him, as it wasn't proper dinner talk, you know."

Ris is nodding at me in agreement. I continue the story filling her in on every detail that I can remember. Everything is still so vivid and clear.

"After dinner, he took me on a tour of his parent's house and their backyard. The entire place is immaculate," I say.

"He kissed me, and I yelled at him for it. He claimed that he was caught up in the moment and all the wine we had at dinner. I said there wasn't a moment at all. He freaked out on me, saying that I wanted him to kiss me. I told I'm that I didn't."

"I kept asking myself time and time again, whether I led him on or not," I resume.

I can see the anger build up in Ris's face as she sits there, silent. I progress.

"He demanded that I kiss him, but I told him that I didn't want to. He grabbed me and tried kissing me again, but I moved away. I rushed back to his parent's house, and he came after me apologizing," I say as I stop and take a deep breath.

Replaying everything is so overwhelming that I need a breather.

Ris stands up, rubbing my arm and telling me it will be okay. She asks if there is more. I nod and continue.

"I made it to the door of the house, but he threw me up against it, holding my hands and face demanding that I kiss him. I end up slapping him, then he violently threw me to the ground, threatening me. Saying I would regret having done that," I tremble as I start to tear up.

It is so painful recalling it all, but relief sets in as I tell Ris.

"He carried me to the pool house and threw me on the floor inside. I tried to run from him, but he caught me. Throwing me back onto the floor," I sigh as a few tears release from my eyes.

I take a deep breath.

"He climbed on top of me and pulled my pants down. I tried to fight, but he was too strong. H-H-He," I manage to get out but lose it.

Ris brings her hand over her mouth, and a tear trickles down her cheek.

"He raped you," she says through exhaled breaths.

Ris is in shock and unable to control her tears. I look up at her, tears flowing down my cheeks as well, and I nod. She grabs me, pulling me into a hug, and we both cry hard.

"Ali, I'm so sorry. I'm so sorry that happened to you," she murmurs in my ear through her sobs.

We talked about how I took the morning after pill that night and that Brady should be clean. Ris mentioned that he sleeps with a lot of women, but he's always been cautious. She said they only had sex unprotected once or twice in the millions of times they've been together. She said she's heard of him forcing women to sleep with him but never anything to this extent. She also never expected that Brady would stoop so low.

She asks if I want to do anything about it, and I say no, because I don't want to jeopardize my job for this or cause any drama, and I'm sure it was most likely my fault. Ris assures me that what Brady did was wrong, and I didn't deserve it or what he did to me at the meeting. She says that no girl deserves to be raped. It's a crime. She tells me she saw his hand in between my legs under the table. She says she is a horrible friend for not making a scene and removing his hand herself. She wishes she would have done that, but she didn't know what to do.

She apologizes and hugs me, telling me how she wants to castrate Brady, then promises to keep quiet about everything. We fix each other's faces and head back to our offices. Ris holds tightly on to my hand the entire way. I am so glad she's by my side through his. Now, I wonder whether I should tell Luke or not.

chapter fifty-seven

The rest of the day goes by rather quickly, considering all the events from this morning. I feel a lot better after telling Ris what happened. I cried my heart out to her, and she comforted and cried with me. She's been working with me in my office on the Christiansen case. We did leave briefly for lunch with a few others to the cute little deli down the street. I did not have much of an appetite, only ordering a small side salad and a fruit smoothie, which I never finished.

There is only two hours left of the day, as Barrett canceled our afternoon meeting. He must be busy on a job or making plans for the celebration dinner tonight. Brady enters my office, and Ris stands up from her chair, acting like my bodyguard.

"What are you doing here?" he asks callously.

"We are working on details of the Christiansen project if you must know," Ris fires back at him.

"You can do that from your own office," he barks as he glares back at her.

He steps farther into my office and makes his way over toward me. I cannot stand him, even more so now. He needs to back the fuck off. Ris walks in front of him, and I get up from my chair. My assistant knocks on the frame of my open door, and we all look in her direction. Thank goodness she has broken the tension building in my office.

"Ms. Garrett, you have a visitor," she says gleefully.

A visitor? Behind her stands, Luke and I instantly light up with joy. He steps into my office looking at me, then to Ris and Brady. His smile is as perfect as I remember. He's wearing dark wash jeans, a tight white t-shirt, and his hair lays neatly up top his head. He looks smoking hot, as usual. I instantly melt.

"Hi!" I shout in excitement.

I walk out from behind my desk toward him, forgetting the intensity that was taking place in my office.

"Who are you?" Brady asks rudely, puffing up his chest.

"Ali's boyfriend!" Ris chimes in with pure attitude behind her voice.

I love Ris and her bluntness. Words can be sharper than actions. I look at Luke to see his reaction to the words that just spewed out of her mouth. His smile doesn't change one bit. He looks at me then turns to Brady, extending his hand out to him.

"Yeah! I'm Luke. Nice to meet you, and you are?" he says.

Luke looks Brady in the eye as he formally introduces himself while firmly shaking his hand. Brady better watch out as Luke will turn him into a cheese sandwich and eat him in one bite.

Yeah! Luke said, yeah, not denying Ris's claim calling him my boyfriend. Holy shit!! I smile.

"Brady, Brady Adams. Senior Designer," he boasts.

Luke is quite a bit taller than Brady, and their bodies look evenly bulk, but Luke makes him look small. Brady seems a little intimidated and slightly taken off his macho high horse. It is funny to see him not be the main attraction.

"Ris, you need to get back to your own office now," Brady snarls.

"It was nice meeting you," he says sharply to Luke.

Then he leaves my office. Ris sticks her tongue out behind Brady's back while flicking him off. Ris will be Ris, and I love her for it.

"Well, ain't he just a pocket full of sunshine and rainbows," Luke chuckles.

"Oh, you have no idea," Ris mumbles angrily.

"It's nice to see you," she says to Luke, giggling, then waves at me as she leaves my office.

Luke nods, then walks closer to me. I throw my arms around him, gripping him tight and resting my head against his chest. I'm so happy he is here; I take in his smell as we embrace, and he rests his chin against my head. I can see Brady staring at us from his office; I turn my head away and close my eyes.

"Oh my God, I'm so excited you are here!" I say in pure glee.

"Me too! This building is insane. So amazingly cool," he states.

I let go of him and check the clock on my desk, it's twenty after four.

"You made good time," I say with excitement.

"Yeah, I left a little earlier than planned. I wanted to see you. I messaged you when I left about ten-thirty or so," Luke replies.

"Sorry, we've been swamped, and I haven't had the time to check my phone at all," I say.

I haven't checked my phone in all the mess of today with how shook I've been until Luke showed up, and now it has all disappeared.

"No worries. I figured you were busy, and I enjoyed the look on your face when you saw me. That was enough for me. It was better as a surprise, anyway," he smirks.

"We've got time for a tour if you'd like one," I ask.

"Hell yeah! Let's do it!" he replies in excitement.

We stroll out of my office, hand in hand. I let my assistants know where I am going after I introduce them to Luke. It's rather amusing watching all the ladies drool over him and not Brady for a change. I grab Ris from her office to accompany us on the tour; she does a lot better job as a tour guide than I do. Showing Luke where I work and the fantastic architecture in this building will be a lot better than the earlier melodramatic experience he encountered.

chapter fifty-eight

Luke is doing exceptionally well with driving in the afternoon traffic in downtown Milwaukee. I forget that he is from San Diego, so he is used to the crazy driving and traffic jam scene. I did not miss it while I was back home. I like being able to go from point A to point B without having to stop a million times along the way. Since I am not behind the wheel, I'm content in this congestion in front of us, plus it gives me ample time to study more of his gorgeous face.

Luke kissed me as soon as we got to his car, I was worried I'd freeze at the gesture, but I didn't. The kiss was so heavenly, with a genuine and sincere passion behind it. The longer he is here; the more what Brady did to me last night fades away to the back of my mind. I also mustered up the courage to tell him about Troy almost as soon as we had left Facade.

He was surprisingly more understanding about it than I thought he'd be, well more understanding than I would be if the situation were reversed. I still have what Ris said floating around in my head when he first arrived, that he's my boyfriend, and Luke didn't deny it. I'm sure I am reading way too much into it, but a "yeah" is technically confirming it. Right? Why am I even contemplating the thought? He's here with me, and I am over the moon!

"Um... I'm sorry about Ris referring to you as my boyfriend today," I say.

I sink into my seat and clench my teeth together in a weird smile thing. I'm not sure what Luke is going say, more so after I told him about Troy. However, he did say it was Troy's loss and his gain. Luke looks at me with his dreamy eyes and gives me his gorgeous smile.

"It's fine. Don't worry about it, relax Turtle!" he replies.

It's fine? What does that mean? Do I continue with this conversation and ask him if he wants to be, or do I let it go? I don't want this to become awkward.

"What time is this dinner thing?" Luke inquires.

"Seventy-thirty. We should have enough time to change then will need to head back out again," I respond.

I tell him to take a left at the next set of lights, then a right a block down into the parking ramp. I love to stare at him; I'm a creeper, but I cannot help it. His forearms are sexy and flex slightly as he grips the steering wheel. The shirt he's wearing displays his abs and pectoral muscles, and you can see the ink from his tattoos through the white of his shirt against his skin.

His profile is impeccable, and his lips; ugh, every inch of him makes me want him. He is one man that God made with complete and utter perfection.

"Where should I park?" he asks, taking me away from analyzing his features.

"Next to my Mustang. Each occupant living here receives two parking spots," I answer.

"Well, that sucks. You wouldn't be able to have a plethora of vehicles!" he smirks.

"I know. They would have to go to a public parking ramp or something. Which would suck balls!" I whine.

Rethinking my choice in words knowing Luke will laugh at the words "suck" and "balls" coming out of my mouth. He probably thinks they aren't too womanly of me to say, but we get a good laugh out of it anyway. Luke grabs his bag from the backseat, and we gallivant toward my apartment. Ris's parents found us a super cute apartment. The rent is a bit steep, but we manage. I like it a lot. We are on the eighth floor of a historic store building.

"Which one are you?" Luke asks.

"C4," I reply.

I open the door to my apartment, and we step inside.

"Wow, this does not look like a little apartment to me at all!" he says in amazement.

"That's because the ceilings are fourteen feet tall," I respond.

Even I was surprised by it's instant appeal when I first moved in here. I give Luke a quick little tour before I start to get ready for the dinner. We walk down the hallway and into my room first. My room is the largest, and it connects to a bathroom that also doubles as the laundry room. Ris didn't like hearing the washer and dryer through the wall, so she took the smaller room across the hall. I find the sound rather soothing.

I tell Luke that Ris's room and bathroom are almost identical, except I have a bathtub/shower combo in mine and the laundry appliances. We walk farther down the hallway into the open floor plan that is our kitchen and dining room. Our living room is on a small loft off the dining area.

"Wow, the view here is—," he starts to say as I interrupt him.

"You should see it at night. It's something else!" I impede.

I leave him to the view of the city from the loft as I saunter to my room to get ready for the dinner party. I stop at Ris's room first to see if I can borrow a pair of her earrings and a necklace, but she's in the shower. I grab them anyway; hopefully, she won't mind. She has everything she is wearing, displayed across her unmade bed.

I make my way back to my room to work on my face. I decide on a subtle smoky eye with the sophistication and sass of my dress and elaborate eyeliner scheme as it makes my green eyes pop. I would have liked Ris to do my eyes, but I didn't do half bad.

I attempt some slight contouring, then finish with my lash-boosting mascara, some rouge, and a light pink lip gloss. I add a small wave to my hair and pin back one side. I put in a pair of small diamond earrings and a short diamond necklace that lays nicely an inch or so above my bust. I contemplate going braless as my dress has adjustable spaghetti straps and is quite tight, which hugs my girls perfectly.

I slip on a black lace thong, then grab my dress off the hanger from the back of my door. It's a little black number that reaches just above my knee on one side. The other side has a frilly ruffled leg flashing slit that travels up a good portion of my thigh. This dress screams class with a shit ton of sass. It's a tad out of my comfort zone, but Ris can be rather persuasive.

My black ankle strap, open toe pumps completes my outfit, complimenting it quite well. I leave my bathroom to make sure Luke is getting dressed. He looks up at me from adjusting his belt, back down to his pants, then quickly back at me again. His mouth drops open, and his eyes go wide.

"What? Do I look that bad?" I say in surprise at his reaction.

I look down at myself and run my hands over my dress. Then bring my eyes back to him.

"Hot damn, girl! You are killing it in that dress!" Ris shouts as she enters my room.

Luke points at Ris, not removing his eyes from me.

"What she said," he mutters in a deep voice.

"Ali, that dress looks smokin' fucking hot on you. It did well!" she boasts.

"I hope it's not too over the top and trashy," I question.

"Nope. It's, ugh," Luke stutters.

"It's fucking sexy as hell, girl!" Ris interrupts.

"And no, it's not trashy at all. Just chill out!"

I walk over to my full-length mirror. I look pretty good, and the slit fits the dress's overall concept, giving it an elegant but edgy appeal. I dig it. I turn to Luke, who is still gawking at me like a horned up teenage boy. He makes me bashful when he looks at me that way.

"How do I look, bitch?" Ris barks as she does a slow spin.

She doesn't need my nod of approval as she rocks every dress she wears. She is wearing a super short strapless black lace dress. It lays perfectly down her curves, and she has the boobs to hold it up. She has on the same shoes that I do, only silver, matching her dangly diamond earrings.

"You look stunning, Ris," I say.

She tromps out of my room after giving me her pressed lip smirk and eyebrow raise. Luke accompanies me to my bathroom for my final hair, makeup, and wardrobe check. His buttoned-up black shirt, medium gray dress pants, and black dress boots accent my outfit perfectly. I'm excited to go to this dinner with my handsome arm candy. Luke couldn't look anymore, suave.

chapter fifty-nine

Ris calls a town car for us. She hates Ubers because she thinks they're gross. I do not see a difference between riding in someone's vehicle that is an Uber vs. riding in a town car; it's a stranger driving an unfamiliar vehicle. She will end up in an Uber tonight regardless, as the clubs don't close until two in the morning, and town cars only run until midnight.

Luke is in front with the driver while Ris and I are in the back seat. We all could've fit back here, but it would have been a bit tight. Ris hands me a few bracelets from her clutch. One is almost like a cuff, it's so thick. I give her a weird look wondering why she is handing these to me. She points at the bruises on my arms that I received last night from Brady. I hope Luke hasn't noticed them. I wore a long-sleeved shirt today so no one would see my arms. I smile at Ris and mouth "thank you" to her. She blows me a kiss, and winks at me, then butts into the conversation that our driver and Luke are having.

I slide the single thin brackets, about eight of them, on one wrist. They shimmy down my arm due to their size and cover my bruises. The cuff fits snug on my other arm, where the largest and darkest bruises are resting. I had put what happened with Brady in the back of my mind when Luke got here, and I haven't thought about it or Brady since.

I hope dinner isn't awkward, and he doesn't try something funny like he did today at the morning meeting. I'm becoming apprehensive thinking about seeing him tonight. I pray Brady behaves himself and Ris doesn't get drunk and cause a scene. I wonder if he is bringing Troy to dinner with him. Troy is his wingman. He told me that Brady never brings a girl with him because it's a huge cock block. Therefore, he brings Troy to help him land the ladies.

Brady makes my skin crawl and thinking about him makes me feel like I need to take a shower. I wish Luke were back here next to me; my thoughts of Brady would disappear. It's still fresh in my mind, but I am trying my best to distract myself from it. Although, I do like seeing Luke's profile and gorgeous teeth while he talks and laughs from back here.

The driver slows down and pulls up in front of the restaurant. It's seven twenty-eight, we made it on time. He gets out of his vehicle to open our doors. He opens my door, and Luke opens Ris's. I thank our driver then walk around behind the car to Luke and Ris. Luke grabs hold of my hand and kisses me on my forehead.

"That's an awesome name for a steakhouse!" Luke chuckles as he looks at the building.

We are at the *Carnivor Steakhouse Moderne.* It is one of the finest steakhouses in Milwaukee. I have only eaten here once before, but the atmosphere and food are quite exquisite. It is said to be Wisconsin's most acclaimed fine-dining destination and consistently tops the year-end "Best Of" list. The building itself is an architect's dream, and the structure and overall concept is captivating.

We enter the steakhouse, and the hostess greets us. Ris tells her we are part of the Facade party and we follow the hostess to the *Raptor Room.* I take in the amazing interior design, lighting, and overall layout of the restaurant that I do not pay attention to all the people from work already here. That is until Ris's loud, obnoxious voice echoes throughout the building.

A few people are already sitting in our private dining area, but most are gathered around the bar that sits off the opening to the room, socializing with a drink in hand. It's always fun to see coworkers outside of a professional work setting. Of course, Barrett is not here yet, he's always the last one to show up. Brady walks up to us, and sure enough, Troy is right behind him.

"Good to see you again and Ali," Brady says.

He shakes Luke's hand then nods at me while looking at me up and down.

"You as well," Luke replies.

If only Luke knew what Brady did to me, he would never be so kind. I am still torn as to whether I want to tell him or not. Although I'm sure if he knew there would be an exchange of words right now or even some fists. Spoiling Barret's party in my team's and my honor is not part of the plan.

"I'm Troy, nice to meet you," Troy says as he shakes Luke's hand.

"Nice to meet you too, I'm—" Luke starts to say before Brady rudely interrupts him.

"Ali's boyfriend. Luke, right?" he says ruthlessly while giving me a sly glare and a wink.

I can see he's going to be an abhorrent prick tonight. Luke is being a gentleman and not feeding into Brady's crudeness. The look on Troy's face when he hears the words "Ali's boyfriend" is heart-breaking to see but not as hard as the look that he gives me next. I look at him with the biggest "I'm sorry" eyes that I have. I didn't want him to find out about Luke and me this way. Fucking Brady.

I am glad that Luke already knows about Troy and me. He doesn't seem to be bothered by having met him or that he is here, which is excellent. He has pulled me tighter to him, though.

"Can I get you two a drink?" Brady asks connivingly.

Why can't he leave me, better yet, us alone! Luke looks down at me; I smile up at him as I bring my hand over our hands that are interlocked.

"Sure, I will have a beer, and she'll have a-" Luke answers but is again interrupted by Brady's smug remark.

"I know what she likes," he replies curtly.

I roll my eyes and turn away from Brady and Troy, skimming the room for Ris. She is toward the back of the dining room near the windows, chatting with the ladies from work. That is when I see Barrett and his wife walking past. Luke hands me my drink that Brady bought; it's white wine, how ironic of him, I bet he roofied it too.

chapter sixty

The room's acoustics become louder as Barrett and his wife enter, everyone follows them from the bar into the dining room. We all take our seats as Barrett stands in the middle of the room. Brady and Troy sit at a table across from us, both looking at me, but with a different look in their eyes. It's very uncomfortable, to say the least because I know the meaning behind both.

"Thank you, everyone, for coming out tonight to celebrate one of the largest accounts that our firm has had the pleasure of landing. Our Commercial division is the heart and foundation of this company. All of you here tonight are the reason for our success, and each of you is greatly appreciated," Barrett says as he looks around the room of over twenty people.

"Ali, will you please, stand," he asks, putting me on the spot.

I look at Luke, smile, and stand from my seat. Ris grabs my hand.

"Ali has been with Facade for four years now. She came to us as an intern in college. We immediately saw her potential and knew that we had to keep her. Upon her college graduation, we offered her a Designer position, which she has taken to heart and has worked hard to fulfill. It's been four amazing years. You are truly an asset to Façade!" Barrett begins to say.

I'm starting to tear up from the kind words that he is saying about me. I love working for Facade and him. I can't imagine being anywhere else. Leaders like him are one in a million. He is an inspiration to me.

"We, at Façade, want to thank her for putting all her projects and clients first, making them feel important and that they matter, which they do. She builds strong relationships with every client, allowing them to place their trust in her and trust in us. We gain loyal customers and build a positive repetiteur. Tonight's celebration is not only to congratulate her on this account but also her achievements of the past four years," Barrett continues.

Everyone in the room begins to applaud. I smile and say "thank you" to Barrett. I feel very honored by his compliments, which are very genuine and sincere.

"I would like to say one more thing before we dive into the delicious meal planned for us tonight, as I can see, some of you look very famished. We have decided to promote Ali to Co-Senior Designer of Commercial alongside Brady Adams. Congratulations Ali! You deserve it! Keep doing what you do, and you'll go very far with us!" Barrett finishes.

My mouth drops wide open, and I cup my hands over it. I cannot believe my ears. This promotion was unexpected; I'm speechless. Looking around the room as everyone is standing and clapping for me is astonishing. Luke is here with me, making the entire moment and evening more special. Even Brady is clapping, he doesn't look too enthused but is standing and applauding. He has to do it reluctantly to come across as a team player. I turn to Ris, who is jumping up and down screaming. We embrace each other tightly. I look at Luke, he hugs me and kisses me firmly on the lips.

"Congratulations, beautiful. You deserve it. We need to have a special celebration tonight of our own if you know what I mean," he says all smiles and gives me a cute wink.

I know what he is hinting toward; however, I don't know if I am ready to engage in anything sexual with him right now. I want to, but I am not sure if I can stomach it or if I am ready to explain my bruises. I'm also not quite sure if he's truly happy for me or just pretending like he is. He's hard to read right now.

I need to focus on what Barrett just said and not worry about what may or may not happen tonight with Luke. Promoted to Senior Designer in only two years is impressive. I wish my dad were here to celebrate with me. He'd be so proud.

I'm so happy and excited, all tingly and jittery. I've been working hard to one day hit this level with the company. It took Brady over five years to reach it. Barrett hugs me then heads to his seat.

Before he sits, he says, "Enjoy your meal this evening and the endless wine!"

Bottles of white and red wine are placed respectively on each table as wait staff begin to take our soup or salad preference. They also ask if we'd prefer steak or fish as our main entrée. I choose a salad and salmon; Luke chooses a salad and filet mignon. He places his hand on my bare thigh, just under the slit of dress. I'm a little startled but welcoming of its presence. He tucks his hand farther down the inside of my thigh between my crossed legs. I look at him with a smile, and he smiles his dreamy smile back at me. I feel safe with him.

Everyone nearby our table personally congratulates me on my promotion. I'm still on a high from hearing it come from Barrett's lips. I'm glad he and his wife are at the table next to us, and thus, I was able to introduce Luke to them. I think they will hit it off well once we can socialize again after our meal. Luke fits in exceptionally well for his first corporate dinner.

After I finish my glass of wine, Luke pours me another glass as our salads arrive. I love Caesar salads, and the one here is delicious. It has Wisconsin's own parmesan cheese topped on it. We are very proud of our cheese.

Once our salad plates are taken, it does not seem too long until our entrées arrive. They are exquisite in their presentation. I almost don't want to eat mine because the plate looks so perfect. I take a bite of my caramelized brussel sprouts, an instant mouth-watering sensation, and it's only one of my sides. Luke's filet mignon looks scrumptious, with the exotic mushrooms and grilled onions draped across the top. I feel like devouring his steak too.

"Can I try a bite of your steak?" I ask Luke as I eye up the hunk of meat on this plate.

"Only if I can have a taste of your salmon," he smiles and winks.

"But of course," I say.

I bring a fork full of salmon to Luke's mouth, and he brings one full of steak to mine. Mmm. This steak is phenomenal; melts in your mouth.

"It's almost as good as yours," I fib.

I am talking with a mouth full like the classy lady that I am. Luke laughs, wiping the corner of my mouth with his thumb, then kisses me. I'm falling head over heels for this man. I felt I was before, but now I know it. The more time I spend with him, the more I feel myself. He casts some spell over me when he is near me.

AFTER WE FINISH OUR MEALS, WE ARE PRESENTED WITH A delightful strawberry-almond cheesecake. I do not know how much more room I have, but it's cheesecake, you can always make room. I can feel the warmth of my body as I start to drink my third glass of wine. I'm becoming a little buzzed. The buzz and being drunk from wine are a lot different than the ones from liquor or beer. I feel like I get classy drunk off wine and make wiser idiotic choices. It sounds ridiculous saying it in my head. Let's have another glass, Ali!.

Luke and I walk up to Barrett and his wife; she asks if I would accompany her to the ladies' room. I accept her invite and leave Luke to get acquainted with my boss. I follow Barrett's wife, Mandy, who is stopped many times on the way by people talking to her. She is so sweet and soft-spoken. She is a fine lady, and she truly inspires me.

We finally make it to the ladies' room.

"Ali, I'm so proud of you. Congratulations again on your hard work and promotion," she says sweetly.

She hugs me before stepping into the stall. I thank her and pee quickly, then check myself over in the mirror. I'm quite flushed, so the wine is kicking in. Mandy steps out from her stall.

"I love that dress you're wearing tonight," I say to her.

"Thank you, Ali. Yours is stunning on you. Though you always look beautiful," she replies with her kind eyes.

That compliment meant a lot coming from such a genuinely classy lady. I'm glad my dress doesn't come off trashy.

"Thank you!" I blush.

"Your boyfriend seems very charming," she adds to our conversation.

"Yes, he is," I reply.

I am so glad Luke has hit it off so well tonight and made an excellent impression on everyone who has met him. She continues asking me about how we met and so on as we make our way back to Barrett and Luke. I see Troy walking toward us, and I excuse myself to speak with him.

"I'm sorry you had to find out this way. I wanted to tell you in person, but Brady beat me to it," I say to Troy with sad eyes.

He deserves an explanation, so I hope he takes it well. Troy keeps walking, not acknowledging me at all. I watch as he passes, then I turn to walk away.

"How long?" he asks sternly.

I turn back to him.

"How long what?" I asked, confused.

"Have you and him been dating?" he replies with disappointment and sadness in his eyes.

I feel bad and ashamed, but we were never really a couple.

"Before or after you told me that you weren't interested in dating anyone?" he asks as he looks me in the eye.

"After," I reply and look at the floor.

He sighs then walks away. I watch him for a bit before I head back to Luke. I feel awful that I hurt Troy; he's so sweet and such a gentleman. I never had that spark with him as I do with Luke.

Barrett and Luke are talking about classic cars when I return. I finish my third glass of wine when Barrett and Mandy excuse themselves for the evening and say their goodbyes to everyone before leaving. Others begin to vacate and those still wanting to stay out gather around Ris, Luke, and I.

It's quarter to eleven. Luke has his arm wrapped around me, and he is swaying a little. I've only seen him have three beers and a glass of wine with his meal. I'm sure he's not quite buzzing yet, well not even close to the way I am.

"Let's go to *Site 1A* then *Lucid,"* Ris shouts.

She loves to party, dance, and get her to drink on. She's a total party animal, and I can tell she is a little buzzed. I ask Luke what he wants to do, and he says that he doesn't care. I told him I don't either, so we decide to go with Ris and the others. I will be leaving Milwaukee soon, Ris and I may not see each other for a few months, so it's a good idea to accompany her wild ass.

chapter sixty-one

We arrive at the Lucid Light Lounge, instead of going to Site 1A first. Lucid happens to be one of the hottest night clubs in Milwaukee. It has been known to have national celebrities make an appearance to enjoy the crazy nightlife. Ris's intern is here with her friends for a Bachelorette party, and they have a VIP Suite. The line is super long to get in, but Ris knows the bouncer at the door so, we won't have to wait.

The rest of our group piles out of an Uber and joins us at the door. Altogether, we have about six people from Facade, well four who work there, and Luke and another Designer's boyfriend. The look on Luke's face seems like he's not too excited to go inside, but I'm ready to dance from how buzzed I am right now.

Ris is her usual party animal self with her short, tight dress and loud, obnoxious voice. We finally get the go-ahead to enter the club. I feel kind of bad that we cut in from of all these people. I'm sure some have been waiting for an hour or so to get in. We all follow Ris upstairs to the VIP section, through the crowd of sweaty drunk people dancing their hearts out.

There are nine VIP sections, and Ris's intern has one of the larger sized ones. As we reach the VIP suite, I notice a very familiar face, it's Brady, and he's macking on her intern. Of course, he's here; he has a thing for interns at Facade. He went after Ris the first time when she was one. If I wasn't already buzzed, I'd tell Luke that I want to leave. Maybe it is a bad idea to be here since Brady is here, but I cannot let him ruin everything for me.

Ris's intern introduces us to her friends and vice versa. We order a round of shots and a few bottles of booze for the suite. Luke and I sit down on the bench; the lighting in our suite is going crazy to the music.

Our shots arrive; we all grab one and make a toast to the girl getting married and my promotion. Brady glares at me then walks off with some chick. Ris takes off with a group of people to go dancing. I sit back and stare at Luke, who is chatting with the dude next to him.

I can feel the shot of straight patron kicking in. I went from a good buzz to drunk in a snap of my finger. I get super giggly when I'm drunk. Luke's never seen me this drunk, and I've never seen him drunk. I'm sure he's buzzing now too after that shot. Luke has his arm around me, and I can't stop staring at him, he's so god damn good looking. I lean in toward him and lick his face, interrupting his conversation. He smiles and grabs me, then we kiss—a passionate kiss on his end, a playful one on mine.

He runs his hand up my thigh under the slit of my dress. I curl my lip and let out a sigh in his mouth. He rubs his hand over my panties, and I instantly become aroused. I want him to fuck me right now and hard. I wish we were back at my apartment, but right now, any place will do—even a swanky nightclub. I grab him through his pants and push myself against him as I massage his tongue aggressively with mine. I'm losing control.

"Settle down, Turtle, we're in public," he whispers in my ear.

"So—," I whisper back at him.

My co-worker, Jade, breaks up my steamy make-out and grope session with Luke to ask if I'd escort her to the ladies' room. I adjust myself, give Luke another kiss, then leave him with her boyfriend, who he seems to get along with quite well. I like that the VIP section has its own restroom, and it's close to our suite—I don't have to stumble too far.

I close the stall behind me, not wanting to break the seal but hover

over the toilet and pee anyways. I can hear moans and groans coming from the stall next to me. Drunk and nosey, I grab my hair in one hand and bend down, looking under the stall. Not to my surprise, I see a pair of high heels facing the toilet and a pair of men's dress shoes facing the same direction behind them. There's nothing like getting fucked in the VIP bathroom at a nightclub. That should be Luke and me right now, I tell myself. I giggle and walk out from the stall over to the sinks.

"I think there are people having sex in here," Jade whispers to me.

I laugh and agree with her, then wash my hands. As I am fixing my hair, the stall of the two people who were fucking opens and out stumbles Brady. He unsteadily rests himself on the door of the stall as one of the girls from the Bachelorette party walks out under his arm, pulling her dress down. He smacks her ass as she makes her way over to look at herself in the mirror next to me.

Jade looks at Brady with wide eyes then to me. She turns to the mirror to apply some lipstick. I freeze, hoping if I don't move, he won't see me as if he's an intoxicated T-Rex. Brady, however, spots me and makes his way toward me. He stops in front of me and raises his finger at me.

"How the fuck do you rate so high to receive a promotion?" he spits as he sways back and forth.

"Your mouth must have some magical sucking powers to have Barrett give you my position."

Not amused by his asinine comment and feeling invincible, I slap him hard for what he just insinuated.

"Fuck you, Brady! I deserve this promotion, and I didn't take your position, we're Co's. That means we have the same position. Now, get the fuck out of my face," I shout back at him.

He grabs the wrist of my hand I slapped him with, and I'm instantly reminded of the night at his parent's house. Fear begins to course throughout my body. I look out of the corner of my eye at Jade, who is watching everything unfold. Oh, my God! Not again. Why did I slap him? I know what it does to him.

"The fuck you do. I am the one who helped you get to where you are today. Without me, you'd be nothing. F-U-C-K-I-N-G- N-O-T-H-I-N-G!" he spews within inches of my face.

I turn my face away from his and tell him to leave me alone. He then grabs my neck as he slams me up against the bathroom wall, pushing his weight against me. I hear Jade gasp.

"You know I'm right, Ali," he growls.

"Get off me, Brady!" I shout.

His weight is way too much for me. I can feel tears well up in the corner of my eyes. I try to knee him and push him off me, but I can't. He puts more of his weight against me and kisses my neck. I am entirely trapped by him again.

"You're just jealous that I wasn't fucking your brains out in that stall. You fucking loved it when I pounded your tight little pussy the other night," he whispers through his teeth in my ear.

"Jade. JADE! Help me. SOMEONE! ANYONE!" I scream, but it seems like it's only a whisper.

"Shut the fuck up! You know you want me. Stop pretending you don't. Every girl wants a piece of this," he snarls as he covers my mouth and runs his tongue up my neck.

Brady is ripped from me and falls hard to the floor. My eyes blurry from my tears that I can barely see what's happening. Jade grabs me and walks me away from where Brady is lying on the floor; someone hovered over him. My eyes adjust, and I watch Luke's elbow cock-back numerous times as he strikes Brady in the face.

chapter sixty-two

The VIP restroom floods with people, onlookers, our group that we came with, and the nightclub staff. Luke is pulled from Brady, and his fist is dripping with blood. Brady looks to be unconscious and is hardly recognizable under all the blood covering his neck and face. His shirt, hair, and the floor are full of blood as well.

Ris grabs hold of me, asking if I'm okay, begging for me to tell her what happened in the restroom. I'm in shock at all the blood surrounding Brady and the crazed look on Luke's face as he tries to break free from the two bouncers trying to restrain him, that I can barely hear her. Everything feels like it's in slow motion.

The police arrive as Jade leaves my side to talk to them. I'm not exactly sure how much she witnessed or heard. Ris is still holding on to me tightly. I look at Luke; he is starting to settle down some now that the police are here. He is yelling at them to let him go so he can see if I'm okay. I am so glad he came to my rescue; I don't know what Brady would've done to me if he hadn't.

I leave Ris, and she grabs my arm, but I move it away from her and keep walking over to Luke. I push one of the police officers out of my way and wrap my arms around Luke's waist, burying my face into his chest. He jerks his arms from the police and wraps them around me, resting his cheek on top of my head. I start sobbing.

"Ali, are you okay? Did he hurt you?" Luke questions.

He grabs the sides of my face, but I hold onto him tighter and cry harder. I want him close to me right now. The paramedics carry Brady out on a stretcher. He's come to and has an ice pack over half of his face. His nose looks broken, and he seems to be missing a tooth. Luke did quite a number on him. I can't say that he didn't deserve it.

The police ask me to sit down and tell them exactly what happened. They say they received a statement from a witness already but wanted one from me since I was part of what just took place. Luke holds me tightly, his arm still wrapped around me. I can see the swelling of his hand with some bruising and blood. Ris is next to me, holding my hand. I decide to sit down and begin to tell them what happened.

They ask if this was our first altercation or if there's been more. Ris squeezes my hand tight and stares at me. I know I should tell them about what happened at his parents' house and this morning at work, but I decide not to. I tell them no, and this is the first time. Ris starts to rub my arm with her other hand.

"Are these bruises from tonight?" one of the officers asks looking at my arm.

I move the bracelets to cover them and lie while nodding yes. I begin to cry again and turn to Ris. She hugs me, while Luke rubs my back.

"He was assaulting you in the women's restroom when your boyfriend came along and stopped it, am I right?" the officer asks.

"That's what she just fucking told you," Ris barks rudely.

"We will need to take him down to the station," the officer resumes.

"He was stopping someone from fucking assaulting her. Why do you need to take him?" Ris yells.

"He saved her from being harmed worse or even raped by that dirtbag. The person who should be charged with anything is that fucking douche bag, Brady. You should take him off the stretcher and lock him up. He's a piece of shit," she shouts as she stands to her feet.

Irate, Ris calls her dad, who is one of the top attorney's in Milwaukee. The police leave us to converse amongst each other as the paramedics check over the bruises on my arms, neck, and back.

RIS'S DAD ARRIVES AND THREATENS THE POLICE. WE ARE all released to him, including Luke. I hug Jade and thank her before we leave with Mr. O'Conner. Luke holds me close as Ris's dad gives us a ride back to our apartment. Ris fills him in on what happened on the way. He tells her it's too late to discuss further details, and he will see us in the morning for breakfast at his house. Mr. O'Connor tells me that he is glad that I am okay and shakes Luke's hand, thanking him for protecting me. I thank him for the ride and also for helping us before leaving his car. Ris stays back to speak with her dad.

Luke and I scurry into my apartment building, up to my floor, and straight to my room. We walk into my bathroom. I ask Luke to remove his blood-stained shirt. I grab a washcloth so I can clean the blood from his swollen hand. He looks at me and tucks my hair behind my ear, then kisses me.

"Let's take a shower," he says politely.

I put the blood-soaked cloth in the sink, walk to the shower, and turn it on. I look back at Luke, who is naked. His perfectly sculpted body is displayed in front of me. I run my hands up his body from his waist, feeling the rippling of his abs under my touch. He places his fingers in mine, bringing my hands up to his face, then kisses the bruises on my wrists and arms. He cups his hands behind my head and kisses me softly.

I release a few tears and open my mouth, inviting in his tongue. He wipes my tears with his thumbs. He slowly moves his hands down my neck to my shoulders, sliding his fingers under the straps of my dress and sliding them down my arms. He runs his hands down my body to the bottom of my dress, grabbing hold of it and pulling it gently up and over my head, tossing it the floor. He tenderly kisses my shoulder, my neck, then my chin as he runs his fingertips up my arms. Then brings his lips back to mine, running his fingers down my chest, and lightly caresses my breasts.

Luke breaks free from our kiss, traveling down my body with his gentle and soft kisses. I break out in goosebumps, and my body begins to tingle. He slides his fingers underneath my thong and pulls it down my hips as he kisses my stomach. My goosebumps heighten, and I feel apprehensive yet safe. I step out of my panties as Luke makes his way back up toward my face. He cups his hands behind my head and passionately kisses me again. He walks us to the shower. As I stand in front of him under the pelting hot water, he soaps up my entire body. He grabs hold of my hair and tucking it over my shoulder as he gently scrubs my back. I'm so relaxed and content right now while he pampers me.

chapter sixty-three

Luke wraps me in a towel, picks me up, and carries me from my bathroom into my bedroom, then lays me down on my bed. He climbs on top of me, opens my towel, and rests himself on his forearms as he cups my cheeks with his soft hands. We look deeply into each other's eyes while he runs his thumb gently across my cheek. I love it when he does that. I close my eyes and feel his touch. His presence here with me makes me feel very secure and at ease.

He gently rubs his thumb across my lips then slowly moves his hand down my chin then down my neck. He continues down to my chest, running his hand over my heart. It's almost as if he has my soul in his hand then kisses my chest just over my heart. He lifts his hand from my chest, bringing it back to my face, and I feel like I'm floating. It's like he has lifted my whole body from the bed, and we are floating, our souls making love above our bodies.

I open my eyes when he tucks my hair behind my ear.

"May I make love to you?" he whispers softly.

A little hesitant, but I am caught up in the moment and still a little under the influence- I permit him. Luke separates my legs with his knee, gently rubbing my clit with his thumb as he passionately massages my tongue with his own. I lift my hands from my bed and slowly run them up the sides of his body. I can feel his skin begin to rise with goosebumps. He amiably inserts his finger inside me. I gasp slightly at the light pressure it brings and grab his wrist. He stops kissing me, halting the insertion, then looks at me with concern.

"Do you want me to stop?" he whispers.

I let a single tear fall. I don't want to falter. I want him to make love to me, so I let go of his wrist; he then continues ever so slowly, moving his finger in and out of me. I close my eyes as I enjoy his soft touch. I can feel myself become wetter from his leisurely swipes inside of me. He removes his finger and kisses me softly. Then he grabs hold of his penis and guides himself inside me. I gasp again, at the intense pressure from his size. He slowly continues sliding farther into me, never releasing his stare from my eyes. Once he is inside me, he brings his hands back to my cheeks.

He moves back and forth gradually, letting out a soft moan and closes his eyes. I run my hand through his hair, and he opens his eyes, looking into mine again. I take a deep breath in and let it out slowly as he continues making love to me. I begin to tingle, intensely, even throughout my face.

Our passion right now and the fact he's making love to me is phenomenal. I could float into the sky or orgasm at any moment. I open my legs wider and bring my legs up the sides of his body. He slides deeper in, keeping his moderately slow pace, and the pressure builds again but feels unbelievably amazing. Luke closes his eyes and passionately kisses me. I open my mouth and slide my tongue into his. I deepen our kiss as he begins moving inside me at a slightly faster pace. He groans deeply into my mouth. Luke has such a healing touch!

I moan and can feel my vagina tighten around the thickness of his cock as I begin to orgasm. He breathes out of his nose and slowly whispers, "I love you" in my mouth. He then tenses his body as he releases inside me. I relax my legs while Luke rests his head on my chest, with his penis still inside me. I open my eyes and look up at the ceiling. Did he just tell me he loves me?

After catching his breath, he lifts his head and looks deeply into my eyes as he runs his thumb over my cheek and under my eye, wiping away a single tear. He kisses me then says in such a sweet and charming voice,

"I'm sorry."

"For what?" I whisper.

Why is he apologizing? I should be doing that and thanking him too, considering he got into a fight because of me at the nightclub.

"Making you cry then coming inside you," he whispers back, still locked on my eyes.

I look deeply into his eyes as another tear slips out. I stare at him for a few seconds—silent.

"That was incredible," I release softly.

I want to cry happy tears. Luke smiles, kisses my nose, and my forehead. He removes himself from inside of me, rolls off to the side, then tucks me inside his body, wrapping his arms around me firmly. I nestle into his bicep, comforted, and protected. I drift off to sleep.

chapter sixty-four

I can feel all of Brady's weight on top of me; I try to thrash my arms and legs to move the slightest bit under his heated bulky physique, but I'm completely frozen. Pure panic washes over my entire body as I am afraid for my life.

"What are you going to do?" I call out in terror.

I can feel the warmth of his breath on the back of my neck as he brings his head closer to mine, and the additional weight from his body crushes me. It's hard to breathe.

"You'll see," he blusters through his teeth.

He shifts his weight again, removing most of it from my body as he rips my pants down over my hips. I want to fight, I need to fight, and I need to break free. I can feel the weight of his body return to mine. I'm unable to move in the slightest bit, and all I can do is scream.

"Brady, stop, please, NO!" I scream at the top of my lungs.

I jolt awake as Luke calls out my name. I look into his concerned eyes as he hovers over me in my bed. I let a single tear tumble down my cheek as flashbacks flood my mind from that unfortunate and painful night with Brady, when he-

"That asshole scared you last night, didn't he?" Luke asks in an angry yet compassionate tone.

I want to tell him that last night at the club wasn't even the icing on the cake. I want to tell Luke that Brady already hurt me before that. I want to tell him that I'm afraid of Brady and he won't stop harassing me since that night at his parent's house. I want to leave and go back to my dad's; no one can hurt me there.

I don't know why Brady is doing this to me. He's always been a pretentious asshole, but he's going above and beyond that persona. I want to speak, but nothing will come out. I don't' know what to say to Luke or how I would say it to him if I were to conjure up the words. I turn away from Luke and lay my head back on my pillow, scooting my naked body back inside his. Luke tucks my hair behind my ear, runs his fingers up and down my arm, then kisses the back of my head. I stare at the wall.

One part of me thinks it's some sick vendetta of Brady's to get me to crack under his disgusting game and give him full control of the Christiansen account, while the other part of me thinks that he is simply this demented and needs some serious help. Whatever his evil plan is, I will never let him sabotage my hard work at Facade. I've built a good rapport for myself; I have established great interpersonal relationships that have opened several doors for me. Brady is just jealous of that and how many new and returning clients go over him to come to me.

Because of his distasteful attitude, arrogance, and lack of people skills, he is falling short. I need to stay strong and stand my ground. I cannot let him break me. I'm stronger than him, and I will fight my way to the top. Nothing can stop me. I've worked way too hard for someone like Brady to take it all away from me. I will succeed, and I will triumph.

Luke grabs hold of my hand, and I'm released from my "*This is Sparta*" clouded bubble. I watch his hand as it interlocks into mine. It's swollen and very bruised. His blood-stained knuckles remind me of what I witnessed him do to Brady's face last night. It's something I can envision he did to his ex-girlfriend's brother when he saw his house engulfed in flames knowing his mother was inside. I can only imagine what he would do to Brady if he were to find out about what he did to me before last night.

I'm worried about what might happen to Luke if Brady decides to press charges. He went to prison the last time he was in a fight and had beaten the guy to a bloody pulp. Brady deserved every second of it, as did that guy who burnt Luke's house down and badly hurt his mother. The justice system doesn't work that way; unfortunately, you cannot defend another's life without receiving consequences.

Do I report how Brady forced himself on me and how he fondled me inappropriately at work yesterday morning to save Luke from another prison sentence? I have no proof that what happened at his parents even took place, other than the bruises on my arms that I lied about and said happened during the club incident. I don't know what to do. All I do know is that I do not want Luke to go to jail again because of me. He was only protecting me.

"Ali, will you, would you, officially be my girlfriend?" Luke stammers in an almost shy way.

My anxiety and stress over the issues that have assembled over the past few days is instantly lifted. I look over my shoulder at Luke. His dreamy eyes and gorgeous lips stare motionless in front of me.

"Yes. I would love to be your girlfriend," I reply with a ginormous smile.

Luke pulls me close to him and kisses me. It's a short but sweet kiss.

"You're so beautiful, Ali," he whispers as he runs his thumb over my bottom lip.

Luke gently crawls on top of me while never breaking his stare. At this very moment, time feels as if it has slowed down, and Luke and I are the only two people alive on the planet. No one else and nothing else matters right now, just us. The way he looks at me brings me to another world; I can forget everything bad happening in my life and be carefree.

He runs his thumbs over my eyebrows, down the sides of my face, across my cheeks and lips, as he holds himself up with his forearms. The rest of his body is lying snug between my thighs. I can feel his flaccid penis against my stomach. I am so hungry for him, but at the same time, I'm content at the very moment we have encountered. It's a sweet, sensual, and special moment that I want to engulf myself in.

I am so consumed by him, by us, and how flawlessly we fit. We are absorbed by one another, and it's very enchanting. I feel like my life has been given back to me, like I'm coming home, into my own body. He unravels all my insecurities and makes me more confident in myself than ever before. I feel so safe with him. I surrender deeply and melt into nothingness.

chapter sixty-five

"Ali, are you guys decent?" Ris calls out as she knocks and slowly opens my bedroom door.

Luke rolls off me as Ris comes into view. I pull the covers up over my chest. It's not like Ris hasn't seen me nude before, but both Luke and I are naked. So it feels a bit awkward.

"Sorry to interrupt you guys, but my dad just called and would like us to head over to his house soon," she states.

"Okay, we will shower quickly and get ready," I reply.

Ris smiles and leaves my room. I wonder if she only filled her father in on what happened last night or if she told him more. I'm not sure how long she stayed with her dad after Luke and I came inside the apartment. I hope Mr. O'Connor can help us keep Luke out of serious trouble.

Luke and I shower, and I try not to think dirty thoughts while we are here, since we need to make it quick. Ris's father is not going to wait around all day for us. We get dressed without any funny business besides, well, some minor distractions, but we still manage to make it out of my room in just under a half-hour.

We head out of the apartment and pile into Ris's Mercedes. It does not take long for us to get to her parent's house. They live in a large condo across town on the historic third ward, on the Kinnickinnic River. The concierge service greets us at the front entrance, but

Ris shoos them away and walks right on by. We enter the foyer, and Ris gestures for us to hurry up. I've been to her parent's condo a few times but not under these circumstances. We reach the thirty-second floor, all of which is her parent's captivating home. Ris doesn't knock but barges in like she owns the place. I hate it when she does that; it makes me feel a tad uncomfortable following her.

Ris's mother is standing against the island in the kitchen with a coffee cup secured firmly in her hand. She is a tall, slender woman like Ris with platinum blonde hair, skin so dark from her obsession with the tanning booth, and lips so full that they may burst from all the filler she injects into them. She is wearing what looks like a black and pink silk sundress, but it could also pass as lingerie. She stops Luke with a halt of her palm against his chest while looking him over as if she will pounce at him at any given moment.

"Gross, mother!" Ris growls at her as she grabs Luke's arm and saves him.

"Your father is in his study," her mother mumbles.

She seductively lifts her head and stares at Luke, then gives him a creepy wink.

"Ew, mom! Just stop," Ris barks rudely at her.

Luke looks at me, and we both laugh. He grabs hold of my hand tightly, and we make our way to Ris's father's study. Ris knocks, and we enter. Her father is sitting behind an elegant cherry oak desk with scrolled molding and is turned toward the windows speaking on his phone. The view is breathtaking; you can see the river and the lake from up here. He turns toward us and gives a wave as he continues with his conversation. He ends his phone call and stands up to shake Luke's hand while nodding at me.

"I just got off the phone with the police department, and Mr. Adam's parents are encouraging him to file charges, but as of right now, he is not in agreement with them. Therefore, we are at a standstill until we get word of his decision," Ris's dad states right out of the gate.

"What will happen if Brady decides to press charges?" I ask with lots of concern and some fear in my voice.

Mr. O'Connor shifts in his chair and brings his hand to his face, making circular motions over his chin with his thumb and pointer finger. Then, he stops and leans forward as he looks at Luke and me.

"Well, with a prior conviction on your record, Luke, one similar to this offense, you may end up seeing more jail time," he sighs.

"Dad, is there anything you can do? He was defending Ali. Brady could have seriously harmed her," Ris shouts,

She becomes quiet when her dad raises his hand to silence her. It's strange seeing her blunt tough-girl shell crumble in the presence of her father, who is tough in his own way. She acts proper around him most of the time, and when her usual self-pokes through, he finds a way to level it. He's not mean to her, but stern and loving. Their relationship is strong, way better than the relationship she has with her superficial mother. Ris and her father are close, a lot like the relationship I had with my father. However, I feel that he was more laid back than Mr. O'Connor.

"Larissa, this is a worst-case scenario I speak of. You know I will do what I can for your friend and her boyfriend," he says.

He gets up from his chair and walks over to her, kissing her on top of the head.

"I need a moment alone with Ali, please."

Luke grabs me and presses his lips against mine. I hug him and lean into his gentle kiss.

"Don't worry! I will keep my freak of a mother away from Luke," she whispers and gives me a wink.

After Luke and Ris leave, Mr. O'Conner asks me to sit next to him on the leather vintage type sofa bench that rests against one of the large windows overlooking the river. I sit next to him and rest my hands in my lap. I'm nervous right now but very comfortable with Ris's dad; I know he's on my, well, our side.

"Ali, I need you to tell me everything you remember from last night and anything else that may have happened before this altercation with Mr. Adams," he says in a soft and calm voice.

I take a deep breath in and sigh loudly as I release my breath. I can feel tears well up in my eyes as I take them off the floor and bring them to Mr. O'Connor's. He leans toward me and places his hand on mine while placing a box of tissues in between us.

"Everything you say is between us, and it will stay confidential unless you want to release it," he says with reassurance.

chapter sixty-six

I start at the beginning, not leaving a single detail out. I tell Mr. O'Connor that I arrived back in the city Thursday afternoon, just in time for the four o'clock meeting at Facade. I disclose to him that Brady did not act any differently toward me or anyone else at work that day than he had in the past four years that I've worked with him. I mention that Brady asked me to dinner, just him and I, claiming it was a business dinner to discuss the Christiansen account that I had recently landed.

I continue to tell Mr. O'Connor that Brady picked me up that evening and brought me to his parent's house, where we dined with them and his little sister. Mr. O'Connor leans back against the window and crosses his leg over his thigh, catching the heel of his foot as he rests his ankle upon his knee, listening attentively.

"We had a lovely dinner, with a few different courses. Each course was accompanied by a different glass of wine that paired well with that particular dish," I say.

"How much wine do you think you consumed yourself?" asks Mr. O'Connor.

"I never finished a full glass before it was taken, and a new one was then set in its place," I reply.

"If I had to guesstimate, all together, I had approximately two glasses, no more than that."

"And how much do you approximate Mr. Adams consumed?" he questions.

"Um... he finished every glass he was given and also had his glass refilled a few times," I answer.

"So, four glasses? Six glasses? How many would you say?" he inquires.

"At least eight, but he did not seem or act drunk from what I recall," I utter.

Mr. O'Conner begins to rub his chin with his thumb and fore-finger back and forth across the jawline of his chin. I take a deep breath in and exhale before I begin to continue to what took place next. I freeze and take another deep breath.

"Take your time, Ali," he whispers warmly.

I hate having to relive this day over and over. I progress forward to what took place in Brady's parent's back yard and how he kissed me. First, blaming the wine and the assumed moment he thought we were having, then somehow turning it around on me in a negative way. I explain what took place next that caused us to argue over me not wanting to kiss him, then me storming off back to his parent's house.

"Mr. Adams was mad you did not want to kiss him after he kissed you, then he apologized for being angry with you over the fact?" Mr. O'Connor asks.

I assume piecing everything I am saying together.

"Yes. Then he pinned me against the door; I slapped him when he tried kissing me again," I swallow.

"After I slapped him, he then threatened me and threw me to the ground," I say about ready to cry.

Mr. O'Conner takes a tissue from the box and hands it to me. I thank him and dab at the corner of my eyes.

"What did he threaten?" he asks.

"He said you're going to wish you never fucking did that, his exact words," I stammer.

"Then, what happened next?" he inquires.

I look down at my lap, where I am fidgeting with the tissue between my fingers. A few tears spill from my eyes, darkening the fabric on my shirt. I take another deep breath and exhale in short, stuttered spurts. Mr. O'Connor uncrosses his legs, putting both feet firmly on the floor, and leans his elbows on his knees as he rests his fist in the palm of his hand.

"He," I take a deep breath and release it.

"He carried me over his shoulder into the pool house. I tried to fight my way down, but he was way too strong for me."

I drop my head down toward my lap and begin to cry, trying to catch most of my tears with the tissue in my hand. It is so painful recalling everything again.

"Did something happen in the pool house, Ali? Something without your consent?" he asks, his voice shaky.

I nod, unable to look back up at him. I continue to cry. He places his hand over mine.

"Are these bruises on your arms from that very night?" he questions.

I nod again. My head still hung down toward my lap, tears flowing down my cheeks like a river.

"Did he—" Mr. O'Connor stops and brings his fist to his mouth.

He then breathes heavily out his nose.

"Did Brady Adams force himself on you in the pool house Thursday night?" he asks with pain and disgust behind his voice.

I slowly bring my eyes from my lap to meet his. He looks deep into my eyes, his shoulders sink, and his eyes gloss over. He stands and walks to the door. I drop my head back toward my lap. I hear him stop before he opens it; I slowly look over at him. He's looking at me and wipes a tear from his eye. He calls Ris in and asks Luke to wait a moment in the hall. She rushes over to me and holds me tight as I cry hard into her chest.

"Did she tell you about the—" Ris begins to say.

"Yes, she told me what happened at his parent's house," her father sighs, feeling quite shaken.

"Did she tell you what he did to her yesterday morning at work? I witnessed it all," she continues.

Her father sits at his desk and cups his hands to his face, right under his eyes. He closes his eyes as he sighs into his hands. Ris then tells him what she witnessed Brady do to me under the table during our morning meeting. I could hear his breathing grow heavier as she spoke about the incident.

"Something needs to be done to that disgusting piece of fucking shit, dad. Excuse my French," Ris growls.

"No!" I whimper. "Please. I don't want any more trouble!"

"Why, Ali? He needs to be punished. He needs to be stopped before he does this to someone else," she yells.

Just as her father tells her to calm down, and I begin to ask that it stay between us, Luke barges through the door. Mr. O'Connor stands from his desk, staring at Luke. Ris looks at him then at me while I stare at him like a deer caught in the headlights.

"He does what to someone else?" Luke demands.

The room goes silent, and Luke walks closer to me.

"Tell him, Ali, he needs to know," Ris says sternly.

"Larissa!" Mr. O'Connor murmurs under his breath.

Luke looks at me, then to Ris, then to her father, and back at me. His face is turning red with fear, and worry grows behind his eyes. I lose it and begin to weep uncontrollably. Ris holds onto me tightly.

"Tell me, please, Ali," Luke begs with concern and vulnerability in his voice.

"Ris? What happened?"

"Brady—"

I gasp as Ris speaks his name, about to tell Luke what happened.

"Brady raped Ali the night she came back to the city," she chokes out then begins to cry.

My tears subside for a short moment as time stands still after the words spill from Ris's lips. I slowly bring my eyes closer to Luke's. He's standing across the room from us. His body has become lifeless, and his voice completely mute. A silence overcomes the large study as all eyes are on him in anticipation of his reaction. He has a blank expression on his face, and he's staring toward the floor. He moves slightly, gradually curling his fingers into fists, and his face is becoming a light shade of bluish-white.

"Luke," I whisper hoarsely as I stand to my feet.

He doesn't move; he doesn't even blink. I can see his chest move up and down with each breath he takes. I walk over to where he stands, stopping a few inches in front of him. His hands still firmly molded into fists so tight his knuckles are white, his jaw clenched shut, and his eyes are burning a hole through the floor.

"Luke," I say again.

My eyes fill with tears, and my body shakes with nerves.

I take a deep breath, then a step closer to him, and bring my hand to touch his face. He steps back from me, bringing his eyes to meet mine. His eyes are narrowed and are carrying a mixture of shock, anger, and sadness. I longed to lose myself in the once beautiful ocean color, but they have lost their vibrant hue and have become dull. His cold gaze sends a shiver up my spine. I need him to move, to speak, something- anything. Luke stares right through me as if I don't exist, yet his eyes are fixated on mine. I blink, and a few tears cascade down my cheeks.

I wish he'd wipe away my tears with his thumbs, kiss me, and hold me while telling me that everything will be okay. Instead, he's motionless, not speaking, and I can see the light once burning inside him has gone dim. I slowly bring my hand to meet his fist. He doesn't step back or dismiss my touch this time. He blinks rapidly as tears build in his eyes, he sniffles, looks at Ris, to Mr. O'Connor, then back down at me. The life I once saw leave his eyes is slowly returning as he peers into mine. The pain, sadness, and anger behind them are unbearable to see, but I can't look away from him. He opens his mouth to say something, but nothing comes out. Luke lowers his eyes from mine, removing his fist from my touch. He turns away from me then walks out the door.

"Luke, wait," I say in a terrified voice, and go after him.

Mr. O'Connor stops me, and Ris hurries to my side.

"Let him go, give him some time. He needs time to process everything," Mr. O'Connor says calmly.

I wrap my arms around Ris and cry hard, so hard that I can barely breathe.

"Dad, what if he goes out looking for Brady?" Ris whispers, with worry in her voice.

"I'll keep a close eye on him, don't you worry. You tend to your friend," he says, kissing Ris's cheek then leaves his study.

Ris wraps her arms around me and rests her cheek on top of my head, rocking us slightly back and forth. I wish all this had never happened. I wish Luke and I decided to go back to my apartment after dinner yesterday instead of going to the club with Ris and the others. I wish I never accepted Brady's dinner invitation. I wish my father had never died.

chapter sixty-seven

Hours have passed, and no sign of Luke. He hasn't shown up at the apartment, Ris's parents, or even the police station. His phone goes straight to voicemail, and his car is still parked next to mine. Where could he have gone? I pace back and forth across our loft as Ris stares out the window from the couch. I know she is worried about me and for Luke. Her father informed us that he hadn't received word of Luke finding Brady. But he did receive a call from the police station that Brady will not be pressing any charges.

He asked if I would like to press charges against Brady for the altercation that took place in the night club as the police are hounding him about it. I tell him no. I want everything to go away and my life to go back to normal. I want Luke here with me. I want to see his gorgeous smile, hear his deep laugh, and have him stare at me the way he does. I need to know he's okay and that we're okay. I lay down on the couch and stare off.

I'm awoken from my sleep when Luke runs his hand across my cheek. I smile, closing my eyes as I take in his touch. He sits down on the couch, shirtless. His body, eyes, smile, and lips are as gorgeous as ever.

"I'm so glad you're back," I whisper.

Luke puts a finger to my lips as he hushes me, then bends down

toward me, and kisses my forehead. He presses his lips against mine in a firm kiss. I open my eyes as he parts from our kiss.
"I love you, Ali," he whispers.

I awake in a panic from the couch, looking around in the darkness. I startle Ris awake from the chair in all my commotion. I scramble to my feet then search the apartment for Luke. No sign of him. His bag of clothes still rests on the floor in my room. I grab my phone, its after midnight. No text or call from Luke; I dial his number, and it goes straight to voicemail again. I rush out to our parking ramp to see his car is no longer parked next to mine. My heart sinks inside my chest as tears well up in my eyes. I didn't think I'd have any left to shed for how much crying I've done lately. He left. He left me.

I want to call Ernie or Jason to see if Luke's made it back, but it's too late. I will call them right away in the morning. I try calling Luke again, but his phone is still off. Ris touches my shoulder.

"Do you want to go see if he is still somewhere in the city?" Ris asks softly.

"I don't know," I reply, wiping the tears from my cheeks.

She tucks her arm underneath mine and walks me back to our apartment. I wish he'd just let me know he's okay, at least.

I stare out the window of our living room with my chin rested on the back of the couch. My mind is entirely blank, and I cannot see any of the twinkling lights from the city perfectly in view. I'm numb. I've lost the one good thing going in my life that made me happy, made me my best self, and made me feel like I could conquer the world.

I WAKE UP AGAIN, FRANTICALLY FROM THE COUCH. RIS IS asleep in the chair next to me. She looks so uncomfortable but is such a good friend to stay out here with me when she could easily be sleeping comfortably in her bed. I check my phone and see that it's quarter after four in the morning. There is still no text or call from Luke.

I walk into the kitchen, yawning and stretching my arms, to make a pot of coffee. I'm going to need it today. I must meet Barrett at Facade to run over my working from home, set up with IT, then drive the five hours back to my dad's.

I wander down the hallway to my room; I enter my bathroom and turn the water on to run myself a bath. I debate whether to add bubbles. Pondering the thought longer then I should, I decide to add some bubble bath.

I throw my hair back in a messy bun on top of my head and pull down on the bags under my eyes as I look myself over in the mirror. I head out of my room back into the kitchen to pour myself a cup of coffee. I hold the sides of my steaming cup of joe as I stare off into space. I snap out of it when I remember that I have a bath running. I rush back down the hallway to my bathroom with the cup of coffee in my hand. The bubbles are high above the tub but are not spilling over. I shut the water off, slowly sliding my clothes down my body, and dip a toe into the tub.

The water is stifling, so I draw my leg back quickly and add some cold water. Once I get the temperature bearable, I step in and sit down with the bubbles hugging me. I glide my hands back and forth across the top of the water before I lean back, resting myself against the cool porcelain of the tub. I close my eyes, taking a deep breath, then exhaling as I try to relax. I drift into a zen-like state as my steamy hot bath engulfs me. Memories of my father from when I was a child fill my mind. He is who I would turn to in situations like this. He's the one who I would cry to about Brady and Luke. He would make everything better, show me a different and more positive way to look at, and approach it all, and it would then set me at ease.

I miss him so much. I need my daddy.

chapter sixty-eight

I try to distract myself with music and plan a place where I will set myself up a little office at my dad's, on my long drive back from Milwaukee. Barrett and IT have provided me with everything I need to successfully have everything run smoothly as it does from my office at Facade. I will be able to video conference with anyone on my team and at work and be virtually present at all meetings. It will be strange not to be there in person, but it's what I need right now to focus.

I called Ernie this morning, and he said he hasn't heard from or seen Luke since he left the shop to see me on Friday, and Jason didn't answer his phone the two times I called him. I'm sure he's sleeping off a weekend of partying. I hope Luke is okay. His phone is still off, and I've probably called him about twenty times already since yesterday.

I pull down my father's long driveway, and it's like a weight instantly lifts from my chest. I can finally breathe and not have to worry about being sexually harassed by one of my co-workers. I get out of my vehicle in the warm evening sun. It's so lovely out here and peaceful—no honking from traffic or busy nightlife, only the sound of mother nature.

I haul my equipment in from Facade, my bag, and the one Luke left at my apartment back in Milwaukee. I notice that the grass has grown exceptionally long, I haven't cut it once since I came back, and I should probably do so soon.

I walk to the small shed that sits off the driveway opposite the barn. It's a cute little shed, made of old barn wood. It has two windows, and for its size, it can store a whole lot of stuff. I turn the knob thing and slide off the latch, opening the shed. My dad and his OCD, I giggle to myself. Everything is organized so neatly and placed almost by size comparison or alphabetically. I pull out the push mower then back out the rider. I check both for gas and see that the rider doesn't have enough to do the entire yard.

I run into the house, grab a shirt, and purse to head to town for some gas and two-stroke engine oil. I don't want to put the gas can in the trunk of my car and have it reek. I rush to the barn with my fingers crossed, my dad took the plow off his plow truck, and it will start. Luckily, the plow is unhooked and off to the side. I hop inside my dad's truck; it's super dusty in here. I haven't been in this truck for a long time. It's a single cab 1996 Ford F150, and a Baja saddle blanket covers the seat. It reminds me of those pullover ponchos from the nineties that everyone had to have.

It starts right up with a little cough before the rumble, over half a tank of gas is still in her. Of course, my dad always told me never to leave a vehicle sit with under half a tank or ever let your tank go under a half a tank in the winter. I push the cassette in as I make my way to town. A song comes blaring across the speakers, *East Bound and Down.* What are the odds that it's this song? I hit eject and look at the tape and see that it's *Jerry Reed's* greatest hits.

I turn on the radio to try and drown out my thoughts of Luke and my urge to want to call him for the umpteenth time since he left Ris's father's study. I drift off, trying to think of places he may have gone if he hadn't come back here. Part of me wants to drive out to his house, but I'm not in the mood to have to explain shit to Jason.

I pull into the gas station and up to one of the pumps. I decide to call Luke before I get out of my dad's truck-straight to voicemail. What the hell? Maybe his phone is dead? I doubt it; it can't be since he has a charger in both of his vehicles. He must not want to talk to me or anyone and wants to be left alone. I'm worried about him. I know what he found out was a lot to handle, but he could at least tell me or someone that he's okay.

I get out of the truck and pump two large gas cans full of gas. I load them into the bed of my dad's truck, then head inside to pay, and grab some oil. As I walk down the aisle with the oil, I can hear an annoying screechy voice. I can recognize it from anywhere; it's Bridget. Why does she have to be working today? I'm not in the mood for her bitchy attitude right now.

I walk up to the counter and set down four bottles of two-stroke oil. Bridget gives me a glare and a quick look over.

"Just the oil?" she asks, quite snooty.

"And the gas on pump three," I mumble.

She gives me a side-eye as she rings me up. I so desperately want to roll my eyes and flick her off, but I keep my cool. As she bags my oil, she eyeballs me again, and I can't bite my tongue any longer.

"What?" I let out rudely.

She looks at me, then adjusts all her weight to one leg and pops out her hip with attitude. She pops a bubble with her gum and says in the bitchiest tone that I've ever heard come out her mouth,

"How's Luke?"

Irritated by our pointless little discord, a tiny ounce of immaturity releases from my lips.

"Wouldn't you like to know," I hiss.

I glare at her, grab my bag of oil, and walk out of the gas station. Ugh, that nosey slut knows how to get under my skin. I hop inside my dad's truck and toss the bag of oil to the floor on the passenger side. I grip tightly to the steering wheel as I drive away. Settle down, Ali, she's not worth getting all riled up over. I take a deep breath, roll down the window, and turn up the music on the radio.

I wonder if Bridget has had any contact with Luke in the last forty-eight hours. I'm sure if she had, she'd have rubbed it in my face just then.

chapter sixty-nine

Mowing the lawn while jamming out to your favorite tunes has its therapeutic qualities. Granted, using a rider makes it easier to reach and fulfill those qualities, but none the less, it's still relaxing. The station I have playing on *Pandora* must know that I am mowing because I've only to skip songs twice during my two-and-a-half-hour mow session.

I return the rider and the push mower to the shed then grab the weed wacker. This contraption scares the shit out of me. Those whips are the least bit forgiving when they connect with skin. My music goes mute as the sound of my ring tone travels through my earbuds. I grab for my phone, hoping it's Luke, but it's only Jason. I let it go to voicemail. My phone has buzzed a few times with messages from Ris and one from Troy, begging me to call him. I don't feel like discussing what he may or may not have heard about what happened between me and his so-called best friend, Brady.

I finish all the yard work as the sun is starting to set. I'm glad my dad had planted some perennials, so there is some color and beauty around the house. I should ask Gladys if she'd like to come over and help me plant flowers in my dad's hanging pots off the deck. I know she loves her flowers.

I go into the house, straight up to the bathroom to remove my sweat-soaked clothes. My feet are stained green. I should've worn some sneakers but am not sure if I have an old pair here. I will have to check for next time. I step into the shower; the hot water burns my arms and shoulders. I must have gotten a little sunburnt while mowing; I didn't even think to put sunscreen on. I turn the dial back a tad, to give the unforgiving sting a breather. The lukewarm droplets hit my skin, allowing me to relax some and take my mind from everything jumbled inside.

I step out of the shower and check my shoulders. They're burnt alright, along with my nose, tops of my ears, arms, and thighs. Lucky me, I get to deal with that itchy stinging pain for a few days. I should know better, but my mind is not in the right place. I apply some soothing aloe vera gel to my red blotchy skin and wonder my way to my room. I gently ease a light t-shirt over my head and slip on some panties.

I give Jason a call, and this time, he picks up on the first ring.

"Alicat!" he answers.

"Hey," I reply.

"What's up? How's it going? Are you back from the city?" he rambles.

I walk into the kitchen and open the fridge, scanning it for something quick and easy to eat.

"Yeah, I'm back. I just finished mowing my dad's yard," I say.

A little preoccupied trying to pull the miracle whip out of the back of the fridge while holding the phone with my shoulder and cheek as I balance the cheese, ham, and mustard in my other hand. It's quite a struggle, but I manage it just fine.

"How did it feel to be back in the city after two weeks of being home?" He strikes up a conversation.

"Interesting," I reply.

If only he knew the half of it. I'm sure he'd flip out and go looking for Brady. Thankfully, he changes the subject, although the change is just as, if not more upsetting.

"Next weekend is the fourth of July and-" Jason pauses right before finishing his sentence.

"It's your dad's birthday."

I put down the cheese, ham, and condiments I wrestled from the fridge. I walk over to the calendar hanging on the wall—Father's

Day. Today is Father's Day. How could I have let this day, the first Father's Day, without my dad almost slip? Too caught up in my stupid drama, is how. God, I'm so fucking selfish. Even after he's dead, my life still trumps his.

"Ali?" Jason's voice rings in my ear.

"Yeah," I reply.

I release a few tears, disappointed in myself.

"Are you okay? I didn't mean to upset you at all," he says softly.

"No, you didn't. I'm fine, just very tired from the past few days," I lie.

Jason goes on to brag about how eventful of a weekend he had, as I go about making myself a sandwich. He mentions that he had the biggest turnout of people he's ever had at his house and that he's having another party this coming weekend-how I must be present. I drift off thinking about how shitty of a daughter I am.

My phone call with Jason ends, and I walk sluggishly into the living room with my sandwich in hand. I sit down on the couch, staring at the carpet. I take a small bite of my sandwich and chew almost in slow motion. I set my ham and cheese sandwich down on the armrest of the couch, as I lay down and curl myself up into a tiny ball. I rock back and forth, humming. I want to cry, but I just can't. I stare at nothing as every part of me becomes numb.

chapter seventy

My alarm chimes and I wake up looking around the dimmed light entering the living room at my dad's. The sun is just starting to rise, and the birds have begun their annoying morning chatters. I reset my alarm for forty-five minutes from now and curl back up in the blanket from the couch.

My alarm sounds again, which feels like five minutes later, and I want to hurl my phone across the room. I sit up on the couch, stretching my arms over my head, then rub the sleep from my eyes. I walk into the kitchen and toss a french vanilla cappuccino k-cup into the Keurig that I insisted my dad buy to keep up with the times. He made his coffee over the stove in an iron kettle. It was as thick as molasses and as dark as my soul.

I walk back into the living room as the water heats up. I sit back down and flick on the TV. I'm not in the mood or the right state of mind to go into the shop today. I don't think I could handle seeing Luke and have him ignore me. I check my phone, and there's still no message or call from him. It's a little after six, which is a little too early to call Maureen at the shop. She doesn't get there until around seven-thirty. I flip through the channels stopping on some stupid game show before I head back into the kitchen to finish up with my cappuccino. I stare out the dining room window as I wait for it to finish.

My phone buzzes. I rush to my phone, praying that it's a message from Luke.

Hey girl, how are you holding up? Have you heard from Luke yet?

A message from Ris reads.

We text back and forth for a good portion of the morning. I call Barrett and let him know that I will miss today's meetings as I am not set up yet. Then I give Maureen a call.

"Rob's Classic Restoration, Maureen speaking," she answers after the second ring.

"Good Morning, Maureen, it's Ali," I say kindly.

"Good Morning, Ali! Are you still in Milwaukee?" she asks in her sweet tone.

"No, I am back at my dad's, but not feeling well, so I won't be coming in today," I reply.

I can hear her fumbling through paperwork and chewing on something. It's probably just her usual morning muffin.

"Oh no, I hope you feel better. Please drink lots of fluids and rest, my dear," she mutters.

"Thank you so much! Have a great rest of your day," I mumble.

"You too, Ali," she says.

I almost hang up from our conversation before blurting out,

"Is Luke at the shop yet?" I ask in a shaky voice.

"No. He called in and took the entire week off," she answers.

He took the week off! Why would he take the week off? Is he that upset over finding out about what Brady did to me? He must be mad at me to not want to talk to me or even come into work. Is he going to quit now?

"Oh. Did he take his vacation?" I ask out of curiosity.

I can hear Maureen clicking the mouse of her computer.

"He wasn't set to take his vacation until the beginning of August. Although he does receive two weeks of vacation a year, the only time on the calendar he has requested off is the first week in August," she informs me.

"Okay, thank you," I say, then end our call.

I'm distraught now. I wish I knew where he was and if he's coming back. I will drive to his house later when I know Jason and Austin are at work, to see if he's packed any of his stuff up. I call him again but the same as all the other times I've called in the past two days, straight to voicemail.

I SLEEP AWAY MOST OF THE DAY, ONLY WAKING TO GO TO THE bathroom, check my phone for a text or call from Luke, and readjust myself on the couch. My dreams are strange, making no sense but don't involve Luke, Brady, or my dad, surprisingly. I silence my phone and try to drift off back to sleep.

At my grandparent's house, a man and woman are rushing me to gather pillows and blankets to bring into a cubby hole through the crawl space on the floor. You can hear the whipping of the wind as it hurls across the roof of the house. Out of the windows, you can see rain darting sideways, the sky is black, and trees are bent almost in half. The man and woman have lanterns and food in their arms as they hurry into the crawl space.

A loud sound like a train overtakes my ears as I hear faint screams come from outside. I crawl down the cubby hole where a man is reaching out to help me down; he grabs the food from the woman after he helps me. I hear glass shatter as she begins to scream and is ripped from the man's hands into the violently circling winds. The man yells and reaches for her then is sucked into the tornado.

I jump down into the depths of the crawl space, throwing a blanket over my head and curling myself into a little ball. I can still hear the screams from the wind and feel the tugging of my blanket as the tornado passes right over me.

I fall to the floor from the couch. I wrestle around, trying to break myself free of the entangled blanket around me. I sit up and look around my father's living room. It's pitch-black, and even the TV has timed itself out. I collect myself, grabbing the blanket, and sitting back on the couch; what an odd dream to have.

I've never met my mother, so I don't know what she looks like, but I kept yelling "mommy" to the woman in my dream, I don't know why. The man was not my father, so I have no clue who he was either. I've never been through a tornado. I've mainly only seen them on the television but know that they've had some touchdown in a few places here. Right now, my life is a tornado with everything that is going on. There is so much disaster happening from all the chaos since my father left this world and me behind. I hope my tornado's aftermath does not destroy my career or what I have built with Luke. He brings so much happiness and joy to my life in what feels like a hollow and depressing time.

I cannot quite figure out what the hell that whole dream was all about and why a woman who seemed to be my mother was in it. I need a distraction from these uncanny images in my mind. I grab my phone and notice I have a few messages and a missed call from Ris, a few messages and a missed call from Troy, a message from Jenna, one of my assistants, and a missed call from Gladys. But nothing from Luke.

chapter seventy-one

The next few days seem to drag at a turtle's pace. I've gotten a lot done, between almost finishing the office remodel, starting the initial designs for the Christiansen's project, and trying to keep my mind busy so I do not think about Luke too much. I wish I knew where he was, or at least that he is okay. It's the weekend, and I had promised Jason I'd come to the party at his house today, even though I don't want to. The more my mind is kept busy, the less I sit and think about Luke and dwell on my selfishness over my father.

Ernie and Luke's custom diamond-plated desks should arrive sometime today or Monday. They are the finishing touches left on my father's old office remodel. I'm proud of how this office has turned out, and I'm sure they will love it. I painted the wall where the door rests a light gray with black, red, and white spin stripping and the wall directly across from it, with all the windows. They are the colors of my dad's shop shirts.

I had wall decal murals made from scanned photos of what the shop used to look like thirty years ago hung on the two remaining walls. I reframed and hung up all the old pictures my dad had back on the wall where the door is. I custom-made corner curio cabinets, faced with diamond plating for all the plaques and trophies my dad and Ernie have received over the years. I hung a new dollar bill in place of the first one my dad's shop made to indicate the first dollar earned after the shop underwent new ownership.

I made sure that the original first dollar was incorporated in Ernie's custom desktop, along with his first shop shirt, pictures with my dad, and other unforgettable memories. Luke's desktop has some sentimental moments with my dad and the shop as well. I had a company come in and lay checkered flag ceramic tiling throughout the office. I also got Luke and Ernie brown leather couches, just like the one my dad had. His one retired to the break room for others to have a little bit of my dad.

I've called Luke every day this week at least twice, sometimes more if I started to miss him or got a weird vibe. Every time, it goes straight to his voicemail. Sometimes I call him to listen to his voice, to hear, you've reached Luke Jameson, leave a message. I wish I knew where he was. I wish he would text me and tell me that he's okay. Even that much would suffice.

I hear a slight commotion as Maureen gets up from her desk, grabbing her things.

"I'm heading out for the day. Have a good weekend," she smiles.

"You too," I smile back.

The shop closes in a half-hour; I will sit and wait until five to see if the desks arrive. I plop my laptop from Facade on Maureen's desk, and I continue working on the Christiansen project designs. It's fantastic, I can handle this project from anywhere I am. It's been nice to see and work with everyone this week without being there in person.

THE DRIVE IS NICE ON MY WAY HOME TO MY DAD'S, I SING along with the radio and let the hot afternoon air race through my car with the windows down. I feel somewhat content today, better than I have all week. Am I losing hope in myself and Luke, or am I coming to terms our short relationship may have come to an end? I know he needs space and time to think, but I need him and his reassurance too.

I bring my purse and laptop into my dad's house, setting my purse on the chair in the entryway. I set my laptop down on the kitchen table, then grab a single box of *Stouffer's* lasagna, and toss it into the microwave. I press the power button on my laptop to reply to client emails and co-worker chats. After I finish my pasta and respond to my final client email for the day, I mosey on upstairs to take a shower and get ready for Jason's party.

My shower is brief, as I did not get too dirty today, and I also did not have much to ponder over. I dry myself off then flip my hair up in a towel. My sunburn has dissipated, leaving a soft gold hue to my skin but still has a slight sting. I plop my suitcase on my bed; I should unpack my shit since I'm here until the end of September. I grab a pair of nude lace boy shorts and my nipple pedals. I slip on my panties and peel the tape from the pedals, securing them over my nipples.

I decide on a floral sleeveless mini dress for tonight; it is hot out, and it should help the uncomfortable sensation of my sunburnt skin. I check myself over in the mirror; this dress is super cute, allowing my skin to breathe. I remove the towel from my head, and I blow dry, straighten, then add some soft waves to my hair. I pin the top half back in a slight poof. I apply some makeup, light and subtle. I'm not really in the mood to go all out with my makeup tonight; I'm not feeling it.

I don't know why I'm getting so dressed up, but I haven't done much involving hair and makeup all week. I go back to my room to put in a pair of pheasant feather earrings, a long dangly necklace, and a bracelet to complete my wardrobe. I check myself over in the mirror then flip my hair out over my shoulders. Maybe part of me thinks I may see Luke tonight, and I want to look somewhat presentable.

I'm a bit nervous about going to Jason's since I decided not to go there at all this week to see if Luke was at his house or if he may have packed up all his belongings. I tried to focus on other things, although I did drive there once but never turned down the dirt road leading to his place. I don't know what I'd do or say if he's at his house tonight. I have so many mixed feelings floating around that it is hard to decipher what possible reaction I would have in such an event.

chapter seventy-two

I follow two cars down the long dirt road. I'm not showing up too late this time around. The butterflies go crazy wild in my stomach as Jason's house comes into view. I can see that he hasn't lit the huge mound made of brush and other shit piled on top of his fire pit. The music is getting louder as I pull up closer toward his garage; I can feel the rumble from the bass as it hits my car.

I look around to see, besides my car and Jason's truck, there are only six other vehicles here. The last party I came to, his place had so many cars that I had to park away from his house. I'm arriving an hour earlier than I did the last time, but I figured there would be more people here by now. At least, I will be able to find Jason right away.

I flip down the visor and check over my makeup and hair; I reapply some lip gloss and flip the visor back up. I open my door and pop my trunk. I picked up two cases of beer and a bottle of *Fireball* on the way. I figured it's the least I could do for all the liquor I drank at the last party I attended here. I set the cases down, adjust my dress, then close my trunk. I walk up the rest of the driveway to the garage.

"Hey Ali, let me help you with those," Austin says as he grabs both the cases from me.

Thankfully, he grabbed those; I was about ready to lose the bottle of *Fireball* I had tucked up under my arm.

"Thanks, Austin," I reply with a smile.

I begin following him up the stairs to the game area above the garage, but I peer down the long driveway that goes past Jason's first. I want so badly to walk down there and see if Luke is here or has been here since he had left Milwaukee almost a week ago.

"Could you grab the door, please," Austin asks.

I pull the door open, and we enter. There are a few more people here than I was led to believe based on the number of cars outside. There are about fifteen or so people here already. Nikki and Mindy among them and three other girls but no sign of Bridget, thank God. The rest are guys from work, High School, and a few that I don't recognize. I don't see Jason, so I set the *Fireball* down next to the other liquors at the homemade bar then turn to leave to find him.

"Hey, where do you think you're going?" Nikki yells from across the room.

I stop and turn back toward everyone. Mindy and Nikki walk up to me; hopefully, they won't be too harsh without their fearless leader. I give them a polite smile as their piercing glares rip holes through my clothes. Why do women have to do that to one another? Why are they so cynical?

"Hey," I say.

I am not enthused what so ever by them judging my hair, makeup, and choice of attire with their annoying glares.

"Aren't you drinking tonight, or are you just running off to your boyfriend," Mindy chimes.

I cannot tell by her tone if she's being friendly or a straight-up bitch, but how does she know Luke is, well was I guess you'd say as of currently, my boyfriend.

"You best hurry because Bridget has already left to go see him, and she's going to beat you to your man," Mindy smirks and laughs, while Nikki shows zero emotion.

Okay, now I know that her tone was bitchy. I don't know what the hell I've ever done to these three girls to cause them to hate me so much. I don't reply; I smile a fake smile and walk away. I make my way down the stairs, and another wave of butterflies hits me.

I cross in front of the garage, which is open but doesn't look to have anyone inside. More cars are coming down the driveway. I stop and stare down the dirt driveway that leads to Luke's place. What if he doesn't want to see me? What if Bridget is down there already and they are- ugh, I don't even want to think about her touching him or worse, him touching her. I couldn't handle walking in on them. That would make me feel grossly uncomfortable and would break me inside.

I hear the door of the house close, and I watch as Jason walks out. I smile and start to walk toward him.

"Damn, Alicat. Why do you have to come dressed all fine and shit?" he says as his eyes practically bug out of his head.

"Shut up, Jay. My outfit isn't that bad," I blush.

"No, no, you look fucking hot. For real," he says, his face a bit flushed.

"Um, thanks," I spit, then giggle.

He tugs at the bottom of my dress, and I swat at him.

"A little fucking short, young lady," he smirks.

I pull my dress down as Jason puts his arm around me, and we head back to the garage. A group of guys comes boisterously, strolling up the driveway toward us along with Bridget. Fucking Mindy tried to start shit between Bridget and me when she wasn't even fucking here yet. These girls still act like we're in damn High School, it's getting old.

Bridget looks at me from the corner of her eye then walks past with the group of guys. Jason removes his arm from around me to fist bump and does some weird handshake with some of them. Jason grabs my hand like he used when we were younger, as we head up the stairs. He always had a hold of me at school and parties as if I were his property, or he was my overly protective big brother.

I walk over to where all the beer and liquor are displayed to get myself a drink. I'm not in the mood for beer and don’t know what I want. I skim over the large selection as if I'm at a mini liquor store. I notice the gold and maroon bottle of *Jeremiah Weed*; I liked this a lot the last time I was here. I search for some lemonade and find a bottle next to the Coke and Sprite. I make myself a weed and lemonade then head back over by Jason, who won't stop checking me out since he first saw me.

We start a game of beer pong, Jason, and I used to be the reigning champs back in our High School days.

We win our first game. I make myself another weed and lemonade as we wait for new opponents. Someone grabs my ass, and I turn to deck them but realize it's Jason. If it were anyone else, I would have lost my shit. The only guy I've let touch me since the night with Brady has been Luke. Even though it was Jason, it still made me cringe and feel a slight bit uneasy. He apologized when he saw the look on my face, so I know it was harmless and something he's done for years.

He talks me into taking a victory shot of tequila. It's so hard to take right off the bat when you've just started drinking; it doesn't go down as smooth. We begin a new game, stopping halfway for Jason and a guy from the opposing team to grab a beer. I mix another drink quickly. Of course, we end up winning again. We both take another victory shot and dive into the next poor souls who dare to play against us. I sink the final cup, and that's three games in a row; we're still the undefeated champs. I'm still set on the more I drink, the better player I become.

We down our third *we are the champions* shot, and Jason dismisses himself, I'm sure, to go find his bed buddy for the night. I giggle as I spoke too soon since he's hovered over the back of the couch with his tongue jammed down Bridget's throat. It's a bit disgusting. I skim the room and notice a lot more people have arrived since we started playing. I walk back to the bar area to make myself yet another drink.

I am quite the popular one tonight, and I know it's because of my dress. I didn't get nearly the amount of attention at the last party when I had worn a sweatshirt and shorts. I pour myself my fourth, or maybe it's my fifth drink, I don't remember, all I know is that I'm feeling fabulous. I look around the room to see all the smiling faces of everyone having a great time. I decide to step outside to grab some fresh air.

I make my way through the crowd of horny male gawkers and some jealous female judgers. I step outside, and a nice warm breeze hits my face. The summer evening breeze is so lovely. I get to the bottom of the stairs, about to head into the garage to bullshit with people that I probably don't know or remember, when I get the brilliant idea to walk down to Luke's place. I'm sure it's all this liquid courage I've gained, but I don't have a single butterfly floating around in my stomach. The driveway seems a lot longer than I remember, and I badly want to sit down, but I keep going. I can see the light from the pole barn come into view. Well, neither his car nor his truck is parked outside.

I trip over a rock or something, probably my foot, and almost take a digger, but I miraculously recover without spilling even a single drop of my drink. I take a sip and continue my very stylish stumble to the door. I put my ear to it to see if I can hear any music or anything, but there's nothing. I get distracted from cupping my hand to my ear, realizing my face feels very warm. I feel around my face for a bit before I bring my focus back to the door. I turn the knob, but it's locked. I walk around the back of the pole barn, using the flashlight on my phone. I try the door on the backside, but it's locked too.

I peer through the window of the door, and it looks pitch black inside. I yell Luke's name a few times and knock on the door like a drunk idiot. I walk back around and stand under the light of the building. I fumble through my phone and tap his name on my screen. I hope and pray he answers this time around. Fingers crossed!

It's ringing, for the first time in six days and a hundred calls later, it's ringing. I pray Luke picks up and doesn't let it go to voicemail or hits ignore.

"Hello!"

Silent for a moment, surprised by what I hear on the other end. A women's voice is ringing through my ear. I hope I'm just really drunk, and Luke sounds like a girl right now.

"Um, may I speak to Luke, please?" I manage to spit out.

"He's indisposed at the moment," she softly replies.

My jaw drops. The words she speaks rip the strings from my heart, *indisposed*, what does that mean, and why is she answering his phone?

"What?" I ask in a confused panic.

Even my drunken state cannot fathom what I am hearing.

"He's currently unavailable," she whispers.

I can feel my heart sink into my chest and the tears well up in my eyes as I stand alone under the light of the pull barn.

"Oh, okay, thanks," I mutter quickly, then hang up.

A few tears race down my face as my vision becomes very blurry. I lean my back up against the door and slide myself gently to the ground. I take a deep breath, exhale slowly, and call him again once my vision has cleared some. It doesn't ring this time but goes straight to voicemail. I shouldn't have called him; he doesn't want to talk to me and is with someone else.

chapter seventy-three

An arm crashes across my shoulder with a loud thud, and landing draped across my chest. My eyes fling open wide, and I look around, frozen in place. I do not recognize the room I'm in at all. Whose arm is this? Oh my God, did I have sex with some random guy from the party last night? I start to panic and think of how the hell I'm going to get off this bed as I continue looking around for clues of who's room this is and where exactly I am.

I continue to lay frozen, conjuring up a plan of escape. I hear a cough, more like clearing of the throat in a deep grumble. There is definitely a guy next to me. How in the hell did this happen! Was I that drunk to not even remember? The last thing I do remember was calling Luke.

The guy removes his arm from my shoulder and rolls over, I'm free to get the hell off this bed and out of wherever I am. I'm incredibly close to the edge, so I ever so slowly inch my body, stopping every movement I make to listen for the person next to me. He's now letting out a light snore, so I continue my quest to get off the bed. I fall off the bed while trying to be as quiet as I can. I land on the floor in a bear stance with a semi-quiet thud. I grimace as I freeze again and close my eyes. The dude is still snoring, so I open my eyes and notice that I'm fully clothed. A sigh of relief washes over my body, knowing I didn't have sex with anyone last night.

I rise to my feet against the wall, in stealth mode. The guy's back is toward me, so I tiptoe around the bed toward the door. I notice my small brown leather crossbody purse that only fits my phone and a few credit cards, is lying on the floor; I grab it and reach for the door handle. I close my eyes as I slowly turn the knob. I hear a faint moan, I freeze, and my eyes go wide. It's a female moan. What in the fuck? I take a deep breath, quietly release it, then calmly look back over my shoulder toward the bed. On it, I see Jason and some random chick that I don't recognize at all. Thankfully, his naked body is partly covered, but she's spread eagle, five-star positioned across the bed. Tits and lady bits are just hanging there, airing out, I suppose.

I giggle, and quickly but quietly let myself out. I cup my hands to my mouth in the open area outside the bedroom and let out an almost full-blown laugh at the sight I just saw. After I collect myself, I look around to notice that I'm in the basement. Jason's room must be the only one down here.

The light of the morning or afternoon sun, whichever it may be, shines through the windows and shows a living room type area. A huge flat-screen TV and a large leather sectional sofa take up most of the space here. A few gun racks on the wall, baseball bats and hockey sticks piled in one corner, and a bookshelf thing full of DVDs and Blu-ray discs in the other. Just off the staircase is a small laundry room-not a bad set up for a dude.

I head upstairs into the actual living room. A smaller flat screen is resting above the fireplace, two couches plus a recliner display at random in the space. The one couch must pull out into a bed because Bridget and a guy I recognize from my dad's shop are canoodling upon it. Man, she sure gets around. A guy is sprawled out on the other couch, and Nikki is in the chair. I make my way to the door and let myself out.

The sun is just about overhead, so it must be damn near noon. The fire pit is still smoldering some from last night, but I don't remember Jason having ever lit it. I come to the edge of the house and step onto the driveway. I begin walking down it toward the garage. I peer in the opposite direction toward where the pole barn is and forgot that I went there last night looking for Luke while hammered. He wasn't there, and when I called him, some woman answered his phone.

I continue past the garage and down the driveway toward my car, thinking about my call to Luke last night. Who was the woman who answered his phone, and where is he? I wipe under my eyes as I'm sure my makeup looks ratchet from all the crying last night. My fingers have black streaks on them when I return them from my face. I pull my phone out, but of course, it's completely dead, so I put it back in my purse. I reach my car, fumbling for my keys. I hear a low growl from the exhaust of a car, and my body flows with tingly butterflies in the hopes that it's Luke driving down the driveway in his Charger.

A car appears, but it's not Luke. I give the guy in the newer Chevy truck a half-hearted smile then get into my vehicle. I sit there for a moment staring off into space. I burst into tears and lay my head on my steering wheel. I let out a sigh and start my car.

A knock at my window startles me from my pity session. I look up to see that it's Jason, standing there in just pants, no shirt, and barefoot. I roll down my window.

"Alicat, are you ghosting me now?" he says in all seriousness.

I am confused as hell by his comment and the blank expression on his face. I open my mouth to ask him what the fuck he means. However, before I can utter a single word, he blurts out.

"You sleep with me then leave. I'm crushed!" he bursts out laughing in the most resonant belly laugh that I've heard from him in forever.

I glare at him and tell him to fuck off. Then, I start laughing myself as he had me going for a second there.

"Let's go get some breakfast," he takes a moment from his laughter to say.

"Um, I'm pretty sure it's lunchtime now, Jay," I reply as I squint to look up at him.

"Well, whatever, let me go grab some shoes," he states as he takes off back to his house in a little jog.

"And a shirt!" I yell.

chapter seventy-four

Jason hops in the passenger seat of my car, fully clothed. His face is a bit scruffy with a chin full of more than a five o'clock shadow. Although he looks quite hot. He can rock out any outfit he wears. The only other person I know who can pull that off is Luke. Good thing I was able to salvage some of my makeup and apply new lip gloss when he ran back into the house.

Jason plays with my radio, and I'm suddenly brought into some crazy deja vu feeling as I vaguely remember a moment like this one with him from back in our High School days. He was once my best friend, and we did everything together. He smiles at me as he turns up the volume to a silly song we used to jam out to and begins doing a little dance in his seat. The song's echoed start brings a huge smile across my face as I watch Jason's goofy moves to

Ssss-Aaaa-Ffff-Eeee-Tttt-Yyyy Safety Dance!

He mouths all the words to me as the song progresses; I laugh, also chiming in here and there to the part when the woman says, "and sing." What a great way to work off a hangover on a Saturday morning.

We head to the local bar and grill since Jason wants a greasy burger as well as a Bloody Mary. Those are so gross, but a greasy burger doesn't sound half as bad right now.

"So, who was the chick in bed with us?" I giggle, making some small talk.

"I honestly have no clue what her name is. She came with some of the other girls last night, but she isn't from around here as far as I know," he says, shrugging his shoulders.

"Classy," I reply, sliding my sunglasses on.

"She has nice tits and a mean blow job, but it was like fucking a warm cup of water," he exaggerates.

Ugh, that's a visual I did not want or need to add to the one I saw of the poor girl this morning that has burnt into my retinas.

"Yuck, Jay," I practically gag.

"What? She was loose as fuck," he smirks.

"Loose or is your dick just that small." I chuckle.

Puffing up his chest, in defense, he lets out, "It was pressed up against your back all morning, so why don't you tell me?"

My mouth drops open as I look over at him with sheer disgust then punch him. He flinches, lifting his leg and arms to shield himself.

"I bet you got a good look at the beast this morning," he laughs.

"You're gross," I growl.

I pull into the bar and grill. As we walk toward the entrance, I pull my dress down, and Jason reaches under it from the back, pinching my ass. I punch him as hard as I can. He laughs while putting his arms up as a truce. I walk behind him since I don't trust his sneakiness. He opens the door for me, and I tuck my dress under my butt to protect myself.

"I hate that fucking dress, by the way," he says through his teeth.

"Why?" I say.

I look back at him as I smile, still covering my rump.

"I have a few reasons," he states while pushing me inside the building by the small of my back.

I raise a brow at him, "Well, enlighten me, please."

We walk through the building, and I can feel Jason watching me as I move toward the bar.

"For starters, it's way too fucking short," he whispers in my ear.

We take a seat at the bar. I look at Jason, he smiles at me then looks around for the bartender. I check the clock as the bartender notices our presence. It's two-thirty already. Holy shit! Jason orders himself a Bloody Mary with all the fixings, two burger baskets, no tomato on mine, and a Shirley Temple for me without the cherry because I'm allergic to them. I can handle artificial cherry, although, like grenadine.

We joke about how he just up and left the girl in his bed as well as everyone else who had passed out last night at his house. I feel bad for that girl, but she brought it on herself. Jason starts bitching about how big of a slut Bridget is and that his ex-girlfriend gets laid more at his house than he does. It's just like hold times, him bitching about Bridget and bragging about his sex life.

As we wait for our food, my eyes bug out of my head when I look over the miraculous Blood Mary sitting in front of Jason. He doesn't even need a burger basket with the six-course meal parading out of his drink. There's a beef stick, hard-boiled egg, an olive, pickles, onion rings, motzi sticks, a slab of steak, and a damn muffin. No wonder Bloody's are so popular. By the time you scarf down all the food, you're so exhausted and thirsty; you slam your drink.

Jason slides the olive off the stick and hands it to me with a wink. He goes back to his conversation with the bartender about a car or something. I drift off a little thinking about Luke and the woman who had answered his phone last night, running every scenario I could think of through my mind. I thought he had asked me to be his girlfriend when he was in Milwaukee and that we were officially dating. Does his disappearance and the woman answering his phone mean that he has broken up with me? I want to call him again, but my phone is in my car charging. I excuse myself to grab it as I watch Jason's eyes follow me then he continues to talk to the bartender.

I walk out to my car, open the door, and lean over my seat to unplug the charging cord from my phone. I feel hands grasp my hips and a body thrust into my ass. I dart into my seat and look up to see that it's Jason laughing.

"Gee, don't be so jumpy, Alicat. It's only me! Sorry," he says as he continues laughing.

I roll my eyes then get out of my car. I push him back with both hands, and I turn on my phone.

"You really shouldn't bend over in that dress," Jason continues.

I glare at him, not amused at all, and head back into the building. Our food is waiting for us at our spots at the bar.

"Are you even still hungry?" I ask, referring to all the food he just ate from his Bloody Mary.

We sit back down. He looks at me as he lifts a brow and takes an overly large bite of his burger while rolling his eyes in the back of his head as he moans "nom-nom." I guess that answered my question. I roll my eyes and shake my head at his childish antics. I add some ketchup and mustard to my burger before placing the bun on top. I take a bite of the greasy burger, and it hits the spot for my hungover growling belly.

After we finish our meal, we play a few rounds of pool. I decide to have a few drinks, which help ease my mind over Luke and my hangover. Jason and I are extremely competitive with each other, so our pool game is strong. Jason pays for our food and bar tab before we leave.

"You okay to drive?" Jason asks.

"I only had two, I should be okay," I reply.

He grabs my hand and drags me across the street.

"Where are we going?" I grumble, badly needing to burp.

"Let's go for a walk in the park, so your food can soak up the alcohol you just drank before you drive," he replies with a smug smile.

I roll my eyes and follow closely behind him to the park. I check my phone to see if Luke has called or messaged me, but Jason grabs my phone and takes off running before I can look. I chase after him, yelling for him to stop being a child and give me back my phone. He zig-zags through the park as I pace myself behind him. Jason is such an ass! I run after him for a little bit then stop to catch my breath. Jason notices and walks up to me.

"Out of breath already, tsk tsk," he says in a whiney girly voice.

"Shut up!" I growl.

I try to snatch my phone from him. He puts his arm over his head, and I jump for my phone. He then switches it back and forth through his hands over his head. I stop jumping and hang my head down in defeat.

"What, you can't go two minutes at all without talking to lover boy," his whiney voice echoes.

I give him a look of a thousand deaths.

"Woah, touchy, aren't we?" he mumbles.

He brings his hands down and hands me my phone. The death stare worked.

"Where is your piece-of-shit knight in shining armor, anyway?" he asks rudely.

I wish I knew. With one eye squinted from the sun, I look at him then look down at the ground. I admit he has me here because I don't have a clue, and I can't even make up an excuse.

"I don't know," I sigh.

An awkward silence takes over for a moment or two before Jason throws me over his shoulder and takes off running through the park. I scream in laughter as his shoulder presses against my bladder, giving me a very sudden urge to pee my pants. I yell for him to put me down before I pee. He sets me down, and I fall over, taking him with me.

He lands on his back, and I land on top of him with my hands pressed against his chest. We both release an "oft" sound as our bodies finally come to a halt. I look up from Jason's chest, into his baby blue eyes. He looks back into mine then reaches his hand toward my face, running it through my hair and resting his thumb just before my ear, then leans in toward my face.

I stare into his eyes, then look down his face to his lips and back up to his eyes. Jason brings his face closer to mine. I can feel the warmth of his breath on my cheek. I part my lips a little when I feel his nose press against my upper lip. I take a tiny breath, release it, then open my eyes wide. I push myself off Jason and stand up, fixing my dress. All I can think about is Luke right now, and kissing Jason would not be the best thing for me to do.

Jason sits up and bends one of his legs while fixing his cap. We are both wafting in awkward silence. I look at him and notice that he's also looking back at me; he is a bit flushed. He gives me a slight smirk.

"Ali, I'm s—" he begins to say as he stands to his feet.

I interrupt him by shaking my head, then grabbing his hat and taking off running. He stands for a second in disbelief at my recent reactions, then he starts to chase me.

chapter seventy-five

The drive back to Jason's place is not as awkward as I thought it would be after we almost exchanged a kiss at the park. He is still being his goofy self and acting as if nothing happened. Well, nothing did happen. I'm glad it didn't, it probably would've ruined our friendship, plus I would've just been another notch on his headboard. We pull down the long driveway to his house. I had a fun afternoon with him; it was like old times minus the moment that almost took place. I missed him and his shenanigans. Although he's grown up a lot appearance-wise, he's still the goofy kid I remember.

I only notice Jason's truck and two other vehicles remain at his house, now that it's after six.

"You're coming back tonight, right?" he asks.

"Um... I don't know if I can handle another night of partying," I give him a side-eye and a smile.

He rolls his eyes as he opens the door and steps out. He closes my door, still holding onto the window frame as he looks around the yard. He then bends down and rests his elbows on the window.

"Please," he says with a pouted lip and puppy dog eyes.

I hate it when he does that. He looks so cute and innocent with those eyes. I huff and roll my eyes at him.

"Fine," I let out an exaggerated sigh almost effortlessly.

I know there is no way I could wiggle out of this as he is persistent. I want to be here if Luke comes back tonight so that I can beat

Bridget to him. Jason makes a "yes" motion with his body then smiles as he stands up and backs away from my car.

"Go wash your face because you look like a clown, and please don't wear a short ass dress this time," he yells with a huge shit grin on his face.

I mouth *fuck you* and flick him off before turning my car around to head back to my dad's. I do need a shower because I stink, and my makeup looks like a kindergartener did it. As I make my way back down the driveway, I start to think about Luke. I want to call him, but I most certainly don't want to listen to that chick's voice on the other end.

Then it hits me, what if the woman who answered his phone last night is the one, he told me about from Colorado; the one he said that he last slept with before me, who he would meet up with every few months. My stomach starts to tie in knots, and I begin to not feel very well just thinking about that. I look down at my phone, just chilling in the cupholder. I grab it and set it on my lap. I contemplate for a solid five minutes whether I should call him or not. I decide to call Ris instead.

"Hey, girl," she answers almost immediately.

"Hey, Ris," I reply to her without hesitation.

"How are you doing? Any news on Luke? Did you find out who that skank was that answered his phone?" she asks, with concern in her voice.

The last two questions I could not answer, and the first one was obvious. I was confused, upset, and conflicted. No matter what, Luke could have just texted me that he needed some time to process things, but he has gone completely MIA.

"I'm okay; spent the afternoon with Jason. He kept my mind off, Luke," I ramble.

"There's still no sign of him. I've come to a possible conclusion on who the girl might be, though."

"Ali, please don't come to any conclusions as they will drive you insane," Ris says sternly.

Since I've thought about the Colorado woman as a possibility, I have made myself sick. But I don't know who else it'd be or why he'd even be with another woman in the first place. I thought he liked me and was even falling in love with me. That's why all of this doesn't add up. It makes zero sense. I want to understand his reasoning, but I can't when he won't talk to me.

"Remember when I told you that he said the last girl he slept with before he slept with me was a chick from Colorado, who he would fool around with every few months. What if it was her?" I ask.

I cringe my teeth waiting for her to explode on me in her Ris way. She is silent for a moment before she speaks. Part of me is thinking that perhaps she agrees with me.

"Girl, trust me when I tell you this. That man is head over heels for you. I have seen the way he looked at you and had to touch you every chance he could. The information he learned at my parents was a lot to process for him. Shit, it was a lot for me when you told me," she states.

Ris loves to give me her philosophical speeches. They usually make me feel better about myself and the situations I am in.

"He needs time to process it. He will be back, and you two will be stronger than ever. Trust me."

I smile as I know she's probably right, and I have nothing to worry about, but I'm still apprehensive over the whole situation. I, as usual, am very likely overthinking everything. I hope she is right.

"Oh, I forgot to tell you," she starts to laugh.

"Brady came into work yesterday as he has taken most of the week off. His face looked so bad. He still had a cut on his eyebrow, nose, and lip. Plus, he had two slight black eyes," she bursts out laughing.

After she catches her breath from her contagious laugher, she continues with her story.

"It was the first time that he's ever looked ugly and like an embarrassed little bitch," she chuckles.

"Good," I reply with some "he deserved it" attitude behind my reply as I laugh with Ris.

Karma is a bitch. He had it coming to him. Just thinking about Brady makes me queasy but a little relaxed to hear about his new makeover.

I pull down my dad's driveway and sit in my car while I continue the conversation with Ris. She goes off more about my relationship with Luke and how we will be just fine once he returns to town. I need to be patient with him and give him some time to process everything. I agree with her, even though it's hard not knowing what's going on with him. I would at least like some acknowledgment from him that he is safe, and we are fine.

After our call ends, I head into my dad's house. The sun is starting to set, so I need to shower and get ready quick to head back over to Jason's for another night of distractions, I hope. I rush up the stairs and head straight for the bathroom. I turn the shower on, and before I step in, I call Luke.

It's ringing. My heart starts to pound. It rings for the second time, then the third, and the fourth. Just as I am about ready to hang up Luke answers.

"Hey."

I freeze as the voice on the other end is Luke's. My heart drops and begins to pound in my chest. I don't say a word but listen.

"Ali?" he says.

A tear slides down my cheek. I lower the phone from my ear, staring down at the floor.

"Ali? Hello?" he says again, muffled from the distance my phone is from my ear.

I press the end call button on my phone and hang up as I rest my arm against my thigh. I stare at the floor as I stand there and cry. I'm still very frozen in shock from the voice I heard on the other end of the phone.

My phone buzzes, and I turn my wrist, which is still hanging down by my thigh. Luke flashes across my screen, and I hit the ignore button. I put my phone on silent then throw it onto the counter of the stink. I slip out of my dress and panties then step into the shower.

Not thinking for one moment about whatever that was that just happened, I start to scrub my face, body, shave my armpits and legs, and wash my hair. I step out of the shower, wrapping myself in a towel and throwing my hair up in one. I walk into my room and turn on my old CD player. An old school metal song comes on, and I turn up the volume.

I grab a shirt that has a low scoop neck and rips up the entire back of it. I used to wear a bright neon sports bra with this shirt, but I decided to live dangerously and not wear one tonight. I grab a pair of white ripped jean shorts and my black sandals. I head back into the bathroom to blow-dry and straighten my hair.

I apply a more smoldering smoky eye than I usually do; I add a thick line of eyeliner, including my bottom inner lid and an extra two coats of mascara. I play eenie-meanie between my brown and bright red lip gloss—the red winning. I do a quick hair flip after I spray myself with my fragrance mist and apply some pit stick to my underarms. I grab my phone, shoving it in my back pocket without checking it, and head out the door.

chapter seventy-six

I don't know what's gotten into me, but I've become very irritated and uneasy, almost angry since I've heard Luke's voice. I stop at the liquor store and grab some vodka and whiskey as I'm in a mood to get annihilated tonight. It's almost ten, so I'm sure I will have some catching up to do.

It's packed at Jason's house like the first night I partied here the day after my dad's funeral. The music is blaring, and the fire pit is blazing. I always feel stupid walking up to his parties by myself and sober, so I open the bottle of vodka and take a swig. I down a few more before I get out of my car. I should get a bit tipsy before going inside. I can feel the burning sensation from the warm vodka traveling down my throat. I burp loud, looking around, but no one heard it, so I laugh at myself then head toward the garage. Jason spots me and comes over. I am glad to see him.

"Woah, Ali, this outfit is—" he starts to say before I interrupt him.

"Let's get drunk. Down for Beer Pong?" I shout and walk up the stairs.

Jason follows behind me.

"Your ass is hanging out of the bottom of your shorts," he announces as he flicks the bottom of my ass cheek.

"Uh, huh," I reply, not giving two shits.

We enter the room where everyone is drinking, shouting, playing games, and having a good ole time. I realize that being sad isn't going to change anything, so why shouldn't I live it up. I walk over to the little bar, set down the vodka and whiskey I brought. I make myself a strong screwdriver and skim the room for Jason. I recognize the girl he's talking to from this morning; well, sort of, since she has clothes on. I walk over and grab his ass. He turns around and puts his arm around me.

"You are feisty tonight," he whispers in my ear.

I do not know quite how to describe the mood I am in right now, but I want to get wasted and not care about anything or anyone. I've had enough of everything.

I give him a raised brow, smile, and shout, "Beer Pong!"

I drink my screwdriver halfway down before we make it to the beer pong table. We find some opponents and begin our first game; of course, we slaughter them badly. Our first four shots were sunk right off the bat. We take our victory shot of patron then dive immediately into the next game. I have Jason make me a new drink before we start. I can feel the warmth of my buzz rising through my body. I'm being unusually flirty with Jason but am liking his attention on me instead of some random hoe from the party.

I bend over the table right in front of him. I can feel his body against mine as I aim my hand at one of our final few cups. I draw my hand back and sink the ball in the cup. I throw my hands up and turn around to jump on Jason.

"Are you not wearing a bra," he whispers in my ear.

He sets me down, and I grab a ball to get ready for my next shot. I dip it in the water cup, then I look back at him and wink.

"Nope," I say in a sort of high-pitched voice, then position myself for my shot.

I make it again. The room shouts as most people crowd around watching Jason and I kick everyone's ass. We win our second game with flying colors, take another victory shot, then start our third game. We switch to the other side of the table this time, and I land my first two balls, missing the third as it hit the cup rim and bounced off the table. I'm on my fourth screwdriver, and I think I had three shots of tequila. I am totally in my zone.

I'm feeling terrific, my attitude and the funk I showed up in has now faded. I'm having a blast and haven't thought about Luke even once since I got here. We end up winning our third game, barely, since Jason is beyond hammered. He keeps burying his head in my neck and grabbing hold of me tightly as his hand travels up and down my bare back under the rips of my shirt plus grabbing handfuls of my ass every chance he can get. I yell that I need a short intermission before we play another game.

Jason whines a little while pulling on my wrist but is quickly preoccupied with some chick. I step away from the table and decide to make myself a weed and lemonade this time before I head outside. Guys keep trying to stop me on my way to the door with praises on my good form, back to back wins, and of course, my skanky choice in attire tonight. I wore it on purpose because I was having a bitch fit earlier.

I open the door and am blasted with warm air. It's cooler than in the room I was just in but still warm. I walk down the stairs, past the garage over to the firepit. Not needing to warm myself but to watch the flames as I take a breather from all the chaos inside. I take a sip of my drink and sway a tad; the drinks and shots are starting to kick in now.

"Ali!"

I hear a voice calling my name from behind me as I stand alone by the fire. I turn around to see Luke standing before me. My mouth opens a tiny bit, my eyes widen, but I stand there staring at him. I drop my drink to the ground as I continue to stare. In the glow from the fire, he looks like a mess, as if he hadn't slept in days. His face is worn and shows melancholy. I want so badly to wrap my arms around him and tell him how much I've missed him, but my current drunken state restrains me from doing so.

"Where in the hell have you been?" I spit, like venom.

The anger is building inside me; I am mad at him and at myself. I'm upset that I didn't know where he was, worrying about him for a week, and finding out he ran to another woman. I am hurt, very hurt because I like him a lot and I expected more.

"I'm sorry. I am so sorry I left, Ali. I didn't know how to deal with what happened, and I needed some time to think. I shouldn't have shut you out," he replies softly. "I don't want to talk about this here and when you are drunk."

"I didn't fucking ask you why. I asked where the hell have you been. Who was that woman who answered your phone?" I demand.

The dejected look on Luke's face as my words continue to spew from my lips burns a hold in my chest. I am melting on the inside because I missed him and am happy, he's here, safe and sound, but I am livid and hateful toward him on the outside.

"What, woman? When did someone answer my phone?" Luke asks.

"Don't play stupid with me, Luke. I called you last night, and a woman answered your phone saying you were busy. What the fuck was that? Who is she?" I shout.

"It's not what you think, Ali," he says.

I cut him off before he has time to conjure up an excuse.

"It's exactly what I fucking think," I hiss. "You find out something horrible that happened to me, you don't say a word, you leave. For a week, a fucking week. I don't hear from you nor does anyone else. Despite everything that has happened between us, you dare to run to another woman."

Luke steps toward me, reaching his hand for mine, but I move away from him.

"Don't fucking touch me," I growl through my teeth.

"You have no clue what I've been going through this past week. I've been a wreck over you. Why? For what? You could care less about me," I cry.

Luke grabs me and wraps his arms around me tight. I throw little punches at his chest, demanding he set me free. He holds me closer. I stop my tantrum and bury myself into his chest as I burst into tears.

"Why did you leave me?" I shudder.

I am so drunk that part of me thinks this is all an illusion, and

Luke is not holding me right now, while the other part of me wants to be wrapped in his arms forever.

"I shouldn't have. I'm sorry. I will never do it again. Please, forgive me," he says with sincerity in his voice.

"I love you, Ali!"

The story continues in...

HER

Please enjoy the following excerpt from **HER**, narrated by Luke.

chapter one

I glance at the clock on my dash, four fifty-two. It's early. I slowly drive down one of the longest and eeriest looking roads I've ever driven down. It is quiet and derelict. Animals must be waking up, with a vast area isolated like this; I should have seen something by now, a bird, a squirrel—anything. The road is quite untraveled. Grass hugs it like a light blanket with little sign of once-tiny rocks coating its existence.

I come upon what looks like the end of an exceedingly long worn driveway to an old wooden barricade. Twenty minutes to trek down a driveway is insane. I see a small house tucked away behind some trees. I get out of my car and make my way down the gravel and grass-covered trail toward the house.

"Luke!" my sister squeals uncontrollably from her front porch.

Cringing inside at the god-awful sound, I walk farther up the trail toward her house, giving her a slight raise of my hand. Why do women make such noise when they are excited? I do not understand the point of shrieking like a dying animal. The falsetto in their pitch is remarkable at times yet annoying as hell. It's worse when there is more than one of them together. Thankfully, my mother is not here, or I would need some ear protection.

HER, available in 2021!

ACKNOWLEDGMENTS

First and foremost, I would like to thank my family for the love and support they have shown me while becoming an author. They allowed me to have time to myself while writing this story and dealing with what came after it to have my work of art published. Without them, this book would have never happened.

Thank you to my friends and acquaintances for the encouragement, support, and the help you have provided during this journey.

An extra special thanks to those who have read the raw version of this story and loved it. The outpour of positivity has been empowering and gave me the shove I needed to have something I wrote published.

Thank you to those behind the scenes proofreading, editing, formatting, and the cover design, for your time, dedication, and patience. I did not realize how much work goes into publishing a story, after the initial manuscript has been completed.

To anyone else who has helped or contributed to my first novel's process and overall success, I thank you from the bottom of my heart.

Last but certainly not least, to you, the reader. Thank you for purchasing my book and reading it. I genuinely hope you enjoyed it.

ABOUT THE AUTHOR

J. M. Elliott is a first-time writer spending her days raising a family in a small town in Minnesota. Secretly, she had always wanted to be an author, even setting numerous New Year's Resolutions to tackle that dream. Between family life and a busy schedule, time to write was out of reach. Until the world was struck by a global pandemic, giving Elliott the extra time, she had longed for to start writing. She is enjoying checking off an item on her bucket list with hopes of writing more books.

Find her at jmelliott.me, on Facebook at J. M. Elliott, on Instagram at @jmelliott2020, and Wattpad as boomeyou.

Made in the USA
Monee, IL
15 December 2020

53064224R00204